M
Burke

Burke, James Lee,
1936-

Last car to Elysian
Fields.

M
Burke

Burke, James Lee,
1936-

Last car to
Elysian Fields.

DATE	BORROWER'S NAME	

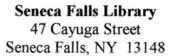

BY THE SAME AUTHOR

White Doves at Morning
Jolie Blon's Bounce
Bitterroot
Purple Cane Road
Heartwood
Lay Down My Sword and Shield
Sunset Limited
Half of Paradise
Cimarron Rose
Cadillac Jukebox
Heaven's Prisoners
Burning Angel
The Lost Get-Back Boogie
The Convict
Dixie City Jam
In the Electric Mist with Confederate Dead
A Stained White Radiance
The Neon Rain
A Morning for Flamingos
Black Cherry Blues
Two for Texas
To the Bright and Shining Sun

Last Car to Elysian Fields

A NOVEL

JAMES LEE
BURKE

SIMON & SCHUSTER
New York   London   Toronto
Sydney   Singapore

SIMON & SCHUSTER
Rockefeller Center
1230 Avenue of the Americas
New York, NY 10020

Simon & Schuster and colophon are registered trademarks
of Simon & Schuster, Inc.

For information about special discounts for bulk purchases,
please contact Simon & Schuster Special Sales:
1-800-456-6798 or business@simonandschuster.com

Designed by Jeanette Olender
Manufactured in the United States of America

10   9   8   7   6   5   4   3   2   1

Library of Congress Cataloging-in-Publication Data is available.

ISBN 0-7432-4542-3

ACKNOWLEDGMENTS

I would like to thank Leslie Blanchard at the Iberia Parish Library and Vaun Stevens and Don Spritzer at the Missoula Public Library for their friendship and generous help over the years.

To my wife, Pearl, and my children,

Jim, Jr., Andree, Pamala, and Alafair

LAST CAR TO ELYSIAN FIELDS

Chapter 1

The first week after Labor Day, after a summer of hot wind and drought that left the cane fields dust blown and spiderwebbed with cracks, rain showers once more danced across the wetlands, the temperature dropped twenty degrees, and the sky turned the hard flawless blue of an inverted ceramic bowl. In the evenings I sat on the back steps of a rented shotgun house on Bayou Teche and watched the boats passing in the twilight and listened to the Sunset Limited blowing down the line. Just as the light went out of the sky the moon would rise like an orange planet above the oaks that covered my rented backyard, then I would go inside and fix supper for myself and eat alone at the kitchen table.

But in my heart the autumnal odor of gas on the wind, the gold and dark green of the trees, and the flame-lit edges of the leaves were less a sign of Indian summer than a prelude to winter rains and the short, gray days of December and January, when smoke would plume from stubble fires in the cane fields and the sun would be only a yellow vapor in the west.

Years ago, in both New Orleans and New Iberia, the tannic hint of winter and the amber cast of the shrinking days gave me the raison d'etre I needed to drink in any saloon that would allow me inside its doors. I was not one of those valiant, alcoholic souls who tries to drink with a self-imposed discipline and a modicum of dignity, either. I went at it full-bore, knocking back Beam or Black Jack straight-up in sawdust bars where I didn't have to make comparisons, with a long-necked Jax or Regal on the side that would take away the aftertaste and fill my mouth with golden needles. Each time I tilted the shotglass to my lips I saw in my mind's eye a simian figure feeding a fire inside a primeval cave and I felt no regret that I shared his enterprise.

Now I went to meetings and didn't drink anymore, but I had a way of putting myself inside bars, usually ones that took me back to the Louisiana in which I had grown up. One of my favorites of years past was Goldie Bierbaum's place on Magazine in New Orleans. A green colonnade extended over the sidewalk, and the rusted screen doors still had painted on them the vague images and lettering of Depression-era coffee and bread advertisements. The lighting was bad, the wood floor scrubbed colorless with bleach, the railed bar interspersed with jars of pickles and hard-boiled eggs above and cuspidors down below. And Goldie himself was a jewel out of the past, a seventy-year-old flat-chested ex-prizefighter who had fought Cleveland Williams and Eddie Machen.

It was night and raining hard on the colonnade and tin roof of the building. I sat at the far end of the bar, away from the door, with a demitasse of coffee and a saucer and tiny spoon in front of me. Through the front window I could see Clete Purcel parked in his lavender Cadillac convertible, a fedora shadowing his face in the glow of the streetlight. A man came in and removed his raincoat and sat down on the other end of the bar. He was young, built like a weightlifter whose physique was earned rather than created with steroids. He wore his brown hair shaved on the sides, with curls hanging down the back of his neck. His eyebrows were half-moons, his face impish, cartoonlike, as though it were drawn with a charcoal pencil.

Goldie poured him a shot and a draft chaser, then set the whiskey bottle back on the counter against the wall and pretended to read the newspaper. The man finished his drink and walked the length of the bar to the men's room in back. His eyes looked straight ahead and showed no interest in me as he passed.

"That's the guy," Goldie said, leaning close to me.

"You're sure? No mistake?" I said.

"He comes in three nights a week for a shot and a beer, sometimes a catfish po'boy. I heard him talking about it on the payphone back there. Maybe he's not the guy who hurt your friend, but how many guys in New Orleans are gonna be talking about breaking the spokes on a Catholic priest?"

I heard the men's room door open again and footsteps walk past me to the opposite end of the bar. Goldie's eyes became veiled, impossible to read. The top of his head looked like an alabaster bowling ball with blue lines in it.

"I'm sorry about your wife. It was last year?" he said.

I nodded.

"It was lupus?" he said.

"Yeah, that's right," I replied.

"You doin' all right?"

"Sure," I said, avoiding his eyes.

"Don't get in no trouble, like we used to do in the old days."

"Not a chance," I said.

"Hey, my po'boy ready?" the man at the end of the bar asked.

The man made a call on the payphone, then ate his sandwich and bounced pool balls off the rails on the pool table. The mirror behind the bar was oxidized an oily green and yellow, like the color of lubricant floating in water, and between the liquor bottles lined along the mirror I could see the man looking at the back of my head.

I turned on the bar stool and grinned at him. He waited for me to speak. But I didn't.

"I know you?" he said.

"Maybe. I used to live in New Orleans. I don't anymore," I said.

He spun the cue ball down the rail into the pocket, his eyes lowered. "So you want to shoot some nine ball?" he said.

"I'd be poor competition."

He didn't raise his eyes or look at me again. He finished his beer and sandwich at the bar, then put on his coat and stood at the screen door, looking at the mist blowing under the colonnade and at the cars passing in the neon-streaked wetness in front of Goldie's bar. Clete Purcel fired up his Cadillac and rattled down the street, turning at the end of the block.

The man with the impish face and curls that hung on the back of his neck stepped outside and breathed the air like a man out for a walk, then got into a Honda and drove up Magazine toward the Garden District. A moment later Clete Purcel pulled around the block and picked me up.

"Can you catch him?" I asked.

"I don't have to. That's Gunner Ardoin. He lives in a dump off Tchoupitoulas," he said.

"Gunner? He's a button man?"

"No, he's been in two or three of Fat Sammy Figorelli's porn films. He mules crystal in the projects, too."

"Would he bust up a priest?" I asked.

Clete looked massive behind the steering wheel, his upper arms like big, cured hams inside his tropical shirt. His hair was sandy, cut short like a little boy's. A diagonal scar ran through his left eyebrow.

"Gunner?" he said. "It doesn't sound like him. But a guy who performs oral sex for a hometown audience? Who knows?"

We caught up with the Honda at Napoleon Avenue, then followed it through a dilapidated neighborhood of narrow streets and shotgun houses to Tchoupitoulas. The driver turned on a side street and parked under a live oak in front of a darkened cottage. He walked up a shell driveway and entered the back door with a key and turned on a light inside.

Clete circled the block, then parked four houses up the street from Gunner Ardoin's place and cut the engine. He studied my face.

"You look a little wired," he said.

"Not me," I said.

The rain on the windshield made rippling shadows on his face and arms. "I made my peace with N.O.P.D.," he said.

"Really?"

"Most of the guys who did us dirt are gone. I let it be known I'm not in the O.K. Corral business anymore. It makes life a lot easier," he said.

Through the overhang of the trees I could see the Mississippi levee at the foot of the street and fog billowing up from the other side. Boat lights were shining inside the fog so that the fog looked like electrified steam rising off the water.

"Are you coming?" I asked.

He pulled an unlit cigarette from his mouth and threw it out the window. "Why not?" he said.

We walked up Gunner Ardoin's driveway, past a garbage can over-flowing with shrimp husks. Banana trees grew against the side of the house and the leaves were slick and green and denting in the rainwater that slid off the roof. I jerked the back screen off the latch and went into Gunner Ardoin's kitchen.

"You beat up Catholic priests, do you?" I said.

"What?" he said, turning from the sink with a metal coffeepot in his hand. He wore draw-string, tin-colored workout pants and a ribbed undershirt. His skin was white, clean of jailhouse art, his underarms shaved. A weight set rested on the floor behind him.

"Lose the innocent monkey face, Gunner. You used a steel pipe on a priest name of Jimmie Dolan," Clete said.

Gunner set the coffeepot down on the counter. He studied both of us briefly, then lowered his eyes and folded his arms on his chest, his back resting against the sink. His nipples looked like small brown dimes through the fabric of his undershirt. "Do what you have to do," he said.

"Better rethink that statement," Clete said.

But Gunner only stared at the floor, his elbows cupped in his palms. Clete looked at me and raised his eyebrows.

"My name's Dave Robicheaux. I'm a homicide detective with the Iberia Parish Sheriff's Department," I said, opening my badge holder. "But my visit here is personal."

"I didn't beat up a priest. You think I did, then I'm probably in the shitter. I can't change that." He began picking at the calluses on his palm.

"You get that at a twelve-step session up at Angola?" Clete said.

Gunner Ardoin looked at nothing and suppressed a yawn.

"You raised Catholic?" I said.

He nodded, without lifting his eyes.

"You're not bothered by somebody hospitalizing a priest, breaking his bones, a decent man who never harmed anyone?" I said.

"I don't know him. You say he's a good guy, maybe he is. There's a lot of priests out there are good guys, right?" he said.

Then, like all career recidivists and fulltime smart-asses, he couldn't resist the temptation to show his contempt for the world of normal people. He turned his face away from me, but I saw one eye glimmer with mirth, a grin tug slightly at the corner of his mouth. "Maybe they kept the altar boys away from him," he said.

I stepped closer to him, my right hand balling. But Clete pushed me aside. He picked up the metal coffeepot from the counter and smashed it almost flat against the side of Gunner Ardoin's head, then threw him in a chair. Gunner folded his arms across his chest, a torn grin on his mouth, blood trickling from his scalp.

"Have at it, fellows. I made both y'all back on Napoleon. I dialed 911 soon as I came in. My lawyer loves guys like you," he said.

Through the front window I saw the emergency flasher on an N.O.P.D. cruiser pull to the curb under the live oak tree that grew in Gunner Ardoin's front yard. A lone black female officer slipped her baton into the ring on her belt and walked uncertainly toward the gallery, her radio squawking incoherently in the rain.

I slept that night on Clete's couch in his small apartment above his P.I. office on St. Ann. The sky was clear and pink at sunrise, the streets in the Quarter puddled with water, the bougainvillea on Clete's balcony as bright as drops of blood. I shaved and dressed while Clete was still asleep and walked past St. Louis Cathedral and through Jackson Square to the Cafe du Monde, where I met Father Jimmie Dolan at a table under the pavilion.

Although we had been friends and had bass fished together for two decades, he remained in many ways a mysterious man, at least to me. Some said he was a closet drunk who had done time in a juvenile reformatory; others said he was gay and well known among the homosexual community in New Orleans, although women were obviously drawn to him. He had crewcut, blond good looks and the wide shoulders and tall, trim physique of the wide-end receiver he had been at a Winchester, Kentucky, high school. He didn't talk politics but he got into trouble regularly with authority on almost all levels, including six months in a federal prison for trespassing on the School of the Americas property at Ft. Benning, Georgia.

It had been three months since he had been waylaid in an alley behind his church rectory and methodically beaten from his neck to the soles of his feet by someone wielding a pipe with an iron bonnet screwed down on the business end.

"Clete Purcel and I rousted a guy named Gunner Ardoin last night. I think maybe he's the guy who attacked you," I said.

Father Jimmie had just bitten into a beignet and his mouth was smeared with powdered sugar. He wore a tiny sapphire in his left earlobe. His eyes were a deep green, thoughtful, his skin tan. He shook his head.

"That's Phil Ardoin. Wrong guy," he said.

"He said he didn't know you."

"I coached his high school basketball team."

"Why would he lie?"

"With Phil it's a way of life."

An N.O.P.D. cruiser pulled to the curb out on Decatur and a black female officer got out and fixed her cap on her head. She looked like she was constructed of twigs, her sky blue shirt too large on her frame, her pursed lips layered with red lipstick. Last night Clete had said she reminded him of a black swizzle stick with a cherry stuck on the end.

She threaded her way through the tables until she was abreast of ours. The brass name tag on her shirt said C. ARCENEAUX.

"I thought I should give you a heads-up," she said.

"How's that?" I asked.

She looked off abstractly at the traffic on the street and at the artists setting up their easels under the trees in Jackson Square. "Take a walk with me," she said.

I followed her down to a shady spot at the foot of the Mississippi levee. "I tried to talk to the other man, what's his name, Purcel, but he seemed more interested in riding his exercise bike," she said.

"He has blood pressure problems," I said.

"Maybe more like a thinking problem," she replied, looking idly down the street.

"Can I help you with something?" I asked.

"Gunner Ardoin is filing an assault charge against you and your friend. I think maybe he's got a civil suit in mind. If I was you, I'd take care of it."

"Take care of it?" I said.

Her eyes squinted into the distance, as though the subject at hand had already slipped out of her frame of reference. Her hair was black and thick and cut short on her neck, her eyes a liquid brown.

"Why are you doing this?" I asked.

"Don't like people who mule crystal into the projects."

"You work both the night and the morning watch?"

"I'm just up from meter maid. Low in standing, know what I mean, but somebody got to do it. Tell the priest to spend more time with his prayers," she said, and started to walk back to her cruiser.

"What's your first name?" I asked.

"Clotile," she said.

Back at the table I watched her drive away into the traffic, the lacquered brim of her cap low on her forehead. Meter maid, my ass, I thought.

"Ever hear of Junior Crudup?" Father Jimmie asked.

"The blues man? Sure," I said.

"What do you know about him?"

"He died in Angola," I said.

"No, he disappeared in Angola. Went in and never came out. No record at all of what happened to him," Father Jimmie said. "I'd like for you to meet his family."

"Got to get back to New Iberia."

"It's Saturday," he said.

"Nope," I said.

"Junior's granddaughter owns a twelve-string guitar she thinks might have belonged to Leadbelly. Maybe you could take a look at it. Unless you just really don't have the time?" he said.

I followed Father Jimmie in my pickup truck into St. James Parish, which lies on a ninety-mile corridor between Baton Rouge and New Orleans that environmentalists have named Toxic Alley. We drove down a state road south of the Mississippi levee through miles of sugarcane and on through a community of narrow, elongated shacks that had been built in the late nineteenth century. At the crossroads, or what in south Louisiana is called a four-corners, was a ramshackle nightclub, an abandoned company store with a high, tin-roofed gallery, a drive-by daiquiri stand, and a solitary oil storage tank that was streaked with corrosion at the seams, next to which someone had planted a tomato garden.

Most of the people who lived at the four-corners were black. The rain ditches and the weeds along the roadside were layered with bottles of beer and pop cans and trash from fast-food restaurants. The people who sat on the galleries of the shacks were either old or infirm or children. I watched a car filled with teenagers run a stop sign and fling a quart beer bottle on the side of the road, ten feet from where an elderly woman was picking up litter from her lawn and placing it in a vinyl bag.

Then we were out in the countryside again and the sky was as blue as a robin's egg, the sugarcane bending in the wind as far as the eye could see, egrets perched like white sculptures on the backs of cattle in a roadside pasture. But inside the loveliness of the day was another element, discordant and invasive, the metallic reek of natural gas, perhaps from a wellhead or a leaking connection at a pump station. Then the wind shifted and it was gone and the sky was speckled with birds rising from a pecan orchard and from the south I could smell the brassy odor of a storm that was building over the Gulf.

I looked at my watch. No more than one hour with Father Jimmie's friends, I told myself. I wanted to get back to New Iberia and forget about the previous night and the trouble with Gunner Ardoin.

Maybe it was time to let Father Jimmie take care of his own problems, I thought. Some people loved adversity, got high on it daily, and secretly despised those who would take it from them. That trait didn't necessarily go away because of a Roman collar.

The state road made a bend and suddenly the endless rows of sugarcane ended. The fields were uncultivated now, empty of livestock, dotted with what looked like settling ponds. The Crudup family lived down a dirt lane in a white frame house with a wraparound veranda hung with baskets of flowers. Three hundred yards behind the house was a woods bordered with trees that were gray with dead leaves and the scales of air vines, as though the treeline had been matted with premature winterkill.

Father Jimmie had set the hook when he had mentioned Leadbelly's name, but I knew as we drove down the road toward the neat white house backdropped by a poisoned woods that this trip was not about the recidivist convict who wrote "Goodnight Irene" and "The Midnight Special" and who today is almost forgotten.

In fact, I wondered if I, like Father Jimmie, could not wait to fill my day with adversity in the way I had once filled it with Jim Beam and a glass of Jax with strings of foam running down the sides.

When I cut my engine in front of the house, I took a Dr Pepper from the cooler on the seat and raked the ice off the can and drank it empty before stepping out onto the yard.

Chapter 2

Junior Crudup's granddaughter had a face like a goldfish, light skin that was dusted with freckles, and glasses that turned her eyes into watery brown orbs. She sat in a stuffed chair, fanning herself with a magazine, her rings of fat bulging against her dress, waiting for me to finish examining the Stella guitar that had lain propped in a corner of her attic for thirty years. The strings were gone, the tuning keys stiff with rust, the sound hole coated with cobweb. I turned the guitar on its belly and looked at three words that were scratched into the back of the neck: *Huddie Love Sarie.*

"Leadbelly's real name was Huddie Ledbetter. His wife was named Sarie," I said.

Junior Crudup's granddaughter looked through a side window at two children playing on a rope swing that was suspended from a pecan tree. Her name was Doris. She kept straightening her shoulders, as though a great weight were pressing on her lungs. "How much it wort'?" she asked.

"I couldn't say," I replied.

"Four or five songs were in the bottom of the guitar case, each with Junior's signature," Father Jimmie said.

"Yeah, what they wort'?" Doris Crudup asked.

"You'd have to ask somebody else," I said.

She gave Father Jimmie a look, then got up from her chair and took my coffee cup into the kitchen, although I had not finished drinking the coffee in it.

"Her husband died three years ago. Last month the social worker cut off her welfare," Father Jimmie said.

"Why?"

"The social worker felt like it. That's the way it works. Take a walk with me," he said.

"I need to get back home."

"You have time for this," he said.

We went outside, into the sunlit, rain-washed loveliness of the fall afternoon. The pecan tree in the side yard puffed with wind and a yellow dog rolled on its back in the dirt while the children swung back and forth above it on their rope swing. But as I followed Father Jimmie down an incline toward the woods in back I could feel the topography changing under my feet, as though I were walking on a sponge.

"What's that smell?" I said.

"You tell me." He tore a handful of grass from the soil and held the roots up to my nose. "They truck it in from all over the South. Doris's lungs are as much good to her as rotted cork. People around here carry buckets in their cars because of their children's constant diarrhea."

I held onto the trunk of a withered persimmon tree and looked at the soles of my shoes. They were slick with a black-green substance, as though I had walked across a factory floor. We crossed a board plank spanning a rain ditch. The water was covered with an iridescent sheen that seemed to be rising in chains of bubbles from the bottom of the ditch. Perhaps twenty settling ponds, layered over with loose dirt, were strung along the edge of the woods, each of them crusted with a dried viscous material that looked like an orange scab.

"Is this Doris's property?" I said.

"It belonged to her grandfather. But twenty years ago Doris's cousin made his 'X' on a bill of sale that had Junior's name typed on it. The cousin and the waste management company that bought the land both claim he's the Junior Crudup of record and Doris is out of luck."

"I'm not following you."

"No one knows what happened to the real Junior Crudup. He went into Angola and never came out. There's no documentation on his death or of his release. Figure that one out."

"I don't want to."

Father Jimmie studied my face. "These people here don't have many friends," he said.

I slipped the flats of my hands in my back pockets and scuffed at the ground with one shoe, like a third-base coach who had run out of signals.

"Think I'll pass," I said.

"Suit yourself."

Father Jimmie picked up a small stone and side-armed it into the woods. I heard it clatter among the tree trunks. Birds should have risen from the canopy into the sky, but there was no movement inside the tree limbs.

"Who owns this waste management company?" I asked.

"A guy named Merchie Flannigan."

"Jumpin' Merchie Flannigan? From New Iberia?" I said.

"One and the same. How'd he get that name, anyway?" Father Jimmie said.

"Think of rooftops," I said.

As I drove back to New Iberia, through Morgan City, and down East Main to my rented house on Bayou Teche, I tried not to think anymore of Father Jimmie and the black people in St. James Parish whose community had become a petro-chemical dumping ground. As sad as their story was, in the state of Louisiana it wasn't exceptional. In fact, on television, the current governor had threatened to investigate the tax status of some young Tulane lawyers who had filed suit against several waste management companies on the basis of environmental racism. The old plantation oligarchy was gone. But its successors did business in the same fashion—with baseball bats.

I fixed an early supper and ate it on an ancient green picnic table in the backyard. Across the bayou kids were playing tag football in City Park and smoke from meat fires hung in the trees. In the deepening shadows I thought I could hear voices inside my head: my adopted daughter, Alafair, away at Reed College; my deceased wife Bootsie; and a black man named Batist, to whom I had sold my bait and boat-

rental business south of town. I didn't do well on Saturday afternoons. In fact, I wasn't doing well on any afternoon.

On some weekends I drove out to the dock and bait shop to see
him. We'd fish the swamp for bass and sac-a-lait, then head home at
sunset, the cypress trees riffling like green lace in the wind, the water
back in the coves bloodred in the sun's afterglow. But across the road
and up the incline from the dock were the burned remains of the
house my father had built out of notched and pegged timbers during
the Depression, the home where I had lived with my wife and daughter, and I had a hard time looking at it without feeling an indescrib-
able sense of loss and anger.

The inspector from the fire department called it "electrical failure." I wished I could accept the loss in terms as clinical as those. But
the truth was I had trusted the electrical rewiring on my home to a
fellow A.A. member, one who had stopped attending meetings. He
filled the walls with cheap switches that he did not screw-wrap and
inserted fourteen-gauge wire into twelve-gauge receptacles. The fire
started inside the bedroom wall and burned the house to the ground
in less than an hour.

I went into the house and looked up Merchie Flannigan's name in
the directory. I had known his parents in both New Orleans and New
Iberia, but I'd never had reason to take official notice of Merchie until I was a patrolman near the Iberville Welfare Project off Basin
Street, back in the days when cops still rang their batons off street
curbs to signal one another and white kids would take your head off
with water-filled garbage cans dropped from a five-story rooftop.

Long before Hispanic and black caricatures acted out self-created
roles as gangsters on MTV, white street gangs in New Orleans
fought with chains, steel pipes, and zip guns over urban territory that
a self-respecting Bedouin wouldn't live in. During the 1950s, the ter-
ritorial war was between the Cats and the Frats. Frats lived uptown,
in the Garden District and along St. Charles Avenue. Cats lived in
the Irish Channel, or downtown or in the projects or out by the In-
dustrial Canal. Cats were usually Irish or Italian or a mixture of both,
parochial school bust-outs who rolled drunks and homosexuals and

group-stomped their adversaries, giving no quarter and asking for
none in return.

In a back-alley, chain-swinging rumble, their ferocity and raw
physical courage could probably be compared only to that of their
historical cousins in Southie, the Five Points, and Hell's Kitchen.
Along Bourbon Street, after twelve on Saturday nights, the Dixie-
land bands would pack up their instruments and be replaced by rock
'n' roll groups that played until sunrise. The kids spilling out the
front doors of Sharkey Bonnano's Dream Room, drinking papercup
beer and smoking cigarettes on the sidewalks, their motorcycle caps
and leather jackets rippling with neon, made most tourists wet their
pants.

But Jumpin' Merchie Flannigan could not be easily categorized as
a blue-collar street kid who had made good in the larger world. In
fact, I always had suspicions that Jumpin' Merchie joined a gang for
reasons very different from his friends in the Iberville. Unlike most of
them, he was not only streetwise but good in school and naturally intelligent. Merchie's problem really wasn't Merchie. It was his parents.

In New Iberia Merchie's father was thought of as a decent but
weak and ineffectual man whose rundown religious store was almost
an extension of its owner's personality. Many nights a sympathetic
police officer would take Mr. Flannigan out the back door of the
Frederic Hotel bar and drive him to his house by the railroad tracks.
Merchie's mother tried to compensate for the father's failure by constantly treating Merchie as a vulnerable child, protecting him, making him wear short pants at school until he was in the fifth grade,
denying him entry into a world that to her was as unloving as her
marriage. But I always felt her protectiveness was of a selfish kind,
and in reality she was not only sentimental rather than loving, she
could also be terribly cruel.

After the family moved to New Orleans and took up life in the
Iberville, Merchie became known as a mama's boy who was anybody's
punching bag or hard-up pump. But at age fifteen, he threw a black
kid from the Gird Town Deuces off a fire escape onto the cab of a
passing produce truck, then outraced a half dozen cops across a series

of rooftops, finally leaping out into space, plummeting two stories through the ceiling of a massage parlor.

His newly acquired nickname cost him a broken leg and a one-bit in the Louisiana reformatory, but Jumpin' Merchie Flannigan came back to Canal Street and the Iberville Project with magic painted on him.

When I called him at home he was gregarious and ingratiating, and said he wanted to see me. In fact, he said it with such sincerity that I believed him.

His home, of which he was very proud, was a gray architectural monstrosity designed to look like a medieval castle, inside acres of pecan and live oak trees, all of it in an unzoned area that mixed pipeyards and welding shops with thoroughbred horse barns and red-clay tennis courts.

He greeted me in the front yard, athletic, trim, wearing pleated tan slacks, half-top, slip-on boots, and a polo shirt, his long hair so blond it was almost white, a V-shaped receded area at the part the only sign of age I could see in him. The yard was covered in shadow now, the chrysanthemums denting in the wind, the sky veined with electricity. In the midst of it all Merchie seemed to glow not so much with health and prosperity as confidence that God was truly in His heaven and there was justice in the world for a kid from the Iberville.

He meshed his fingers, as though making a tent, then pointed the tips at me.

"You were out at the Crudup farm in St. James Parish today," he said.

"Who told you?" I asked.

"I'm trying to clean up the place," he replied.

"Think it might take a hydrogen bomb?"

"So give me the gen on it," he said.

"The Crudup woman says she was cheated out of the title."

"Look, Dave, I bought the property three years ago at a bankruptcy sale. I'll check into it. How about some trust here?"

It was hard to stay mad at Merchie. I knew people in the oil business who were openly ecstatic at the prospect of Mideastern wars or subzero winters in the northern United States, but Merchie had never been one of them.

"Been out of town?" I said.

"Yeah, Afghanistan. You believe it?"

"Shooting at the Taliban?"

He smiled with his eyes but didn't reply.

"The woman in St. James Parish? Her grandfather was Junior Crudup," I said.

"An R&B guy?"

"Yeah, one of the early ones. He did time with Leadbelly. He played with Jackie Brenston and Ike Turner," I said. But I could see him losing interest in the subject. "I'd better go. Your place looks nice. Give me some feedback later on the Crudup situation, will you?" I said.

"My favorite police officer," I heard a woman say.

The voice of Theodosha Flannigan was like a melancholy recording out of the past, the kind that carries fond memories but also some that are better forgotten. She was a member of the LeJeune family in Franklin, down the Teche, people whose wealth and lawn parties were legendary in southwest Louisiana, and she still used their name rather than Merchie's. She was tall, darkly beautiful, with hollow cheeks and long legs like a model's, her southern accent exaggerated, her jeans and tied-up black hair and convertible automobiles an affectation that belied the conservative and oligarchical roots she came from.

But in spite of her corn bread accent and the pleasure she seemed to take in portraying herself as an irreverent and neurotic southern woman, she had another side, one she never engaged in conversation about. She had written two successful screenplays and a trilogy of crime novels containing elements that were undeniably lyrical. Although her novels had never won an Edgar award, her talent was arguably enormous.

"How you doin', Theo?" I said.

"Stay for coffee or a cold drink?" she said.

"You know me, always on the run," I said.

She curled her fingers around the limb of a mimosa tree and propped one moccasin-clad foot against the trunk. Her breasts rose and fell against her blouse.

"How about diet Dr Pepper on the rocks, with cherries in it?" she said.

Don't hang around. Get away now, I heard a voice inside me say.

"I'm just about to fix some sherbet with strawberries. We'd love to have you join us, Dave," Merchie said.

"Sounds swell," I said, and dropped my eyes, wondering at the price I was willing to pay in order not to be alone.

On the way into the backyard Theodosha touched my arm. "I'm sorry about your loss. I hope you're doing all right these days," she said.

But I had no memory of her sending a sympathy card when Bootsie died.

I went to an early Mass the next morning, then bought a copy of the *Times-Picayune* and drank coffee at the picnic table in the backyard and read the newspaper. I read three paragraphs into an article about an errant bomb falling into a community of mudbrick huts in Afghanistan, then closed the paper and watched a group of children throwing a red Frisbee back and forth under the oak trees in the park. A speedboat full of teenagers roared down the bayou, swirling a trough back and forth between both banks, splintering the air with a deafening sound. I heard my portable phone tinkle softly by my thigh.

The operator asked if I would accept a collect call from Clete Purcel.

"Yes," I said.

"Streak, I'm in the zoo," Clete shouted.

In the background I could hear voices echoing down stone corridors or inside cavernous rooms.

"What did you say?"

"I'm in Central Lock-Up. They busted me for assaulting Gunner

Ardoin. I feel like I've been arrested for spraying Lysol on a toilet bowl."

"Why haven't you bonded out?" I asked.

"Nig and Willie aren't answering my calls."

I tried to make sense out of what he was saying. For years Clete had chased down bail skips for Nig Rosewater and Wee Willie Bimstine. He should have been out of jail with a signature.

I started to speak, but he cut me off. "Gunner is a grunt for Fat Sammy Fig, and Fat Sammy is connected up with every major league piece of shit in Louisiana. I think Nig and Willie don't want trouble with the wrong people. Arraignment isn't until Tuesday morning. Been down to Central Lock-Up lately?"

I took the four-lane through Morgan City into New Orleans. But I didn't go directly to the jail. Instead, I drove up St. Charles Avenue, then over toward Tchoupitoulas and parked in front of Gunner Ardoin's cottage. His Honda was in the driveway. I walked down to a corner store and bought a quart of chocolate milk and a prepackaged ham sandwich and sat down on Gunner's front steps and began eating the sandwich while children roller-skated past me under the trees.

I heard someone open the door behind me.

"What the fuck you think you're doin'?" Gunner's voice said.

"Oh, hi. I was about to ask you the same thing," I said.

"What?" he said. He was bare chested and barefoot, and wore only a pair of pajama bottoms string-tied under his navel. The breeze blew from the back of the cottage through the open door. *"What?"* he repeated.

"Toking up kind of early today?"

"So call the DEA."

"Father Jimmie Dolan was your basketball coach. Why did you say you didn't know him?"

"'Cause I can't remember every guy I knew in high school with a whistle hanging out of his mouth."

"Father Jimmie says it wasn't you who attacked him, Gunner. But I think somebody told you to bust him up, and you pieced off the job to somebody else. Probably because you still have qualms."

"Is this because I filed on your friend?"

"No, it's because you're a shitbag and you're going to drop those charges or I'll be back here tonight and jam a chainsaw up your ass."

"Look, man—" he began.

"No, you look," I said, rising to my feet, shoving him backward through the door into the living room. "Fat Sammy is behind the job on Father Jimmie?"

"No," he said.

I shoved him again. He tripped over a footstool and fell backward on the floor. I pulled back my sports coat and removed my .45 from its clip-on holster and squatted next to him. I pulled back the slide and chambered a round, then pointed the muzzle at his face.

"Look at my eyes and tell me I won't do it," I said.

I saw the breath seize in his throat and the blood go out of his cheeks. He stretched his head back, turning his face sideways, away from the .45.

"Don't do this," he said. "Please."

I waited a long time, then touched his forehead with the gun's muzzle and winked at him.

"I won't. I'd think about my request on those charges, though," I said.

Just as I eased the hammer back down, his bladder gave way and he shut his eyes in shame and embarrassment. When I looked up I saw a little girl, no older than six or seven, staring at us, horrified, from the kitchen doorway.

"That's my daughter. I get her one day a week. I've known some cruel guys with a badge, but you take the cake," Gunner said.

The charges against Clete were dropped by three that afternoon. I drove him from Central Lock-Up to his apartment on St. Ann, where he fell asleep on the couch in front of a televised football game. Fat Sammy Figorelli's home was only three blocks away, over on Ursulines. The temptation was too much.

Fat Sammy had grown up in the French Quarter, and although he owned homes in Florida and on Lake Pontchartrain, he spent most of his time inside the half city block where the Figorelli family had lived since the 1890s. It seemed Sammy had been elephantine all his life. As a child the balloon tires of his bicycle burst under his weight. His rump wouldn't fit in the desk at the school run by the Ursuline nuns. In high school he got stuck inside his tuba while performing with the marching band at an LSU football game. The paramedics had to scissor off his jacket, smear him with Vaseline, and pry him loose in front of ninety thousand people. In his senior year he mustered up the courage to invite a girl to the Prytania Theater. A gang of Irish kids in the balcony rained down a barrage of water-filled condoms on their heads.

As an adult he filled his body with laxatives, tried every diet program imaginable, trained at fat farms, sweated to the oldies with Richard Simmons, attended a fire-walker's school run by a celebrity con man in California, almost died from liposuction, and finally had a gastric bypass. The consequence of the latter was a weight loss of 170 pounds in a year's time.

All of the wrong kind.

He lost the blubber, but under the blubber was a support system of sinew that hung on his frame like curtains of partially hardened cement. If this was not enough of a problem, Fat Sammy had another one that was equally egregious and beyond the scope of medicine. His head was shaped like a football, his few strands of gold hair brushed like oily wire into his scalp.

I twisted an iron bell on the grilled door that gave onto a domed archway leading into Fat Sammy's courtyard.

"Who is it?" a voice said from a speaker inside the gate.

"It's Dave Robicheaux. I've got a problem," I said.

"Not with me, you don't."

"It's about Gunner Ardoin. Open the door."

"Never heard of him. Come back another time. I'm taking a nap."

"There're some movie people in New Iberia. They want to work with some local guys who know their way around," I said.

The speaker box went dead and the gate buzzed open.

The courtyard was surfaced with soft brick, the flower beds blooming with yellow and purple roses, irises and hibiscus and Hong Kong orchids. Banana and umbrella trees and windmill palms grew along the walls, and the balconies dripped with bougainvillea and passion vine. Fat Sammy lay in a hammock like a beached whale, a Hawaiian shirt unbuttoned on his chest, his skin glazed with suntan lotion. A portable stereo and a mirror and a hairbrush sat on a glass-topped table next to him. The stereo was playing "Clair de Lune."

"Who are these movie people?" he asked.

"Germans. They're making a documentary. I think you're the man to show them around," I said.

I pulled up a deep-backed wicker chair and sat down without being asked. He sat up in the hammock and turned down the volume on the stereo, his scalp glistening in the sunshine. He wiped his head with a towel, his eyes neutral, his mouth down-turned at the corners. "Documentary on what?" he asked.

"Let me clear the decks about something else first. Somebody beat up a priest named Father Jimmie Dolan. It's a lousy thing to happen, Sammy, something no respectable man would be involved in. I thought you'd want to know about it."

"No, I don't."

"In the old days elderly people in New Orleans didn't get jack-rolled and their houses didn't get creeped and nobody murdered a child or abused Catholic clergy. If N.O.P.D. couldn't take care of it, we let you guys do it for us."

His eyes were hooded, like a frog's. "You were kicked off the force, Robicheaux. You don't speak for nobody, at least not around here." He paused, as though reconsidering the tenor of his rhetoric. "Look, this used to be a good city. It ain't no more."

When I didn't speak he took a breath and started over. "This is the way it is. I make movies. I build houses. I'm developing shopping centers in Mississippi and Texas. You want to know who's running New Orleans? Flip over a rock. Welfare pukes hustling bazooka and blacks and South American spics and bikers muleing brown skag out of Florida. Nothing against the blacks or the spics. They're making it just like we did. But I wouldn't be in a room with none of them people unless I was encased in a full-body condom."

"Who did the job on Father Dolan?"

His eyes were pale blue, almost without color, his expression like that of a man who had never learned to smile. "Somebody saying it's on me? This guy Ardoin you mentioned?"

I looked at a strip of pink cloud above the courtyard. "You're the man in New Orleans," I said.

"Yeah, every whore in the city tells me the same thing. I wonder why. I ever jerk you around, Robicheaux?" he said.

"Not to my knowledge."

"Then I ain't going to now. That means I didn't have nothing to do with hurting a priest, and what I might know about it is my own business."

"I'm a little disappointed, Sammy. Within certain parameters you were always straight up," I said. I got up to go.

He brushed at his nose, his pale blue eyes burrowing into my face. "You lied your way in here? About them movie people?" he said.

"That was on the square." I handed him a business card that had been given to me by a member of a visiting German television crew the previous week. "These guys are doing a story on the New Orleans connection to the assassination of President Kennedy. They believe it got set up here and in Miami."

"You saying I—" His voice broke in his throat. "I voted for John Kennedy."

"I'm saying nothing had better happen to Father Dolan again."

Fat Sammy rose from the hammock, wheezing in his chest, like an angry behemoth that couldn't find its legs. I had forgotten how tall he was. He picked up a glass of iced tea from the table, gargled with it, and spit it in the flower bed.

"You own your soul?" he asked.

"What?"

"If so, count yourself a lucky man. Now get the fuck out of here," he said.

. . .

I ate dinner with Clete at a small restaurant up the street from the French Market, then shook hands with him and told him I had better head back for New Iberia. I watched him walk across Jackson Square and pass the cathedral, pigeons flapping in the shadows around his feet, and disappear down Pirates Alley. I started to get into my truck, but instead, for reasons I couldn't explain, I sat down on one of the iron benches by Andrew Jackson's equestrian statue, and listened to a black man playing a bottleneck guitar.

It was the burnt-out end of a long day and a longer weekend. The wind was cold off the river, the light cold and mauve colored between the buildings that framed the square, the air tinged with the smell of gas from the trees and flower beds. The black man worked the glass bottleneck up and down the frets of his guitar and sang, "Oh Lord, my time ain't long. Rubber-tired hack coming down the road, burial-ground bound."

An N.O.P.D. cruiser pulled to the curb on Decatur. A black woman in uniform got out and fixed her cap, adjusted the baton on her belt, and walked toward me. She positioned herself between me and the sun, like an exclamation point against a fiery crack in the sky. I picked at my nails and didn't return her stare.

"Can't stay out of town?" she said.

"I have an addictive personality," I replied.

She sat down on the corner of the bench. "You got a bad jacket for a cop, Robicheaux."

"Who the hell are you?" I said.

"Clotile Arceneaux. See," she said, lifting her brass name tag with her thumb. "Your friend, Father Dolan? He's an amateur, and they're going to take his legs off—yours, too, you keep messing in what you're not supposed to be messing in."

"I'm not big on telling other people what to do. I ask they show me the same courtesy," I said.

The baton on her hip kept banging against the bench. She slid it out of the ring that held it and bounced it between her legs on the cement. Her pursed lips looked like a tiny red rose in the gloom. I thought she would speak again, but she didn't. The sun went down behind the buildings in the square and the wind gusted off the levee, smelling of rain and fish-kill in the swamps.

"Can I buy you coffee, officer?" I said.

"Your friend is off the hook on the assault beef. Time for you to go home, Robicheaux," she said.

Home, I thought, and looked at her curiously, as though the word would not register in my mind.

Chapter 3

On Monday I left the department at mid-morning and checked out a history of Louisiana blues music and swamp pop from the city library and began reading it in my office. It was raining outside, and through my window I could see a freight train, the boxcars shiny with water, wobbling down the old Southern Pacific tracks through the black section of town. The longtime sheriff, an ex-marine who had marched out of the Chosin Reservoir, had retired and been replaced by my old partner, Helen Soileau.

I saw her stop in the corridor outside my office and bite her lip, her hands on her hips. She tapped on the door, then opened it without waiting for me to tell her to come in.

"Got a minute?" she asked.

"Sure."

"A couple of N.O.P.D. plainclothes picked up a prisoner this morning. They said you and Clete bent a pornographic actor out of shape. They thought it was funny."

"Pornographic actor?" I said vaguely.

"Ardoin was his name."

"Clete flattened a coffeepot against the side of the guy's head, but it wasn't a big deal," I said.

She had the muscular build of a man and blond hair that she cut short, tapering it on the sides and neck so that it looked like the freshly cropped mane on a pony. She wore slacks and a white, short-sleeve shirt, a badge holder hooked on her belt. She sucked in her cheeks and watched a raindrop run down the window glass above my head.

"Not a big deal? Interrogating people outside your jurisdiction, banging them in the head with a coffeepot? Dave, I never thought I'd be in this situation," she said.

"Which one is that?"

She leaned on the windowsill and looked at the lights of the freight caboose disappearing between a green jungle on each side of the tracks.

"You and Cletus work it out, but I don't want anybody, that means *anybody*, dragging N.O.P.D.'s dogshit into this department. I don't want to be the dartboard for those wise-asses, either. We straight on this?" she said.

"I hear you."

"Good."

"Remember an R&B guitarist named Junior Crudup?" I asked.

"No."

"He went into Angola and never came out. I think his granddaughter got swindled out of her land over in St. James Parish. I think Merchie Flannigan is mixed up in it."

She straightened her back, then looked at me for a long moment. But whatever she had planned to say seemed to go out of her eyes. She grinned, shaking her head, and walked out into the corridor.

I followed her outside.

"What was that about?" I asked.

"Nothing. Absolutely nothing," she said. "Streak, you're just too much. God protect me from my own sins."

Then she laughed out loud and walked away.

Monday night I listened to two ancient .78 recordings made by Junior Crudup in the 1940s. As with Leadbelly, the double-strung bass strings on his guitar were tuned an octave apart, but you could hear Blind Lemon and Robert Johnson in his style as well. His voice was haunting. No, that's not the right word. It drifted above the notes like a moan.

There are some stories that are just too awful to hear, the kind that people press on you after A.A. meetings or in late-hour bars, and later you cannot rid yourself of. This is one of them.

Oldtime recidivists always maintained that the worst joints in the country were in Arkansas. Places like Huntsville and Eastham in the Texas penal system came in a close second, primarily because of the furious pace at which the convicts were worked and the punishment barrels they were forced to stand on throughout the night, dirty and unfed, if a gunhack decided they were dogging it in the cotton field.

But Angola Pen could lay claims that few other penitentiaries could match. During Reconstruction Angola became the model for the rental convict system, one emulated throughout the postbellum South, not only as a replacement for slave labor but as a far more cost-efficient and profitable successor to it. Literally thousands of Louisiana convicts died of exposure, malnutrition, and beatings with the black Betty. Each of the camps made use of wood stocks that were right out of medieval Europe. The scandals at Angola received national notoriety in the 1950s when convicts began slashing the tendons in their ankles rather than stack time on what was called the Red Hat Gang.

I drove up Bayou Teche to Loreauville, where the black man to whom I had sold my boat and bait business now lived with his daughter on a small plot of land not far from town. His house was set back in the shadows, on the bayou's edge, the tin roof almost entirely covered by the overhang of pecan and oak trees. I parked my pickup truck in the trees and walked up to the gallery, where he sat in a wood rocker, a jelly glass filled with iced coffee in his massive hand.

His name was Batist, and he was both older than he would concede and yet indifferent to what the world thought of him. He had worked most of his life as a farmer, a muskrat trapper and commercial fisherman with my father, and as a packer in several canneries. He could not read or write, but he was nonetheless one of the most insightful people I had ever known.

A fat, three-footed raccoon named Tripod was eating out of a pet bowl on the steps.

"What's the haps, 'Pod?" I said to the raccoon, scooping him up in my arms.

Batist's whiskers were white against his cheeks. He removed a cigar from the pocket of his denim shirt and slipped it into his jaw but didn't light it.

"You ain't come to see me this weekend," he said.

"I had to take care of some business in New Orleans," I said. "Years ago, you knew Junior Crudup, didn't you?"

He raised his eyebrows. "Oh yeah, ain't no doubt about that," he replied.

"What happened to him?"

"What always happened to his kind back then. Trouble wherever he went."

"Want to be a little more specific?"

"Back in them days there was fo' kinds of black folks. There was people of color, there was Negroes, and there was colored people. Under all them others was niggers."

"Crudup was in the last category?"

"Wrong about that. Junior Crudup was a man of color. Called hisself a Creole. He wore an ox-blood Stetson, two-tone shoes, and a shirt and suit that was always pressed. Used to have a cherry red electric guitar he'd carry to all the dances. If a man could be pretty, that was Junior."

"How'd he end up in Angola?"

"Didn't fit. Not in white people's world, not in black people's world. Junior had his own way. Didn't take his hat off to nobody. He'd walk five miles befo' he'd sit in the back of the bus. Back in them days, a black man like that wasn't gonna have a long run."

Tripod was struggling in my arms and kicking at me with his feet. I set him down and looked at the fireflies lighting in the trees. The air was cool and breathless, the surface of the bayou layered with steam. An electrically powered boat hung with lanterns was passing through the corridor of oaks that lined the banks. Batist's attitudes on race were not conventional ones. He never saw himself as a victim, nor did he ever act as the apologist for black men who were forced into lives of crime, but by the same token he never told less than the truth about the world in which he'd grown up. So far I could not determine where he stood on Junior Crudup.

"It started at a dance at the beginning of the Depression," he said.

"Junior was about t'irteen or fo'teen years old, working in a band for a black man had the most beautiful voice you ever heard. They was playing in a white juke by Ville Platte, on a real hot night, the place burning up inside. The singer, the man wit' the beautiful voice, he was playing the piano and singing at the same time, sweat pouring down his face. A white woman come off the dance flo' and patted her handkerchief on his brow. That's all she done. That's all she had to do.

"After the juke closed up, five white men drunk on moonshine caught the singer out on the road and beat him till he couldn't get off the ground. But that wasn't enough for them, no. They was in an old Ford, one wit' them narrow tires, and they run the tire right acrost his t'roat and busted his windpipe. Man never sung again and died in the asylum. Junior seen it all, right there on the side of the road, and couldn't do nothing about it. I don't t'ink there was a person in the whole round world he trusted after that."

"Why'd he go to the joint, Batist?"

"Got caught sleeping wit' a white man's wife. That was 1934 or '35. But you want to know what happened in there, we got to talk to Hogman."

"Batist, I'd really like to keep this simple."

"They put Junior Crudup on the Red Hat Gang. Every nigger in Lou'sana feared that name, Dave. The ones come off it wasn't never the same."

Hogman Patin was a big, powerful man, an ex-con musician who had done time at the old camps in Angola with Robert Pete Williams, Matthew Maxey, and Guitar Git-and-Go Welch. His arms were coal black and laced with pink scars from a half dozen knife beefs inside the prison system. Now he ran a cafe in St. Martinville, appeared once a year at the International Music Festival in Lafayette, and sold scenic postcards with his signature on them for a dollar a piece. Batist and I sat with him in his side yard, a mile up the bayou, while he threw scrap wood on a fire and told us about Junior Crudup and the Red Hat Gang.

"See, Junior run the first year he was on the farm. Gunbull put a half cup of birdshot in his back, but he whipped a mule into the water and held onto its tail till it swum him all the way acrost the Miss'sippi," Hogman said, flinging a board into the fire, the sparks fanning across the bayou's surface. "A young white doctor on the other side picked the shot out of his back and tole Junior he had a choice—he'd give Junior ten dollars and forget he was there or the doctor would carry him on back to the penitentiary.

"Junior said, 'They'll whup me with the black Betty if I go back.'

"The doctor say, 'No, they ain't. I'm gonna make sure they ain't.'

"The doctor carried him on back to the farm and tole the warden he was gonna come see Junior every mont', and if Junior was whupped, the doctor was gonna have the warden's job.

"When Junior come out of the infirmary, they sent him to the Red Hat Gang. There was two captains running the Red Hat Gang then, the Latiolais brothers. First day they tole Junior they knowed they couldn't whup him, but by God they was gonna kill him.

"See, there was several t'ings special about the Red Hat Gang. Everybody wore black-and-white stripes and straw hats that was painted red. But didn't nobody walk. From cain't-see to cain't-see, it was double-time, hit-it-and-git-it, roll, nigger, roll.

"The Latiolais brothers was both drunkards. One of them might drink corn liquor under a tree and take a nap, then wake up and point his finger at a man and say, 'Take off, boy.' The next t'ing you'd hear was that shotgun popping.

"If a man fell out under the sun, he'd get put on an anthill. If a man was dogging it on the wheelbarrow, the captain would say, 'I need me a big wet rock.' There was a mess of rocks piled up down in the shallows, see. A convict would have to find a big one, a twenty-five pounder maybe, wet it down, and run it back up the slope to the captain befo' it was dry. Course, the faster the convict run, the quicker the rock got dried.

"So one day the captain tole Junior he was dogging it and he better get his ass down on the river and bring the captain the biggest wet rock he could find. Now, them rocks was a good half mile away and the captain knowed Junior was gonna be one wore-out nigger by the end of the day.

"Except Junior toted the rock on up the slope, then when the captain wasn't looking, he ducked behind some gum trees and pissed all over it. Then he holds up the rock to the captain and says, 'This wet enough for you, boss?'

"The captain touches the rock and looks at his hand and smells it. He cain't believe what Junior just done. Everybody on the Red Hat Gang started laughing. They was trying to hide it, looking at the ground and each other, but they just couldn't hold it inside. It was so funny they thought for a minute even the captain would laugh. They was sure wrong about that."

"What happened?" I asked.

Hogman wore a strap undershirt that hung like rags on his body. His eyes took on a melancholy cast.

"The captain took Junior to the sweatbox on Camp A. It was an iron box no bigger than a coffin, standing straight up on a concrete pad. They kept that boy in there seven days, in the middle of summer, no way to go to the bat'room except a bucket between his legs," he said.

"What became of Junior?" I asked.

"Don't know. He was in and out of 'Gola a couple of times. Maybe they buried him in the levee. I reckon there's hundreds in that levee. I don't study on it no mo'," he said.

His eyes seemed to focus on nothing, his forehead glistening in the firelight.

Early the next morning I picked up my mail in my pigeon hole at the department and sorted through it at my desk. In it was an invitation, written in a beautiful hand on silver-embossed stationery.

Dear Dave,

Can you come to Fox Run Saturday afternoon? It's lawn tennis and drinks and probably a few self-satisfied people talking about their money. In fact, it's probably going to be a drag. But that's life on the bayou, right? Merchie and I do want to see you.

Call me. Please. It's been a long time.

Until then, Theodosha

A long time since what? I thought.

But I knew the answer, and the memory was one I tried to push out of my mind. I dropped the invitation into a drawer and glanced out the window at a car with two men in it, pulling to the curb in front of the courthouse. The driver wore a black suit and a Roman collar. His passenger twisted his head about, his face bloodless, like someone on his way to the scaffold.

Two minutes later the pair of them were at my door.

"Phil came to the church and made his reconciliation," Father Jimmie said, closing the door behind him. "If you don't mind, he'd like to talk over some things with you. Maybe in private."

Gunner Ardoin, whom Father Jimmie referred to as Phil, looked at me briefly, then out the window at a trusty mowing the grass.

"You want to tell me something, Gunner?" I asked.

"Yeah, sure," he replied.

Father Jimmie nodded and left the room. I told Gunner to take a seat in front of my desk. He breathed through his mouth, as though he were inside a walk-in freezer.

"I'm doing this for Father Dolan," he said.

"You're doing it to save your ass," I said.

His eyes didn't look at me but his face hardened.

"You went to confession?" I said.

"They call it reconciliation now. But, yeah, I went," he said.

"So who put the contract on Father Jimmie?"

"I got a phone call. From a guy named Ray. He don't have another name. He just said I was supposed to take care of Father Dolan. When I got a delivery to make, Ray is the guy who calls me. I told Ray I didn't do stuff like that. He says I do it or I find a new source of income. So I called up a guy. He rolls queers in the Quarter and at some sleaze joints on Airline. For a hundred bucks he does other kinds of work, too."

"Do you have any idea what you did to a decent and fine man?"

"You want the guy's name?"

"No, I want Ray's last name and I want the guy Ray works for."

"Man, you don't understand. Father Dolan's got enemies all over New Orleans. He's trying to shut down drive-by daiquiri windows and trash incinerators and these guys who been dumping sludge out in the river parishes. He told the *Times-Picayune* these right-to-life people were committing a sin by putting these women's pictures and names on the Internet."

"What are you talking about?"

"These anti-abortion nutcases. They take pictures of women going into abortion clinics, then put the pictures and the women's names and addresses on the Internet. Father Dolan spoke up about it, a Catholic priest. How many enemies does one guy need?"

"Our time is about up, Gunner," I said.

"The queer-bait from the Quarter was supposed to scare Father Dolan, not go apeshit with a pipe. Hey, are you listening? It's on the street I snitched off Sammy Fig. You must have given up my name to Fat Sammy."

"Sammy says he never heard of you. You shouldn't have anything to worry about."

"I knew it." His face turned gray. He wiped his mouth and looked at the trusty gardener clipping a hedge outside the window. "Why you staring at me like that?" he said.

"I think you're using the seal of the confessional to keep Father Dolan from testifying against you."

"Maybe that was true at first. But I'm still sorry for what I done. He's a good guy. He didn't deserve what happened to him."

I glanced at my watch. "We're done here. So long, Gunner," I said.

He rose from his chair and walked to the door, then stopped, his shoulders slightly stooped, his impish features waiting in anticipation, as though an act of mercy might still be extended to him.

"What is it?" I said.

"Call Sammy Fig. Tell him I didn't rat him out."

"What's Ray's last name?" I asked.

"I don't know."

"*Adios,*" I said.

I went back to reading my morning mail. When I looked up again, he was gone. A moment later Father Jimmie stuck his head in the door, his disappointment obvious.

"You couldn't help Phil out?" he asked.

The next day I called the warden's office at Angola Penitentiary and asked an administrative assistant to do a records search under the name of Clarence "Junior" Crudup.

"When was he here?" the assistant asked.

"In the forties or fifties."

"Our records don't go back that far. You'll have to go through Baton Rouge for that."

"This guy went in but didn't come out."

"Say again?"

"He was never released. No one knows what happened to him."

"Try Point Lookout."

"The cemetery?"

"Nobody gets lost in here. They either go out through the front gate or they get planted in the gum trees."

"How about under the levee?"

He hung up on me.

At noon I walked past the whitewashed and crumbling brick crypts in St. Peter's Cemetery to Main Street and ate lunch at Victor's Cafeteria, then returned to the office just as the sun went behind a bank of thunderheads and the wind came up hard in the south and began blowing the trees along the train tracks. There were two telephone messages from Theodosha Flannigan in my mailbox. I dropped them both in the dispatcher's wastebasket.

At 4:00 P.M., in the middle of a downpour, I saw her black Lexus pull to the curb in front of the courthouse. She popped open an umbrella and raced for the front of the building, water splashing on her calves and the bottom of her pink skirt.

I went out into the corridor to meet her, feigning a confidence that masked my desire to avoid seeing her again.

"Did you get my invitation?" she said, her face and hair bright with rain.

"Yes, thanks for sending it," I replied.

"I called earlier. A couple of times."

Two deputies at the water cooler were looking at us, their eyes traveling the length of her figure.

"Come on in the office, Theo. It's been a little busy today," I said.

I closed the door behind us. "If you can't come Saturday, I understand. I need to talk to you about something else, though," she said.

"Oh?"

"I've got a problem. It comes in bottles. Not just booze. Six months ago I started using again. My psychiatrist gave me the keys to the candy store," she said.

Her voice was wired, the whites of her eyes threaded with tiny veins. She let out a breath in a ragged sigh. Her breath smelled like whiskey and mint leaves, and not from the previous night. "Can I sit down?" she asked.

"Yes, I'm sorry. Please," I said, and looked over my shoulder at Helen Soileau passing in the corridor.

"Dave, I have little men with drills and saws working in my head all day. Sometimes in the middle of the night, too," Theodosha said.

"There's a meeting tonight at Solomon House, across from old New Iberia High," I said.

"I've been in treatment twice. I was in analysis for seven years. I get a year of sobriety, then things start happening in my head again. My most recent psychiatrist shot himself last week. In Lafayette, in Girard Park, while his kids were playing on the swings. I keep thinking I had something to do with it."

"Where's Merchie in all this?"

"He makes excuses for me. He doesn't complain. I couldn't ask for more. You know, he's not entirely normal himself." She took a handkerchief from her purse and blotted the moisture from her eyes. "I don't know what I'm doing here. Merchie's bothered because you think he's dumping oil waste around poor people's homes. He looks up to you. Can't you come out to Fox Run Saturday?"

"I'm kind of jammed up these days."

"How long were you drunk?"

"Fifteen years, more or less."

"You didn't want to drink when your wife died?"

"No," I said, my eyes leaving hers.

"I don't know how anybody stays sober. I feel dirty all over."

"Why?"

"Who cares? Some people are born messed up," she said. "I'm sorry for coming in here like this. I'm going to find a dark, hermetically sealed, air-conditioned lounge and dissolve myself inside a vodka collins."

"Some people just ride out the hangover. Today can be the first inning in a new ballgame."

"Good try," she said, rising from her chair.

I thought she was about to leave. Instead, she fixed her gaze on me, waiting. Her hair had the black-purplish sheen of silk, the tips damp and curled around her throat.

"Is there something else?" I asked.

"What about Saturday?" Her face softened as she waited for an answer.

Chapter 4

That evening, at twilight, a Buick carrying three teenage girls roared around a curve on Loreauville Road, passed a truck, caromed off a roadside mailbox, then righted itself and slowed behind a school bus as someone in the backseat flung a box of fast-food trash and plastic cups and straws out the window. The truck driver, a religious man who kept a holy medal suspended from a tiny chain on his rearview mirror, would say later he thought the girls had settled down and would probably follow the church bus at a reasonable speed into Loreauville, five miles up Bayou Teche.

Instead, the driver crossed the double-yellow stripe again, into oncoming traffic, then tried to cut in front of the church bus when she realized safe harbor would never again be hers.

Helen Soileau, four uniformed deputies, two ambulances, and a firetruck were already at the accident scene when I arrived. The girls were still inside the Buick. The telephone pole they had hit was cut in half at the base and the downed wires were hanging in an oak tree. The Buick had slid on its roof farther down the embankment, splintering a white fence before coming to rest by the side of a fish pond, where the gas tank had exploded and burned with heat so intense the water in the pond boiled.

"You run the tag yet?" I said.

"It's registered to a physician in Loreauville. The baby-sitter says he and his wife are playing golf. I left a message at the country club," Helen said.

She wore her shield on a black cord around her neck. The wind shifted, blowing across the barns and pastures of the horse farm where the Buick had burned. But the odor the wind carried was not of horses and alfalfa. Helen held a wadded-up piece of Kleenex to her nose, snuffing, as though she had a cold. Two firemen used the jaws-of-life to pry apart the window on the driver's side of the Buick, then began pulling the remains of the driver out on the grass.

"The bus driver says the Buick was swinging all over the road?" I asked.

"Yep, they were having a grand time of it. Life on the bayou in 2002," Helen said.

The water oaks along the Teche had already lost their leaves and their branches looked skeletal against the flattened, red glow of the sun on the western horizon. A spruce green Lincoln with two people in the front seat approached us from the direction of Loreauville, slowing in the dusk, pulling onto the shoulder. The driver got out, looking over the top of his automobile at the scene taking place by the fish pond, his face stenciled with a sadness that no cop, at least no decent one, ever wishes to deal with.

I reached through the open window of Helen's cruiser and picked up a pair of polyethylene gloves and a vinyl garbage bag.

"Where you going?" she said.

"Litter patrol," I replied.

I walked back along the road for two hundred yards or so, past a line of cedar trees that bordered another horse farm, then crossed the road to the opposite embankment where a spray of freshly thrown trash bloomed in the grass. I picked up chicken bones, half-eaten dinner rolls, soiled paper napkins, a splattered container of mashed potatoes and gravy, three blue plastic cups, three lids and straws, and broken pieces of a plastic wrap that had been used to seal the lids on the cups.

There were still grains of ice in the cups, along with the unmis-takable smell of sugar, lemon juice, and rum. I found a paper sack and placed the cups and lids in it, then deposited the sack in the garbage bag.

When I got back to the accident scene, Helen was talking to the father and mother of the girl who had driven the Buick. The father's face was dilated with rage as he pointed his finger at the drivers of both the truck and the church bus, both of whom had said his daughter was speeding and crossing the double-yellow stripe.

"Maybe you boxed her off, too. Why would she go off the left-hand embankment unless you wouldn't let her back in line? Answer me that, goddamnit," he said.

An ambulance containing the bodies of the three girls was working its way around the other emergency vehicles, its flashers beating silently against the dusk.

I dropped the evidence bag in Helen's cruiser and drove home, passing a rural black slum at the four corners, where several cars and pickup trucks were lined up at the service window of a drive-by daiquiri store.

Early the next morning, when the streets were still empty and the light was gray and streaked with mist in the backyards along the bayou, Fat Sammy Figorelli parked his Cadillac in front of my house, puffed on a cigarette while studying the live oaks and antebellum homes that lined East Main, then walked up on my gallery and began knocking so hard the walls shook.

"You mad at my door?" I said.

"I need to straighten you out about a certain issue," he said.

I stepped outside, barefoot, still unshaved, dressed only in a T-shirt and khakis. He wore a rust-colored shirt and brown knit necktie and knife-creased slacks. He stood a half-head taller than I, his porcine face shiny with cologne.

"A little early, isn't it?" I said.

"I get up at four every morning. I think sleep sucks," he said.

"I see. Then you wake up other people. Makes sense."

"What?" he said.

"Why are you here, Sammy?"

"I got this punk Gunner Ardoin calling me up, telling me he didn't rat me out, that he's got a little girl, that he can't afford to lose work 'cause he's in the hospital."

"Why tell me about it?" I asked.

"Thanks to you and that animal Purcel, my name is getting drug into all this."

"Into what?"

"Stories about a priest getting bashed. I don't want to hear my name coming up no more in regard to Father Jimmie Dolan. This guy is a world-class pain in the ass and I got nothing to do with him. What kind of priest punches out the owner of a health salon, anyway?"

"I hadn't heard that one."

"He probably left it out of his homily."

"I'll try to remember all this. Thanks for dropping by," I said.

Sammy looked at me for a long time, his nostrils swelling with air, his small mouth a tight seam, as though he had been talking futilely to either a deaf or stupid man. A delivery truck smelling of donuts or freshly baked bread passed on the street. Fat Sammy watched the truck turn the corner by a huge, redbrick, tree-shaded antebellum home called the Shadows and disappear down a side street.

"This is a nice town," he said.

I realized that whatever was really bothering him was probably not within his ability to explain. He watched a blue jay lighting on a bird feeder that hung from an oak limb in the yard. Then, like every mainstream American gangster I had ever known, almost all of whom struggle to hold onto some vestige of respectability, he unknowingly opened a tiny window into a childlike area of his soul.

"I talked with them German film people who's doing a documentary. They say you told them I used to be on a first-name basis with a Miami guy who helped kill President Kennedy. It's true, you told them people that?" he said.

"You know the same stories I do, Sammy. They just sound better coming from you. You were born for the screen, partner," I said.

He seemed to think about my explanation, but showed no indication of wanting to leave my gallery.

"You care to come inside and have some coffee?" I said.

"Got any donuts?" he said.

I opened the door for him and watched his enormous bulk move past me into my house. I could smell an odor like testosterone ironed into his clothes.

That morning I drove to the high school that the three dead girls had attended up the bayou in the little town of Loreauville. The registrar gave me a copy of the yearbook from the previous year and I found the three girls' photographs among members of the junior class. All three had been either class officers, prom queens, members of the drama club and speech team, or participants in Madrigals. They had been scheduled to graduate in the spring.

But one of the girls had a different kind of distinction. The driver, Lori Parks, had been on probation for possession of Ecstasy and had been driving with a restricted license for a previous DWI. By late afternoon the forensic chemist at our crime lab had matched a latent print from one of the plastic cups I had picked up two hundred yards from the crash site. The latent belonged to Lori Parks.

There is no open-container law in the State of Louisiana. It is supposedly illegal to drink and drive in the state, but a vendor can sell mixed drinks at drive-by windows to people in automobiles, provided the container is sealed. Wrapping a piece of plastic around the lid of a daiquiri cup satisfies the statute, and the passengers in the automobile are allowed to open the cups and consume any amount of alcohol they wish as long as they do not give alcohol to the driver.

If the driver is drinking and sees a state trooper or sheriff's deputy hit his flasher, he only needs to hand his cup to a passenger and instantly he comes into compliance with the law.

The only person legally liable for any violation of the statutes governing the drive-by window sale of mixed drinks is the clerk who actually makes the sale, never the owner. Sometimes the clerk, who is usually paid no more than minimum wage, is fined or jailed or both for selling to underage customers. But the daiquiri windows remain open seven days and nights a week, positioned on each end of town, thriving on weekends and on all paydays.

Just before I started to drive out to the daiquiri store at the four corners on Loreauville Road, the phone rang on my desk. It was the administrative assistant in the warden's office at Angola Penitentiary, the same man who had hung up on me when I had mentioned the possibility of Junior Crudup being buried under the levee along the Mississippi River.

"I did some digging around," he said.

I laughed into the receiver.

"You think this is funny?" he said.

"No, sir. I'm sorry."

"Ever know an old gunhack by the name of Buttermilk Strunk?"

"Cain't-See to Cain't-See Double-Time Strunk?" I said.

"That's the man. He was working levee gangs from Camp A in 1951. He says Crudup was a big stripe back then and on the shit list of a couple other gunbulls who wanted to make a Christian out of him, get my meaning?"

"I think so," I said.

"They worked him over pretty bad. Strunk says that's about the time a man came to the penitentiary and made recordings of some of the convicts. According to Strunk, this man probably saved Crudup's life."

"You mean John or Allen Lomax, the folk music collectors?"

"No, this guy lives in Franklin. You ought to know him. He only owns about half the goddamn state."

"Who are we talking about?" I said, my impatience growing.

"Castille LeJeune. Strunk says LeJeune came to Angola with a man from a record company and got Crudup pulled off the levee gang. He doesn't know what happened to him after that. . . . You still there?"

"Castille LeJeune saved the life of a black convict? I'm having a hard time putting this together."

"Why's that?"

"He's supposed to be a sonofabitch."

"Remind me not to waste my time on bullshit like this again," the administrative assistant said.

. . .

That night my old enemy was back. According to his friends, Audie Murphy fashioned a bedroom out of his garage in the hills overlooking Los Angeles and slept separately from his wife, a loaded army-issue .45 under his pillow. After World War II he had become convinced that, before he could sleep a full night again, he would have to spend five days in peacetime for every day he had spent on the firing line. For him that meant twenty years of sleeplessness.

I couldn't offer my limited experience in Vietnam as the raison d'etre for my insomnia. I drank before I went there and I drank more when I came back. Now I did not drink at all and my nocturnal hours were still filled with the same visitors and feelings; they simply took on different shapes and faces.

The night seemed alive with sound—the clatter of red squirrels on the roof, a dredge boat out on the bayou, a brief rain shower that swept across the trees in the yard. When I finally fell asleep I dreamed of my dead wife Bootsie and Father Jimmie Dolan and the three girls who had died in a burning automobile and of a Negro convict who had been ground up in a system that loathed courage in a black man.

What were the dreams really about? An imperfect world, I suspect, one over which death and injustice often seemed to hold dominion. But what kind of fool would surrender his sleep over a condition he could not change?

Sleeping with a .45 did not bring Audie Murphy peace of mind, nor did gambling away millions in Las Vegas. I had slept with firearms, too, and invested substantial sums of money in the parimutuel industry at racetracks all over the country, but I was no more successful in my attempt at redress with the world than he was. That said, I did have an answer for insomnia, one that was surefire and one that Murphy evidently did not try. But just the thought of its coming back into my life made sweat pop on my forehead.

When I went to the office in the morning a faxed message was waiting for me from the Department of Public Safety and Corrections in Baton Rouge. Since there was no record of Junior Crudup's discharge from Angola or his death while on the farm, it was the department's contention he had served his full sentence and gone out "max time," which meant he would have been released without parole stipulations or supervision sometime in 1958.

It was pure blather.

I called Father Jimmie Dolan at his rectory in New Orleans and was told he was working in the garden. Fat Sammy had said Father Jimmie was a global-size pain in the ass. The archdiocese must have felt the same. He had been assigned to an ancient, downtown church in a dirty, dilapidated neighborhood off Canal, where Mass was still said in Latin, women in the pews covered their heads, and communicants knelt at the altar rail when they received the Eucharist, as though the 1960s reforms of Vatican II had never taken place.

Last year, when I remarked to Father Jimmie on the obvious bad judgment if not punitive intention on the part of the diocese in placing a minister such as himself in a parish with an anachronistic mindset, he replied, "Some people can't accept change. So the church lets a few wall themselves up in a mausoleum and pretend the past is still alive. Know anybody else who has that kind of problem?"

"Excuse me?" I said.

"They're not bad guys," he said, grinning from ear to ear.

My mind came back to the present and I heard Father Jimmie scrape the phone receiver off a hard surface.

"Fat Sammy Figorelli says you punched out the owner of a health salon," I said.

"Not exactly."

"How 'not exactly'?"

"The guy we're talking about runs a massage parlor and escort service. He forced a seventeen-year-old Vietnamese girl from our parish to give a blowjob to one of his customers. Is this why you called?"

"The Department of Corrections says Junior Crudup's last sentence was up in 1958. They say he wasn't paroled and he didn't die inside the prison, so he must have gone out max time in '58."

"He was probably killed and buried on the farm. But I doubt if we'll ever know."

"There's more. An oldtime gunbull says a man by the name of

Castille LeJeune got Junior off the levee gang around 1951. But that's where the trail ends."

"Castille LeJeune, in Franklin? That's Theodosha Flannigan's father. She's married to Merchie Flannigan."

"How'd you know that?" I said.

"She used to live in New Orleans. She was one of our parishioners. Can we have a talk with Mr. LeJeune?"

"I don't like to get too close to Theodosha."

There was a beat, then he said, "Oh, I see."

Way to go, Robicheaux, I thought.

That afternoon I went to each drive-by daiquiri store in New Iberia. Each of the stores used the same type of blue plastic cups that I had picked up near the accident scene, the same type lids, the same type sealing wrap. I showed each of the clerks working the window the yearbook photographs of the three girls killed on Loreauville Road. Each clerk looked at them blankly and shook his head. At the first three stores I believed the denials given me by the clerks. At the fourth my experience was different.

The store was a boxlike, plywood structure, painted white, located inside an oak grove just outside the city limits. I parked my cruiser in the trees and waited in the shade while the clerk, a kid probably not much over legal age himself, serviced three drive-by customers. Then I walked to the window, which had a flap on it propped up by a stick. I opened my badge on him.

"What's your name?" I said.

"Josh Comeaux."

"You work here every evening, Josh?"

"Yes, sir. Unless I have a basketball game. Then Mr. Hebert lets me off," he answered.

I flipped the high school yearbook open to a marked page and showed him pictures of two of the dead girls.

"You know either one of these girls?" I asked.

"No, sir, I can't say I do," he said. He wore khakis and a starched, print shirt, the short sleeves folded in neat cuffs on his upper arms.

His hair was black, combed back with gel, boxed on the neck, his skin tanned.

"Can't or won't?" I said, and smiled at him.

"Sir?" he said, confused.

I turned to another marked page in the yearbook and showed him a picture of Lori Parks.

"How about this girl?" I said.

He shook his head, his eyes flat. "No, sir. Don't know her. I guess I'm not much help on this. These girls do something wrong?"

"You seem out of breath. You all right?" I said.

"I'm fine," he said, and tried to smile.

"What time did you serve her?" I asked.

"Serve who?"

"Lori Parks," I said, tapping the picture of the driver.

"I haven't said I did that. I haven't said no such thing. No, sir."

"The autopsy on this girl indicates she was alive when the gasoline tank on her car exploded. She was seventeen years old. I think you're in a world of shit, partner."

He swallowed and looked at the smoke hanging in the trees from a barbecue joint. He opened his mouth to speak, but a middle-aged, balding man who wore a cowboy vest and a string tie and hillbilly sideburns that looked like grease pencil cupped his hand on the boy's shoulder and glared at me through the service window.

"You saying we served somebody under age?" he asked.

"I know you did," I said.

"Every young person who comes by this window has to show ID. That's the rule. No exceptions," he said.

"You the owner?" I said.

He ignored my question and addressed his clerk. "You serve anybody who looked like a minor yesterday?"

"No, sir, not me. I checked everybody," the clerk said.

"That's what I thought," the man in the vest said. "We're closed."

"How did you know the problem sale was yesterday?" I asked.

He pulled out the support stick from under the window flap and let it slam shut in my face.

. . .

While I had spent the afternoon questioning the employees of New Iberia's drive-by daiquiri stores, an unusual man was completing his journey on the Sunset Limited from Miami into New Orleans. He had small ears that were tight against his scalp, narrow shoulders, white skin, lips that were the color of raw liver, and emerald green eyes that possessed the rare quality of seeming infinitely interested in what other people were saying. He sat in the lounge car, wearing a seersucker suit and pink dress shirt with a plum-colored tie and ruby stick pin, sipping from a glass of soda and ice and lime slices while the countryside rolled by. An elderly Catholic nun in a black habit sat down next to him and opened a book and began reading from it. She soon became conscious that the man was watching her.

"Could I help you with something?" she asked.

"You're reading *The Catholic Imagination* by Father Andrew Greeley. A fine book it is," the man said.

"I just started it. But, yes, it seems to be. Are you from Ireland?"

He considered his reply. "Umm, not anymore," he said. "Are you going to New Orleans, Sister?"

"Yes, I live there. But my parents came from Waterford, in the south of Ireland."

But he didn't seem to take note of her parents' origins. His eyes were so green, his stare so invasive, she found herself averting his gaze.

"Would you be knowing a Father James Dolan in New Orleans?" the man asked.

"Why, yes, he's a friend of mine."

"I understand he's a lovely man. Works in a parish where they still say a traditional Mass, does he?"

"Yes, but he's—"

"He's what?"

"He's not a traditional man. Excuse me, but you're staring at me."

"I am? Oh, I beg your pardon, Sister. But you remind me of a mother superior who ran the orphanage where I once lived. What a darlin' sack of potatoes she was. She used to make me fold my hands like I was about to pray, then whack the shite out of me with a ruler. She was good at pulling hair and giving us the Indian burn, too. Have you done the same to a few tykes?"

He drank from his glass of ice and soda and lime, an innocuous light in his eyes. "Not running off, are you? You forgot your book. Here, I'll bring it to you," he said.

But she rushed through the vestibule into the next car, the big wood beads of her fifteen-decade rosary clattering on her hip, the whoosh of the doors like wind howling in a tunnel.

On Saturday afternoon Father Jimmie and I went together to the Flannigan lawn party at Fox Run, down Bayou Teche, in St. Mary Parish. The home had been constructed during the early Victorian era to resemble a steamboat, with porches shaped like the fantail and captain's bridge on a ship and cupolas and balconies on the upper stories that gave a spectacular view of the grounds, the antebellum homes on the opposite side of the bayou, and the sugarcane fields that seemed to recede over the rim of the earth.

Live oaks draped with moss arched over the roof of the house, and palm trees grew in their shade to the second-story windows. A visitor to the lawn party could ride either western or English saddle around a white-fenced track by the horse stables, or play tennis on either a grass or red-clay court. The buffet tables groaned with food that had been prepared at Galatoire's and Antoine's in New Orleans. The drink table was a drunkard's dream.

The guests included the state insurance commissioner, who was under a federal grand jury indictment and would later become the third state insurance commissioner in a row to go to prison; petro-chemical executives from Oklahoma and Texas whose wives' voices rose above all others; two New York book editors and a film director from Home Box Office; an ex-player from the National Football League who rented himself out as a professional celebrity; career military officers and their wives who had retired to the Sunbelt; the former governor's mistress whose evening gown looked like pink champagne poured on her skin; and state legislators who had once been barbers and plumbers and who genuinely believed they shared a common bond with their host and his friends.

Father Jimmie had worn his Roman collar, and the consequence was that he and I stood like an island in the middle of the lawn party while people swirled around us, deferential and polite, touching us affectionately if need be but avoiding the eye contact that would take them away from all the rewards a gathering at Castille LeJeune's could offer.

After a half hour I wished I had not come. I went inside the house to use the bathroom, but someone was already inside. A black drink waiter in the kitchen directed me to another bathroom, deeper in the house, one I had to find by cutting through a small library and den filled with fine guns and Korean War–era memorabilia.

A steel airplane propeller was mounted on the wall, and under it was a framed color photograph of Castille LeJeune and a famous American baseball player, both of them dressed in Marine Corps tropicals, standing in front of two vintage Grumman Hellcat fighter planes parked on a runway flanged by Quonset huts and palm trees. In another photo LeJeune stood at attention in his dress uniform while President Harry Truman pinned the Distinguished Flying Cross on his coat.

But the photos that caught my eye were not those of Castille LeJeune's career as a Marine Corps pilot. A picture taken at his wedding showed him and his young wife, in her bridal gown, standing on the steps of a church. She was tall, dark featured, and absolutely beautiful. She also looked like the twin of her daughter, Theodosha.

When I went back outside the sun was setting beyond the trees on the bayou, the sugarcane fields purple in the dusk, the air cool and damp, thick with cigarette smoke and smelling of alcohol that had soaked into tablecloths or had been spilled by the guests on their clothes.

In my absence Father Jimmie had cornered both Castille LeJeune and Merchie Flannigan and was talking heatedly with them, his coat separating on his chest when he raised his arms to make a point, one foot at a slight angle behind the other, in the classic position of a martial artist.

"Let me finish if you would," he said when Merchie Flannigan tried to speak. "You say you're cleaning up the Crudups' property? The place is floating in sludge."

"I'm sure Merchie is doing his best. Why don't you help yourself to the food, Father?" Castille LeJeune said.

He was a trim, nice-looking man, with a lean face and steel gray hair that he combed straight back. He wore a white sports coat and dark blue shirt and a gold and onyx Mason's ring on his marriage finger.

"No, thanks," Father Jimmie said, wagging two fingers as though brushing Castille LeJeune's words from the air. "So let me see if I understand correctly. In 1951 you took a friend to Angola Prison to record Junior Crudup, but you have no idea what happened to Junior later?"

"I was doing a favor for my wife. She was fond of folk music. That was a long time ago," LeJeune answered, his eyes crinkling at the corners, his gaze wandering among his guests.

"But a retired guard, a man named Strunk, says you got Junior pulled off the levee gang."

"I don't remember that. I wouldn't have had that kind of influence," LeJeune said.

"Really?" Father Jimmie said. "You wouldn't throw a fellow a slider, would you?"

The insult to a man of his age and position seemed not to register in LeJeune's face. Instead, his eyes crinkled again. "Have a good time," he said. He placed his hand warmly on Father Jimmie's arm and walked away.

"Let me get you a beer, Father," Merchie Flannigan said.

"Shame on you for what you're doing to those black people in St. James Parish," Father Jimmie said.

Father Jimmie's heart might have been in the right place, but it was embarrassing to listen to him berate Merchie Flannigan in front of others and I didn't wait to hear Merchie's reply. I walked out of the backyard and into the oak trees, then witnessed one of those moments when you realize that each human being's story is much more complex than you could have ever guessed.

Between the horse stables and the bayou was a white-railed, sloping green pasture containing a fish pond and a small dock. A gas lamp mounted on a brass pole burned above the dock, and I could see moths flying into the flame, then dropping like pieces of ash into the water. As I stood among the trees I saw Theodosha watching the same scene, one hand on the fence railing. The electric lights were on in the stables and I could see her face clearly in the illumination, her brow knitted, the muscles in her throat taut, her hand gripped tightly on the rail.

I walked toward her but her attention had been distracted by the strange red reflection of the sun's afterglow on the bayou. A little boy and girl, not older than four or five, climbed through the fence on the opposite side of the fish pond and ran giggling toward the dock. I had no way of knowing the depth of the pond, but a spring board was attached to the end of the dock, which meant the depth was certainly over a child's head.

Theo looked back from the sunset at the pond and saw the children almost the same time as I. She bit her lip and raised her hand as though to warn them off, but she remained outside the fence, frozen, as though an invisible shield prevented her from entering the pasture. The children thumped onto the dock and danced up and down, then bent over the edge of the dock and peered at the fish feeding on the moths dropping from the flame in the gas lamp.

Theodosha heard me walk up behind her. She turned abruptly, startled, her expression one of both fear and shame.

"That water is fairly deep, isn't it?" I said.

"Yes," she said, turning back toward the pond. "Yes, those children shouldn't be out there. Where are their parents?"

I started to climb through the fence.

"No, I'll do that. I'm sorry. I'm—" She didn't finish whatever she was going to say. She ducked under the top rail of the fence and ran awkwardly onto the dock, then returned, clasping each of the children by the hand.

The children's faces were hot, angry, a bit frightened, their cheeks pooled with color.

"We didn't know we did anything wrong, Miss Theo," the little boy said.

"You shouldn't go near a lake or pond or the bayou without your mother or father. Don't you ever do this again," Theo said, and shook him.

Both of the children began to cry.

"Hey, you guys, let's get a soft drink," I said.

I took them by the hand and walked them to the drink table and asked the waiter to give each of them a Coca-Cola. Through the trees I saw Theodosha walking rapidly toward the back of her house, her arms clinched across her chest, as though the temperature had dropped thirty degrees.

I decided I'd had enough of the LeJeune family for one evening. I told Father Jimmie I'd say good night to our hosts for both of us and went to find Theodosha inside the house. I didn't have to look far. She was in the den with her father, sitting on a stuffed leather footstool beneath the mounted airplane propeller, her face in her hands. Castille LeJeune stood above her, stroking her hair, his eyes filled with pity.

Neither one of them saw me. I backed out of the doorway and joined Father Jimmie outside.

"Do you know where Merchie is?" I asked.

"He and another man went to the stables. The other guy seems to have his own Zip code," he said.

"Let's go, Father."

"I was too hard on Flannigan?"

"What do I know?" I said.

We got in my pickup truck and headed down the long driveway toward the state road. I thought the bizarre nature of my visit to the plantation home of Castille LeJeune was over. It wasn't. In the glare of floodlamps, by a long white, peaked stable, Merchie Flannigan was perched on top of a fence, drinking from a bottle of Cold Duck, while a tall, gray-headed, crew-cropped, angular man in cowboy boots and western-cut slacks was lighting strings of Chinese firecrackers and throwing them in the air while a group of children screamed in delight. In the background, a half-dozen thoroughbred horses raced back and forth across a fenced pasture.

Merchie flagged me down and walked toward my truck, slightly off balance.

"Not leaving, are you?" he said.

"Looks like it. Thanks for having us out," I said.

Merchie bent down to window level to see across me. "I'm a bum Catholic, Father. But I try," he said.

"You were in the reformatory?" Father Jimmie asked.

Merchie's face reddened. "Yeah, I guess I was."

"We'll compare stories sometime," Father Jimmie said.

The tall, crew-cropped man lit another string of firecrackers and threw it popping into the air. One of the thoroughbreds struck the fence and knocked a slat onto the grass.

"Why are you letting that guy panic those horses like that?" I said.

"That's Will Guillot. Those are his kids," Merchie replied, then seemed to look into space at the vacuity of his words. "Will does things for my father-in-law. You don't know him?"

"No."

"You should," he said.

"Why?"

"You're a police officer," he said. He leaned on his arms against the side of my truck, his eyes slightly out of focus, his breath like a wine vat.

Chapter 5

The telephone call to Father Jimmie came on Sunday afternoon, while he was watching a pro football game on television at the rectory. It was raining, and through the window he could see the rainwater cascading off the roof, pounding the small garden he tended in the green space between the gray, back wall of the church and the alley where the sanitation service picked up the garbage.

"I need to go to confession, Father," the voice said.

"Reconciliation is scheduled every afternoon at four, except Sundays," he said.

"I need to go now."

Father Jimmie looked over his shoulder at a quarterback completing a thirty-yard pass on the television screen.

"Can it wait?" he asked.

"I have to get something of a serious nature off my conscience."

In the silence Father Jimmie could hear the man breathing into the receiver. "I'll be in the confessional at four o'clock," he said.

He finished his sandwich in front of the television, and a half hour later walked down the center aisle of the church toward the three confessionals that were inset in a side wall at the rear of the building. The inside of the church was magnificent. Twin balconies draped with brilliant red tapestries extended all the way from the choir to the altar area. The pulpit was hand-carved from teak wood and had been constructed high above the laity, in a time when there were no microphones to magnify the minister's voice. Whenever the sunlight struck the stained-glass windows, the effect inside the church was stunning. The celestial scenes on the ceiling and the paintings depicting Christ's passion in the Garden of Gethsemane and his ordeal by scourge and mockery and spittle and finally crucifixion made the viewer swallow in both reverence and trepidation.

The front doors of the church were open, and Father Jimmie could see the grayness of the afternoon out on the street and the drabness of the neighborhood and the rainwater welling up from the storm sewers. Perhaps a dozen people were in the pews, all of them old, their clothes shabby, their rosary beads wrapped around their hands. Some nodded at him and smiled as he passed. Their faith was genuine, he thought, their level of devotion long since proven by the lives they had led, but if they did not have this place to visit, where they could say their beads and confess sins that were either imaginary or inconsequential, he knew they would have no lives at all.

A homeless man slept in a back pew, curled up in a fetal position, his odor rising from his clothes like a living presence. A bottle of fortified wine had fallen from his coat pocket and was precariously balanced on the edge of the pew.

Father Jimmie picked it up, tightened the cap, and placed it on the floor, within arm's reach of the sleeping man.

Then, on the far side of the church, he saw a man he had never seen before. The man wore a tight-fitting tan raincoat buttoned to his neck, like a prison on his body. His face was beaded with water, his ears like small cauliflowers, his hair cut short, combed neatly, reddish in color. He was sitting rather than kneeling, his hand resting on a domed, black lunch box. His eyes never made contact with Father Jimmie's.

Father Jimmie went into the vestibule of the church and smelled the wind and rain and leaves blowing in the street. He wished he had not answered the phone in the rectory. It was a gray, wet day, with a touch of winter in the air, but it reminded him of Kentucky in the late fall, just before Advent, when a great dampness would settle on the Cumberland Mountains and the color would drain out of the sky and the fields and the leaves of the hardwoods would turn to flame in the hollows. It should have been a day to watch football and eat soup and hot bread and perhaps jog in Audubon Park. But he could not refuse a request for reconciliation, no matter how neurotic, self-absorbed, or irritating the source was.

He opened the door to a side corridor that led to the back entrance of a confessional, placed his stole around his neck, and sat down inside. He heard someone open the door to the adjoining box and the person's weight depress the kneeler that was attached to the partition separating the penitent from the confessor. Father Jimmie pushed back the wood slide that covered the small, grilled, gauze-covered window through which the penitent, in this case a man who smelled of street damp and hair tonic, would make his confession.

But the man did not speak.

"Are you the gentleman who called the rectory?" Father Jimmie asked.

"That I am, Father."

"What is it you'd like to tell me?"

Father Jimmie could see the outline of the man's head. The ears looked like they had been carved around the edges with a paring knife. He heard the man snuff down in his nose and shift his weight on the kneeler.

"Been a while since I've visited one of these," the man said.

"Yes?"

"I'm a bit flummoxed. Hold on a bit, Father, while I organize my thoughts."

Father Jimmie heard what he thought was the man's lunch box clattering open inside the confessional. "What are you doing in there?" he asked.

"Nothing." The man was breathing hard now. "I met a Catholic sister on the train. I was rude to her. She's a friend of yours. So I apologize for that."

"Oh, you're the fellow. Well, she already called me. I'll pass on your apologies. Is that it?"

"I scared the shite out of her. She tell you that?"

"Don't do it anymore and it won't be a problem. Is that all you have to tell me. Because if it is—"

"No, it is fucking not, sir."

"*What* did you say?"

The man was breathing hard through his nose now, a ray of light from outside the confessional glimmering on the planed surfaces of his face.

"I said give me a fucking minute, if you please," he said.

"Are you drunk?"

The man did not reply. He seemed to burn with energies he couldn't express. He rocked on the kneeler and twisted his head from side to side, then made a grinding noise in his throat. The lunch box clattered with sound again, as though the man had dropped a heavy object in it and snapped the latch on the lid.

"Tell the nun she's a splendid woman and I hope she lives long enough to have a bishop for a son. Send up a thanks to your patron saint, Father. Maybe buy a Powerball ticket while you're at it," the man said.

He flung open the door of the confessional and stalked through the vestibule and out the front of the church. Father Jimmie followed him as far as the front steps and watched him walk toward Canal, a golfer's cap pulled down on his head, his narrow shoulders hunched forward in the rain, his lunch box glistening with moisture. The man looked back over his shoulder at Father Jimmie, his face contorted, as though he had just fled a burning building.

It had rained through the night in New Iberia, and in the morning the sun rose like a pink wafer out of a blanket of fog that covered the cane fields. When I got to the office the parents of Lori Parks were waiting for me. Sometimes the survivors of family members who meet violent deaths have no place to direct their anger and loss other than at the police officer who is assigned to help them. Their rage is understandable, particularly when a cop is straight up and informs them the percentages are not in favor of justice being done. But sometimes the anger of the survivors has more to do with guilt than grief.

The father was sandy haired and tall, with an aquiline nose, the tops of his forearms sun freckled, his hands long and tapered. The wife was built like a stump, a ring of fat under her chin, her hair dyed dark red, her perfume a chemical fog.

"I hear you're questioning the employees of the daiquiri shops in town," the father said.

"Yes, sir, that's correct," I said.

He and his wife had not taken a seat when I offered them one. They looked down at me, from across my desk, stolid, angry, their defenses and denial rooted in concrete.

"Are you saying our daughter was DWI?" he asked.

"That's the conclusion of our lab."

He nodded silently, the color in his eyes deepening, the skin around the rim of his nostrils whitening.

"So the truck and bus drivers are off the hook?" he said.

"I don't think they're players in this," I said.

"Excuse me?" the wife said.

"I think your daughter and her friends were served alcohol illegally. I'd like to put the people in jail who empowered them to drink and drive. But to be truthful I don't think that's going to happen."

"Our daughter is responsible for her own death? Is that it? A seventeen-year-old girl burns to death and it's her goddamn fault?" the father said.

I leaned forward on my desk and picked up a paper clip from the ink blotter, then dropped it. "Dr. Parks, I'm sorry for your loss. Your daughter had a history. It's one a lot of kids have today. But the fact won't go away that she'd had her license suspended previously and she was on probation for possession of Ecstacy. Was she ever in any kind of treatment program?"

"How dare you?" the wife said.

"How about it, sir?" I said to her husband.

"You're scapegoating my daughter, you sonofabitch," he said.

"We're done here," I said. I folded my hands on my desk blotter and avoided eye contact with them.

"We'll be back," the father said.

"I have no doubt about that," I replied.

At mid-morning I walked down the street, across the railroad tracks, and had coffee and a piece of pastry at Lagniappe Too on Main. When I got back to the department a black woman in blue slacks, a beige shirt, and polished black shoes was waiting for me by the dispatcher's cage. She carried a zippered satchel under her arm.

What was her name? Andrepont? No, Arceneaux. Clotile Arceneaux. Clete had said she looked like a black swizzle stick with a cherry stuck on the end. He should have been a writer rather than a chaser of bail skips, I thought.

"Got a minute?" she said.

"For you, anytime," I said.

She walked with me to my office. I closed the door behind her. "N.O.P.D. hasn't busted you back to meter maid, have they?" I said.

"Thought I might show you some photos of an interesting guy who just got to town," she said.

"You want to tell me who you are?"

She smiled at me with her eyes and removed a manilla folder from her satchel. "You ever see this guy before?" she asked.

There were four black-and-white photographs inside the folder, three taken with a zoom lens, one taken in the garish light of a Toronto booking room. The man in the photographs made me think of a ring attendant at a boxing gym or a horse groom at the track. "Nope, I don't know him," I said.

"His name is Max Coll. He's been questioned or been a suspect in thirty-two homicides. Not one conviction. Interpol thinks he worked for the IRA but they're not sure. Miami P.D. says he's freelance and jobs out for the Mob. We had a tail on him yesterday, but he shook it. We think he showed up at your friend Father Dolan's."

"Think?" I said.

"A detective talked to Father Dolan. Seems like Father Dolan has got us mixed up with the bad guys," she said.

"Why you showing me this stuff?"

"Hate to see your friend get clipped 'cause he's a poor listener. That goes for you, too, handsome."

"You're with the G?"

"We think the priest was lucky yesterday. What we can't figure is why. Max Coll is a lot of things but fuck-up isn't one of them," she said.

"You're DEA?"

She looked up into my face, her head tilted at an angle, her teeth white behind her grin. "I heard you had a cinder block for a head," she said.

"Have you had lunch yet?" I said.

"Some people are all work and no play. That's me, Robicheaux. Max Coll uses a silencer, sometimes an ice pick. You heard it first from your ex–meter maid friend at N.O.P.D."

"Right," I said.

She stuck a business card in my shirt pocket and hit me on the hip with her satchel. "See you around, darlin'," she said.

I walked with her to the front door of the building and watched her get in her automobile and drive away. Helen Soileau was standing behind me.

"What's with Miss Hip-Slick?" she said.

"She's with N.O.P.D.," I said.

"The hell she is. She's a state trooper. She used to work undercover narcotics in Shreveport. She got into a firefight with some dealers about ten years ago and shot all five of them."

Later, while I was out of the office, Clete Purcel left a message that he had checked into the old motor court on East Main, one that had long served as his field office in southwest Louisiana and his home away from home. The motor court was located inside a massive bower of live oak trees and slash pines on the bayou, and when I drove through the entrance that evening I saw Clete in front of the last cottage, barechested, wearing shorts with dancing elephants on them, flip-flops, and a Marine Corps utility cap, drinking from a bottle of Dixie while he flipped a steak on a flaming grill.

"Running down bail skips?" I said.

"No, I just had to get out of the Big Sleazy for a while. Gunner Ardoin is driving me nuts," he said.

"What's happening with Gunner?"

"He thinks somebody's going to clip him. Maybe he's right. So I . . ."

"So you what?"

"Gave him my apartment."

"Your apartment? To Gunner Ardoin?"

"His wife skipped town and left his little girl with him. What was I supposed to do? Quit looking at me like that," he said. He picked up a can of diet Dr Pepper from an ice chest and tossed it at me.

I sat down in a canvas chair, out of the smoke from the grill. Through the trees the sunlight looked like gold foil on the bayou. A tugboat passed, its wake slapping against the bank.

"Ever hear of a button man by the name of Max Coll?" I said.

"A freelance guy out of Miami?"

"That's the one."

"What about him?"

"That black patrolwoman who answered the complaint in Ardoin's kitchen, Clotile Arceneaux? She's an undercover state trooper. She told me this guy Coll tried to kill Father Dolan yesterday," I said.

"Dolan thinks he walks on water. You might tell him the saints died early deaths."

"He's not a listener," I said.

"Yeah, like somebody else I know," Clete said.

I walked down in the trees and watched the boats pass on the bayou while Clete finished grilling his steak. On the opposite bank two black laborers were trenching a waterline while a white man in a straw hat supervised them. When I walked back out of the trees Clete was laying out two plates, paper napkins, and knives and forks on a picnic table.

"I don't want to steal your supper," I said.

"Don't worry about it. My doctor says when I die I'll need a piano crate just to put my cholesterol in," he said.

"I'm trying to find out what happened to a convict in Angola back in the fifties. A guy named Junior Crudup. He went in and never came out," I said.

"Yeah?" Clete said, dividing up his steak, looking at a woman in a bathing suit on the bow of a speedboat.

"Father Jimmie and I were at the house of Castille LeJeune Saturday evening. LeJeune got Crudup off the levee gang back in 1951. But he said he has no memory of it," I said.

"You're talking about stuff that happened a half century ago?" Clete said.

"Crudup's family got swindled out of their property."

Clete plopped a foil-wrapped potato on my plate and sat down. He looked at me for a long time. "So you think this character LeJeune is lying?" he said.

"I couldn't tell."

"Wake up, big mon. Rich guys don't care whether the rest of us believe them or not. That's why they're great liars."

"His daughter saw two kids about to fall into a fish pond. But she was afraid to climb inside a fence and get them," I said.

"Is Father Dolan part of this?"

"He took me out to the Crudup place in St. James Parish."

"This guy is playing you, Dave. He knows you don't like authority or rich people and you're a real sucker for a sob story. How about letting Dolan and the Throw-ups or whatever clean up their own shit?"

"*I'm* getting played? You just gave a pornographic actor your apartment. The same guy you hit in the head with a coffeepot. You go from one train wreck to the next."

"That's why I never listen to my own advice."

He drank from his bottle of Dixie beer, his green eyes filled with an innocent self-satisfaction, his jaw packed with steak.

. . .

The next morning I drove to the house of Josh Comeaux, the clerk who I believed had sold daiquiris to Lori Parks and her friends the afternoon they burned to death. He lived with his mother in a small, weathered frame house not far from the Southern Pacific railway tracks. In the front yard was a post with hooks on it, from which vinyl bags of garbage hung so they would not be torn apart by dogs before the trash pickup.

Josh pushed open the screen door and stepped out on the gallery. He was barefoot and wore recycled jeans without a belt and a black T-shirt with the sleeves cut off. A heart with a circle of thorns twisted around it was tattooed high up on his right arm. Through the screen I could see a fat woman in a print dress watching a television program.

"You come to arrest me?" he said.

"Not yet. Who bruised up your face?"

He touched the yellow-and-purple discoloration below one eye.

"Dr. Parks did. Last night. After I got off from work."

"Lori's father?" I said.

"Yes, sir. That's why I figured you were here."

"He knocked you around?"

"I went in for gas at the all-night station. He walked me out in the shadows and hit me. He was pretty mad."

"Are you telling me you confessed something to Dr. Parks?"

"Yeah. I mean yes, sir. I told him what I did."

"Before you go any farther, I need to advise you of certain rights you have, the most important of which is your right to have an attorney."

"Who is that?" the fat woman in the chair yelled through the screen.

"Just a guy, Mom," Josh said, and walked out into the yard, out of earshot from his mother. "I told Dr. Parks I sold daiquiris to Lori and her friends. They were there three times that afternoon. It's not the only time I've sold to underage kids, either. Mr. Hebert tells us not to hold up the line 'cause somebody can't find their driver's license. But what he means is on weekend nights don't pass up any business."

"Mr. Hebert is your employer?"

"Yes, sir. At least till this morning. He fired me when I told him I'd served Lori and the other girls."

"Did Lori give you an ID of any kind?"

He shook his head. "When Lori Parks wanted something, you gave it to her. She was the prettiest girl in Loreauville."

"Josh, I'm placing you under arrest. Turn around while I hook you up."

"Am I going to prison?"

"That's up to other people, partner," I said, and put him in the backseat of the cruiser, my hand on top of his head.

As we drove away I saw his mother walk out on the gallery and look in both directions, wondering where her son had gone.

That afternoon I called Lori Parks's father at his office. His receptionist told me he was not expected in that day.

"Is the funeral today?" I asked.

"It was yesterday," she replied.

"Would you give me his home number, please?"

"I'm not supposed to do that."

"We can send a cruiser out there and bring him in, if you like," I said.

When I called his home no one answered and the message machine, if he had one, was turned off. I checked out a cruiser and drove to Loreauville, nine miles up the Teche, and found his house in a wooded, hilly area on the bayou, just outside of town.

The one-story house was long and flat and constructed of what is called South Carolina brick, torn down from nineteenth-century buildings and shipped to Louisiana for use in custom-built homes. Apple green wood shutters that were ornamental rather than operational were affixed to the walls on each side of the windows and looked as if they had been painted on the brick. The porch ran the width of the house and was intersected with a series of miniature fluted columns. With its flat roof and squeezed windows, the house looked like a constipated man crouched back in the trees. It had probably cost a half million dollars to build.

Dr. Parks stood on a shady knoll overlooking the bayou, slashing golf balls across the water into a grove of persimmon trees. When I walked up behind him, leaves crackling under the soles of my shoes, he glanced at me for only a moment, then whacked another ball into the persimmons.

"I arrested Josh Comeaux this morning," I said.

"Glad to hear it," he said. His face was heated, freshly shaved, even though it was late in the day. He picked another ball out of a bucket and set it on a tee.

"He says you knocked him around."

"What's your business here, Detective?" He rested his driver by his foot. He wore doeskin gloves that had no fingers and a long-sleeve maroon polo shirt and casual slacks that accentuated the flatness of his stomach and the graceful line of his hips.

"I'd like to see the owners of these drive-by daiquiri stores run through a tree shredder. But you're taking out your anger on the wrong person, Dr. Parks," I said.

"I moved my family here from Memphis. We thought small-town America wouldn't have drugs and political officials on the take and bastards who sell children booze to kill themselves with. I've been a stupid man."

He took his position on the tee, lifted his golf club with perfect form, and whipped it viciously into the ball.

"Don't add to your grief, sir," I said.

He turned and faced me. "You have any idea of what it might have been like inside that car?" he said.

"The tox screen showed traces of marijuana in Lori's blood," I said.

"So what?"

"Maybe Josh Comeaux is a victim, too."

"I must have done something wrong in a former life," he said.

"Pardon?"

"My daughter was burned alive and the cop who should be kicking somebody's ass is a goddamn titty-sucking liberal. You need to leave my property."

I took my sunglasses out of their case, then replaced them and stuck the case back in my shirt pocket. The wind was cold blowing out of the trees and I could smell the heavy odor of the bayou in the shadows. The skin under Dr. Parks's right eye seemed to twitch uncontrollably.

"Are you hard of hearing?" he asked.

"The judge will probably go light on Josh's bond. That means he'll probably be back home in a day or so. Are we clear on the implication, sir?" I said.

"That I'd better not hurt him?"

He waited for an answer but I didn't give him one. I fitted on my sunglasses and walked back to the cruiser, my shoes crunching through the leaves the doctor had raked into piles, only to see them blown apart by the wind. The doctor's wife emerged from the front door, wearing a house robe and slippers, a drink in her hand, the makeup on her face like a theatrical mask.

"You think I care about that boy? You think that's what this is about? Where are your brains, man?" the doctor shouted after me.

The following evening I ate supper in the backyard, then went to the old cemetery by the drawbridge in St. Martinville where Bootsie was buried. The air was cold and smelled of distant rain, the sky yellow with dust blown from the fields. Several of the houses bordering the cemetery had signs on the galleries announcing TOMB PAINT FOR SALE. In south Louisiana we bury the dead on top of the ground and it's a tradition to whitewash the crypts of family members on All Saints Day. But it wasn't November yet. Or was it? I had to look at the calendar window on my watch to assure myself the month was still October.

Bootsie's crypt was located by the bayou, and standing next to it I could look downstream and see on the opposite bank the ancient French church and the Evangeline Oak where she and I had first kissed as teenagers and the stars overhead had swirled like diamonds inside a barrel of black water.

I removed the three roses I had placed in a vase two nights previous and washed and refilled the vase under a tap by the gravel path that led through the cemetery. Then I put three fresh roses in the vase and set it in front of the marble marker that was cemented into the front of Bootsie's crypt. The roses were yellow, the petals edged with pink, the stems wrapped in green tissue paper by a young clerk at the Winn-Dixie store in New Iberia. When he handed me the roses I was struck by the bloom of youth on his face, the clarity of purpose in his eyes. "I bet these are for a special lady," he had said.

I sat on a metal bench with a ventilated backrest for a long time and drank a bottle of carbonated water I had brought from home. Then the wind came up and scattered the leaves from a swamp maple on the bayou's surface, and inside the sound of the wind I thought I heard a loon calling.

I finished the bottle of carbonated water, screwed the top back on, and pitched the bottle at a trash barrel. But the bottle bounced on the rim of the barrel and fell on the gravel path. Rather than get up from the bench and retrieve it, I looked at it dumbly, all my energies dissipated for reasons that made no sense, the light as cold and brittle as if the sun were layered with ice.

I heard footsteps behind me.

"I wasn't going to disturb you but I have to get back home," Theodosha Flannigan said.

"Pardon?" I said.

"Your neighbor told me you'd be here if you weren't at home," she said. "I was parked in my car, waiting for you to come out. Merchie doesn't know where I am. He ducks bullets in Afghanistan, then gets strung out if he breaks a shoelace. It's because of his mother. I think she was lobotomized. That's not a joke."

I couldn't follow what she was saying. I started to get up, but she put her hand on my shoulder and sat down beside me.

"It's about Saturday night. Those two children were in danger of falling in the pond and I just stood there and watched it happening. I feel like shit," she said.

"'Bravery' and 'fear' are relative terms. What counts is you went after them," I said.

"I have some bad memories about that pond," she said. She bit on a hangnail and stared into space. "I never go inside that fence. You must think I'm an awful person."

But the truth was I didn't want to talk about Theo's personal problems. I stood and picked up the plastic bottle that had bounced off the trash can and dropped it inside. When I sat back down I felt the blood rush from my head.

"Are you okay?" she said.

"I still have bouts with malaria sometimes," I said.

She wore a scarf tied under her chin, the points of her hair pressed flat against her cheeks. "Something else is bothering me, too, Dave. I think I make you uncomfortable," she said.

"No, that's not true. Not at all," I said, focusing my eyes on the bayou.

"That night we had the little fling? We'd both been drinking our heads off. Neither one of us was married at the time. I admit I thought you might come back around, but you didn't. So I wrote it off. It's no big deal."

"You're right, it's no big deal. I didn't say it was a big deal," I replied.

"Then why are you so—"

"It's not a problem. That's really important to understand here," I said.

"I'm afraid I've intruded upon you."

"No, you haven't. Everything is fine. Give Merchie my best."

"Will you come out to dinner?"

I pinched my temples and looked down the bayou at the Evangeline Oak looming over the water and at the spire of the old French church, a sliver of moon rising behind the steeple.

"Maybe we can talk about it later," I said.

"Sure. I'm sorry for being here like this. Since my psychiatrist died . . . No, that's the wrong word. Since he shot himself I feel this terrible sense of guilt. I've got two days' sobriety now. That's pitiful, isn't it? I mean, taking pride in staying off the hooch for two days, like I invented the wheel?"

"I'll see you, Theo."

She exhaled her breath and I felt it touch my skin. She raised her eyebrows, staring inquisitively into my face, as though I needed to supply the endings to all her unfinished thoughts. Then she seemed to give it up and kissed the tips of two fingers, pressed them against my cheek, and walked out of the cemetery, a solitary firefly lighting in a tree above her head.

In the morning I called a homicide detective at the Lafayette City Police Department by the name of Joe Dupree. He had been in the 173 Airborne Brigade in Vietnam, but never spoke of the war and ate aspirin constantly for the pain he'd carried in his knees for thirty-five years. He was also one of the most thorough investigators I had ever known.

"What do you have on this psychiatrist who shot himself in Girard Park?" I said.

"Dr. Bernstine? It's going down as a suicide. Why do you ask?"

"A woman named Theodosha Flannigan has brought it up a couple of times."

"Merchie Flannigan's wife?"

"Yeah, how'd you know?"

"Her name was in Bernstine's appointment book," he replied.

"You don't buy the suicide?"

"He took two .25 caliber rounds in the right side of the head. The muzzle burns were an inch apart, just above the ear. If the second round was discharged as a spastic reaction, why were the entry wounds almost identical?"

"Any witnesses?" I asked.

"None who could give a visual. But a kid said he heard two pops. At first he said they were a few seconds apart. Then he said they were together. Finally he said he couldn't be sure what he heard. Anyway,

Bernstine had powder residue on his right hand. I'd like to say he was left-handed so my suspicions would have more basis. But he was ambidextrous."

"What's bothering you, besides the kid originally saying there was a time lag between the shots?"

"Bernstine died on a Saturday. The Flannigan woman was scheduled to see him the following Tuesday. But there was no case record on her in his files."

"Maybe he had just started seeing her."

"No, I called Ms. Flannigan. She said she'd been going to Bernstine for six months. Anyway, Bernstine's wife calls me every day and tells me no way in hell he shot himself. Maybe not. But he'd lost his butt in the stock market and rumor has it he was messing around on his wife. So it's going down as a suicide."

"Thanks for your time, Joe."

"You haven't told me what Ms. Flannigan said to you."

"For some reason she feels guilty about Bernstine's death," I said.

"Think she was in the sack with him?"

"If she had been, she would have told you about it. She's a little neurotic," I said.

"I'm shocked you'd know anybody like that, Dave."

The following Monday Father Jimmie Dolan had just returned to the rectory after saying a 7:00 A.M. Mass when the phone rang in his office.

"Hello?" he said.

There was no reply. He heard a streetcar bell clanging in the background.

"Hello?" he repeated.

"Oh hello, Father. Sorry. I couldn't get the bloody door closed on the booth," a voice said.

"It's you again, is it?"

"Father, you've put me seriously in the shitter."

"I think you need counseling, my friend."

"Sir, you're a prelate and hence I believe a man of honor. Can you give me your word you won't continue to interfere in certain enterprises that are fully legitimate and doing little if any harm to anyone?"

Father Jimmie shuffled some papers around on his desk, then picked up a page torn off a note pad. "Your name is Max Coll?" he said.

"The coppers must have paid you a visit."

"Are you on Canal or St. Charles?"

There was a pause, then Max Coll said, "Now, how would you be knowing where I am?"

"There's only one streetcar line in operation today. It runs only on those two streets. So that means you're not too far away from me."

"You're a mighty intelligent man. But I need to—"

"You stay out of my church."

"Sir?"

"You heard me. If you ever bring a weapon into my confessional again, I'll tear you apart."

"Excuse me for saying this, Father, but that is a fucking mean-spirited statement for a Christian minister to make."

"Be thankful I don't have my hands on you," Father Jimmie said, and hung up.

Then he stood motionlessly by his desk, his heart hammering against his chest.

Chapter 6

That same evening, Leon Hebert, the daiquiri-store operator who had fired Josh Comeaux, had to handle the window by himself because Josh's replacement had called in sick. Hebert didn't like to work alone, at least not at night. He was a cautious man, both with money and people, and had made his living over the years on the soiled edges of society wherever he had gone. If there was any group of people he understood in this world, it was his clientele.

After he was discharged from the United States Navy, he had owned a liquor store on South Central Avenue in Los Angeles. The profits were huge and, except for the insurance, the overhead minimal. He accepted food stamps, welfare grocery orders, and even Bureau of Public Assistance bus tokens in place of money. After 2:00 A.M. he and a hired man would drive a panel truck down to East Fifth Street and sell eighty-nine-cent bottles of fortified wine, called short dogs, for two dollars apiece to the desperate souls who could not wait for the bars to open at 6:00 A.M.

But Leon Hebert learned there was a downside to running a business in a ghetto. On a warm summer night a white L.A. patrolman tried to hook up a drunk driver and force him into the back of a cruiser. In five minutes bricks, bottles, and chunks of curb stone were being flung into the traffic on Century Boulevard. This was in the era before the Crips and Bloods, but their predecessors—the Gladiators, Choppers, Eastside Purple Hearts, Clanton 14, and the *Aranas*—rose to the occasion and strung fires all over the south and east sides of Los Angeles.

A Molotov cocktail crashed through the window bars and front glass of Leon Hebert's store. The inventory went up like gasoline.

In the riot only two groups of white-owned businesses were spared: funeral homes and the offices of bail bondsmen. The lesson was not lost on Leon. When he got back to New Iberia, his birthplace, he sold burial insurance to people of color, collecting their half-dollar and seventy-five-cent premiums weekly, wending his way without fear through every back-of-town slum in south Louisiana.

Then he discovered the fast lane to prosperity was still available. He didn't have to go into the ghetto to sell his wares, either. The ghetto dwellers came to him, inside a shady grove on the four-lane, their gas-guzzlers smoking at his drive-by window, his ice-packed daiquiris, sweet and cold, ready to go at five bucks a pop.

He should have felt good about his situation, he told himself. He'd saved every cent he'd made peddling burial insurance and put it in a surefire franchise that gave him 60 percent of the profits. He made people happy, didn't he? Why did these damn kids from Loreauville get themselves killed with his cups in their car? And how about Josh Comeaux telling the physician, what was his name, Dr. Parks, teen-agers were always served at Leon's drive-by?

Mondays were slow and Leon thought about closing up early. What was it that was bothering him? The doctor? The sheriff's detective who got in his face? He looked out the service window into the dusk and saw blue-collar families leaving a barbecue-and-po'boy place on the corner of the short span of asphalt that joined the east-bound and westbound highways, between which he operated his store. The evening was warm and fireflies floated in the oak trees. He watched the people from the barbecue place getting into their cars and pickups, their children bouncing up and down on the seats. For just a moment he wanted to join them and free himself from whatever presence it was that seemed to cling to his skin like road film.

Three spoiled brats from Loreauville run themselves off the road into a telephone pole and he's in the toilet. There was no justice, he told himself.

A junker car filled with black men pulled to the window and Leon removed six plastic-sealed daiquiris from the ice compartment of his giant refrigerator and handed them one by one through the driver's window.

Leon waited for the car to pull away, but it didn't. The driver continued to stare into Leon's face, a toothpick in the corner of his mouth. A passenger in the backseat was smoking a cigarette, the ash glowing in the darkness. The passenger by the right front window held a metallic object in his lap, one that glinted dully in the light from the dashboard.

"I'm not alone. I got a man here with me," Leon said, his pulse quickening.

"What you talking 'bout, man?" the driver said.

The passenger by the right front window lifted a Zippo from his lap and lit a cigarette with it.

Leon let out his breath. "Y'all want something else?" he said.

"Yeah, you ain't give me my change," the driver said.

Three hours later Leon Hebert put his money bag in the floor safe, locked the doors, and turned off the lights. It was a beautiful night. The wind rustled in the trees overhead and the constellations were stenciled across the sky. An eighteen-wheeler passed on the highway, then an ambulance with its flashers on. The ambulance continued on past the hospital and turned onto the drawbridge and the state high-way that fed into Loreauville Road, where the three girls had been trapped inside their burning Buick.

Why did he have to think in images like that? *He* didn't do it, he told himself. That kid who worked for him, Josh Comeaux, had a boner in his pants for the Parks girl and would have let her slam it in the car door if she'd wanted to. Why didn't they put *that* in the pa-per? he said to himself.

No justice, he thought.

Someone started a pickup truck in front of the barbecue place and backed out of the parking lot, then headed slowly down the asphalt strip toward Leon Hebert's store, pieces of gravel clicking under the tires.

Leon fished his car keys out of his pocket, then dropped them in the darkness. When he bent over to retrieve them, the driver of the pickup turned into the oyster-shell loop that curved past Leon's drive-by service window.

"We're closed," Leon said, the high beams of the pickup burning red circles into his eyes.

But there was no response from inside the truck.

"Who is that?" he said, trying to smile.

A figure opened the truck door and stepped out on the oyster shells. Leon raised his hand to shield his eyes and squinted into the brilliance of the headlights. "My clerk already went to the bank. There's nothing here for you," he said.

The first pistol shot hit him high up on the chest with an impact like an anvil iron, knocking him backward, the hard-packed oyster shells slamming into the back of his head. The shooter had cut the lights on the pickup and was walking toward him, stooping for just a second to pick an object off the ground. The shooter stared down at Leon, perhaps realizing a mistake had been made, that the wrong person had been shot, that Leon Hebert should not have had a fate like this imposed upon him.

The figure leaned over him, blotting out the sky. Leon tried to speak, but the only sound that issued from his body was the air wheezing through the hole in his lung.

Then his mouth was pried apart and something that was stiff and bittersweet and crusted with dirt was shoved between his teeth and forced deep into his throat. Leon's right hand tried to clasp the shoe of the figure bending over him, to somehow telegraph the plea for mercy that his lungs and throat could not make. At that moment he looked into the face of his tormentor and knew what his final moments on earth would be like. He twisted his head sideways and looked desperately out at the highway, wondering how the world of normal people and normal events could be only a heartbeat away.

No one reported the shooting until just before sunrise, when a tramp who had been sleeping in the weeds by the railway track crossed the road and tripped over the body. Helen Soileau picked me up at my house in a cruiser and handed me a thermos filled with coffee and hot milk. She hit the flasher and we rolled through town to the crime scene.

"You're the skipper now. You don't have to do this early A.M. stuff anymore," I said.

"Somebody has to keep you guys on your leash," she replied.

Her eyes looked straight ahead, her expression flat. We passed a long row of shacks, the reflection of the flasher rippling across the house fronts.

"This isn't a robbery-homicide, is it?" I said.

Cane trucks packed to the top were already on the road when we got to the crime scene, snarling traffic at the intersection by the drawbridge. The early sun was red through the trees and mist was rising off the bayou behind the hospital. Leon Hebert lay on the oysters shells a few feet from his drive-by window, a bullet wound in his chest, a second one puckered in the center of his forehead, a third through the eye. A blue daiquiri cup had been compressed into a cone and stuck in his mouth.

An ambulance and three sheriff's department vehicles were parked outside the yellow crime-scene tape that had been strung through the oak trees. The coroner had not arrived but our forensic chemist, Mack Bertrand, was kneeling beside the body, slipping plastic bags over the hands of the dead man. A small man in tattered clothes and tennis shoes without socks sat outside the tape, his back against a tree trunk, his knees drawn up before him.

"How do you read it, Mack?" I said.

"The shooter used a revolver or he picked up his brass. I'd say the wounds were made with either a .38 or a nine-millimeter," he replied. He had ascetic features and wore a clip-on bow tie, suspenders, a crinkling white shirt, and a briar pipe in a little leather holster on his belt.

He lifted the dead man's right wrist. "It looks like there's shoe polish under his fingernails," he said. "My guess is the first round was fired from a distance and hit him in the chest. Then the shooter walked up close and put the next two in him point-blank. The victim probably looked up into the shooter's face and grabbed his shoe before he died."

"Why would he do that?" Helen asked.

Mack shook his head. He popped open another plastic bag and with a pair of tweezers lifted the coned plastic cup from the dead man's mouth, then dropped it inside the bag. "Take a look at this," he said, getting to his feet. "There's blood on the bottom of the cup. That means the victim's heart was probably still pumping when the cup was shoved into his mouth."

"Meaning?" Helen said.

"Who knows?" he said.

"No forced entry on the building?" I said.

"None that I could see," he said.

"How about tire impressions?" Helen asked.

"Probably every kind of tire made in the western world has been through here. Did y'all know this guy?" Mack said.

"He moved back here from L.A. He used to sell burial insurance," Helen said.

I looked at the small man in tattered clothes sitting against the tree trunk outside the tape. "Is that the guy who found the victim?"

"Yeah, good luck. I get the impression he's a traveling wine connoisseur," Mack said.

I stepped outside the crime-scene tape and squatted down eye-level with the man in tattered clothes. His skin was grimed with dirt and he wore a greasy cap crimped down on his head. Like all men of his kind, his origins, the people who had conceived him, the place or home where he grew up had probably long ago ceased being of any importance to him.

"You were sleeping by the tracks?" I said.

"I fell off the train. I was pretty much knocked out," he said.

"Did you see or hear anything that might be helpful to us?" I asked.

"I told it to that other guy." He nodded toward Mack Bertrand.

"Nothing bad is going to happen to you, podna. You're not going to jail. We're not holding you as a material witness. All those things are off the table. Just tell me what you saw."

He wiped his nose with his wrist. "Late last night I heard something go 'pop.' Then I heard it again. Maybe twice. Then a pickup truck drove off."

"Did you see the driver?"

"No."

"What did the pickup truck look like?"

"Just a truck. It was going down toward the bridge there."

"Why'd you come across the road this morning?"

"They got free coffee at the hospital," he replied.

My knees ached when I stood up. I took two dollars from my wallet and gave it to him. "There's a donut shop back toward town. Why don't you get yourself something to eat?" I said. I started to walk away from him.

"I seen something go flying out the truck window. Under the streetlight. Down toward the drawbridge. I don't know if that's any help to you or not," he said.

A few minutes later the coroner arrived. Later, the paramedics unzipped a black body bag and placed the remains of Leon Hebert inside it and lifted it onto a gurney. Mack Bertrand fiddled with his pipe and put it between his teeth, upside down. He was a family man, a Little League coach and regular church goer, and usually not given to a public expression of sentiment.

"You asked why the victim grabbed the shooter's shoe," he said. "He was asking for mercy."

I waited for him to continue. But he didn't.

"Go on, Mack," Helen said.

"That's all. He had a sucking chest wound and couldn't speak. It was probably like drowning while somebody watched. So he tried to beg with his hand. He must have been a bad judge of character."

"How's that?" I asked.

"Whoever did this poor bastard wanted him to go out as hard as possible," Mack said.

Helen and I and a uniformed deputy searched along the edges of the road by the drawbridge, looking for the object the hobo said he had seen thrown from the fleeing pickup truck. But we found nothing of consequence. Helen dropped me at my house and I shaved and showered and drove to the office. At 9:15 A.M. I called the office of Dr. Parks. The receptionist said he would not be in. I called his home.

"What do you want, Mr. Robicheaux?" he said.

"How did you know it was—"

"Caller ID. What's the problem now?"

"I'd like to come out to your house a few minutes."

"You're not welcome at my house."

"Sorry to hear you say that," I replied.

I drove up Loreauville Road, through horse-farm country and fields bursting with mature sugarcane, under a hard blue sky you could have scratched with a nail. The air was cool and sweet smelling, like cinnamon burned on a woodstove, and through the cypress and oak trees that lined the Teche the sunlight glittered like goldleaf on the water's surface.

But when I turned into Dr. Parks's driveway I seemed to enter a separate reality. His house was covered with shadow, the air cold, the birdbaths and empty fishpond and flagstone walkways moss stained and smelling of night-damp. The back end of a battered beige pickup truck stuck out of a shed in the rear of the house. Next to it was a stack of hay bales with a plastic bull's-eye pinned to them and a dozen arrows embedded in the straw. I had to ring the bell twice before he answered the door.

He was unshaved, the whites of his eyes shiny with a yellow cast, as though he had jaundice, a sour odor emanating from his clothes.

"Say it," he said.

"May I come in?" I asked.

"Suit yourself," he said, and walked deeper into the house.

We entered a large, cheerless room with an unlit gas log fireplace and dark paneling on the walls and windows covered by thick velvet curtains. Track lights on the ceiling were focused on a huge gun case that was filled with both modern and antique firearms.

"That's quite a collection," I said.

"Get to it, Detective," he said.

"Somebody waxed Leon Hebert last night. Somebody who really had it in for him."

"That breaks me up."

"You own a .38 or a nine-Mike?"

"A what?"

"A nine-millimeter."

"Yeah, a half dozen of them."

"You drive your pickup truck last night?"

"No."

"Where were you last night?"

"Home, with Mrs. Parks. And that's the last question I'm answering without my attorney being present."

We were standing no more than one foot apart. I could see the fatigue in his face, the sag in his skin, the manic shine of grief and anger in his eyes.

"My second wife died at the hands of violent men, Dr. Parks. The sonsofbitches who did it are all dead and I'm glad. But their deaths never brought me peace," I said.

"Is that your evangelical moment for the day?"

"I recommend you not leave town."

"One question?" he said.

"Go ahead."

"Did Hebert see it coming? Because I hope that motherfucker suffered just the way my daughter did before he caught the bus."

I left his house without answering his question. There are times as a law officer when you wish you did not have to look into the soul of another, even a grieving victim's.

That afternoon a seventeen-year-old black kid by the name of Pete Delahoussaye came into my office. Pete was over six feet and walked like he was made from coat hanger wire, but he had a fast ball that came down the chute like a B.B. and LSU and the University of Texas had both offered him athletic scholarships. Seven days a week, at 5:00 A.M., Pete and his widowed mother delivered the Baton Rouge *Morning Advocate* from one end of town to the other.

He stood in front of my desk, a paper sack hanging from his left hand.

"What's happenin', Pete?" I said.

"Found something early this morning. Thought maybe I should bring it in," he said.

"Oh?"

"Yeah," he said, sticking his hand in the bag. "I was passing Iberia General, going toward Jeanerette, when something come sailing out of a pickup."

"Whoa," I said, rising from my chair, just as he lifted a blue-black, pearl-handled revolver from the paper sack. I could see the leaded ends of bullets inside the cylinder. I stepped away from the muzzle and took the gun from him.

"How much have you handled this, partner?" I asked.

"A little bit," he replied, his eyes leaving mine.

"Did anyone else handle it?"

"No, suh."

"Did you see the person inside the truck?"

"No, suh, I ain't."

"What kind of pickup was it?"

"Just a beat-up old truck. Brown, I think. I would have brought the gun in this morning, but I had to go to school."

"You did fine."

"Mr. Dave?"

"Yeah?"

"I didn't know about the man getting killed at the daiquiri drive-by till this afternoon. My mother thinks I'm in trouble."

"You're not. You're a good guy, Pete. Mind if we fingerprint you?"

"So you won't get my prints mixed up with somebody else's?"

"You got it."

"That's it?"

"That's it."

I watched him walk down the hall, grinning, his day back in place. Keep playing baseball, kid, and don't ever grow up, I thought.

Mack Bertrand, our forensic chemist, called me from the lab the next afternoon. "We've got a ballistics match on the .38," he said.

"How about latents?" I asked.

"They all belong to Pete Delahoussaye," he said.

"None on the rounds in the cylinder?" I asked.

"Absolutely clean. I think that gun was oiled and wiped down before it was fired."

"What did you get off the plastic cup?"

"Smudges that had dried dirt on top of them. I'm sure they were there long before our shooter arrived."

"Anything else?"

"The victim had shoe polish and grains of leather under the nails of his right hand. But we knew that at the crime scene. Except for the discarded weapon, I'd say our perp was a professional."

"Thanks, Mack. By the way, what would you say the value of the gun is?"

"It's a single-action army Colt, fairly rare. A lot of collectors have them. Maybe fifteen hundred dollars."

I walked down to Helen's office and opened the door. She was just getting off the phone. "I'd like to get a warrant on Dr. Parks's house," I said.

"Looking for what?" she asked.

"Mack Bertrand says there were leather scrapings under the victim's nails."

"Think Parks is our man?"

"He had both motivation and opportunity."

Her eyes searched my face. "That isn't what I asked," she said.

"I went out to his house yesterday. He didn't attempt to hide his hatred of the victim. He even wanted to know if Hebert suffered. Later I wondered if it was an act."

"Like he's trying to brass it out?"

"Maybe. What doesn't make sense is the shooter throwing the gun out his truck window right by the drawbridge. Unless he wanted us to find it."

"Why do perps do anything?" She glanced down at the legal pad by her telephone. "We ran the serial number on the gun. It's registered to a William Raymond Guillot. He lives in Franklin."

"Guillot?" In my mind's eye I saw a tall, gray-headed, crew-cropped man by a slat fence, lighting a string of firecrackers, pitching it into the air, while behind him a half-dozen thoroughbreds thundered back and forth across a pasture.

"You know him?" Helen said.

"If it's the same guy, I saw him with Merchie Flannigan at Castille LeJeune's place."

She bit down on the corner of her lip. "I think the ante just got raised on us," she said.

"Say again?"

"I checked out Hebert's liquor license with the state board. He didn't own the daiquiri shop. It's part of a corporation called Sunbelt Construction. Guess who's listed as the CEO?"

Before I could answer, she said, "You got it, bwana. Castille Le-Jeune. Hope you enjoy charging howitzers with a popgun."

Chapter 7

Max Coll could not believe his bad luck. Not only had he blown the job on the priest in the confessional, his efforts at researching the priest's schedule for another run at the situation had been blessed with an electric storm from hell. By late Wednesday afternoon the streets of New Orleans were flooded and lightning had crashed into an oak tree on St. Charles, dropping most of the canopy into the center of the avenue. The consequence was a traffic jam from Canal all the way uptown to Carrollton Avenue. Max could not even get a taxi from the edge of the Quarter to Father Dolan's church and had to walk ten blocks in a driving rain, a scoped and silenced .223 carbine banging against his rib cage.

He looked like a drowned rat when he entered the church. Water poured out of his shoes and each time he coughed he experienced a sensation like a sawblade splitting his sternum. He began sneezing and couldn't stop. He honked his nose into a wad of paper towels until he was light-headed, then was almost run down by a beggar woman pushing her way out of the vestibule with a shopping cart.

Why had he taken this job? It was jinxed from the start. New Orleans wasn't a city. It was an outdoor mental asylum located on top of a giant sponge.

Get a hold of yourself, he thought. Take care of business, do a proper job of it, and never come back here again. It was almost 6:00 P.M. and the sky outside was absolutely black. The priest had finished his afternoon stint in the confessional and was no doubt having his supper, Max told himself. If the priest was true to his schedule, he would be saying his evening prayers in a front pew soon, his wide back presenting itself in lovely fashion to Max's crosshairs up in the choir. It was all going to be neat and tidy, nothing personal involved, no unnecessary pain. We all got to earn our keep, Father, he said to himself.

Max waited until the vestibule was empty, then darted up the side stairs into the choir area. Ah, that was easy enough, he thought, looking down on the half dozen or so old people praying in the pews. Through a side window he saw lightning leap above the adjacent rooftops, illuminating the fire escape and the alleyway down below. Max did not like lightning. It brought back memories and catechism lessons he saw no point in reliving. He blew his nose softly, unbuttoned his raincoat, and unsnapped the carbine from the sling under his armpit. When he sat down in a chair among a pile of hymnals in the corner he unconsciously glanced upward at the celestial paintings on the ceiling, then quickly shifted his attention back to the nave of the church before he got lost in troubling thoughts that would be of no help in concluding the business at hand.

He surveyed the marble pillars, the tapestry-draped banisters on the balconies, the apse over the altar, the hand-carved pulpit. The place looked like it had been transported from the Middle Ages and dropped from a hundred-thousand feet into the middle of a slum, he thought. Even the parishioners could have been street beggars out of the fifteenth century. All the place needed was Quasimodo swinging on the bells. What was the matter with these people? Hadn't they heard of modern times? And how about this Father Dolan, threatening him with physical violence over the telephone? Now, that was a sad state of affairs, an Irish-American priest berating a man who had worked in the service of the IRA. Pitiful, Max thought.

"What are you doing, Mister?" a little boy's voice said.

Oh shite, he thought.

"Are you here for choir practice?" the child said. He was not over nine or ten and wore long pants and a white shirt with a tie. His hair was wet and freshly combed, his nails pink and trimmed.

Max closed his raincoat, covering his carbine. "Choir practice? Not exactly," he said.

"Then what are you doing?"

"Examining the roof for rain leaks. I work for the bishop."

"How come you're all wet?"

"I told you. Now get lost."

"I'm here with my mother for Father Jimmie's choir practice. I don't have to do what you say."

"Now, you listen, you malignant pygmy—" Max said.

"Screw you," the little boy said.

Max coughed violently into his palm. His head was splitting, his nose running. "Here's five dollars. Go buy yourself a hot chocolate," he said.

"Screw you twice," the little boy said.

"How would you like your dork stuffed in a light socket?" Max said.

"Make it ten bucks," the little boy said.

"What?"

The little boy peered over the balcony. "Here comes Father Dolan now. Ten bucks or I start screaming," he said.

Max shoved the money in the boy's hands and watched him run down the stairs. The little bastard, he thought. I hope the vendor pours Liquid Drano in his hot chocolate.

Then Max heard footsteps, many of them, clopping up the wooden stairs. Either this is not happening or I'm being fucked with a garden rake, he thought.

He jerked open the window on the fire escape and climbed outside into rain that was now mixed with hail, closing the window halfway behind him. The icy pellets pounded his head, scalded his face, and slid down his coat collar inside his clothes. And if that wasn't enough, a bolt of lightning crashed into the alley, filling the air with the stench of sulphur and scorched electrical wiring. Jesus God, why was this being visited upon him? Then he looked down below and realized there were no steps below the fire escape, only rusted fastenings in the stone wall where a steel extension had once been in place. He was trapped like a rain-soaked parrot on a perch in an electrical storm, while inside the church Father Dolan's parishioners were dry and warm, passing out hymnals to one another.

Well, maybe it was time to spread the discomfort around a little bit, forget neat and tidy and simply splatter the good father's porridge and be on his way, Max thought. Why not? Click off the safety, burn the whole magazine if need be, then haul ass right through the choir and on downstairs into the street. Father Dolan's singing parishioners would be too busy climbing under the furniture or shaking the crab cakes out of their drawers to worry about describing Max Coll to the authorities.

He knelt down in a shooting position on the fire escape, squinted into the carbine's scope, and saw the priest's magnified face swim into the crosshairs. In fact, the magnification of the priest's head was so great Max could not make out detail but see only hair and skin and perhaps just a touch of beard stubble. The hail clattered and danced like mothballs on the steel mesh of the fire escape, stinging the backs of Max's hands, drumming softly on his cap.

The carbine was loaded with soft-nose rounds and two of them impacting inside the priest's face would undoubtedly blow the back of his head into the wall like pieces from a broken watermelon. Max ground his molars, breathed hard through his nose, and felt his finger tighten inside the trigger guard. Squeeze it off, he told himself. Do it, do it, do it.

But he froze again, his hands trembling, just as they had trembled inside the confessional.

He was disgusted with himself. As he started to get to his feet, the silencer on the muzzle of the carbine scraped against the window glass. Suddenly he was not only looking straight into the priest's face, the priest was actually charging toward him.

There was no place to run. The priest jerked the window open, ripped the carbine from Max's hands, then gripped the stock with both hands and drove the steel-plated butt into Max's mouth. Max felt his lip burst like a grape against his teeth, then the guardrail behind him peeled from its fastenings. In the wink of an eye he was plunging backward through space, his arms outspread, preparing himself for the impact on the brick-paved alley below.

Instead, he crashed into the middle of an opened Dumpster loaded to the gunnels with rotten produce and the leftovers from a parish shrimp boil. He stared upward from the garbage like a crucified man, right into the angry face of Father Dolan, who peered down at him from the edge of the broken fire escape. Max extracted himself from the softness of garbage that seemed to be sucking him into its maw and began pulling himself over the side of the Dumpster.

"Don't forget this," he heard Father Dolan call.

Max looked up in time to see his carbine plummeting through the rain and hail, just before it bounced off his uplifted face.

On Thursday morning I took the four-lane into Franklin, then checked in with the St. Mary Parish Sheriff's Department and was given directions to the home of William Guillot. It was a lovely old Victorian house, located in a tree-covered, residential neighborhood, one of deep green lawns and hydrangeas and impatiens blooming in the shade and wide galleries hung with porch swings. But the gardener told me Guillot wasn't there and I could probably find him at the subdivision he was building not far from the four-lane.

It wasn't hard to find. Five hundred yards from the road, where two tin-roofed farmhouses had once stood amidst cedars and poplar trees, bulldozers had scoured a thirty-acre wound in the earth for the construction of houses that looked as if they had been designed by a man with delirium tremens. At the entrance to the subdivision-in-progress a workman was spreading kerosene on a huge pile of oaks and slash pines that had been recently lopped into segments with chainsaws.

I parked my cruiser in a cul-du-sac flanked by three framed structures that several electricians were wiring. The man I had seen throwing firecrackers in the air by Castille LeJeune's horse barns was talking with a truncated, moon-faced workman in a yellow hard hat.

When the workman saw me, he turned his face away, mounted the steps of a framed structure, and busied himself with a nest of wiring hanging from the back of a breaker box.

William Guillot wore shined cowboy boots and dark blue western slacks with high pockets and a gray snap-button shirt. He seemed to be one of those men to whom age was an asset and maturity a source of power and confidence. His skin was grainy, his profile rugged; in fact, he had all the handsome characteristics of the archetypical western horseman, except for a purple birthmark that was like dye that had leaked from his hairline into the corner of his left eye.

"Help you?" he said.

"My name's Dave Robicheaux. I'm a detective with the Iberia Sheriff's Department. Are you William R. Guillot?" I said, my gaze wandering from him to the electrician in the yellow hard hat.

"Call me Will. What can I do for you?" he said.

"Where were you Monday night, Mr. Guillot?"

"At my fish camp. Down at Pecan Island."

"Anybody with you?"

"Maybe. What is this?"

"We're in possession of a revolver that's registered in your name. It's a single-action Colt .38. You own a weapon like that, sir?"

His hazel eyes fixed on mine and never blinked. "Say that again."

I repeated my statement.

"Yes, I do own one. But it's at my house," he said.

"Not anymore."

"Bullshit," he said, half smiling.

"I think we'd better take a ride to your house and check it out."

"If you haven't noticed, I'm building a subdivision."

"You an architect?"

"No."

"The revolver registered in your name is part of a homicide investigation, Mr. Guillot. If I were you, I'd get my priorities straight."

"Homicide?" he said, genuinely surprised.

"You own a brown pickup truck?"

"I don't. The company does. What about it?"

But I was looking at the back of the electrician who had walked away, and was not listening to William Guillot anymore.

"Did you hear me? What the hell is going on? Why are you staring at my electrician like that?"

"Is he your subcontractor?"

"What about it?"

"He installed defective wiring in the walls of my house. It burned to the ground," I said.

Guillot's eyes narrowed and dropped briefly to my person, as though he were filing away my inventory in a private compartment. "Follow me to my house," he said.

Twenty minutes later I stood in his home office, the sunlight breaking through a pecan tree by the side window, while he searched his desk, a wall safe, and the drawers of a gun cabinet. "It's gone," he said.

"You have a break-in recently?"

"Six or seven months ago."

"You reported it?"

"Yeah, but I didn't miss the .38. Why would somebody steal only the .38 and none of my other guns?"

"Write down the names of the person or persons you were with Monday night."

"Maybe I don't want to do that."

"I see. Maybe you can work through that problem in a jail cell."

He wrote a woman's name and address and telephone number on the top page of a scratch pad and handed it to me. "My wife and I are separated. Her lawyer is trying to clean my clock. This isn't information that will help my situation," he said.

"It's not our intention to compromise your privacy," I said.

But his eyes grew heated, as though he were remembering an unfinished, angry thought. "Back there at the house site, you made a serious accusation about my electrician. Did you file charges against him?" he said.

"In New Iberia we have no inspection system outside the city limits. Also, in Louisiana an electrical contractor has no liability one year after the work is done. You like building homes in Louisiana, Mr. Guillot?"

"I think you've got an ax to grind, Mr. Robicheaux. Let me say this up front. When I get pushed, I push back."

"Really?"

"Yeah, really," he said.

I tossed my business card on his desk. "Give me a call when I can be of service," I said.

That same afternoon the phone rang on the desk in Father Jimmie Dolan's office. He stared at the phone as it rang four times, then listened to the voice that came through the speaker on the message machine.

"Are you there, Father? Excuse me if I sound strange, but I have a broken nose, a mouth that looks like a smashed plum, and a tooth knocked out of my head. All done by a Catholic priest," the voice said.

In the background Father Jimmie could hear piano music and the sounds of street traffic.

"I know you're listening, Father. Would you please have the courtesy to pick up the fucking phone," the voice said.

"What is it this time?" Father Jimmie said.

"Because of you I'm up to my bottom lip in Shite's Creek and the motorboat is about to go roaring by."

"Could you do something about your language, please?"

"My language?" Coll said, his voice like a nail being pried out of dry wood. "I took ten thousand dollars up front for the whack on you. Now I have to pay it back or prepare to go through life with no thumbs."

"Then return it."

"I lost it at the dog track."

"Change your way, Coll."

"Sir, please don't be talking to me like that. I'm miserable enough."

"I called the police on you yesterday. If you won't worry about your soul, you might give some thought to what New Orleans' finest will do to you."

"If there's a trace on your line, it won't help. I'm on a cell."

"You're close by the little alcove in the French Market. I know the pianist who plays there. She's playing her theme song, 'Down Yonder,' right now."

"You leave a man no dignity. Can you help with the ten thousand? Maybe I could borrow it from one of your charities?"

"I'm hanging up now. I don't want you to contact me again."

"Oh, sir, don't do this to me. Don't fucking do this to a man who—"

"Who what?"

"Maybe wants to remember who he used to be."

Father Jimmie replaced the receiver in the phone cradle, the plastic surface as warm as human tissue against his palm, his hand trembling for reasons he couldn't readily explain.

Early the next morning I drove to Abbeville and interviewed Gretchen Peltier, the woman whose name had been given to me by Will Guillot as his alibi witness. She was middle-aged, slightly overweight, her hair dyed a deep black to hide the white roots. She worked as a secretary for an insurance agency and her hands trembled on the desktop when I asked her about her whereabouts Monday night. Her employer was inside a glass-windowed office, his door closed.

"Can't we do this somewhere else?" she said.

"Sorry," I replied.

"I was with Mr. Will. At his camp. We're friends."

"What hours were you with him?"

"I left his camp at dawn. The next day. Does that satisfy you?" Her eyes were filmed with embarrassment.

Later the same morning, Helen Soileau and I and another plain-clothes served the search warrant on Dr. Parks at his home. His face looked sleepless; he had just finished shaving and a piece of bloody tissue paper was stuck to a cut on his chin. He stared at the warrant incredulously. "Search for what?" he said.

"Let's start with your shoes. Take them off, please," I said.

He stared long and hard at me, then the resolution seemed to go out of his eyes. He sat on a footstool in the living room and unlaced each of his black dress shoes and handed them to me. The shoes were new and the leather on them was buffed and smooth and bright as mirrors. "Let's take a look in your closet, Doctor," I said.

We went inside the master bedroom. The curtains were closed, the air oppressive. I felt almost claustrophobic inside the room. "Could you open the curtains, please?" I said.

He started to turn on the overhead lighting.

"No, sir. Open the curtains," I said.

"Why?" he said.

"Because I see better with natural light," I said.

When he pulled back the curtains the room was immediately flooded with sunshine. The window gave onto a patio and a beautiful view of the bayou and the live oaks in the side yard. But the potted plants on the patio were dead, the glass-topped table marbled with dirt and the dried rings of evaporated rainwater. Helen and I pulled all the shoes out of the closet and bagged two pairs of black ones.

Dr. Parks sat on the side of the bed, his shoulders rounded. His wife opened the bathroom door, looked at us briefly, then closed it again. "Look, you've got your job to do. I accept that. But I heard . . ." he said.

"Heard what?" I said.

"You people found the gun that killed the daiquiri-shop operator," he said.

"The man who owns the weapon makes a convincing case it was stolen," I said.

"You think I go around stealing guns from people?"

"You attend gun shows, Dr. Parks?" Helen asked.

"Sure. All over the country."

"Ever buy a firearm at a tailgate sale?" she asked.

He rubbed his brow. "It's hopeless, isn't it?" he said.

"What do you mean?" I said.

"I've heard about stuff like this. You can't make your case and you zero in on the survivors of the victim," he said.

There were many rejoinders either Helen or I could have made. But you don't break off the barb of a harpoon in a man who has already been ripped from his liver to his lights.

We got back in the cruiser and crossed the drawbridge in Loreauville, then headed up the state highway toward New Iberia. We passed cane trucks and the old Negro quarters left over from plantation days and an emerald green horse farm with big red barns and pecan trees next to a white house.

"Why'd you want the curtains open back there?" Helen asked, watching the road.

"Their bedroom was like a grave. I couldn't breathe."

She glanced sideways at me.

"You didn't feel it?" I asked.

"You worry me, bwana," she said.

Chapter 8

On Saturday morning I drove with Clete to New Orleans to check out his apartment, which he had loaned to Gunner Ardoin and his little girl. We crossed the Atchafalaya on the arched steel bridge at Morgan City, the docked shrimp boats and old brick buildings and tile roofs and palm-dotted streets of the town spread out below us in the sunshine. Then we drove into rain that seemed to blow out of the cane fields like purple smoke, and by the time we approached the giant bridge spanning the Mississippi, Clete's Cadillac was shaking in the wind, the fabric in the top denting with hailstones.

We drove into the French Quarter and parked in front of his apartment on St. Ann. He ran through the rain and went upstairs into his apartment. A few minutes later he was back in the car, his brow knitted.

"Gunner taking care of the place?" I said.

"Yeah, everything looks fine," he said.

"What's wrong?" I said.

"He left a message on the machine. He said an Irish guy was asking around in the neighborhood a couple of days ago. A weird-looking dude with little ears. Gunner thought maybe this guy had business with me."

"Max Coll?" I said.

"Yeah. I think Gunner's got it wrong, though. Coll doesn't have any reason to be interested in me. Gunner might get himself popped."

"Where's Gunner now?"

"He didn't say. How do I get involved in crap like this?"

"Let's have a talk with Fat Sammy."

"I can't stand that guy. He looks like a blimp after all the air has gone out of it."

"There're worse guys in the life."

"Oh, I forgot, he gives discounts to the meth whores who work in his porn films," he said.

He fired up the Caddy, the rust-eaten muffler roaring against the asphalt, and we drove in the rain to Fat Sammy's house on Ursulines.

I rang the iron bell at the entrance.

"Who is it?" Sammy's voice said from the speaker inside the archway.

"Dave Robicheaux," I replied.

He buzzed open the gate and we walked through the flooded courtyard to the door of his house, which he had already unbolted and left ajar. I had not told Sammy that Clete was with me. When we stepped inside the living room he was lying on the floor, dressed in purple gym trunks and a strap undershirt, watching an opera on cable TV while he curled dumbbells into his chest. His massive legs were as white and hairless as a baby's, his pale blue eyes looking at us upside down.

"What's the haps, Sammy?" Clete said.

"Who said you could come in here, Purcel?" Fat Sammy asked.

Clete looked at me. "I'll wait in the car," he said.

"Clete's my friend, Sammy."

Sammy set down the dumbbells and got to his feet, his lungs wheezing. The living room was dark, the windows covered with thick velvet curtains. Through a side door I could see two men, neither of whom I recognized, shooting pool. Sammy looked down from his great height at both me and Clete.

"So you want to watch some opera?" he asked. He spread his feet and began touching his toes.

"You know a guy named Max Coll?" I said.

"Do I know him? No. Do I know who he is? Yeah, he works out of Miami 'cause it's suppose to be an open city there. Here's the short version. You want somebody clipped, there's guys in Little Havana who work for a service. You want it done right, you ask for this Irish character. Except some people say he's a wacko."

Out of the corner of my eye I saw Clete staring intently through the side doorway at the two men shooting pool.

"Wacko how?" I said.

"I don't know, 'cause I don't keep company with them kind of people," Sammy said. "Look, what I hear is the wacko screwed up a job in New Orleans and stiffed the wrong people. That means if he goes back to Miami he might float up in a barrel. Now, we done with this?"

"The guy in there with the patent-leather hair? Is that Frank Dellacroce?" Clete asked.

"What about it?" Sammy said.

"Nothing. I thought he was down on a murder beef in Texas. Maybe George W. slipped up during his days as chief needle injector," Clete said.

Sammy's eyes looked at nothing while he scratched at his cheek with three fingers. "Come back another time, Robicheaux," he said.

Outside, rain was sluicing off the rooftops while Clete and I ran for his Cadillac. We got inside and slammed the doors. "Why do you always have to start up the garbage grinder?" I said.

"That greaseball shooting pool put his infant daughter in the refrigerator and held a gun to his wife's head while he did it. You think Sammy is on the square? I think he's a fat douche bag who should have been blown out of his socks years ago."

"You don't listen, Clete. It's hopeless. You'll never change."

"Neither will you, Dave. You'd like to splatter every one of these shitheads, but you won't admit it. Bootsie's death is eating your lunch. You talk about getting honest at meets? Why don't you stop stoking up your own fires?"

We drove over to Decatur in silence, wrapped in anger, with no destination, the sky as gray as dirty wash. Rainwater was spouting from the sewer grates, the guttural roar of the ruptured muffler vibrating through the Cadillac's frame.

"If you want to attack me, Clete, do it. But don't drag my wife's death into it," I said.

"I'm finished talking about it. Live your own life," he replied.

At the traffic light in front of the Cafe du Monde I got out of the car, slammed the door behind me, and ran through the rain to the pavilion. When I looked back over my shoulder Clete was gone and Jackson Square looked as cold and stark as a black-and-white photograph taken in the dead of winter.

I ordered coffee and hot milk and a plate of beignets, but couldn't eat. I walked the streets in the rain, keeping under the balconies, threading through the tourists carrying street-sale ten-dollar umbrellas. I looked through steam-coated windows of cafes and bars where people were watching Saturday-afternoon football on television. On Dauphine I went into a bar that was packed with gay men, all of them shouting in unison to punctuate the gyrations of a famous transvestite dancing on the stage. The bartender wore a pencil-line mustache and earrings and a black leather cap and leather vest without a shirt. He stared at me across the bar.

"You have coffee?" I asked.

"This look like a Starbucks?" he replied in a New England accent.

"Give me a soda with a lime twist," I said.

He fixed my drink and set it on the bar. He smiled to himself, but not offensively.

"On the job?" he said.

"No, not on the job," I said.

"No problem, sir," he said.

I closed my eyes as I drank down the soda and lime in the glass. I could have sworn I tasted the traces of bourbon in the ice. I used the rest room and walked back out on the street, my skin and clothes reeking of cigarette smoke, my head buzzing with sounds like an electric wire popping in a rain puddle.

I lost track of time. It stopped raining toward evening and a wet fog settled on the French Quarter and drifted like colored smoke off the neon lights over the clubs. Bourbon Street, which was closed at night to automobile traffic, became filled with college boys drinking beer out of plastic cups, conventioneers and tourists strung with cameras peering into strip joints that featured both topless and bottomless performances, and black kids tap dancing like minstrel caricatures or running a shuck that begins, "Bet you five dollars I can tell you where you got your shoes at."

I walked along the river where bums sat on stone benches with sack-wrapped bottles of fortified wine between their thighs. I turned up Esplanade and walked all the way to the ragged edge of the Quarter at Rampart, past a hallelujah mission with a neon cross above its door, past Louis Armstrong Park, a place no white person in his right mind enters either day or night, over to Basin Street and the long white wall that fronted St. Louis Cemetery. Through the gates I could see row upon row of whitewashed crypts and stone crosses, framed against the sodium lamps of the Iberville Project that burned in the fog with the incandescence of pistol flares.

I sat down on a bus bench next to a huge man with a wild beard and head of black hair. He wore a suit that looked like it had been pulled from a garbage can, a tie knotted like a garrote in the collar of his flannel shirt. His skin was so grimed with dirt it was hard to tell his race. His eyes made me think of the renegade Russian priest Rasputin.

"You got any money?" he said.

"What do you need it for?" I answered.

"Something to eat. Maybe a drink or two."

I found four dollars and seventy-three cents in my pocket and gave it to him. He clenched it in his hand but remained seated on the bench. "I got me a dry place in one of the tombs. The mission is all full on Saturday nights," he said.

I nodded. A group of tourists were walking by, talking among themselves about either *A Streetcar Named Desire*, the play by Tennessee Williams, or the original streetcar itself, which today sits like an immobile and disconnected anachronism on a cement pad down by the river.

The disheveled man stood up and began waving his arms at them. "That streetcar didn't go out to Desire," he yelled. "It went out to Elysian Fields. It was the last car that still run out to Elysian Fields. All these streets here was Storyville. It was full of colored whorehouses and women who killed themselves with morphine. Hey, don't you go in them crypts! The kids from the Iberville Project climb over the wall and bust people like you in the head. Are you listening to me? This ain't New Orleans. You're standing in the city of the dead. You just don't know it yet."

The tourists walked quickly up the street toward Canal, their faces ashen.

A minute later Clete Purcel's Cadillac came around the corner, oil smoke leaking from under the frame, a hubcap rolling loose across the asphalt, like a paean to the disorder in his life. He pushed open the passenger door.

"Want to go back to New Iberia?" he said.

"Why not?" I said, and got inside. I looked through the back window at the silhouette of the disheveled man receding behind us.

"Sorry I got on your case. But I think Fat Sammy has been putting the slide on you," Clete said.

"Maybe he has."

"No maybe about it, Streak. Every ounce of meth going into the projects has Sammy's greasy prints all over it. He makes me think of a giant snail trailing slime all over the city."

"You're one in a million, Cletus."

He looked at me uncertainly, a pocket of air in one cheek, then roared up the ramp onto I-10. We poured it on all the way back to New Iberia, like two over-the-hill low riders who no longer look at calendars or watch the faces of clocks.

On Monday morning Mack Bertrand called me from the lab and said the shoes we had removed from Dr. Parks's house were not the source of the leather scrapings found under the fingernails of the dead daiquiri vendor, Leon Hebert. A few minutes later Helen came into my office and I told her of the lab's findings.

"So where does that leave us?" she said.

"A revenge killing of some kind. The daiquiri cup stuffed down the victim's throat indicates a high level of rage. Dr. Parks had motivation."

"You don't sound convinced," she said.

"Parks has so much anger I doubt he'd deny killing the man if he did it."

"How about this guy Guillot?"

"He's a poster child for obnoxiousness. But why would he shoot someone and throw the weapon, registered in his name, on the side of the road?"

"We're talking about middle-class people, Streak. Career perps are predictable. Dagwood and Blondie aren't."

Beautiful.

But I believed there were other factors at work in this case that were more complex than a simple act of vengeance. It was too much for coincidence that Castille LeJeune's corporation owned the daiquiri store where Leon Hebert had been murdered and that the murder weapon belonged to Will Guillot, one of his employees.

But Helen was right. We were dealing with middle-class people who didn't have the proclivities and personal associations of career criminals, most of whom were basket cases who left a paper trail through the system from birth to the grave.

Why had Theodosha Flannigan been afraid to climb through the fence surrounding the fish pond on her father's property? Why did Castille LeJeune say he had no memory of using his influence to get Junior Crudup off the levee gang at Angola? People denied evil deeds, not good ones.

And how about the suicide of Theodosha's psychiatrist? If she was his regular patient, why wasn't her case file in his records?

I long ago became convinced that the most reliable source for arcane and obscure and seemingly unobtainable information does not lie with government or law enforcement agencies. Apparently neither the CIA nor the military intelligence apparatus inside the Pentagon had even a slight inkling of the Soviet Union's impending collapse, right up to the moment the Kremlin's leaders were trying to cut deals for their memoirs with New York publishers. Or if a person really wishes a lesson in the subjective nature of official information, he can always call the IRS and ask for help with his tax forms, then call back a half hour later and ask the same questions to a different representative.

So where do you go to find a researcher who is intelligent, imaginative, skilled in the use of computers, devoted to discovering the truth, and knowledgeable about science, technology, history, and literature, and who usually works for dirt and gets credit for nothing?

After lunch I drove to the city library on Main and asked the reference librarian to find what she could on Junior Crudup.

She looked thoughtfully into space. She had a round face and wore glasses with pink frames and parted her hair down the middle. "I have a history of blues and swamp pop here. That might be helpful," she said.

"I've already used that. This guy disappeared from Angola about 1951. There's no record anywhere of what happened to him."

"Wait here a minute," she said.

I watched her moving around in the stacks, sliding a book off a shelf here and there, then clicking on a computer keyboard. A few minutes later she waved for me to join her at a back table, where she had spread open several books that contained mention of Junior Crudup.

"I looked at those already, I'm afraid," I said.

"Well, there's a photographic collection in Washington, D.C., that might be worth looking at," she said.

"Pardon?"

"In the forties and fifties a photographer who once worked with Walker Evans photographed convicts all over the South. He had a penchant for black musicians. He tracked some of their careers for decades. There are hundreds of photographs in his collection."

"Is he still alive?"

"No, he died twenty years or so ago."

"How do we get a hold of the collection?"

"All the ones he took of Crudup or of Louisiana prisons are downloading and printing right now. You need anything else?"

The photographs were stunning, shot with grainy black-and-white film in Jim Crow jails and work camps, when the convicts still wore stripes and the hacks carried lead-weighted walking canes and made no attempt to hide the spiritual cancer that lived in their faces. Nor was there any attempt to hide the level of severity and privation that characterized the lives of the prisoners in the photographs. In each photo the camera caught an image or a detail that left no doubt in the viewer's mind about what he was seeing: a wheeled cage tiered with bunks parked inside a swamp; a convict sitting in the bottom of a wood sweatbox, a forced grin on his face, a waste bucket by his foot; a work gang assembled at morning-bell count, while in the background two men tried to balance themselves barefoot atop a case of empty pop bottles; a mounted gunbull in a cowboy hat framed against a boiling sun, his arm pointed, yelling a command at a convict pulling a fourteen-foot cotton sack behind him.

It was called stacking time on the hard road.

But in each of the photographs the reference librarian had downloaded, Junior Crudup was obviously the odd piece in the puzzle box, regardless of his surroundings. In a ditch with a dozen other convicts, he was the only light-skinned man, the only one with an etched mustache, and the only one to look directly into the camera. His eyes were clear, his face marked by neither resentment nor grandiosity. I suspected he was one of those for whom the gunbulls did not have a category, which would not have been good news for Junior Crudup.

But some of the photographs were taken outside of prison. One showed him with Leadbelly, the two of them laughing at a joke in front of what appeared to be a practice session of Cab Calloway's orchestra. Another showed him at a crowded table in a supper club, a beautiful black woman in a pillbox hat and polka-dot organdy dress, with an orchid pinned to her shoulder, seated next to him. Everyone in the picture was grinning at the camera, except Junior Crudup. He was dressed in a tuxedo, his tie pulled loose, a cigarette trailing a line of smoke from between two fingers. There was a half grin on his mouth, his eyes focused on a neutral spot, as though he were not entirely connected to the environment around him.

I got a manilla envelope from the reference librarian and began slipping the printouts of the photos inside it. Then a detail in the last photo caught my eye and made me pull it back out. The photo was far less dramatic than the others and showed eight or nine convicts in denims, not stripes, plowing under cane stubble with mules in a sugarcane field that sloped down to a bayou.

An obese white man in a straw hat, with a doughlike face and a shotgun propped on his thigh, was watching them from atop his horse. Junior was staring up at the gunbull, a hoe at an odd angle over his shoulder, his face puzzled, as though he had just been told something that made no sense. It was wintertime and the bayou was low, the roots of the cypress trees exposed along the banks. A stump fire was burning on the edge of the field, the smoke drifting like a dirty smudge across the sun. Across the bayou, on the edge of the picture, was the back of a Victorian home that had obviously been built to resemble a steamboat.

The home of Castille LeJeune.

A half hour later I rang the bell on his front porch, without having called or gone through his corporate office in Lafayette. "I thought you might be interested in this photo. According to the cutline on it, it was taken in 1953," I said when he opened the door.

His eyes dropped to the photo briefly but he did not take it from my hand. "Mr. Robicheaux, how nice of you to drop by," he said.

"That's Junior Crudup in the picture, Mr. LeJeune. That's your house in the background."

He wore slacks and a tie and a blue sweater with buttons on it. His eyes fixed on mine, twinkling. "I'm sure what you say is true. But the burning issue here seems to escape me."

"You said you had no memory of getting Crudup off the levee gang. But here he is, harrowing your sugarcane field across the bayou from your house."

He tried to suppress a laugh. "Let's see if I understand. You've driven out here to talk to me about a photo taken of convicts almost fifty years ago?"

"Did you rent convict labor back then, Mr. LeJeune?"

"The people who ran my family's agricultural interests might have. I don't remember." He looked at his wristwatch and raised his eyebrows. "Oh heavens, I'm supposed to leave for New Orleans shortly."

His patrician insouciance, his disingenuousness and contempt for the truth were part of a lifelong attitude on which there were no handles. I could feel words breaking loose in my throat that I didn't want to say. "You received the Distinguished Flying Cross from Harry Truman, did you?"

"Do you wish me to confirm what you already know, or do you wish to ask me a meaningful question?" he said, his eyes gazing benignly out on the flowers and palm and oak trees in his yard.

I could feel my left hand opening and closing against my thigh, the veins tightening in the side of my head. Don't get into this, I heard a voice say in the back of my mind. "I met Audie Murphy once. It was a great honor," I said.

"I'm happy to hear that," he said.

"Thank you for your time, Mr. LeJeune," I said.

He made no reply. Even though I had managed to control my anger I felt like a fool, one of that great army of salaried public servants who were treated by the very rich as doormen and security guards. I got in my cruiser and began backing down the long, shaded driveway to the state road, the sun flashing through the canopy like the reflection off a heliograph. When I reached the entrance to the state road I had to wait for a long line of cane trucks to pass, the wagon beds swaying heavily with the enormous loads they carried. In the meantime Castille LeJeune had gotten into his Oldsmobile and was driving toward me.

I got out of the cruiser and walked to his car, then waited for him to roll down the window. "I'm sorry, I forgot to leave you a business card," I said, and placed it on his dashboard. "I think something real bad happened to Junior Crudup. Please be advised there's no statute of limitation on murder in the state of Louisiana, Mr. LeJeune. By the way, it was an honor to meet Audie Murphy because he seemed to be both a patriot and a straight-up guy who didn't try to get by on bullshit."

On Tuesday morning Helen called me into her office. "I just got off the phone with Castille LeJeune's attorney. He says you made a nasty accusation yesterday at LeJeune's house," she said.

"News to me."

"You think you can jam a guy like Castille LeJeune?"

"He's lying about Junior Crudup."

"The R&B convict again?"

"Right."

"How about we concentrate on crimes in this century? Starting with the homicide at the daiquiri store."

"No matter what avenue we take, I think it's going to lead back to LeJeune."

"Maybe because you want it to."

"Say again?"

"You hate rich people, Dave. You can't wait to get into it with them."

"No, I just don't like liars."

"Can you do me a favor?"

"What?"

"Go somewhere else. Now."

That afternoon Father Jimmie Dolan was at a basketball practice in a Catholic high school gymnasium not far from his church, when his cell phone rang inside his gym bag. "Father Dolan," he said into the receiver.

"I need only a quick word. Don't be hanging up on me now," the caller said.

"How did you get this number?"

"Told the secretary at the rectory I was your grandfather. I need something from you."

"What could I possibly have that you want?"

"I was paid to take out this fellow Ardoin. But I'm not going to do it."

"You didn't answer my question. What is it you want?"

"There's an open contract on me, Father. That means I'm anybody's fuck. But they messed with the wrong fellow, you get my drift?"

"No, and I don't want to."

"I'm going to loosen some people's earthly ties."

Father Jimmie stared listlessly across the gym at the boys who were taking turns laying up shots under the basket. He had a sore throat and fever and wanted nothing else in life at that moment except a glass of whiskey and a warm bed to lie down in.

"You know what I'm asking from you, don't you?" Max Coll said.

"I think you want absolution for your sins, Max. But you can't have it. Not over the phone, certainly. And perhaps never, not unless you give up your violent ways."

The cell phone was silent.

"Did you hear me?" Father Jimmie said.

"I think I've misjudged you. Under it all you're a hard-nosed bastard of a kind I remember only too well, one whose cassock and collar come before his humanity. Shite if you're not a disappointment to me."

The transmission went dead. Father Jimmie's cheek stung as though it had been slapped.

Chapter 9

That evening I fixed a bowl of milk for a stray cat and watched him drink it on the gallery. He was a hard-bodied, short-haired, un-neutered white cat with chewed ears and pink claw scars inside his coat. His tail was as thick as a broom handle. When I petted him he looked at me blankly, then went back to his milk.

Theodosha Flannigan pulled her Lexus into the driveway and parked under the pecan tree by the side of the house. A guitar in an expensive case was propped up in the backseat. She wore loafers and a blue terry cloth blouse and jeans low on her hips so they exposed her stomach. The wind gusted and leaves swirled around her, and a single band of dusky sunlight cut across her face.

"What's the name of your little friend?" she asked, sitting down on a step next to the cat.

"He didn't say," I replied.

She picked the cat up in her arms and kissed him on top of his head. Then she flipped him on his back and set him in the crevice formed by her thighs and straightened his body by pulling his tail as though it were a strap on a piece of luggage. She scratched him between his ears and under his chin. "We're going to call him Mr. Adorable. No, we're going to call him Snuggs," she said.

"What's happenin', Theo?" I said.

"I heard about your visit to my father's house."

"Your father has a problem with the truth. He doesn't think he needs to tell it."

"He says you talked to him as though he were a criminal."

"I talked to him as though he were an ordinary citizen. He didn't like it. Then, rather than confront me about it, he used his attorney to report me to the sheriff."

"He comes from a different generation, Dave. Why don't you have a little compassion?"

Time to disengage, I said to myself. The streetlights were coming on under the oak trees, and the air was cool and damp and I could smell an odor like scorched brown sugar from the mills. Theo set down the cat and stroked his back, then stood up. "You want to see my new guitar?" she asked.

"Sure. I didn't know you played," I said.

She came back from the car with her guitar and unsnapped the case. "I'm not very good. My mother was, though. I have some old tapes of her singing some of Bessie Smith's songs. She could have been a professional. The only person I've ever heard like her is Joan Baez," she said.

Theo removed the guitar from its case and sat down again on the steps. She made a chord on the neck and brushed her thumb across the strings, then began singing "Corina, Corina" in Cajun French. She had been much too humble about her ability. Her voice was lovely, her accompaniment with herself perfect as she ran each chord into the next. In fact, like all real artists, she seemed to disappear inside the thing she created, as though the identity by which others knew her had nothing to do with the inner realities of her life.

She smiled at me when she finished, almost like a woman delivering a kiss after she has made love.

"Gee, you're great, Theo," I heard myself saying.

"My mother used to sing that. I don't remember her well, but I remember her singing that song to me before I went to sleep," she said. She began putting away her guitar.

The cat she had named Snuggs nuzzled his head against her knee. The wind riffled through the oak and pecan trees overhead, and a group of children on their way to the library rode by on bicycles, laughing, the streetlights glowing in the dampness like the oil lamps in a Van Gogh painting. There was not a mechanized sound on the street, only the easy sweep of wind and the scratching of leaves on the sidewalk. I didn't want the moment to end.

But like the canker in the rose or the serpent uncoiling itself out of an apple tree, there had been an element in Theo's song that disturbed me in a way I couldn't let go of.

"The melody for 'Corina, Corina' is the same as 'The Midnight Special,'" I said.

"Un-huh," she said vaguely.

"That was Leadbelly's song. The Midnight Special was a train he rode into the Texas State Penitentiary at Huntsville. According to the prison legend, the convict who saw the headlight on the locomotive shining at him in his sleep was going to be released in the coming year."

But I saw she had still not made the connection.

"Your father didn't want to answer questions about Junior Crudup, Theo," I said. "Crudup was Leadbelly's friend inside Angola. They probably composed songs together. I think Crudup was a convict laborer on your father's plantation."

She continued snapping her guitar case shut and never looked at me while I spoke. But I could see what I thought was a great sadness in her eyes. She reached over and petted the cat good-bye, then turned toward me. "You have an enormous reservoir of anger inside you, Dave. I guess I feel sorry for you," she said.

The next morning events kicked into overdrive, beginning with a phone call from Clotile Arceneaux, the black patrolwoman who Helen said was an undercover state trooper.

"We've got Father Jimmie Dolan in custody," she said.

"Are you serious?" I said.

"As a material witness. He won't give up Max Coll's whereabouts."

"Which administrative moron is behind this?" I said.

She paused before she spoke again. "Coll tried to kill the priest but he won't press charges. So a couple of detectives figured Father Jimmie is not a friend of N.O.P.D. and decided to put the squeeze on him. Look, the word on the street is there's an open contract on Max Coll. We need this guy out of town or in lock-up. We also don't need trouble from Catholic priests."

"Can't help you," I said, and hung up the phone.

She called back three hours later. "Guess who?" she said.

"Same answer as before," I said.

"Try this. We just heard from Miami-Dade P.D. Max Coll flew into Ft. Lauderdale, whacked two greaseballs who were getting laid on a yacht, then caught the last flight back to New Orleans. At least that's what they think. Get Dolan out of Central Lock-Up. Better yet, get him out of the state," she said.

But I didn't have to spring Father Jimmie. The bishop and Father Jimmie's conservative colleagues at his church came through for him, evidently making trouble from the mayor's office on down through the chain of command at N.O.P.D.

Father Jimmie called me at home that evening. "You know the story of Typhoid Mary?" he said.

"A nineteenth-century cook or kitchen helper who caused problems everywhere she went?" I replied.

"The bishop is recommending I travel somewhere that's quiet and rustic. Maybe do a little bass fishing. I think anywhere outside of New Orleans would be fine with him," he said.

I shut my eyes and tried not to think about what he was obviously suggesting. "Straight up, Jimmie. Do you know where Max Coll is hiding?"

"Absolutely not," he said.

"Why didn't you file charges against him?"

"The cops need a Catholic minister to tell them Coll's a killer?"

I rubbed the back of my neck. "Want to entertain the bass?" I asked.

Father Jimmie moved into a back room of my house and the weekend passed uneventfully. On Monday Clete called the department and asked me to meet him for lunch at Victor's Cafeteria.

It was crowded with noontime customers, the wood-bladed fans turning high above us on the stamped-tin ceiling, the steam tables arrayed with Friday specials featuring shrimp or catfish or étoufée. Clete's plate was piled with dirty rice and brown gravy, kidney beans, and two deep-fried pork chops. He wore an electric blue shirt and white sports coat, his face red with sunburn from a tarpon-fishing trip out on the salt. "Dolan's at your place, huh?" he said.

I nodded, waiting for him to begin one of his lectures. But he surprised me.

"There's an N.O.P.D. snitch I pay a few bucks to. He called me this morning about a bail skip who's hid out in Morgan City. Then he mentions this guy Max Coll. He says Coll capped two high-level Miami greaseballs and there's a fifty thou open whack on him. Which means every street rat in New Orleans is crawling out of the sewer grates."

"Yeah, I heard about it."

"Right," Clete said, feeding a half piece of bread into his mouth. "Well, tell me if you've heard this. At seven this morning either Frank Dellacroce or his clone was in the donut shop by the railway tracks."

"Here, in New Iberia? The guy you saw shooting pool in Fat Sammy's house?"

"He came out of the donut shop just when I was going in. At first he couldn't believe his bad luck. Then he puts on a wise-ass grin and says, 'You fish for green trout over here, Purcel?' I go, 'No, I'm looking for a needle dick who puts his own child in a refrigerator. Know anybody like that, Frank?'

"He goes, 'That story is a lie my wife's lawyer spread about me during our divorce. So why don't you either pull your head out of your ass or mind your own fucking business?'"

People around us were quietly picking up their plates and trays and moving to tables farther away from us.

"Just then two more greaseballs come out of the donut shop. One used to be a shooter for the Giacanos. The other one I don't know."

"How do you read it?" I asked.

"They think Dolan knows where Coll is hiding. Any way you cut it, big mon, you've let Dolan piss in your shoe."

"Can we take our food to the park?" I said.

"What's the problem?"

"I think we're about to get thrown out of here."

"What for?" he said, still chewing, his face filled with puzzlement.

After I returned from lunch I went into Helen's office. She was talking on the phone, standing up, a pair of handcuffs pulled through the back of her belt. Before she hung up I heard her say, "You don't have to tell me." Then she looked at me blankly. "What is it?" she said.

"Clete says three New Orleans wiseguys are in town. They're after a rogue button man by the name of Max Coll," I said.

"They're staying at the Holiday," she said.

"How do you know that?"

"The manager called earlier. The greaseballs have hookers in their rooms and are scaring the shit out of the staff. I was about to tell you about it but I got a call from a guy at the chamber of commerce. He says you and Clete Purcel had a conversation in Victor's Cafeteria that made a third of the room move their tables."

"I'm sorry."

"Dave, I've told you before, we have enough problems of our own. What does it take to make you understand that?"

The room was silent. I heard a warning bell clanging at the railroad crossing and a freight train clattering down the tracks. "You want the wiseguys out of town?" I said.

"I hate to tell you what I want," she said.

"Just say it, Helen."

She spit a hangnail off her tongue. "Meet you outside," she said.

We arrived in four cruisers at the Holiday Inn out by the four-lane. My experience with the Mob or its members had never been one that possessed any degree of romance. In fact, my encounters with them always made me feel as though I had walked inside the drabness and urban desperation of an Edward Hopper painting. Although it was Monday and the motel was almost empty, Frank Dellacroce and his two friends had taken a row of rooms in back, facing the highway, where road noise echoed off the windows and doors of their building. Their cars were brand new, waxed and shining, but were parked by an overflowing Dumpster, out of which trash feathered in the wind and scudded across the asphalt. The sun was barely distinguishable in the sky, the air close with an odor like fish roe that has dried on a beach; the only sign of life in the scene was a palm tree whose yellowed fronds rattled dryly in the wind.

Helen got out of her cruiser, her arms pumped, her shield hanging from a black cord around her neck. A cleaning woman was passing on the walkway, a plastic bucket filled with detergent bottles on her arm. "You smell marijuana coming from that room?" Helen asked.

"Ma'am?" the cleaning woman said.

"That's what I thought," Helen said. She banged her left fist on the door of the room registered to Frank Dellacroce, her right hand resting on the butt of her holstered nine-millimeter. "Iberia Parish Sheriff's Department! Open the door!" she shouted.

With few exceptions, television and motion pictures portray members of the Mafia or the Mob or the Outfit as dapperly dressed, Plotinian emanations from an ancient ethnic mythos. They are not only charismatic—they take on the proportions of protagonists in Elizabethan tragedy, with accents from Hell's Kitchen.

The truth is most of them are stupid and at best capable of holding only menial jobs. They use dog-pack intimidation to get what they want, whether it involves preferential seating in a restaurant or taking over a labor union. On a personal level their sexual habits are adolescent or misogynistic, their social behavior inept and laughable.

In terms of health, they're walking nightmares. Listen to any surveillance tape: After age fifty, they complain constantly about clap, AIDS, obesity, impotence, emphysema, clogged arteries, ulcers, psoriasis, swollen prostates, the big C, and incontinence.

The room door opened and a man with black, freshly barbered

hair and pale features and dark eyes stepped outside. He was barefoot and wore slacks without a shirt. His chest was triangular in shape and covered with a fine patina of hair, his upper arms well developed. He started to pull the door shut behind him.

Helen pushed the door back on the hinges. "Your name Della-croce?" she said.

"Frank Dellacroce, yeah. Why the roust?" he said.

"We have a complaint you're soliciting prostitution and using narcotics in the motel. Place both your hands against the building and spread your legs, please," she said. She crooked a finger at a figure inside the room. "You need to come out here, Miss. Bring your purse with you."

The girl who emerged from the room was probably not over nineteen, dressed in sandals; skintight, cut-off jeans; and a Donald Duck T-shirt that hung on the points of her breasts. She wore no makeup and her hair was bunched on the back of her head with a rubber band. "I didn't do anything," she said.

"Get out your ID," Helen said.

The girl's hands were shaking as she removed her driver's license from her billfold and handed it to Helen.

Helen looked at the photo and the birth date on the card, then gave it back to her. "Beat it."

"Ma'am?"

"Your trick is a guy who put his infant child inside a refrigerator. You want a fuckhead like that in your life?" Helen said.

The girl walked hurriedly across the parking lot toward the street. The uniformed deputies had pulled Dellacroce's two friends out of the adjoining rooms and were shaking them down against a cruiser. But they found no weapons or dope on them and none in their rooms.

Dellacroce was still leaning against the wall, his feet spread. "We done with this?" he said.

Helen didn't answer. I could see the frustration building in her face.

"Hey, we're here for the tarpon rodeo. We ain't broke any laws. You get off squeezing my sack, fine. But I want a lawyer," Dellacroce said.

"Better shut up," I said.

"I'd show you where to bite me, but I'm holding up the building here," he said.

"Helen, could I have a word with Mr. Dellacroce?" I said.

"Please do," she replied.

Dellacroce took his hands off the wall and watched her and the deputies get back in their cruisers. I told Dellacroce's two friends to go inside their rooms and to keep their doors shut. Dellacroce stared at me, a cautious light in his eyes.

"My house is off-limits to you, Frank. So is Father Jimmie Dolan," I said.

His slacks hung just below his navel. He traced the tips of his fingers up and down the smooth taper of his stomach, almost as though he were caressing a woman's skin. "You were Purcel's partner in the First District?" he said.

"At one time."

"Mind if I get my shirt?" he said.

"No, I don't mind," I said.

He reached inside the door and picked up a long-sleeve pink shirt and began drawing a sleeve up his arm. His hair was tapered, lightly oiled, iridescent on the tips. "Purcel was on a pad for us," he said.

"Yeah?" I said.

"That's all. He made himself a little change."

"What are you saying, Frank?"

"Nothing. Just talking about the history of your friend."

"Tell me, is that story about your infant child true?"

"No," he said. His eyes held on mine, devoid of any sentiment or moral consideration I could see, indifferent to the lie they either contained or did not contain. His mouth was slightly parted and his teeth were wet with his saliva. I could feel his breath puff against my skin like a presence released from a poisonous flower. Involuntarily I stepped back from him.

"Word of caution, Frank. Max Coll was a shooter for the IRA," I said.

"The what?"

"I hope you find Coll. I really do. Have a nice day," I said, and grinned at him.

The sun came out late in the afternoon, the wind died, and the sky was marbled with crimson clouds. When I got home from work Father Jimmie was raking leaves in the backyard.

"Clete and I are going to throw a line in. How about joining us?" I said.

"Not today," he said. He picked up a huge sheaf of blackened pecan and oak leaves and dropped them on a fire burning inside a rusted oil barrel. The smoke rose in thick curds and twisted through the canopy like a yellow handkerchief.

"Never knew you to pass up a fishing trip," I said.

"I saw Max Coll," he said.

"Don't say that."

"I was coming out of Winn-Dixie. He was standing across the street."

"Maybe you're imagining things."

"No, I saw him, Dave."

"Then he'd better not come around here."

"He's a sick man. He needs help."

"I'm not buying into this discussion," I said, and walked away.

When I looked back out the kitchen window Father Jimmie was heaving more leaves onto the fire, his clothes and skin auraed with smoke and dust in the shafts of sunlight breaking through the trees.

God protect me from martyrs and saints, I thought.

Clete and I hitched up my boat trailer to the back of my pickup and a half hour later slid the boat into the water at Bayou Benoit in St. Martin Parish. The surrounding water shed looked both enormous and desolate in a strange, autumnal way. There wasn't a sound from the bays or the inlets, not even the flopping of a bass or a gator back in a cove. A painter would have called it a beautiful evening. The western sky was still pale blue, the clouds like strips of fire, the leaves of the cypress and willow trees golden and motionless in the dead air. But the closed shutters on the houseboats and the lines of ducks and geese transecting the sun made something sink in my heart, as though I were the last man standing on earth.

As we headed across a long bay into a flooded woods, Clete sat in the bow, humped over, his back to me, the collar of his denim coat pulled up, his Marine Corps utility cap snugged down on his head. He ripped the tab off a can of beer and drank it, then began eating a Vienna sausage sandwich. I cut the engine and let the boat drift on its wake into the trees. Clete reached into the ice chest and tried to hand me a diet Dr Pepper.

"No, thanks," I said.

He clipped a Mepps spinner on his monofilament and cast it deep into the cove. "Something happen today?" he asked.

I told him about my encounter with Frank Dellacroce at the motel, about his attempt to put me on a pad, about his mention that Clete had once taken juice from the Mob. Clete retrieved his lure, his face never changing expression.

"So what's the point?" he said.

"I don't like a degenerate bad-mouthing my friends. I don't like being offered a bribe," I replied.

He waited a long time before he spoke again. "I don't think that's the problem, noble mon," he said.

"Oh?"

"You think all this belongs in a time capsule," he said, making a circle in the air with his hand. "Outsiders aren't supposed to come here, particularly greaseballs and Wal-Mart and these cocksuckers grinding up the trees with bulldozers. It's always supposed to be 1950."

"I see."

"The truth is you wish you had all these bastards locked in your sights inside a free-fire zone."

"Glad you've figured it all out."

"At least I don't sleep with a nine-millimeter anymore."

"Don't be offended when I say this, but, Clete, you can really piss me off sometimes."

"You worry me, mon. I think you're going into a place inside yourself that people don't come out of."

I saw a bass roll among the flooded trees, like a green-gold pillow of air violating the symmetry of the surface. I cast my Rapala above the place he had broken the water, hoping to retrieve it across his feeding area. Instead, the balsa wood lure clacked against the trunk of a willow and the treble hooks went deep into the bark.

"I'll row us over there," Clete said.

"Not on my account," I said. I jerked the monofilament with my hand and snapped it off. The sun disappeared on the horizon like a flame dying on a wet match.

Way leads on to way.

I tried to go to bed early that night but I couldn't sleep. Rain began to click on the trees, then on the tin roof of my house, and I dressed and drove up the bayou road in the rain to St. Martinville. On the edge of the black district I went into a brightly lit cafe and ordered a cup of coffee and a small bowl of gumbo at the counter. A door with a beaded curtain was cut in one wall, and in the adjoining room a man was playing an accordion, while another man, with thimbles on his fingers, accompanied him on an aluminum rub board that had been molded to fit the contours of his chest.

The people in the other room were all light-skinned people of color, often called Creoles, although originally the term *Creole* had denoted a person of French or Spanish ancestry who had been born in the New World. The people in the next room were blue-collar mulattos whose race was hard to determine. They drifted back and forth across the color line, married into both white and black families, still spoke French among themselves, and tended to be conscious of manners and family traditions.

Seated in one corner by himself was Frank Dellacroce, a shot and a glass of beer by his hand, his legs crossed, his silk shirt unbuttoned in order to expose his chest hair and the gold chain and medallion that rested on it. He tossed back the whiskey and flexed his mouth as though he had just performed a manly act. Then he tilted back his head, the small of his back against the seat of the chair, and seemed to resume his concentration on the music. The song the accordionist was playing was "Jolie Blon," the most haunting and unforgettable lament I have ever heard. Then I realized that the object of Frank Dellacroce's attention had nothing to do with music, or a song about unrequited love and the loss of the Cajun way of life: Frank Dellacroce's attention was fixed on the shapely form of a young Creole woman dancing by herself.

Her name was Sugar Bee Quibodeaux. Her eyes were turquoise, her hair the color of mahogany, fastened in back with a silver comb, her gold skin dusted with sun freckles. She also had the mind of a seven year old. She had conceived her first child when she was twelve and at age fifteen was taken to a state hospital by her grandparents and sterilized. Sometimes a local cop or a kind neighbor or business person tried to protect her from herself, but ultimately no one could restrain Sugar Bee's love of boys and men and the excitement and joy her own body gave her.

I finished eating and paid my check at the register. Through the beaded curtain I could see Sugar Bee sitting at Frank Dellacroce's table, a bottle of beer and a glass in front of her. She was leaning forward, listening to something he was saying. He leaned forward, too, his hand deep under the table. Then the two of them stood up and she picked up her purse, one with white sequins and tassels on it, and hung it by a string from her shoulder. They walked through the beaded curtain toward the front door.

"That's far enough, Frank," I said.

He turned around, half smiling. "You following me?" he said.

"Nope."

"Then we got no problem here. Right?"

"Yeah, I think we do," I said.

"No, no, man," he said, wagging his finger. "I ain't done nothing wrong."

"That's a matter of definition, Frank," I said.

"We talking about a racial issue here?"

"You're going back to your motel, Frank. You're going back alone. Got the drift?"

"I checked you out, Robicheaux. You're an A.A. rum-dum people around here feel sorry for. But that don't mean you get to beat up on guys like me 'cause I'm Italian or from New Orleans or whatever the fuck it is about me that bothers you."

I looked at my watch. "Your coach is about to turn into a pumpkin," I said.

He stepped toward me. "This is a free country. You don't like what me and the lady are doing, I say suck my dick. Now, you get out of my face and out of my space 'cause I really fucking don't like you, man."

"At this point I'm placing you under arrest. Put your hands behind you and turn around, please," I said.

"Arrest? For what?" he said, his face incredulous.

"Disturbing the peace, creating a public nuisance, using profanity in public, that sort of thing. I'll think of some more charges on the way down to the jail," I said.

"This ain't even your jurisdiction," he said.

But I wasn't listening now. I turned him toward the wall and hooked him up, then pushed him out the door into the parking lot. It had stopped raining, and the air was cold and wet, and fog was rolling out of the trees across the road. Sugar Bee and several other patrons of the cafe and bar had walked outside and were watching us.

"You armed, Frank?" I said.

"Want to search my crotch? Be my guest," he replied.

I fitted my hand under his arm and moved him toward the hood of my truck. That's when he hawked phlegm out of his throat and spat it in my face.

I felt it in my eyelashes, on my mouth, in my hair, like a skein of obscene thread clinging to my person. I picked him up by his belt and slammed him into the fender of the truck, then drove his head down on the hood. But Frank Dellacroce was not one to give up easily;

though his wrists were cuffed behind him, he brought one hand up and clenched it into my scrotum.

I smashed his head into the hood again, then got my handcuff key out of my pocket and unhooked him. I spun him around and drove my fist into his mouth, throwing all my weight into the blow, snapping his head back as though it were on a spring. I saw his lip burst against his teeth, and I hooked him in the eye with a left, caught him on the jaw and in the throat and on the nose as he went down.

He was whipped, but I couldn't stop. I picked him up by his shirt and hit him again, rolled him off a car fender and drove my fist repeatedly into his kidneys. He collapsed in a mud puddle and tried to drag himself away from me. But I knelt beside him and twisted his shirt in my left hand and drew back my fist to hit him again. He tried to speak, his ruined face pleading. I heard people screaming and felt Sugar Bee slapping at my head with a shoe, her voice keening in the damp air.

A light on a pole burned overhead. I stared at the circle of faces around me, like a drunkard coming out of a blackout. Their eyes were filled with fear and pity, as though they were watching a wild animal tear his prey apart inside a cage. But there was one man in the crowd who did not belong there. He was white and had narrow shoulders and wore a seersucker suit with a pink tie. His ears were small, convoluted, hardly more than stubs on the sides of his head. His face and expression made me think of the bleached hide on a baseball.

As I looked up into his eyes I had no doubt in the world who he was, no more than you can doubt the presence of death when it suddenly steps into your path. I got to my feet and helped Frank Dellacroce up, then propped him against the grill of an ancient gas guzzler, no more than five feet from the man in the seersucker suit.

"Frank, meet a guy you've probably been looking for all your life," I said.

Then I walked off balance to my truck and drove away.

Chapter 10

Early the next morning I soaked my hands until the swelling had gone out of my fingers, then I put Mercurochrome on the cuts in my knuckles and tried to cover them unobtrusively with flesh-colored Band-Aids. I picked up the morning paper off the gallery and went through it page by page, just as I had done for years when I was coming off a drunk, wondering what kind of carnage I may have left in an alley or on a rain-swept highway.

But this morning the paper seemed filled with cartoons and sports and wire-service and local feature stories that had nothing to do with events in front of a cafe-and-bar on the St. Martin Parish line. Snuggs, my newly adopted cat, followed me back inside and I opened a can of food for him and put it in his bowl and sat with him on the back porch while he ate. The wind was cool and damp and sweet smelling through the trees, but each time I closed my eyes I saw the terrified, blood-streaked face of Frank Dellacroce and wondered who lived inside my skin.

Father Jimmie was still asleep, so I drove over to Clete's cottage at the motor court and took him for breakfast at the McDonald's on Main Street. Then I cleared my throat and told him about the previous night—at least most of it.

"Wait a minute," he said, raising his hands from his food. "You had your piece and your cuffs with you?"

"Right," I said.

"Why?" he said.

I shrugged.

"Maybe because you were looking for trouble when you left home?" he said.

I looked at an oak tree out on the street, one that was strung with moss and lighted by the pinkness of the early sun. "I saw Max Coll there," I said.

"You did what?"

"In the crowd. I've seen pictures of him. It had to be Coll. His head looks like a used Q-tip," I said.

Clete's eyes studied my face. They seemed to contain a level of sorrow that I could not associate with the man I knew. "What are you doing to yourself, Streak?" he said.

At 11:30 A.M. Helen leaned her head in my door. "Pick up line two. See how much this has to do with us. If it doesn't, don't let it get on our plate," she said.

The man on the other end of the line was a St. Martin Parish plainclothes named Dominic Romaine. He was a big, fat, sweaty man, known for his rumpled suits, horse-track neckties, and general irreverence toward everything. He had emphysema and his voice wheezed into the phone when he spoke.

"That guy you beat the shit out of last night, Frank Dellacroce?" he said.

"Uh, there's a bad connection, Romie. Say again."

"Pull on your own joint, Robicheaux. I don't know why you busted this guy up, but it don't matter. In other words, you're not gonna be up on an IA beef."

"Sorry, I'm just not reading you, partner."

I heard him take a deep breath, the air in his lungs whistling like wind in a chimney. "After you got finished with Dellacroce, he drove to a cabin by Whiskey Bay. It's actually a fuck pad a bunch of greaseballs out of Houston use. Get this"—he broke off and started laughing, then fought to catch his breath again—"he was behind the wheel of his car, sucking on a bottle of tequila, while this mulatto broad was giving him a blowjob, when a guy comes out of the dark and parks a big one in the back of his head. I mean a big one, too, like a .44 mag. His brains were still running out his nose when we got there."

Dominic Romaine started laughing again. I felt my vision go in and out of focus. Outside, an ambulance passed the courthouse, its siren screaming. "You still there?" he said.

"Who was the shooter?"

"No idea. No description, either. The mulatto handing out the blowjob is retarded or something. Dave, there's a question that needs to go into my report."

"I didn't see Dellacroce after my encounter with him," I said.

"Got any speculations on the shooter?"

My head was pounding, my stomach churning. "Check with N.O.P.D. Dellacroce was a hitman and fulltime wise-ass. I think he was a grunt for Fat Sammy Figorelli."

"It sounds like his passing will go down as a great tragedy. Hey, Dave? You know that song by Louie Prima? 'I'll be standing on the corner plastered when they bring your coffin by'? I love that song. Hey, Dave?"

"What?"

"Next time you go looking for a punching bag, make sure it ain't in St. Martin Parish," he said.

I barely got through the day. I tried to convince myself the man I had seen in the crowd the previous night was not Max Coll. I had seen only photos of him, taken through a zoom lens or in a late-night booking room. The man in the crowd could have been a tourist, or someone who had walked over from the convenience store next door, I told myself. And even had it been Max Coll, was I my brother's keeper, particularly if my "brother" was a dirtbag like Frank Dellacroce?

But I knew in my heart my thought processes were self-serving and futile and that I had helped set up a man's death. I worked late at the office, past sunset, then turned out the light on my desk and drove home, just as it began to rain.

I pulled into my drive, expecting to see Father Jimmie's car under the porte cochere. Instead, I saw Theodosha Flannigan's Lexus parked in the shadows and a light burning in the kitchen. The trees in the yard and the bamboo along the edge of the driveway were shrouded in mist, and yellow leaves floated in the rain puddles. The front door and the windows of the house were open, and I thought I could smell the odor of freshly baked bread. In fact, the entire scene, the dark cypress planks in the walls of the cottage, the rusted tin roof, the black-green overhang of the oaks and pecan trees, and the warm radiance emanating from the kitchen windows, all made me think of the house where I had lived many years ago with my father and mother.

As soon as I stepped into the house I saw Snuggs resting on the arm of the couch, his eyes shut, his paws tucked under his chest, a red satin bow tied around his neck. I walked into the brightness of the kitchen and stared woodenly at Theodosha, who was lifting a loaf of buttered French bread out of the oven. Behind her, steam curled off a pot of gumbo. Her mouth parted slightly when she saw me, as though I had dragged her away from a troubling thought.

"I fixed you some supper. Hope you don't mind," she said.

"Where's Father Jimmie?" I asked.

"He went to Lafayette. He said he's probably going to stay over."

"Is Merchie here?" I said.

"I'm not sure where he is. He's just out being Merchie. Do you want me to go?"

"No, I didn't mean that. I'm just a little disconnected today."

She began setting the table as though I were not there. Her hair looked like it had just been cut and shampooed. She wore Mexican sandals and khakis with big pockets and a denim shirt embroidered with roses and stovepipe cactus. In fact, as I looked at her moving about the room, I realized what it was that drew men to her. She was one of those women whose intelligence and élan and indifference to public opinion allowed her to give symmetry and order to what would have been considered chaos in the life of a lesser person.

"Theo, I'd feel a lot better if we could ask Merchie over," I said.

"I knew you'd say something like that."

She set a gumbo bowl on the table and stared at it emptily. She removed a strand of hair from the corner of her mouth and walked to within a foot of me. She started to touch me, then folded her arms in front of her, as though she had no place to put her hands. Her breath was cold and smelled of bourbon and orange slices.

"I was going to a meeting today. I had no plans to drink. I swear. I drove twice around the block, then went into a bar and drank for two hours." She looked up at me desperately. "Dave, I'm seriously fucked up. Nothing I do works."

She lowered her head and inverted her palms and clasped them around my wrists. She stood on my shoes with her sandals and her stomach touched my loins. I could smell the shampoo in her hair and the perfume behind her ears. She pulled my hands to her sides and held them there. I could feel a thickness growing in me, a dryness like confetti in my mouth. She slipped her arms around my waist and pressed her face sideways against my chest.

"Dave, why didn't you ask me to marry you?" she said.

"This is no good, Theo."

"We had fun together. Why did you go away?"

"I was a drunk. I would have made any woman unhappy."

Her eyes were wet against my shirt. I patted her on the back and tried to step away from her. Then she turned up her face to be kissed.

"I'll see you," I said.

"What?"

"I have to go back to the office," I lied. "I just came home to get something. I don't even remember what it was."

Then I left my own house, feeling stupid and inadequate, which was perhaps an honest assessment.

When I returned to the house two hours later she was gone. The kitchen was immaculate, the food she had fixed carted away. I didn't fall asleep until after midnight. Then I woke at three in the morning and sat on the edge of the mattress, my skin filmed with sweat, my loins like concrete, the darkness creaking with sound. I put my loaded .45 under the pillow and when the sun came up the hardness of the steel frame was cupped in my palm.

Later, I ate a bowl of Grape-Nuts and milk and sliced bananas on the kitchen table, then heard Snuggs at the back screen. I opened the door for him and he walked to his pet bowl under the kitchen sink and waited for me to fill it with the box of dry food I kept on top of the icebox. The red silk bow Theodosha had tied around his neck was coated with mud. I took a pair of scissors from the dresser in the hallway and snipped the bow loose from his fur. "It looks like Theo's concern for you was limited, Snuggs," I said.

Somehow that thought made me feel more comfortable about leaving her and the meal she had prepared for me the previous night. I returned the scissors to the dresser drawer. But before I shut it I glanced down at the box where I kept all the sympathy cards that had been sent to me when Bootsie died. A corner of an envelope stuck out of the pile and the return address on it made me wince inside. On my visit to Theo and Merchie's house several weeks ago she had expressed her sympathies about Bootsie's death, but I'd had no memory of her sending a card and had concluded her sentiments were manufactured.

But her card was in the pile and the statements on it were obviously heartfelt. I picked up Snuggs and set him on the countertop and patted his head. "How can one guy's thought processes be this screwed up?" I asked.

Snuggs rubbed against me, brushing his stiffened tail past my nose, and made no comment.

The phone on the counter rang. I started to pick it up, then hesitated and stared at it, my heart quickening, because I knew who it was, who it would *have* to be, if he was the obsessed and driven man I thought he was.

"Hello?" I said.

"Is the good father there?" the voice asked.

"No, he's not."

"Would you be knowing his whereabouts?"

"No, I don't. But I recommend you not call here again."

"Oh, do you now?"

"Mr. Coll, I'm a lot less tolerant about you than Father Dolan. You drag your sickness into my life and I'm going to put a can of roach spray down your throat."

"*I'm* the sick one? Two nights ago you kicked the bejesus out of that poor fuck in front of the bar. I'd say you're a piece of work, Mr. Robicheaux."

Use the cell phone to call the office and get the line open, I told myself. But Max Coll was ahead of me. "I'm not on a ground line, sir. You needn't fiddle around with technologies that will serve no purpose. Tell Father Dolan he and I share a common destiny."

"Are you insane? You're talking about a Catholic priest."

"That's the point. It's the likes of me who keep him in business. Thanks for your time, Mr. Robicheaux. I hope to meet you formally. I think you might be my kind of fellow."

He hung up.

"So the guy's a nutcase," Clete said at lunch.

I pushed my food away. We were in a place called Bon Creole, a small family-owned cafe that specialized in po'boy sandwiches. It was two in the afternoon and the other tables were empty. "I've got another problem, Clete," I said.

"No kidding?"

"It's not funny."

"Look, big mon, Frank Dellacroce's mother was probably knocked up by leakage from a colostomy bag. He got what he deserved. Stop thinking about it."

"I'm not talking about Dellacroce."

"Then maybe you should take whatever it is to Father Dolan. I don't know what else to say."

He waited for me to reply. When I didn't, he widened his eyes and opened his hands, as if to say, *What?*

I want a drink. Worse than I've ever wanted one in my life, I heard a voice say.

Clete's next remark did not help. "I'm a bad guy to ask for advice. I always handled my problems with a pint of Beam and a six-pack of Dixie, then I wake up the next morning with a Bourbon Street stripper whose idea of world news is the weather channel." He read the expression on my face and grimaced. "Sorry, Streak. Sometimes I don't know when to shut up," he said.

When I got back to the office, Wally, our three-hundred-pound, hypertensive dispatcher, gestured at me from the cage. Long ago every plainclothes in the department had become inured to Wally's sardonic sense of humor and his comments about our bumbling ways and collective lack of intelligence. But this afternoon he was different. His eyes were evasive, his smile like an incision in clay. "Been to lunch, huh?" he said.

"Yeah. What's up?"

"That fellow Flannigan was in here."

"Merchie Flannigan?"

"He was pacing up and down for an hour, like he was about to piss his pants. When he got ready to go I axed him if he wanted to leave a message." Wally shifted in his chair, arching his eyebrows.

"Would you just spit it out?" I said.

"He said tell Dave not to be running his pipeline under the wrong man's fence. The district attorney and some Chamber of Commerce people was in the waiting room. So was Helen."

A woman passed us and looked back at me briefly. "Okay, Wally, I appreciate it," I said, and started to walk away.

"Hey, Dave?" he said.

"Yeah?"

"I never liked that guy. He's a bum. Put a cork in his mout'."

I walked back to the cage. "What are you telling me?" I said.

Wally picked up a pencil and went back to his paperwork. "Nothing. I didn't mean to mix in nobody's bidness," he replied.

I went into my office and stood at the window, tapping my fingers on the sill. I had no doubt Merchie wanted trouble. Otherwise he would not have brought his complaint into the place where I worked.

Well, sometimes the best way to deal with the lion is to spit in the lion's mouth, I told myself. At 5:00 P.M. I drove to Merchie and Theo's home on the edge of town.

Even though I had passed the house a thousand times, I still could not get over the juxtaposition of imitation thirteenth-century battlements with a boiler works across the highway. But perhaps the conjuncture of nouveau riche vulgarity with pecan orchards and horse barns and the softly lit ambiance of Bayou Teche was the perfect stageset for a man like Merchie Flannigan. Strip away the guise of the reformed street hood and self-made egalitarian success story, and there was little difference between Merchie and his father-in-law, Castille LeJeune. They didn't go after their enemies head-on; they poisoned the environment where they worked.

I saw Theo look out the living room window as I parked my truck.

"What's wrong, Dave?" she said, opening the front door.

"Merchie was looking for me at the department. He seems to think I'm causing a problem in his marriage," I said.

"Come in."

"Where is he?"

"At my father's. Wait, don't leave like this."

"Straighten him out on this, Theo," I said.

Her face slipped by the driver's window as I turned around and headed back out the driveway.

A half hour later, I pulled up to the front of Fox Run, Castille LeJeune's home outside of Franklin. I rang the front doorbell, but no one answered. The wind was balmy out of the south, smelling of brine and schooled-up speckled trout at Cote Blanche Bay, the setting so tranquil that my anger at Merchie, which I had fed all the way down the road, made me feel like a spiritually unclean visitor inside a church. The house itself was deep in shadow, the oak trees creaking overhead, but the surrounding fields and horse pasture were still lit by the last rays of the sun, and in the distance I thought I saw Merchie walk from behind a row of abandoned cabins to a promontory that overlooked the bayou.

I went around the fenced pond that Theo feared for reasons she did not share and walked past a row of shotgun cabins that were probably built in the 1890s for the black people who planted and harvested the LeJeune family's sugarcane and drove it to the grinding mill in mule-drawn wagons without a member of the LeJeune family ever putting a hand on it. The cabin doors were gone, the tin roofs buckled loose from the joists, the plank floors blown with grit and scoured by the hooves of livestock. The privies were still standing, the eaves clotted with the nests of yellow jackets and mud-dobbers; the wood seats, once streaked with urine, now dry and smooth as old bone; the grass around the walls a bright green.

I wondered if Junior Crudup had once slept in these cabins or used these privies, coming in hot and dirty from the fields, perhaps in leg irons, his evening meal a jelly glass of Kool-Aid and a tin plate of greens, fried ham fat, corn bread and molasses. I wondered how many lyrics in his songs had their inception right here, among these desiccated shacks that perhaps told more of a people's history than anyone wished to remember.

I had left work ready to bend Merchie's day out of shape and now I had managed to link him in my mind with his father-in-law and the cruelties and racial injustices of Louisiana's past. What was my motivation? Easy answer. I didn't have to think about the fact I had deliberately put Frank Dellacroce in Max Coll's gunsights.

Merchie was standing on a grassy knoll, his back turned to me, and did not hear me walk up behind him. A solitary white crypt, closed in front by a black marble slab that was chiseled around the edges with strings of flowers and clusters of angels, rested at a slight angle in the softness of the ground. Merchie squatted down with an orchid he inserted in a green water vase. The name on the slab was Viola Hortense Flannigan, Merchie's mother, the strange, neurotic, possessive woman who used to wash out his mouth with soap and whip his bare legs with a switch until he danced.

Earlier I had been ready to tear him apart. Now I felt my anger lift like ash from a dead fire.

"I apologize for intruding on you," I said.

"You're not," he said, rising from his crouched position, a bit like a man waking from sleep.

"You were looking for me at the department?"

He scratched the top of his arm idly and looked at the wind blowing in the grass. "I get hot under the collar sometimes. Things aren't always right with me and Theo. So I take it out on the wrong people," he said.

"No harm done," I said.

He combed his hair and put his comb away, then watched a flock of black geese freckle the sun. "My mother always wanted to be a southern lady. She told people she grew up in the Garden District in New Orleans. The truth was her old man ran a produce stand in the Irish Channel. So I bought this little piece of land from my father-in-law and buried her in it."

I nodded, my eyes averted. In the distance I could see the railed fish pond that caused Theo such fear she had almost let two children drown rather than climb through a fence and approach the water.

"What happened at that pond, Merchie?" I asked.

He opened and closed his hands, the veins in his forearms filling with blood. "This place is a living curse. I'd like to set fire to it and plow its earth with salt. Outside of that, I don't have much to say about it," he said. Then he walked away, accidently kicking over the vase into which he had placed an orchid for his mother.

Chapter 11

Some people seem to be born under a bad sign.

At 8:30 A.M. the following day an arson inspector called me at the office. In the early hours of the morning a fire had broken out in Dr. Parks's game room and had quickly spread through the roof, destroying the back third of his house. "I know the guy just lost his daughter, but he's hard to take. How about coming out here, Dave?" the inspector said.

"What's the deal?" I said.

"Parks is convinced somebody tried to burn him out."

"My relationship with Dr. Parks isn't a very good one."

"You could fool me. He seems to think you're the only guy around here with a brain."

I drove up to Loreauville and crossed the drawbridge there and followed the state road to the shady knoll where Dr. Parks's home sat among the trees like a man with an angry frown. A solitary firetruck was still there and two firemen were ripping blackened wood out of a back wall with axes. Dr. Parks approached me as though somehow I were the source of all the problems and missing solutions in his life. "I want an arson investigation initiated right now," he said.

"That's a possibility, but so far there doesn't seem to be enough evidence to warrant one." I raised my hand as he started to interrupt. "No one is saying your suspicions don't have merit. These guys just haven't found an accelerant or a—"

"It's connected to my daughter's death."

"No, it's not, sir." I fixed my eyes on the blackened back of his house and the roof that had caved in on the kitchen and master bed-room. It was so quiet I could hear my watch ticking on my wrist.

"Look here, Mr. Robicheaux, I asked that you come out because I know about some of the losses in your own life. I thought you would understand what's going on here," he said.

I tried to ignore the personal nature of his statement. "These fire-men are good guys. You can trust what they tell you. I think you've just had a lot of bad luck," I said.

"There's no such thing as luck," he replied.

Just then an unshaved, mustached fireman in rubber pants and suspenders and a big hat walked from behind the house with a clutch of fried electrical wiring in his hand. "We got an ignition point," he said.

"What?" Dr. Parks said.

The fireman spread the wires across his palm and cracked open the insulation on them. "These were in the wall of your game room. See, they're burned from the inside out," he said.

"That's impossible. I just had that game room added on two years ago," Dr. Parks said.

"It's not impossible if somebody installed oversized breakers in your breaker box," the fireman said.

"Who did the work on your house, Doctor?" I said.

"Sunbelt Construction," he said.

I tried to walk away from him, as though I were preoccupied with the destruction at the back of his home. But he grabbed my arm roughly. "What do you know about Sunbelt Construction?" he asked.

"It's owned by Castille LeJeune," I replied.

"Who the hell is Castille LeJeune?"

"His company owns the daiquiri store where your daughter and her friends bought their drinks on the day they died," I said.

Had I just set up another man, in this case Castille LeJeune? I asked myself on the way back to the department.

No, I had simply told the truth.

But that did not change the fact I had let Frank Dellacroce take the big exit at the hands of Max Coll.

Later I went home for lunch and found Father Jimmie on a ladder, screwing a basketball hoop to the back of the porte cochere.

"You do open-air reconciliations?" I said.

"Yeah, hold the ladder for me. What's the problem?" he replied, still concentrated on his work.

"It's not overdue library books," I said.

He looked down at me.

"I think Max Coll capped a wiseguy out at Whiskey Bay. I probably could have prevented it," I said.

He climbed down from the ladder and replaced his tools in a metal box and clicked it shut. "Run that by me again," he said.

We walked toward the bayou while I told him what had happened —the abiding anger that had made me seek out a violent situation, the savage beating I had given Frank Dellacroce, my recognizing Coll among the crowd in front of the cafe, and, most serious of all, my releasing Dellacroce from custody when I knew, with a fair degree of certainty, I was turning him over to his executioner.

Father Jimmie picked up a pine cone and tossed it into the middle of the bayou. "Dave, if you share responsibility for this man's death, then so do I," he said.

"How?"

"I was uncooperative with N.O.P.D. I could have worked with them and helped bust Coll. He would have been past history now."

I sat down on a stone bench by the edge of the bayou. Its surfaces felt cold and hard through my trousers. The wind gusted and red and yellow leaves tumbled out of the trees into the water. "You going to give me absolution?" I asked.

"You were forgiven as soon as you were sorry for what you did. But you need to tell this to someone else or you'll have no peace of mind."

"Sir?"

"What's the new sheriff's name? The woman who used to be your partner? Let me know how it comes out," he said.

He walked back up the slope and removed a basketball from a

cardboard box and swished it through the hoop. You got no free lunch from Father Jimmie Dolan.

Helen listened quietly while I told her about the events of the night I beat Frank Dellacroce within an inch of his life. Her elbows rested on the ink blotter, her chin resting on her thumbs, her fingers knitted together. "This guy Coll is wanted in Florida on two murders?" she said.

"For questioning, at the least."

"What do you think he's doing around here?"

"That's open to debate," I said.

"Meaning what?"

"He has an obsession with the priest who's staying at my house. He's obviously hunting down the people who are trying to take him out. His brains were probably in the blender too long. Take your choice."

She stood up from her chair and stared out the window, her fingers opening and closing against the heel of her palm. "So far there's no evidence it was Coll who shot Dellacroce?" she asked.

"No."

"And you never saw Coll in person?"

"Only in photographs."

"I think you're under a lot of strain. And that's where we're going to leave it for now."

She had given me a temporary free pass, a complicitous wink of the eye; all I had to do was acknowledge it. "My perceptions aren't the issue here. Coll called me at my house. He told me he was in the crowd the night I busted up Dellacroce."

"Coll called you?"

"That's right."

"This isn't police work. It's a soap opera. Are you drinking?"

"No."

"Dave, you either get your act together or we seek other alternatives. None of them good."

"You want my shield?"

"I won't be a party to what you're doing," she said.

"Doing *what*?"

"Ripping yourself apart so you can get back on the bottle. You don't think other people read you? Give yourself a wake-up call." She wadded up a piece of paper and tossed it angrily at the wastebasket.

That evening I went to an A.A. meeting in a tan-colored, tile-roofed Methodist church, not far from the railway tracks. From the second-story window I could see the palm trees in the churchyard, the old brick surfacing in the street, the green colonnade of an ancient firehouse, the oaks whose roots had wedged up the sidewalks, and the strange purple light the sun gave off in its setting.

Across the railway tracks was another world, one that used to be New Iberia's old redlight district, whose history went back to the War Between the States. But today the three-dollar black prostitutes and five-dollar white ones were gone and the cribs on Railroad and Hopkins shut down. Instead, white crack whores, called rock queens, and their black pimps worked the street corners. The dealers, with baseball caps reversed or black silk bandannas tied down skintight on their scalps, appeared in the yards of burned-out houses or in the parking lots of small grocery stores as soon as school let out. After sunset, unless it was raining, their presence multiplied exponentially.

They offered the same street menu as dealers in New Orleans and Houston: weed, brown skag, rock, crystal meth, acid, reds, leapers, Ecstasy, and, for the purists, perhaps a taste of China white the customer could cook and inject with a clean needle in a shooting gallery only four blocks from downtown.

Down the hall, on the second floor of the Methodist church, was a Narcotics Anonymous meeting. Most of the attenders there had been sentenced by the court. Few were people you would normally associate with criminality. Almost all of them, in another era, would have been considered run-of-the-mill blue-collar people whose lives had nothing to do with the trade on Hopkins and Railroad avenues.

But on that particular evening I was not thinking about the ravages of the drug trade. Instead, I was wondering how long it would be before I walked into a saloon and ordered four inches of Black Jack or Beam's Choice with a long-neck Dixie on the side.

Then I looked across the room and saw a man who was geographically and psychologically out of place. He saw me staring at him and raised one meaty paw in recognition. His eyes were like merry slits, his jowls glowing with a fresh shave, his sparse gold hair oiled and flattened into his pate. I crossed the space between us and sat in the chair next to him.

"This is a closed meeting of A.A. What are you doing here?" I said.

"I checked it out. It's an open meet. Besides, I belong to Overeaters Anonymous, which means I probably got trans-addictive issues. That means I can go to any fucking meeting I choose," Fat Sammy Figorelli replied.

"That's the worst bullshit I ever heard. Get out of here," I said.

"Fuck you," he said.

"Is there a problem over there?" the group leader said.

Sammy didn't speak during the meeting. But afterward he helped stack chairs and wash coffee cups and put away all the A.A. literature in a locker. "I like this place," he said.

"You're about to have some major trouble," I said.

"*I'm* gonna have trouble? You're beautiful, Robicheaux. Take a walk with me," he said.

I followed him down the stairs, into the darkness outside and the odor of sewer gas and wet leaves burning. "If you're using A.A. to—" I began.

"You drunks think you're the only people who got a problem. How would you like food to be your enemy? Anybody can stay off booze a hunnerd percent. Try staying off something just part way and see how you feel," he said.

"What's your point?"

"My sponsor says I got to own up to a couple of things or I'm gonna go on another chocolate binge, which don't do my diabetes a lot of good. Max Coll not only cowboyed a couple of high-up guys in Miami, he stiffed the sports book they owned for a hundred large. The word is he's gonna be hung by his colon on a meat hook. Last point, there's a guy around here you don't want to mess with."

He stopped and lit a cigarette. The cigarette looked tiny and innocuous in his huge hand. He watched a car full of black teenagers pass, their stereo thundering with rap music, his face clouding with disapproval.

"Which guy?" I said.

"A guy who hurts people when he don't have to. You want to find him, follow the cooze. In the meantime, don't say I ain't warned you."

Then he labored down the sidewalk toward his Cadillac, his football-shaped head twisted back at the sunset.

"Come back here," I said.

He shot me the finger over his shoulder.

I thought I was finished with Sammy Fig for awhile. Wrong. The phone rang at 2:14 in the A.M. "There's something I didn't tell you," he said.

I sat on the edge of the bed, the receiver cold against my ear. Outside, the moon was bright and glowing with a rain ring behind the sculpted limbs of a pecan tree. "Time to desist, Sammy. That means join Weight Watchers or go to the fat farm, but stay out of my life," I said.

"Frankie Dellacroce's family is in Fort Lauderdale. A couple of them are on their way here."

"So long," I said, and started to lower the receiver from my ear.

"They got you made for the pop on Frankie."

"Me?"

"You broke his sticks in front of a bunch of colored people earlier in the night. Later the same night he catches a .44 mag in the head. You're a cop. Who would you put it on?" he said.

I could hear my breath against the receiver. "This is crazy," I said.

"I got to get some sleep. You're lucky you ain't got insomnia," he said, and hung up.

In the morning I confronted Father Jimmie at the breakfast table. "Sammy Figorelli says a couple of Frank Dellacroce's relatives might be coming around," I said.

"What for?" he said.

"They think I killed him."

"Not too good, huh?"

"Where can I find Max Coll, Jimmie?"

"If I knew, I'd tell you," he replied.

"I'd like to believe that. But I'm starting to have my doubts."

"Want to repeat that?" he said, chewing his food slowly.

"He's going to call again. When he does, I'd like for you to set up a meet with him."

I saw his brow furrow. "I can't do that," he said.

"You sentimental about this guy?"

"He's a tormented man," he said.

"Tell yourself that the next time he empties somebody's brainpan." I picked up my cup of coffee and took it with me to work.

Except I did not go to work. I turned around in the parking lot and drove to the cemetery in St. Martinville, where Bootsie was buried in a crypt right up the bayou from the Evangeline Oak. I sat on the ventilated metal bench in front of the crypt and said the first two decades of my rosary, then lost my concentration and stared woodenly at the bayou and the leaves swirling in the current and the ducks wimpling the water around lily pads that had already turned brown from early frost. My skin felt chafed, as dry as paper, my palms stiff and hard to close. I replaced my rosary in my coat pocket and put my face in my hands. The sun went behind a cloud and the wind was like ice water on my scalp.

Why did you go and die on us, Boots? I heard myself say, then felt ashamed at the selfish nature of my thoughts.

An hour later I walked into the department, washed my face in the men's room, then undertook all the functions of the working day that give the illusion of both normalcy and productivity. Clete Purcel dropped by, irreverent as always, telling outrageous jokes, throwing paper airplanes at my wastebasket. He even used my telephone to

place an offtrack bet. By noon the day seemed brighter, the trees outside a darker green against blue skies.

But I could not concentrate on either the growing loveliness of the
day or the endless paperwork that I was sure no one ever looked at after it was completed.

We had no one in custody for the shooting of the drive-by daiquiri
store operator, even though we had a suspect with motivation in the
form of Dr. Parks, and a connection, through the murder weapon, to
an employee of Castille LeJeune. In the meantime a Celtic killing
machine like Max Coll was running loose in our area; I had been
made by the family of Frank Dellacroce for the murder of their relative; and Theo and Merchie Flannigan continued to hover on the
edge of my vision, chimeric, protean, like the memory of a college
prom that, along with youth, belongs in the past.

It was the kind of criminal investigation in which thinking served
no purpose. The motivation in most crimes was not complex. Usually people steal and cheat because they're either greedy or lazy or
both. People kill for reasons of money, sex, and power. Even revenge
killings indicate a sense of powerlessness in the perpetrator.

At least that was the conventional wisdom of duffer cops who think
psychological profiling works best in films or TV shows that have little to do with reality.

But where did Junior Crudup fit into this? Or did he? Maybe Helen was right, I just wanted to nail the Daddy Warbucks of St. Mary
Parish, Castille LeJeune, to a tree.

I spread the photos of Junior Crudup given me by our reference librarian on my desk blotter. Did you dream at night of the black Betty
slicing across your back? I wanted to ask him. Didn't you learn you
can't beat the Man at his own game? What happened to you, partner?

I picked up the last photo in the series and looked again at the image of Junior staring up at a mounted gunbull, across the bayou from
Castille LeJeune's home, his hoe at an odd angle on his shoulder, his
face puzzled by a world whose rules ensured he would never have a
place in it. But the focus of my attention was not Junior. In the win-
try background, guiding a single-tree plow through the cane stubble,

was a muscular, coal black convict, with the clear detail of welted scars on his forearms, the kind a convict might earn in a half dozen knife beefs.

I held a magnifying glass to the grainy black-and-white image. I was almost sure the face was that of a youthful Hogman Patin, the long-time recidivist who had been on the Red Hat Gang with Junior but had said he did not know Junior's fate.

I picked up the telephone and called my house.

"Hello?" Father Jimmie said.

"Want to check out some Louisiana history you don't find in school books?"

"Why not?" he said.

Chapter 12

Wherever Hogman lived, he created a bottle tree, for reasons he never explained. During winter, when the limbs were bare, he would insert the points of the branches into the mouths of colored glass bottles until the whole tree shimmered with light and tinkled with sound.

Father Jimmie and I parked in the front yard of his house on the bayou and walked around to the back, where Hogman was hoeing weeds out of a garden next to his bottle tree. He stopped his work and smiled, then saw my expression.

"Why'd you jump me over the hurdles?" I said.

"You mean about Junior?" he said.

"You got it," I replied.

"Junior punched his own ticket. You might t'ink he was a hero, but back in them days, if a nigger got mixed up wit' a white woman, all of us had to suffer for it."

"How about spelling that out for me?" I said.

The year was 1951. Hank Williams and Lefty Frizzell played on every jukebox in the South, and across the ocean GIs packed snow on the barrels of .30 caliber machine guns to keep them from melting while they mowed down wave after wave of Chinese troops pouring into North Korea.

But in central Louisiana, a group of black convicts who knew little or nothing of the larger world suddenly found themselves transferred from Angola Penitentiary to a work camp for nonviolent offenders deep down in bayou country. The camp had been created out of the remnants of what had been called the quarters on Fox Run Plantation. None of the convicts knew what to expect. The first morning they found out.

They were given clean denims, soap, toothpaste, good work shoes, and were told to burn their striped pants and jumpers in a trash barrel behind the camp. The beatings with the black Betty, the sweatboxes and anthill-treatment, the fecal-smelling lockdown units, the killings by guards on the Red Hat Gang, became only a memory at Fox Run. Sometimes a truculent inmate was forced to wear leg irons or stand all night on an upended bucket, and the food they ate—the greens, fatback, beans, corn bread, and molasses—was the same fare served at Angola; but the guards were not allowed to abuse them, and at night the inmates slept in cabins with mosquito screens on the windows, boiled coffee in the fireplace, played cards and listened to radios, and on holidays had preserves and cookies to eat.

The humane treatment they received was due solely to one person: Miss Andrea, as they called her, the wife of Castille LeJeune.

The other inmates had been in the camp six months when Junior transferred in from the Red Hat Gang. The first time he saw her he was in the bottom of an irrigation canal with Hogman Patin, raking mounds of yellowed weeds out of the water and flinging them up on the embankment. She was riding English saddle on a black gelding, her long hair tied behind her head, her white riding pants skintight across her rump and thighs. Her small hand was cupped around a braided quirt.

"That's her, huh?" Junior said.

"Who?" Hogman said.

"Miz LeJeune," Junior said.

"What you care who she is?"

"She wrote me a letter."

"Shit."

"That's right. Up at the joint. Tole me how much she liked my music. She's a fine-looking woman."

"You get them t'oughts out of your head, nigger," Hogman said.

"You boys eye-balling down there?" the guard said from horse-back.

Among Junior's few possessions was a guitar, a twelve-string Stella he had bought in a New Orleans pawnshop. He tuned the double-strung E, A, and D strings an octave apart so that the chords rever-berating out of the sound hole gave the impression of two guitars being played simultaneously. Each evening, after supper, he played on the front steps of his cabin, his steel finger picks glinting in the setting of the sun, his voice rising into a sky filled with clouds that looked like colored smoke.

Then, one spring night, while he played on the steps, he saw her car stop on the road. It was a purple 1948 Ford convertible, with an immaculate white, buttoned-down top. She was smoking a cigarette behind the wheel, her skin softly lit by the green illumination of the dashboard. She listened to him play until she had finished her ciga-rette, then she dropped it outside the window, restarted her engine, and drove away.

In July, on a languid Saturday morning, a guard by the name of Jackson Posey told Junior to put on a fresh change of state blues, to brush his shoes, comb his hair, bring his guitar, and get in the guard's pickup truck. As the two of them drove toward the big house, Junior could feel the guard's irritation like a palpable presence inside the cab.

"What's going on, boss?" Junior asked.

Jackson Posey did not reply. Although he was often called boss, he held the rank of captain, one he had earned by shepherding convicts under the gun for two decades, pulling almost the same kind of time as his charges. But the fact he was a captain was a matter of great pride to him, because it meant he was literate and had administrative duties within the penal system. His forearms were pocked with early indications of skin cancer, the top of his forehead half-mooned like a sliver of melon rind where he normally wore a hat. He put three fin-gers into a pouch of Red Man and inserted the string tobacco into his jaw, then drove around to the back of the big house and parked under a mulberry tree.

Junior could see Andrea Castille seated on the patio, a pitcher of lemonade on a glass table beside her. A recording machine, the kind that made use of wire spools, rested on the brickwork by her foot, an extension cord running back through the French doors into the house. Inside the living room a little girl, a miniature of her mother, played on the rug with wood blocks.

"I always treated you fair, ain't I?" the guard said.

"Yes, suh," Junior said.

"Then it don't hurt to tell Miss Andrea that, does it?"

"No, suh."

"You stay where I can see you," he said.

"Wouldn't have it no other way, boss."

Jackson Posey narrowed one watery blue eye, as though squinting down a rifle barrel. "You sassing me?" he said.

Junior shut the truck door behind him and approached Andrea Castille with his guitar cradled under his right arm. She wore a pink sundress and dark glasses and a gold cross on a chain around her throat. "Can you play 'Goodnight Irene'?" she said.

"Yes, ma'am, I learned it from the man who wrote it," he replied.

"I'd like to record you while you do it. That is, if you don't mind."

"No, ma'am, I'm glad to."

"Would you like to sit down?"

"Standing is just fine, ma'am."

He slipped the cloth strap of the guitar around his neck and sang for her, feeling foolish at the contrived nature of the situation, wondering if the guard's eyes were burrowing into his back or if Andrea Castille's husband was watching him from an upstairs window.

"You have a wonderful voice," she said. "Sit down. Please, it's all right."

"Ma'am, I'm a convict." Involuntarily his eyes swept across the back windows of the house.

She seemed to resign herself to his recalcitrance. "Would you sing another song?" she said.

He sang one of his own compositions. The breeze had dropped and his shirt was damp against his skin. He could not see her eyes behind her dark glasses, but he believed they were invading his person. His fingers were moist and clumsy on the frets, his voice uncertain. A muscle spasm sliced across his back from the odd angle in which he was holding the Stella.

He stopped and blotted his face on his sleeve, his heart beating. Why was he behaving like this?

But he already knew the answer. He wanted her approval—just like an organ grinder's monkey.

"I hurt my back in the field yesterday. Just ain't myself," he said.

"Maybe you can come another time, when you're feeling better," she said.

He shook his head negatively, his eyes lowered, his frustration and anger at himself rising. But she didn't give him time to speak. "I have something for you. I'll be just a minute," she said.

He waited patiently in the dappled sunlight, the heat rising from the bricks around him. What was she up to? He had known white women like her in the North, he told himself. They liked to stick their hand in the tiger cage. Sometimes they even brought the tiger into their bed. Well, if that was what she wanted, maybe she might just find out who sticks what in who, he said to himself.

She emerged from the French doors with a narrow, blue-felt, brass-hinged box in one hand. She removed her dark glasses and handed him the box. For the first time he saw her eyes. They were the color of violets, like none he had ever seen, and there was a kindness and honesty in them that caused a thickening sensation in his throat.

"I've heard you play these on your records. I didn't know if you had one now or not," she said.

He pried the lid back stiffly and looked down at a chrome-plated harmonica cushioned inside the white satin interior of the box.

"It's an E-major Marine Band," she said.

"Yes, ma'am. I know. This is a fine instrument, Miss Andrea."

"Well, thank you for coming to my house," she said. Then she shook his hand, something no southern white woman had ever done.

On the way back to the camp, the guard, Jackson Posey, kept turning and staring at the side of Junior's face. Junior looked straight ahead, the harmonica case gripped in his palm. Just before they drove past the wire into the cluster of cabins that made up the improvised work camp, Posey braked the truck and shifted the floor stick into neutral. A cloud of dust floated by his open window.

"You got no control over what that woman does, so I ain't holding it against you," he said.

"Suh?" Junior replied.

"You know what I'm talking about. Her husband's coming home from the arm service next week," the guard said.

"Yes, suh," Junior said, still uncertain about the direction of the conversation.

"I ain't gonna lose my job 'cause I let his wife shake hands with a nigger convict. You hearing me, Junior?"

Junior could feel the softness of the felt box in his fingers. "You don't like what she done, lock me down, bossman," Junior replied.

"You just earned yourself a night on the bucket. Sass me again, and Miss Andrea or no Miss Andrea, you're gonna be the sorest nigger in the state of Lou'sana."

Two weeks later, while Junior and Hogman were pulling stumps on the far side of the bayou, he saw Andrea LeJeune and her husband cantering their horses through a field of buttercups. They clopped across a wood bridge that spanned a coulee, disappearing into a grove of live oaks. A few minutes later she emerged by herself, her face pinched with anger, and slashed her quirt across her horse's flank. She galloped past Junior toward the drawbridge, her thighs crimped tightly into the horse's sides, dirt clods flying off her horse's hooves. She was so close Junior could have reached out and touched her leg.

But if she saw him, she showed no recognition in her face.

That night another convict in Junior's cabin was looking at the pages of a newspaper that had blown from the road into the camp's wire fence. A photograph on the front page showed Castille LeJeune in a dress Marine Corps uniform with a medal hanging on a ribbon from his neck. "That's the man own Fox Run, ain't it?" the convict said. His name was Woodrow Reed. He wore a goatee that looked like a cluster of black wire on his chin, and the other inmates believed he could tell fortunes with a greasy pack of cards he carried in his shirt pocket.

"That's the man," Junior replied.

"What it say about him?" Woodrow asked.

"He saved a bunch of lives, then he shot down a Nort' Korean name of Bed Check Charley."

"Bed Check who?"

"That's a guy used to fly over the Americans in a Piper Cub and drop hand grenades on them. The F-80s couldn't nail him 'cause they was too fast. But Mr. LeJeune went after him in a World War II plane that was a lot slower and blew his ass out of the sky."

"How come you know all this?" Woodrow asked.

"Read about it in a magazine."

"You somet'ing else, Junior," Woodrow said.

But secretly Junior did not feel he was something else. One out of three of his adult years had been spent in prison. He had made race records in Memphis, been interviewed in *Downbeat* magazine, and performed with Cab Calloway's orchestra in New York City, all before he was thirty years old. But what had he done with his success? Rather than build upon it, he had gotten into trouble every place he went. Now he was the man with one eye in the country of the blind, sassing redneck prison guards, a hero to hapless, illiterate, and superstitious men because he could read a magazine.

One month later, on a Saturday afternoon, Andrea LeJeune had him brought to the big house again. This time her husband was with her on the patio, seated under an umbrella, a tropical drink in his hand. Their daughter, who must have been around three or four years of age, was throwing a ball back and forth on the lawn with a black maid.

"This is my husband, Junior. He'd love to hear you sing 'Goodnight, Irene,'" she said.

LeJeune's legs were crossed. He wore socks with his sandals and seemed to be studying the points of his toes.

"Huddie Ledbetter done it a lot better than I can," Junior replied. He shifted his weight and felt the belly of the guitar scrape hollowly against his belt buckle.

"Then play something of your own choosing," Castille LeJeune said, his gaze still fixed on the end of his foot.

"Suh, I ain't all that good," Junior said. His eyes met LeJeune's briefly, then slipped away.

"You uncomfortable for some reason?" LeJeune asked.

"No, suh."

"Then play. Please," LeJeune said.

He sang "Dig My Grave with a Silver Spade," running quickly through the verses, leaving out the treble string improvisations he usually ran high up on the guitar's neck. When he finished he looked at nothing, the guitar strap biting into the back of his neck. He could smell the exhaled smoke from LeJeune's cigarette drifting into his face.

"You seem to be a man of considerable accomplishment. How is it you spent so many years in jail?" LeJeune said.

"Don't rightly know, suh. Guess some niggers just ain't that smart," Junior replied.

He heard the guard's shoes crunch on the gravel drive, as though the guard were experiencing a tension he had to run through the bottoms of his feet into the ground. But LeJeune seemed to take no notice of any sardonic content in Junior's remark.

"Maybe you should have joined the military and found a career for yourself that didn't get you into trouble," LeJeune said.

"I served in the United States Navy, suh. Under another name, but in the navy just the same."

"You were a stewart?"

"No, suh. I was a munitions loader. I loaded munitions right next to Harry Belafonte."

"Who?"

"He's a singer, suh."

"Obviously my knowledge of pop'lar music isn't very extensive," LeJeune said, and smiled self-indulgently at his wife.

Why had Junior just told LeJeune of his military record or the fact he had known Harry Belafonte? It was like flipping a piece of gold through a sewer grate. At that moment he hated LeJeune more than any human being he'd ever met.

"Would you like something to eat before you go?" LeJeune said. He held up a crystal plate on which a thick ring of crushed ice was embedded with peeled shrimp.

"No, thank you, suh."

"I insist," LeJeune said. He used a fork to scrape a pile of shrimp and ice on a paper plate, then inserted a toothpick in a shrimp and handed the plate to Junior. "Go back yonder and sit in the shade and eat these."

Junior looked at the yard, the absence of chairs or scrolled-iron benches on the grass or even a glider hanging from an oak limb. "Where, suh?" he said.

"Behind the carriage house. There's a box you can sit on. Enjoy your snack and then Mr. Posey will take you back to the camp," LeJeune said.

"You sit right here at the table. I'm going to get you some gumbo and a Coca-Cola from the house," Miss Andrea said. "Did you hear me? Put your guitar in the chair and sit down."

"I think Mr. Crudup knows where he should eat," her husband said.

"Castille, if you weren't so miserably stupid and insensitive, I think I'd shoot you," she replied. Then she added "God!" and went inside the house.

LeJeune got up from his chair and walked to the driveway, where he talked quietly with the guard, Jackson Posey. Junior Crudup felt as though he were sliding to the bottom of a dark well from which he would never emerge.

Jackson Posey did not drive the pickup truck directly back to the work camp. Instead, he crossed the bayou on the drawbridge and parked between a sugarcane field and a persimmon grove, out of sight of either the LeJeune home or the camp. He breathed hard through his nose, his mouth a tightly crimped line.

"Get out of the truck," he said.

"I ain't did nothing, boss."

"You got that sonofabitch on my ass. You call that nothing?"

"Not my fault, boss."

They were both standing outside the truck now. The sky was hot and bright and wind was blowing dust out of the cane field and birds were clattering in the persimmon trees. Jackson Posey reached behind the driver's seat. Junior heard something hard clank against metal.

"Drink it," Posey said.

But Junior shook his head.

"Good 'cause now I can send your skinny black ass right back up to 'Gola."

"Ain't nobody in the camp supposed to get the Mussolini treatment. Miss Andrea don't allow it."

"Miz LeJeune don't write the rules now. What's it gonna be? Don't matter to me one way or another." Posey shook a cigarette loose from a package of Camels and inserted it in his mouth.

Junior took the bottle of castor oil from the guard's hand and unscrewed the cap. The bottle was brown and heavy, the oil as viscous as syrup. He began to drink, then gagged and started again. The guard looked at his watch.

"All of it," Posey said.

"Ain't right, boss."

"You messed up the man's pussy. What do you expect him to do? Like my daddy used to say, life's a bitch, then you die. Chug it down, boy."

Posey watched while Junior finished the bottle, then fingered a reddish purple scab on his arm, one that had not been there only two days ago. He drew in heavily on his cigarette, his eyes draining, as though he were purging himself of any intimations of his own mortality.

"It ain't nothing personal, Junior," he said.

"It's real personal, boss."

The guard stared emptily at the heat waves bouncing off the bayou and flicked his cigarette into the wind.

By the time Junior got back to the camp his bowels were collapsing inside him.

Hogman stopped his account and picked up a bottle that had fallen from his bottle tree. He wedged it in the fork of the tree and seemed to lose interest in both Father Jimmie and me and the story he had been telling.

"Go on, Hogman," I said.

"Junior started believing he was gonna have a life besides jailing and road-ganging. Gonna get a pardon from the governor and be a big star up Nort'. Just like Leadbelly."

"Andrea LeJeune was going to work a pardon for him?"

"That's what he t'ought. She made Jackson Posey keep taking Junior up to the house when Mr. LeJeune was gone. Junior talked about her all the time, how pretty she was, what she smelled like, how she had all these fine manners, how she knew everyt'ing about his music. A whole bunch of people come up from New Orleans to hear him sing and play his twelve-string in the backyard."

"What happened to him, Hogman?"

"Don't know. I got paroled. Last time I seed Junior he was playing 'Goodnight Irene' on the steps of his cabin, waiting to see if Miss Andrea was gonna drive by in her li'l convertible."

"I think you're holding out on me, partner."

"Miss Andrea got killed in a car wreck two or t'ree years after I left the camp. Mr. LeJeune lived up in that big house wit' just himself and his li'l girl. Junior disappeared. Ain't nothing left of him but a voice on scratchy old records. Nobody cared what happened back then. Nobody care now. You axed for the troot'. I just give it to you."

Hogman walked inside the back of his house and let the screen door slam behind him.

Chapter 13

Ordinary people sometimes do bad things. A wrong-headed business decision, a romantic encounter in a late-night bar, a rivalry with a neighbor over the placement of a fence, any of these seemingly insignificant moments can initiate a series of events that, like a rusty nail in the sole of the foot, can systemically poison a normal, law-abiding person's life and propel him into a world he thought existed only in the perverse imaginings of pulp novelists.

At sunrise on Saturday morning the sky was pink and blue, the trees in my yard dripping from a thunder shower during the night, and I took a cup of coffee and hot milk and a bowl of Grape-Nuts out on the gallery and read the morning paper while I ate. When I was halfway into the editorial page Dr. Parks pulled his battered, beige pickup to the curb and got out. His jaws were heavy with beard stubble, one eye clotted with blood; he wore no socks and jeans that were grass-stained at the knees.

"I need help," he said.

"In what way?"

He sat down on a step, a few inches from me. His long, tapered hands rested between his legs and his body gave off an odor like sour milk. His mouth began to form words, but nothing came out.

"Take it easy, Doctor. This stuff will pass with time. A guy just needs to put one foot in front of the other for a while," I said.

"There's no justice. Not for anything," he said.

"Pardon?"

"My daughter's death. The electrical fire at my house. I bought a home warranty policy from Sunbelt Construction. The policy is underwritten by a bunch of criminals in Aurora, Colorado. I tried to talk to the Louisiana insurance commissioner about it and was told he's on his way to the federal pen."

Like most people whose lives have been left in disarray by events so large he couldn't even describe them to himself, his rage against the universe had now reduced itself to the level of a petty financial quarrel with a fraudulent home warranty company.

"There might be a state senator or two we can call on Monday. How about a cup of coffee?" I said. I rested my hand on his shoulder and tried to smile, then I saw the green cast in the skin under his eyes and the detached stare that made me think of soldiers I had known many years ago.

"I was on a medevac at Khe Sanh. I was in two crashes and one shoot-down. I put my best friends in body bags. It was all for nothing. This goddamn country is going down the sewer," he said.

"I was over there, too, Doc. We can always be proud of what we did and let the devil take the rest of it. Sometimes you've got to throw the bad times over the gunnels and do the short version of the Serenity Prayer. Sometimes you just say full throttle and fuck it."

But my words were of no value. He got to his feet like a man walking in his sleep, then turned and extended his hand. "I insulted you at my home and in your office. I didn't mean what I said. My wife and I are better people than we seem," he said.

He pressed the fingers of one hand against the side of his head, like a man experiencing a pressure band or a level of cerebral pain that gave him no relief. He pulled open the door of his pickup and got inside, holding the steering wheel to steady himself. I walked to the passenger window.

"Where you headed?" I asked.

"To confront the people who cheated me, the ones who put defective wiring in my house, the ones who shouldn't be on the goddamn planet."

"I don't think that's a good idea, Doc."

"Stand away from the truck," he replied. He ground the transmission into gear and swung the truck into traffic, almost hitting an automobile packed with Catholic nuns.

I went back inside and called the dispatcher. Wally happened to be on duty. "You want us to pick up this guy, Dave?" he asked.

I thought about it. Roust Dr. Parks now, in his present state of mind, and we would probably only add to his grief and anger. With luck he would eventually go home or at worst get drunk somewhere, I told myself. "Let it go," I said.

Helen Soileau called me just after lunch. "How busy are you?" she said.

"What's up?"

"It's Dr. Parks. Wally said you called in on him earlier."

"What about him?"

"Evidently he went looking for Castille LeJeune. He didn't find him, so he went after this guy Will Guillot."

"What do you mean 'he went after him'?"

"With a cut-down double-barrel twelve-gauge."

"He shot Guillot?" I said.

"You got it backwards. Parks is dead. Say good-bye to our prime suspect in the drive-by daiquiri shooting."

"Wait a minute. I can't get this straight. Parks is *dead*?"

"At least he was five minutes ago. Get pictures if you can," she said.

When I got to the home of Will Guillot emergency vehicles were still parked along the street and barricades set up to prevent the curious and the voyeuristic from driving past the house. The incongruity of the images there would not fit in time and place. In a tree-covered neighborhood of nineteenth-century homes and thick St. Augustine lawns, where the hydrangeas and impatiens and Confederate roses were softly dented by the breeze, and blue jays and robins sailed in and out of the live oaks, Dr. Parks lay on his side in the driveway, his mouth and eyes locked open, one cheek pressed flat against the cement, a pool of dried blood issuing from a ragged hole in his throat into the sunlight. Six inches from his outstretched hand lay a cut-down twelve-gauge, the stock wood-rasped and sanded into a pistol grip.

The crime-scene investigator was a nervous, tightly wrapped man with a strong cigarette odor by the name of Dale Louviere. When I ducked under the crime-scene tape he glared into my face, as though challenged, nests of green veins pulsing in his temples. Before he had entered law enforcement he had been a gofer and point man for a notorious casino operator in Lake Charles.

"What do you want, Robicheaux?" he said.

"Dr. Parks was part of an Iberia Parish homicide investigation. Where's the coroner?" I said.

"Him and the sheriff fish together on Saturday. We're still waiting on them," Louviere replied.

"Are there any witnesses?"

"Yeah, the shooter, Will Guillot. He's in the kitchen."

"How do you read it?" I asked.

"Open and shut. The vic went nuts about a house fire or a home warranty policy or something. He came here to wax Guillot and instead caught a .45 in the throat. The round hit the oak tree in front."

I leaned over to look more closely at the cut-down twelve-gauge. I couldn't see a brand name on it, but the steel around the magazine was incised with delicately engraved images of ducks and geese in flight. "Handsome gun to chop down with a hacksaw," I said.

"Get some mud in the barrel and that's what people do, Robicheaux," Louviere replied.

"Except this guy was a collector. How many collectors spend their time converting their firearms into illegal weapons?"

"The next time I investigate a homicide, I'll have the crime scene shipped to Iberia Parish so you can supervise it," he said.

I walked through the porte cochere to a back door and entered the kitchen without knocking. Will Guillot was at the counter, gazing out the back window into the yard, while he ate a ham-and-lettuce sandwich. A tall, half-empty glass of milk rested by his sandwich plate. He turned and looked at me quizzically, the birthmark that drained like purple dye from his hairline to the corner of his eye almost obscured by shadow, so that one side of his face looked like the marred half of a large coin.

"You were in fear for your life, were you, Mr. Guillot?" I said.

"Yeah, I guess that describes it," he answered, one cheek stiff with a piece of bread. "You have jurisdiction here?"

"You don't have to talk to me if you don't want to."

"I don't want to."

"Fair enough. On an unrelated subject, are you a hunter or a gun collector?"

"I hunt. Why?"

"No reason. Were you in 'Nam?"

"No. What's that have to do with anything?"

"Dr. Parks was on a medevac. He had his problems, but I don't think he was a violent man. I don't think that cut-down twelve on the driveway was his, either."

"This conversation is over, Mr. Robicheaux, and you can get out of my house."

"Does it bother you?" I said.

"*Bother* me? That I defended myself against a lunatic?"

"His daughter was burned alive after buying liquor illegally at one of Castille LeJeune's daiquiri shops. His house burned after you put bad wiring in it, and you shot him to death after he came here to complain about a fraudulent home warranty policy you sold him. It's hard to believe one guy can have that much bad luck, isn't it? Enjoy your sandwich, Mr. Guillot. I'll be in touch," I said.

"Kiss my ass," he said.

Sunday Father Jimmie had gone to Lafayette to collect signatures on a petition to shut down drive-by daiquiri windows and had stayed the night at a retreat house in Grand Coteau. I ate a plate of clam spaghetti at a cafe in Jeanerette, then went to sleep reading T.E. Lawrence's *Seven Pillars of Wisdom*, with Snuggs on the foot of the bed. My windows were open and in my sleep I heard the wind in the trees, a solitary pecan husk rattle on the tin roof, a workboat chugging heavily on the bayou. The air was cool and clean smelling with ground fog, rainwater ticking in the trees, and I felt Snuggs walk across my back so he could sniff the breeze blowing through the screen. Just after midnight, my bowels constricted as though I had swallowed a piece of broken glass. I went into the bathroom and sat on the toilet, my thighs trembling with nausea.

Then I heard someone wedge a tool between the back door and the jamb, splinter the deadbolt, and enter the house. Whoever it was moved quickly toward the band of light at the bottom of the bathroom door, opened it slightly, and looked in at me.

"I wasn't planning to meet you like this, but I couldn't resist the opportunity. Can I be getting you anything? You don't look too well," the figure said.

"Coll?"

"Right you are. No, don't get up. Take care of business while I have my say, then I'll be off." His hand came through the opening and removed the key from the lock. He shut the door and locked it from the outside.

"What do you think you're doing?" I said.

I heard him go into the bedroom, then scrape a chair into position. "This is a fine cat you have here. Been in a few fights, has he?"

"Listen, Coll—"

"He's got a real pair of bandoliers back there."

My face was cold with sweat, a bilious fluid rising from my stomach. Gray spots danced before my eyes.

"Father Dolan and I have nothing to do with your life," I said.

"Oh, but you do. Two rather nasty cretins just arrived in town, Mr. Robicheaux, the cousins of Frank Dellacroce. Stone killers, they are, sir, with no parameters and no charitable impulses. Evidently a few of the greaseballs think you blew poor Frank's head off. Would you like to hear what they did to a friend of mine?"

"No."

"Took a blowtorch to him. What's the name of your cat?"

"Snuggs."

"What a fine little fellow. Built like a fucking fire hydrant. It's a shame the innocent suffer. But maybe that's the only thing that causes us to take action."

I could feel my heart quicken. "What are you saying?"

"I didn't make the world. I just live in it as best I can. I'll be going now."

"You leave that cat here."

But he didn't reply. I heard his chair scrape but did not hear him set Snuggs down. "Coll? Did you hear me?" I yelled.

I heard him banging about in the kitchen, then a hard, clunking sound and his footsteps going heavily through the house and out the front door. By the time I was able to climb out the bathroom window, the yard and the street were empty, the ground puffing with fog, the moon as bright as a white flame behind the skeletal outline of a water oak.

I went around back and entered the house through the kitchen door. A pitcher of milk rested on the drainboard and Snuggs was lapping from a bowl next to it, one Max Coll had filled with both milk and dry cat food.

I started to dial 911, then gave it up, propped a chair against the kitchen door, and went back to sleep, my .45 under my pillow.

At 8:05 Monday morning Clotile Arceneaux walked into my office. She wore a pair of navy blue slacks, a blouse printed with tropical flowers, and a polished black gunbelt with her badge holder hung from the front and her cuffs pushed through the back. She had the blackest hair and wore the brightest lipstick I had ever seen.

"How's life in the Big Sleazy?" I said.

She grinned broadly, then sat down without being asked. "You're a magnet, Robicheaux," she said.

"For what?"

"Trouble. We keep a few people at the New Orleans airport, watching to see who comes and goes, know what I mean? Three days ago a couple of greaseballs from Ft. Lauderdale got into town, spent the night with some hookers, then caught a flight to Lafayette. Guess what their last names are?"

"Dellacroce?"

"How'd you know?"

"Max Coll was at my house last night."

"Say again?"

"He was walking around inside my house. He talked to me through the bathroom door."

She looked up at one corner of the ceiling, her eyelids fluttering. Then she scratched her neck and looked at me. "I brought mug shots of the Dellacroces. They're brothers, Tito and Caesar. Tito's friends call him the Heap, 'cause he looks like a haystack with eyes. But the mean one is Caesar. He's short and not very bright."

"He uses a blowtorch on people?"

"You do know about these guys."

"Max Coll is tops when it comes to intel."

"I've got to get a job over here. New Orleans just doesn't cut it."

"Want to go to lunch later?"

"Like to, slick, but the Big Sleazy calls. I've got a little more here on your man Coll."

"He's not my man. He's a meltdown you guys shipped to New Iberia."

She raised her eyebrows and made an innocent face as she opened a manilla folder in her lap. "The Coll family was hooked up with the IRA for generations," she said. "Some of them may have been behind the bombing of a pub in Belfast. Some Protestant militants decided to get even and took Max's whole family out, including an older brother who was a Catholic priest."

"That's how he ended up in the orphanage," I said, more to myself than to her.

She looked down again at the open folder in her lap. "Yeah, that's right. He was there until he was fifteen," she said.

"Go to lunch with me," I said.

She thought about it. "Make it a beignet and a cup of coffee," she said. She studied me with one eye half closed.

That afternoon I looked down at the booking photos of Tito and Caesar Dellacroce she had left on my desk. Tito, known as the Heap by his peers, stared back at me with eyes that were like cups of black grease. His brother made me think of a ferret in need of a haircut. Both Max Coll and Fat Sammy Figorelli had indicated Frank Dellacroce's relatives had put his death on me. Maybe. But I believed their real target was still Max Coll, and Max was in New Iberia for reasons other than a religious obsession with Father Jimmie. I believed Max had intimations about where the hit on Father Jimmie had come from, and Max blamed that same person for putting a contract on him and had come to our area to wipe the slate clean.

Or perhaps he was simply crazy.

Regardless, it was time to dial up Max's head and see how he liked having things turned around on him. I called the *Daily Iberian* and scheduled an ad to run in the next day's personal notices.

"Let me read this back to you," the clerk said. "'Max, you owe me $57.48 for the damage you did to my back door. Why don't you pay your debts instead of acting like a window-licking voyeur who breaks into people's houses and molests their pets? Tito and Caesar just blew into town and seem upset because you canceled their cousin's ticket. Have a nice day—Dave.'"

"Perfect," I said.

"Mr. Robicheaux, this ad doesn't make much sense."

"It does if you're morally insane," I replied.

Did you ever have a song in your mind you couldn't get rid of? For me, at least on that Monday afternoon, it was "Goodnight Irene." I kept thinking of Junior Crudup sitting on the steps of his cabin in the work camp, playing his twelve-string guitar, singing the words to Leadbelly's most famous composition, while he waited to catch a glimpse of Andrea LeJeune's purple Ford convertible passing on the dirt road. Did she arrange for him to return to the house again? Did the guard, Jackson Posey, continue to torment him because of the hatred Posey felt for himself and the lot the world had dealt him?

If God in that moment looked down upon His creations, I wondered if He wasn't terribly saddened by the level of madness that had become the province of His children.

The song was still in my head when I went that afternoon to Baron's, the health club where I worked out, and saw Castille LeJeune seated on a hardwood bench in the dressing room, his face bright with sweat from his racquet ball game, a towel wrapped around his neck. He was jovial and expansive, sipping from a glass of icewater while he talked with a group of businessmen, although a sign on the wall stated no glass containers were allowed in the room. It was 5 P.M. and both black and white workers from the salt mines out in the wetlands and the sugar mills that ringed the town burst loudly into the dressing room. Instead of being intimidated by LeJeune's presence, they treated him as they would a celebrity, greeting him as "Mr. Castille." Somehow he was one of them, at least for the moment, a patrician who knew them by their first names and spoke both demotic French and English without being patronizing.

There were great differences in the room, but not between the races. The black and white working men spoke the same regional dialect and shared the same political attitudes, all of which had been taught them by others. They denigrated liberals, unions, and the media, considered the local Wal-Mart store a blessing, and regularly gave their money to the Powerball lottery and casinos that had the architectural charm of a sewer works. They were frightened by the larger world and found comfort in the rhetoric of politicians who assured them the problem was the world's, not theirs. And most heartening of all was the affirmation lent them by a genteel person like Castille LeJeune, a Distinguished Flying Cross recipient who, unlike many members of his class, showed no fear or lack of confidence in their midst, which told them of his respect for their humanity.

I dressed in a corner of the room, my back turned to LeJeune and the cluster of men around him. Maybe I was wrong about him, I thought. Maybe Helen and Theodosha were justified in their criticism of my attitudes. I was born in the late Depression and bore an ingrained resentment toward the wealthy and the powerful. All drunks fear and desire both power and control, and sometimes even years of sobriety inside A.A. don't rid alcoholics of that basic contradiction in their personalities. Why should I be any different?

When I had almost thought my way into a charitable attitude toward Castille LeJeune, I felt a hand touch my shoulder. "Would you like to play a round of racquet ball, Mr. Robicheaux?" he said.

"Never learned how," I said.

"Do you have any idea why this deranged physician, what's-his-name, Parks, would have come to my home, then to my foreman's?"

So you're a showboat as well as a hypocrite, I thought. "His daughter was served illegally at your daiquiri shop before she died in a car crash. Your company defrauded him on the house-remodeling job it did at his home. He also said you sold him a bogus warranty on his house. Maybe that might have something to do with it," I replied.

"I'd like to say your reputation precedes you, Mr. Robicheaux. But your potential seems to have no limits," he said.

"Your deceased wife brought a black convict to your house out of respect for his musical talent, an event evidently you couldn't abide. That same convict, Junior Crudup, disappeared from the face of the earth. I suspect, on the day of your death, his specter will be standing by your bed."

The only sound in the room was the hum of the overhead fans.

"How dare you?" he said.

I'm going to get you, you sorry sack of shit, I said to myself, my eyes fixed six inches from his.

The days were growing shorter, and by 6 P.M. the sun had set, the sky was black and veined with lightning, and Bayou Teche was high and yellow and chained with rain rings in the glow of the lamps along the banks of City Park. Father Jimmie walked about in the backyard, his hands in his pockets, examining the sky, the wind swirling leaves around his ankles. He came back in the house smelling of trees and humus, his eyes purposeful.

"I need to work things out with Max Coll," he said.

"You have to do *what*?" I said.

"He's in New Iberia because I'm here. Now, these other criminals

are showing up because *he's* here. Where does it end? One man is already dead."

"Frank Dellacroce sexually exploited a retarded girl. I think he got
off easy."

"I had to own up to some things at the retreat, the big one being
pride."

"In what?"

"My feeling of virtuous superiority to others," he said.

"You don't call self-flagellation a form of pride?"

"You're a hard sell, Dave."

The phone rang like a providential respite. Or at least that's what I
thought until I realized who was on the other end of the line.

"Where do you get off embarrassing my father in a public place?"
a woman's voice said.

"Your father is neither a victim nor a martyr. Cut the crap, Theo,"
I said.

"Your anger taints everything in your life. You disappoint me in
ways I can't describe."

I heard a sheet of rain clatter across the tin roof. I wanted to pretend I was impervious to her words, but the element of truth in them
was like a thorn pressed into the scalp. "Where are you?" I said.

"In a bar." She gave the name, a box of a place squeezed between
shacks in New Iberia's worst neighborhood.

"How much have you had?" I asked.

"I'm drinking a soda and lime, believe it or not. But I'm about to
change that. Why, you want to get loaded?"

"You wait there," I said.

As I backed out of the driveway, the canopy of oaks over the street
stood out in lacy, black-green relief against the lightning rippling
across the sky. I did not pay particular attention to the car that
rounded the corner and followed me past the Shadows.

Inside the house Father Jimmie tore the wrapper off his hangered
dry cleaning and discovered his black suit was missing. He would

have sworn it had been with his other things when he had brought them from the laundry three days ago. He searched the rack, then checked the top drawer where he kept his Roman collar and rabat, the backless garment that serves as a priest's vest.

Both collar and rabat were gone.

Chapter 14

I drove to the bar Theodosha had called from and parked on the street. The bar was a gray, dismal place, ensconced like a broken matchbox under a dying oak tree, its only indication of gaiety a neon beer sign that flickered in one window. She was at a table in back, the glow of the jukebox lighting her face and the deep blackness of her hair. She tipped a collins glass to her mouth, her eyes locked on mine.

"Let me take you home," I said.

"No, thanks," she replied.

"Getting swacked?"

"Merchie and I had another fight. He says he can't take my pretensions anymore. I love the word 'pretensions.'"

"That doesn't mean you have to get drunk," I said.

"You're right. I can get drunk for any reason I choose," she replied, and took another hit from the glass. Then she added incongruously, "You once asked Merchie what he was doing in Afghanistan. The answer is he wasn't in Afghanistan. He was in one of those other God-forsaken Stone Age countries to the north, helping build American airbases to protect American oil interests. Merchie says they're going to make a fortune. All for the red, white, and blue."

"Who is *they*?"

But her eyes were empty now, her concentration and anger temporarily spent.

I glanced at the surroundings, the dour men sitting at the bar, a black woman sleeping with her head on a table, a parolee putting moves on a twenty-year-old junkie and mother of two children who was waiting for her connection. These were the people we cycled in and out of the system for decades, without beneficial influence or purpose of any kind that was detectable.

"Let's clear up one thing. Your old man came looking for trouble at the club today. I didn't start it," I said.

"Go to a meeting, Dave. You're a drag," she said.

"Give your guff to Merchie," I said, and got up to leave.

"I would. Except he's probably banging his newest flop in the hay. And the saddest thing is I can't blame him."

"I think I'm going to ease on out of this. Take care of yourself, kiddo," I said.

"Fuck that 'kiddo' stuff. I loved you and you were too stupid to know it."

I walked back outside into a misting rain and the clean smell of the night. I walked past a house where people were fighting behind the shades. I heard doors slamming, the sound of either a car backfiring or gunshots on another street, a siren wailing in the distance. On the corner I saw an expensive automobile pull to the curb and a black kid emerge from the darkness, wearing a skintight bandanna on his head. The driver of the car, a white man, exchanged money for something in the black kid's hand.

Welcome to the twenty-first century, I thought.

I opened my truck door, then noticed the sag on the frame and glanced at the right rear tire. It was totally flat, the steel rim buried deep in the folds of collapsed rubber. I dropped the tailgate, pulled the jack and lug wrench out of the toolbox that was arc-welded to the bed of the truck, and fitted the jack under the frame. Just as I had pumped the flat tire clear of the puddle it rested in, I heard footsteps crunch on the gravel behind me.

Out of the corner of my eye, I saw a short, thick billy club whip through the air. Just before it exploded across the side of my head, my eyes seemed to close like a camera lens on a haystack that smelled of damp-rot and unwashed hair and old shoes. I was sure as I slipped into unconsciousness that I was inside an ephemeral dream from which I would soon awake.

. . .

I knew it was sunlight when I awoke. I could feel its warmth on my skin, see its red-edged radiance at the corners of the tape that covered my eyes. Along with the chemical odor, perhaps ether or chloroform, that still clung to my face I could smell dead fish and ponded water that had gone stagnant inside shade and blackened leaves freshly broken by someone's shoes. I was seated in a chair, my wrists cuffed behind me with a plastic band. I turned my head into a breeze blowing from a window or door, like a blind man entering his first day without sight, vainly hoping the world around him was not filled with adversaries.

A motorboat passed a short distance away. When the sound of the wake sliding through flooded trees died, I heard two men talking about a football game in another room. I tried to rise from the chair, then realized both my ankles were strapped to the legs. "Asshole is awake," I heard one of the men say.

A door opened and I felt the planks under my feet become depressed by the weight of the men entering the room. "How you feel?" one of them said.

"You're kidnapping a police officer," I said.

"I asked you how you felt."

"All right. I feel all right," I replied.

"Hear that? He's all right," the second man said. "Frank Dellacroce is not all right. Somebody blew most of his head off."

"It wasn't me," I said.

"It wasn't him," the second man said. "That's good to hear, 'cause people say you kicked the shit out of him the night he was killed. While he was in handcuffs."

"You got it wrong," I replied.

"He says we got it wrong. That's good, 'cause what we hear about you ain't so good. We hear you got a hard-on 'cause you can't drink, that you like to beat up people, that you got some kind of problem with Italians in general," the same voice said.

"I haven't seen you. I don't know who you are. I think what we have here is a misunderstanding. I'm ready to let it go at that," I said.

"He's ready to let it go. I like that. We're talking about a generous man here," the same voice said. "You want a beer?"

"No."

"Yeah, you do."

I turned my face toward the voice. "Why pull a federal beef down on yourselves? Use your head," I said.

"Oh, we'll use our head, all right. You bet your life," the same man said.

I heard a tab being torn loose from a pressurized can, then smelled beer and heard foam splattering on the floor. I could hear someone drinking from the can, swallowing thirstily. He pressed the can against my mouth, clicking it against my teeth, then forcing the aluminum rim between my lips.

"Don't do that," the first voice said.

"He wants it. He just don't know it yet," the second man said.

Someone, I think the second man, pulled loose my belt, then inserted his fingers between my trousers and stomach and poured the remnants of the can into my underwear. "You already pissed your pants while you were asleep, so I'm just cleaning you up," he said.

I felt the beer run down my thighs and calves. The wind blew through the windows and puffed the room and tin roof with air that smelled of brine and ozone and thunderheads out on the Gulf. Try to think clearly, I told myself. If they simply wanted to kill you, you would already be dead. They're not using their first names with one another and your eyes are taped because eventually they're going to release you. Don't change their agenda, I thought.

"Where's this guy Max Coll?" the first man said.

"If you find out, I'd like to know. He creeped my house," I replied.

"He creeped a cop's house?" the same man said.

"He's not your ordinary button man," I said.

"What's he look like?"

"I never saw him," I lied.

"He's a Mick, though, right?" the same voice said.

"We know he's in the area. We think he popped Frank Dellacroce. But we don't have much information on him."

Suddenly a steel instrument bit into my left thumb and mashed the tissue and veins into the joint. I tried to clench my jaws on the scream that came out of my throat.

"That's what happens when you try to jerk us around," the second man said. He was behind me now, his breath touching the back of my ear. "Guess where these pliers are going next?"

"No more of that," the first man said.

"He killed Frank," the second man said.

"Maybe. But we wait on the man and see what he wants. Get out of the way," the first voice said.

I smelled his presence in front of me, like hair with sweat dried in it and clothes with soap still in the fabric. Then his huge hand molded a chemical-soaked towel over my face and I felt myself floating to the bottom of a dank well where laughing faces stared down at me from a circle of blue overhead.

I lay sideways on a floor through most of the afternoon, my eyes still taped, my knees and ankles now wrapped tightly with tape as well. In my mind's eye I tried to see the faces of all the people who had been important in my life. I thought of my mother and father, illiterate Cajuns who had done the best they could with what little they owned and who struggled through the Depression and the war years to create a decent home for themselves and their only son. I thought of the two Catholic nuns who had been my first- and second-grade teachers and the time when I accidently walked into a room where they were jitter-bugging to a phonograph, their beads and habits flying. The other clergy I had known in my early years had disappeared from memory, but those two remained with me, as though framed inside a secular holy card.

I thought about the members of my platoon, deep in Indian country, blade faced, stinking of funk and rotted socks and mosquito repellant, their skin twitching as they worked their way down a night trail strung with toe-poppers and booby-trapped 105 duds. I thought about my dead wives, Annie and Bootsie, who were always my steadfast friends as well as spouse and lover, and I thought about Alafair, my adopted daughter, studying at Reed College in Portland, and wondered if I would ever see her again.

I thought about the country in which I had grown up and which I had served as a soldier and police officer. It was the best country on earth, the most noble, egalitarian, democratic experiment in human history. It was a grand and wonderful place to live, well worth the fighting for, as Ernest Hemingway would say. Thomas Jefferson knew that, and so did Woody Guthrie, Dorothy Day, Joe Hill, Molly Brown, and the IWW.

To hell with the likes of my warders, who I was sure were Tito and Caesar Dellacroce. Let them do their worst, I told myself. And to hell with all the politicians on the take and the princes of industry who lionized Third World bedbugs in order to carry out their agenda of inculcating fear in the electorate at home. America was still America, the country everyone in the world wanted to emulate, where rock 'n' roll and the Beat lyrics of Jack Kerouac would outlive all the venal interests that threatened her.

Dying wasn't so bad, not if you faced it bravely, with a clear conscience and your principles still intact. But maybe it wouldn't come to that, I told myself. The tape was still on my eyes, my tormentors ostensibly still unidentifiable.

At least that is what I told myself.

Then I heard movement in a room beyond the door of the room in which I lay, and the muffled voices of at least three men talking, and I felt my sense of personal resolve begin to drain like water from the bottom of a gunnysack.

The door opened and two sets of hands lifted me into a chair. The room was silent, the tin roof creaking from the cooling of the day. Someone wrapped tape both around my waist and the back of the chair.

"I don't know where Max Coll is. What purpose would I have in concealing his whereabouts?" I said, although no one had spoken to me.

"See, he knows what we want. He don't even wait to be asked the question. That shows us he's a smart guy who can look into the minds of other people. That shows us he's smart and we're dumb," said the voice of the man who had applied a pair of pliers to my thumb.

"How you want this to play out, 'cause we got a flight to catch?" said the voice of the other man, who I now believed to be Tito Dellacroce, also known as the Heap. But he was speaking to someone else, and not to his brother, either.

Whoever he asked the question of did not respond. Instead, I heard the soft sound of a clothing zipper sliding on its track, followed by a pause, just before a warm stream of urine splashed in my face and ran down inside the tape that bound my eyes. I twisted my head from side to side, but the person urinating on me painted my mouth, hair, and neck and drenched my shirt before he zipped up his fly again.

"We're naming this place Yellow Springs, Louisiana, in your honor, Robicheaux," said the voice of the man with the pliers.

They left the room and closed the door behind them. I leaned forward and spit, then sucked saliva out of my jaws and spit again. I heard a car door slam and the car drive away. Two men reentered the room and one of them grabbed a corner of the tape and ripped it loose from my eyes and the back of my head.

"You're shit out of luck," said the man with the tape hanging from his fingers. He was short, with a pointed face, and small, energized, deep-set eyes, his hair scalped above his ears like bowl-cut animal fur.

Next to him was his brother, Tito the Heap. His hair was braided in dreadlocks that hung to his shoulders, which sloped away from his thick neck like the sides on a tent. One jawbone kept flexing like a roll of pennies.

The room was bare, except for a table on which a tool box and a camcorder rested. The walls and floor were constructed of rough planks, and through the screen window I could see a woods strung with air vines and dotted with palmettos and beyond the tree trunks a bay and the red sun low on the horizon. In the distance somebody was firing a shotgun, perhaps popping skeet over the water.

"Are you listening, asshole? The man says the whack goes down an inch at a time. You get to be in your own movie," said the short man, whom I recognized from his mug shot as Caesar Dellacroce.

"Get it over with," I said.

"I think if you knew what was coming, you wouldn't say that," Caesar said.

I looked into space, my eyes slightly out of focus with fatigue and hopelessness and now resignation.

"I'm talking to you," Caesar said. He popped my cheek with his hand.

"I figure I'm done, so what I'm about to tell you is the truth. I didn't smoke Frank Dellacroce, but I wish I had. He was a punk and a bully and somebody should have put the electrodes on him and blown out his grits a long time ago. When you get finished with me, Clete Purcel is going to turn over every rock in New Orleans and Fort Lauderdale until he finds you, then make you wish your mother had flushed you down the toilet with the afterbirth."

Caesar stared at me, his mouth parted slightly, his jaws slack. "Say that again?"

"Go fuck yourself," I said.

"You believe this guy?" Caesar said to his brother. But he was clearly distracted now, not quite in charge anymore.

"We wasted too much time on this," Tito said reflectively. His eyes, like his brother's, were inset deeply in the skull, his nostrils flaring when he breathed, as though the plates of muscle on his chest and shoulders were squeezing the air from his lungs. "Here's what it is, ace. You rolled the dice with the wrong guy and lost. We ain't responsible for this. So take your medicine like a man. I'll make it short and sweet as possible. You want to say anything?"

"No," I replied, and fixed my gaze out the window on a watery, red sunset barely showing behind the thin trunks of trees that had already turned dark with the gloaming of the day. Tito Dellacroce pushed a sponge into my mouth with the heel of his hand, then began winding tape around my head.

"Hang on," Caesar said, staring out the same window but at a different angle.

"What?" Tito said.

"There's a priest out there," Caesar said.

"Where?"

"Walking down off the levee. He's carrying a briefcase. Look for yourself. He's got a bandage around his throat," Caesar said.

Tito went to the window, then pulled a curtain across it. "You ever seen a priest around here?" he asked.

"Yeah, lots of priests hung out at Frank's old fuck pad."

"His fuck pad was up the road. Our father used to take us fishing here. It ain't a fuck pad," Tito said.

"Enough, already. It's a priest carrying a pro-life petition around or something. It ain't a big deal," Caesar said.

"Get outside."

"Do it yourself. The mosquitoes out there eat cows for lunch." Caesar peeked through the side of the curtain. "See, he's gone."

Just as he dropped the curtain back in place someone in heavy shoes walked up on the porch and banged hard on the door. Tito and Caesar looked at each other. Then the visitor on the porch banged even harder, shaking the entire cabin. "I'll get rid of him. Stay with asshole," Caesar said.

He removed a .25 caliber automatic from his side pocket, snicked a round into the chamber, set the safety, and replaced the gun in his pocket. He opened the door and stepped into the front room. Tito Dellacroce stood behind me, one huge hand resting on my shoulder, the lower portion of his stomach touching the back of the chair. I could hear him breathing and smell the food he had eaten for supper on his skin. Caesar had left the door between the rooms ajar so Tito could listen.

"What can I do for you, Father?" I heard Caesar say.

The reply was muffled, a wheezing sound, like a man speaking through a rusty clot in his windpipe.

"What's that?" Caesar said.

The priest tried again, his voice barely a whisper.

"You're signing up people for a retreat?" Caesar said. "No, we belong to a church in Florida. We're just doing some fishing. Here's five bucks for your missions or whatever. No, I don't need no holy card."

The priest spoke again.

"We ain't got a bathroom. Just a privy out back no white person would want to slap his keester on. Try the filling station up on the state road. Okay, *vaya con dios*. That's Latin for 'see you around,' right?"

A moment later Caesar came back through the door that separated the two rooms of the cabin.

"So?" Tito said.

"So nothing. The guy had a tracheotomy or something. He sounded like all his gas was coming out the wrong end," Caesar said.

"Check."

"On what?"

"On where he is. I got to draw a picture on your forehead?"

"You worry too much," Caesar said irritably, and jerked the window curtain aside again. Then he froze. "I told him not to go back there."

"Go back where?" Tito said.

"To our privy. I told him not to do that."

"Give me your piece. Get away from the window," Tito said.

The wind gusted off the water, stressing the tin roof against the joists. Then someone stepped onto the back porch. Tito jerked the .25 caliber automatic from his brother's hand and clicked the safety off with his thumb. "Is that you, Father? 'Cause if it is this is getting to be a headache we don't need—"

The door burst open and, framed against the light, dressed in a black suit and Roman collar and black rabat, was a compact, well-groomed man with a 1911 U.S. Army model .45 automatic in each hand.

"Oh, it's a darling pair we have here. Suck on this," he said. He began firing with both guns, shooting Tito in the mouth and through the throat, hitting his brother Caesar Dellacroce in the sternum and thigh.

Tito crashed into a wall and collapsed on his spine, his legs spread, his jaw torn loose from his head. Caesar tried to crawl away from the rounds that blew the sole of his shoe off his foot, tore through a buttock, and splattered blood off his shoulder in a horsetail on the floor.

The room was littered with ejected shell casings when Max Coll finally stopped firing. He nudged Tito in the chest with his polished shoe, satisfying himself that Tito was dead, then leaned down and studied Caesar's face. "Oops, looks like you're still on board, little fellow," he said, and fired a round into the side of Caesar's head, stepping back to avoid the splatter.

He stood erect and took my measure, his cheeks rosy, a cleft in his chin slick with sweat. He pulled the sponge from my mouth. "You all right, Mr. Robicheaux?" he asked.

My heart was pounding, my ears almost deaf. "Cut me loose," I said.

"Can't do that, sir. You're a copper through and through. You'd figure out a way to have me in cuffs for sure. Give my best to Father Dolan. He's a bit hard-headed, but under it all I think he's a fine man of the cloth. His kind make me proud I'm a Catholic," he said.

And with that he was gone.

Fifteen minutes later three cruisers from the St. Martin Parish Sheriff's Department arrived at the fish camp, having been notified of my situation from a payphone by Max Coll.

Chapter 15

On Wednesday afternoon, after sleeping almost fifteen hours, I drove with Clete Purcel in his Caddy to City Park and sat under a barbecue pavilion in the rain on the banks of Bayou Teche.

"A guy pissed in your face?" he said.

"No, first he pissed in my face. Then he pissed all over me," I replied.

He lit a Lucky Strike and spit a piece of matter off his tongue. A moment later he flipped the cigarette into the bayou and watched it float away. "Don't let me light one of these again," he said.

"I won't."

"The Flannigan broad set you up," he said.

"I don't believe that."

"She got you out of your house and into a bar. What's that, working the Steps one drink at a time?"

"It was my idea to go over there."

"Why? You got some big obligation to keep other people from drinking if they want to?"

I didn't answer. I tried to avoid his eyes. "Are we talking about boom-boom out of times past?" he said.

"Why don't you give some thought to the way you talk to other people, Clete?"

"Did you ever get it on with her or not?" he asked.

"Maybe."

"Maybe?" He nodded profoundly. "So after you made your ex-punch's father look like a vindictive prick in front of his friends, you don't think she would lure you to a slop chute in hopes you'd either get killed or drunk again? Perish the thought."

I stared at the rain dimpling the surface of Bayou Teche. "Theo isn't connected with people like Tito and Caesar Dellacroce," I said.

"Merchie worked for the Teamsters in Baton Rouge. They'd force guys to buy a union book, then get them fired after a month so they could crank up their membership numbers. That's how he got into the pipeline business."

"That doesn't mean he's mobbed up today."

"A guy who trucks oil waste into black neighborhoods? Not a chance. When I was a kid we had a rumble with the Ibervilles. It was supposed to be fist, feet, and elbows, no shanks, no chains. Merchie opened a switchblade and busted it off in my cousin's arm. In my opinion he's still a project street rat as well as full-time punk and gash hound. Quit defending these assholes."

"Gash hound?" I said.

"Forget it, big mon. I don't want to talk about it anymore. Your head is encased in cement."

I had long ago learned there was no point in arguing with Clete or expecting him to understand that the people he resented most were those who came from the same background he did. He pushed his porkpie hat down on his brow and stared disgustedly at the rain. "I'm going to cripple the motherfuckers behind this, Dave. I mean that literally," he said.

He walked away under a dripping live oak toward his Caddy, his sports coat stretched to splitting on his huge shoulders.

He dropped me off at the house and I went inside and lay down on the bed in the back room. Earlier I said I had slept for fifteen hours. The truth is a little different. I could not rid myself of the sense of violation I had experienced at the hands of Tito and Caesar Dellacroce and the man who had urinated on me. I felt that soap could not cleanse my skin or my hair. When I closed my eyes and began to drift into sleep, I didn't dream of the Dellacroces but instead of a war few people are interested in today. I heard automatic weapons fire, the thropping of helicopter blades, and I saw strings of white light fountaining inside jungle foliage from the explosion of a phosphorus round. I felt a medic from Staten Island tying my wrists so I would not tear at the compress on my side. I smelled the odor of blood and feces in the uniforms of both the living and the dead being piled around me on the floor of an overloaded slick piloted by a nineteen-year-old warrant officer who had taken a steel splinter in one eye.

Sleep occurred in ten-minute intervals, and each time I awoke I wanted four inches of Black Jack straight up, vodka that had been at least twelve hours in a freezer, beer that hit the back of the throat like a spray of golden needles, yellow mescal with a thick green worm in the bottom of the bottle.

An hour after Clete had dropped me off I sat on the side of the bed with a head full of cobwebs, my mouth dry and tasting like bitters. Helen had told me not to come back to work until the following Monday. But memory was the enemy, and solitude and inactivity gave me no respite from it. I called N.O.P.D. and left a message for Clotile Arceneaux. A half hour later she called me back. "What's happenin', baby cakes?" she said.

"Baby cakes?"

I heard her laugh. "What can I help you with?" she said.

"What have you got on Merchie Flannigan?"

"A pipeline or oil guy, grew up in the projects, did some time when he was a kid?"

"That's the one."

"I'll check but I think he's pretty inactive."

"Clete thinks maybe Merchie and his wife might have been mixed up with the Dellacroce brothers."

"What about the Dellacroces?"

"They're dead. Max Coll smoked them both."

"So much for inner-department communications. Coll killed them?"

"He's posing as a priest and carrying a couple of .45 autos in a briefcase. Tito and Caesar Dellacroce abducted me. They took me to a fish camp not far from where Coll killed their cousin." It sounded foolish when I said it.

She paused a moment. "What did they do to you at this fish camp?" she asked.

"Nothing. Coll capped them."

She paused again and I could tell she didn't believe me. "Let me give you a tip. Screw Max Coll and screw the Dellacroces. The issue is porn and crystal meth. Everything else is secondary. New Orleans was made for it. You with me on this?"

"No."

"That's what I thought."

"Sorry to bother you," I said.

"Don't give me any of your guff, Robicheaux. You doin' okay over there?"

"Why?"

"'Cause you don't sound like it," she said.

So that's why she was undercover at N.O.P.D., I thought after I hung up. Some cops were probably on a meth pad and maybe the pornographers had gotten to a few of them, too. Porn had always been there, in one form or another, and sex and the economics of New Orleans tourism were longtime business companions. The Mob maintained they didn't traffic in porn, just as they claimed they didn't deal in narcotics. But they lied. They were involved in every pernicious enterprise in the United States, and decades ago had branched into shipping, the meat industry, and coal mining. The numbers racket used to be the lubricant that fueled and greased all their other machinery, but since state lotteries and legalized gambling had replaced numbers as their chief source of money, the progeny of Lucky Luciano and Benny Siegel had shifted gears to keep up with the times.

Not only had the Internet provided huge new markets for porn producers, their businesses had a built-in edge on dope trafficking. They had the First Amendment to hide behind, and most zoning boards had no problem in allowing them to open their businesses in neighborhoods where the residents, usually the poor and elderly, had no power.

The overhead was low. Junkies, demented sluts, and perverts of every stripe couldn't wait to take off their clothes in front of the camera, convinced their acting careers were just beginning.

The subject of pornography brought to mind Fat Sammy Figorelli again. He had warned me about a man he said hurt people without cause, although Sammy, in his self-serving fashion, managed not to mention the man's name. Clete was right. I had given Sammy a free pass too long. I called Clotile Arceneaux again.

"I need a favor," I said.

"What kind?"

"While my eyes were taped shut a guy urinated in my face. I think Fat Sammy Figorelli knows who he is."

"Say all that again?"

I did, this time in detail. She was quiet a long time. "What do you want from me?" she said.

"Help me jam up Sammy Fig."

"Can't do it."

"Why not?"

"We think Fat Sammy might be talking to us soon."

"As an informant?"

"Think FBI and Witness Protection."

"These guys were going to burn my kite, on film, one frame at a time. I'm not too interested in hearing about federal needs right now."

"Too bad. Stay in New Iberia, Robicheaux. That's not just a cautionary statement, either," she said.

That evening I took Clete to dinner at the Patio in Loreauville. After we ate we walked to the iron bridge over Bayou Teche and stared down at the water. The sky was crimson, full of birds, the air heavy with the smell of the sugar mills grinding cane. In the distance I heard a boat horn blowing on the water.

"I'm worried about you, noble mon," Clete said.

"You shouldn't."

"You fool lots of people. But you never fool your old podjo. Tell me I'm wrong."

I couldn't, so I changed the subject. "Fat Sammy knows who put the hit on me," I said.

"I told you he was a grease bag."

"I need to put the squeeze on him. N.O.P.D. was no help."

"You mean the black broad, what's-her-name, Clotile Whatever?"

"She's got her own problems."

"Save the St. Francis of Assisi routine for another time. What's to-day?"

"Wednesday," I said.

Clete put a stick of gum in his mouth and looked at the shadows the trees made on the bayou's surface. "You really want to put a freight train up Sammy's cheeks?"

"I couldn't have said it better."

"Remember Janet Gish? Used to be a dancer out on Airline?" he said.

"What about her?"

"She was Gunner Ardoin's costar in one of Fat Sammy's films. You like Italian opera?"

During the next two days Clete made several phone calls to New Orleans and was mysterious about all of them. But taciturnity in Clete, at least with me, usually meant he was working on a scheme that was so outrageous no sane person would involve himself in it. No one who reviewed Clete's record could doubt his creativeness when it came to spreading mayhem and chaos wherever he went. He not only shot a federal witness to death in a hog lot, he filled a New Orleans' gangster's vintage convertible with cement, destroyed a half-million-dollar home out on Lake Pontchartrain with an earth grader, pinned a hitman on the floor of the Greyhound depot's men's room and poured the contents of a liquid soap container down his throat, dropped a Teamster steward off a fourth-floor hotel balcony into a dry swimming pool, handcuffed a U.S. congressman to a fire hydrant on St. Charles, cuffed a dirty cop to the conveyor chain in a car-wash and hot-wax machine, and was believed to have put sand in the fuel tank of an airplane that crashed and exploded in the mountains of western Montana, stringing the spruce trees with the remains of several Galveston and Las Vegas mobsters.

He considered his own behavior perfectly reasonable and did many of the above deeds and others that were worse with a lopsided grin on his face, thinking them hardly worthy of mention.

His best friends were drunks, grifters, and brain-fried street people, his girlfriends strippers and junkies. Gangbangers, pushers, strong-arm robbers, and dirty cops crossed the street when they saw him coming. He swallowed his blood and ate his pain and never flinched in a fight, no matter what his adversaries did to him. He was the bravest and most loyal man I ever knew, and also the most irreverent, reckless, irresponsible, and self-destructive.

I tried not to think of how Janet Gish could be a player in Clete's plan to jam up Fat Sammy Figorelli. Friday evening I found out.

He told me to meet him in Metairie, in front of a rented hall on the edge of a middle-class neighborhood. Metairie had become a white-flight refuge during the mass exodus from New Orleans in the 1970s, known for its strict law-and-order attitudes and the distinction of having given David Duke his start in the state legislature.

I waited for Clete in the parking lot, the sky ribbed with strips of pink cloud, the trees ruffling in the yards of the modest homes beyond a shopping mall, the rental hall filling with families dressed as though they were going to church. The scene made me think of Levittown but not in a bad way. The rental hall, with its gravel roof and artificial brick shell, seemed to transcend its own cheapness, like an excursion back into an earlier era when American neighborhoods had sidewalks and were defined by their sense of community and generational continuity.

I looked again at my watch. Where was Clete? The light was fading, the air growing cold. From inside the hall I could hear someone adjusting the volume on a microphone. Then I saw Clete's lavender Cadillac coming hard down the street, the front and back seats packed with people, slowing down for a stop sign just before he bounced into the parking lot, dust and exhaust fumes rising like a dirty halo from the car frame. When he cut the engine the entire car body seemed to gasp and shrivel like an animal that had been mortally wounded. The windows were open and I could smell a heady, thick odor, like burning leaves, drifting out on the wind, then someone flicked a marijuana roach sparking onto the pavement.

Clete got out of the car and closed the door behind him, then leaned down to the window. "Crack open another six-pack and go easy on the stash. I'll be right back," he said.

"Where's the fucking opera? You said we were gonna see an opera," a woman in back said.

"I've got reserved seats. Trust me. Just be cool. Everything's copacetic," he replied.

He walked past me, so I would have to follow him, out of earshot of the people in the car. He lifted his shirt off his chest and sniffed at it. "Do I smell like a whorehouse?" he asked.

"What's going on?" I said.

"Fat Sammy belongs to this group of amateur opera singers. They perform once a month at the hall. It's Ozzie and Harriet night by way of Palermo. The archbishop is a big fan and sits up on the front row. Starting to get the picture?"

"No."

"You want to squeeze Fat Sammy, forget conventional methods. Sammy's a geek and closet pervert who always wanted people to like him. So he comes out here and pretends he's a normal member of the human race. That's about to end."

"Who's in the car?"

"Janet Gish and Big Tit Judy Lavelle and four others who got bonds with Willie Bimstine and Nig Rosewater. Either Sammy gives up the guy who put the whack on you or I'm marching all of them right up the front aisle and turning them loose."

"This doesn't sound too good, Clete."

"Oh, Sammy Fig as victim, I forgot. Every one of those broads has worked in either his porn films or his massage parlor. Ask them how they like giving twenty-dollar blowjobs to conventioneers from Birmingham."

I walked back to the Cadillac and looked inside. "How y'all doin'?" I said.

"Hey, Robicheaux, Clete say you taking us to supper at Galatoire's," a black woman in shades said. She called herself Cody Wyoming, although she had grown up on Prytania Street in New Orleans, not far from where Lillian Hellman was born.

"He hasn't filled me in on that yet," I replied.

"You might be getting old, Streak, but I bet you still got the thrust under the hood," she said. Everybody in the car roared.

I walked back to Clete. "Galatoire's?" I said.

"Nig and Willie owe me a thousand for running down a skip in Mobile. Except they say they don't owe me anything because I told Willie to write the bond on this guy when I knew he was mainlining six balloons a day. So I told them they pay for the dinner at Galatoire's, I tell the girls it's on Willie and Nig, which means they'll tell all the other hookers in New Orleans Willie and Nig are great guys, and we call it even."

"I don't think this is going to work."

"It'll work. Ever hear that story about Sammy taking a girl to the Prytania and a bunch of kids in the balcony hitting them with water bombs made from condoms? I was one of the kids in the balcony. I guess I'm sorry for what we did, but that's the way it was back then. Come on, Streak, this is the life we chose."

On that note I walked through the double doors of the hall into the heart of middle America, cloistered, far from the inner city, passenger jets decelerating overhead as they approached the airport, a bustling shopping mall close by, and a freeway streaming with headlights to reassure everyone God was in His heaven and all was right with the world.

Clete had not lied to Janet Gish and her friends about reserved seating. Eight folding metal chairs in the front row remained empty, a program resting on the seat of each one. Otherwise the house was packed. Sammy Figorelli stood resplendent on the stage with his fellow singers, beaming, stuffed inside a summer tux, the footlights surrounded by bouquets of plastic flowers. Clete took out his cell phone and pushed a button on the speed dial.

"I'm down in front, Janet. I'll wave to you when I'm sure we've got the right seats. Yeah, wait for me to wave. It's mass confusion here," he said, and clicked off his phone.

By now Sammy had seen us and was watching us out of the corner of his eye while he tried to hold a conversation with the other singers. Clete mounted the wood steps that led onto the stage as though he were part of the production, stepping carefully over the plastic flowers clumped around the footlights. "Got a second, Mr. Figorelli?" he said.

Fat Sammy walked toward him, his eyes like hot BBs. "What do you think you're doing, Purcel?" he asked.

"Check out the ladies in the doorway at the back of the hall. They've been doing a little weed, so I hope they don't get too giggly," Clete replied.

Sammy stared at the back of the hall like a man witnessing the erection of his own gallows. His cheeks bladed with color and pinpoints of sweat popped on his forehead. He labored down the steps, forcing Clete to follow him. "You get rid of them people," he said hoarsely.

"And miss the reception afterwards? You kidding? Can we get introductions to the archbishop?" Clete said.

"What are you after?" Sammy said, his breath coated with funk.

"Give us the name of the guy who sicced the Dellacroces on Dave."

Sammy's face was shiny with a greasy film now, his boutonniere like a red wound on his jacket. "You got no right to do this to me, Purcel," he said.

"I'm counting to three, then waving Janet Gish into action."

"The guy's out there now, you dumb Mick."

"Where?" Clete said, twisting his head to survey the crowd.

"Don't do that. You're gonna get me clipped," Sammy said.

"I don't see anybody out there I know. Do you, Dave?"

"We're done here," I said.

"No, no. Sammy's going to give us a name," Clete replied, waving a finger.

"Sammy's going down with the ship. Right, Sammy?" I said.

But Sammy Fig's embarrassment was such he could no longer speak. In fact, I thought he was on the edge of having a coronary attack. The fatty layer under his chin trembled, his chest heaved, and sweat ran like hair oil into his shirt collar. I was convinced, at that moment, that inside every adult human being the child was still present, in this case an obese little boy struggling to free himself from the metal coils of a tuba while a packed football stadium laughed at his discomfort.

"We're going to boogie. Tell the guy who pissed on me I'll be looking him up," I said.

"You already burned me. Y'all don't know what you've done," Sammy said.

"That's the breaks. Anything else happens to Dave, I'm going to see you first. That means you're going to be the deadest douche bag in New Orleans," Clete said, jabbing Sammy in the chest with his finger.

We left Sammy standing numb and shaken in front of his audience and rounded up Janet Gish and her friends and headed for Galatoire's on Bourbon Street.

On the way out of the rental hall I searched the crowd for a familiar face, one that might belong to the man who had crisscrossed me from head to foot with his urine. But if he was there, I did not see him.

"You blew it, Dave. Fat Sammy would have cracked," Clete said later.

"What did Sammy do when you and your friends threw water-bomb condoms at him and his girlfriend?" I said.

We were coming out of Galatoire's, into the pre-Christmas holiday atmosphere of late-night Bourbon Street. The street was loud with music, the neon like purple and pink angel hair inside the fog blowing off the river. "He cried and came at us with both fists," Clete said.

"He's still the same kid."

"All of us are. Except Fat Sammy became a pimp and dope pusher. It's only rock 'n' roll, Dave. Everybody dies. Go with the flow and try to have a few laughs," Clete said. He propped his shoe on a fire hydrant and buffed the tip with a cloth napkin he had taken from the restaurant.

Chapter 16

I went back to work Monday morning. I took a legal pad from my desk drawer and wrote Junior Crudup's name at the top of it, then drew a circle around it. This is where it had all started, I thought, both for me and the LeJeune family. Under Junior's name I wrote the names of Castille LeJeune, Theodosha, Merchie, and Theodosha's psychiatrist in Lafayette, the man who supposedly committed suicide.

Then I angled a line from Castille LeJeune's name to the names of Will Guillot and the dead daiquiri shop operator and Dr. Parks, who had died in Will Guillot's driveway.

To one side I placed the names of the New Orleans players—Father Jimmie Dolan, Max Coll, the Dellacroce family, and Gunner Ardoin, the part-time porn actor.

The connections between the names and the deeds associated with them seemed byzantine on the surface, but for me the answers in the investigation lay in the past and the key was still the first name on the page, Junior Crudup.

Helen opened my office door. "The Lafayette Sheriff's Department just called. Get this," she said. "The archdiocese is having a clerical conference of some kind. One of the out-of-towners happened to be an Irish priest. His jokes were a big hit. Then a pistol fell out of his shoulder bag in the lobby of the Holiday Inn."

"Our man Max?"

"What's with this guy?"

"He's nuts."

"That's the best you can do?"

"Got a better explanation? Where'd he go?"

"They don't know. They think he was driving a rental."

"He'll be back."

"You sound almost happy."

"He saved my life. Maybe he has redeeming qualities," I said, grinning at her.

"The guy who said 'suck on this' and blew away two people?"

"It's only rock 'n' roll," I said.

"Fire your psychiatrist," she said, and closed the door.

I studied the names and lines on my notepad. Years ago, after the murder of my wife Annie, I went twice a week to sessions with an analytically oriented therapist in Lafayette. He was one of those who believed most aberrations in behavior and personality development were caused by fairly obvious dysfunctions in the patient's environment. The problem in treating them, he maintained, was that they were so obvious the patient usually would not buy the connection between the cause and the problem.

Theodosha had told me her husband, Merchie, was having what she called another flop in the hay and that she couldn't blame him for it. I took that to mean she had a sexual problem of her own, one that had sent her husband elsewhere. But I also remembered a remark our dispatcher Wally had made about Merchie Flannigan, as well as one made by Clete Purcel.

I walked up front and leaned on the half-door that enclosed Wally in the dispatcher's cage. He was writing on a clipboard, the top of his head and his neatly parted, little-boy haircut bent down. His shirt pocket was stuffed with cellophane-wrapped cigars. "What chu want, Dave?" he asked without looking up.

"You told me Merchie Flannigan was a bum, that he was a guy you never liked. Let's clear that up," I said.

"So I got a big mout'," he replied.

"This is part of a murder investigation, Wally. I'm not going to ask you again."

"He's got a wife, but he messes around on the side."

"A lot of men do."

"He was driving my wife's niece home. She was working at his office in Lafayette. She was seventeen years old at the time. He axed her if she wanted to go swimming at his club. It was late and the club was closed, but he said it didn't matter 'cause he had a key and the owner and him was golf buddies. She didn't have a suit, but he said that wasn't no problem 'cause they'd get one from behind the counter and put it on his tab.

"There wasn't no lights on in the pool when she came out of the dressing room. She started swimming back and fort' across the shallow end, then he come up to her and axed her if she could swim on her back. She said she always got water up her nose, and he says just turn over and rest on my hands and I'll show you how to do it."

I waited for him to go on but he didn't.

"What happened?" I said.

"He tole her how pretty she was, how she had to be careful about young boys only got one thing on their mind. She tole him she was cold and she better go back inside and get dressed. He said it was okay, they'd come back another time, that she was the prettiest girl he'd ever seen."

He stopped again, ticking his pencil on the clipboard, looking at nothing.

"That was it?" I said.

"It was enough for her daddy. He was gonna go over to Flannigan's house and break his jaw but his wife hid the car keys. So the next morning he walked into Flannigan's office and made sure the door was open so everybody could hear it and tole him his daughter wouldn't be coming back to work no more."

"Thanks, Wally."

"What do I know?" he said.

A lot, I thought.

I went back to my office and started in on the paperwork that had built up during the days I was off. The phone on my desk rang.

"Tell me what I'm hearing isn't true," the voice of Clotile Arceneaux said.

"I'm not too keen on rumors."

"Did you and your buddy Purcel brace Sammy Fig out in Metairie Friday night?"

"Maybe."

"Some federal agents are seriously pissed off about this, as well as somebody else, meaning myself. What gives you the right to go into another jurisdiction and intimidate other people's witnesses?"

"I don't read it that way."

"Well, read this. Sammy Fig thinks either I or federal agents gave you information that sent you over to Metairie. He says he'll no longer be cooperating with us and we can shove Witness Protection up our ass."

"That's the way it flushes sometimes."

"I love your metaphors. I even like you. But right now I'd like to push you off a tall building."

"Where's Sammy now?"

"I left that part out, did I? We have no idea. Gone. My guess is he's gonna try to take it to them before they get to him first."

"Take it to whom?"

"To *whom*? I love talking to cops who need to show me how educated they are. How would we know, since eighteen months of casework just got dumped in the toilet? You're something else, Robicheaux. I hope you come out of this all right, but remind me to be on vacation the next time I catch a case you're involved with. Did you and Purcel really take a bunch of hookers to Galatoire's?"

"I think we've got a bad connection. Let me call you back later."

"Not necessary. I've had all the horse shit I can take in one day," she said.

Top that.

At noon I signed out of the office and drove up the bayou to Hogman Patin's house. He was building a chicken coop under a pecan tree in his side yard and pretended not to see me when I turned into the drive. He slipped his hammer through a hole in a leather pouch on his belt, looking intently at his creation, then walked around the back of his house, out of sight.

I left my truck on top of the oyster-shell drive, the engine ticking with heat, and followed him. He was sitting on his steps, his big hands cupped on his knees, the knife scars on his arms like the backs of worms that had burrowed under the skin. The sun's reflection wobbled brightly on the bayou's surface, but he stared at it without blinking. "Ain't goin' to let the past alone, are you?" he said.

"You have to confront it to get rid of it, Hogman," I replied.

"I done tole you almost all I know. Why don't you let it be?"

"What happened to Jackson Posey, the guard who had to keep taking Junior up to Miss Andrea's house?"

"Cancer eat him up. Heard he died at Charity Hospital in Lafayette. Died hard, too."

I picked up a handful of moldy pecans from a shady, damp area and began chunking them into the bayou. "You've never told anybody why you made a bottle tree in your backyard, have you?" I said.

"Ain't nobody else's bidness."

"You're a religious man, Hogman. Each one of those bottles represents a different prayer. Every time the wind makes the glass sing in the branches, a prayer goes up from each of those bottles, doesn't it?"

He lowered his eyes and pared one of his fingernails with a toothpick. "What a man do in his home is what he do in his home," he said.

"You helping cover up a murder, Hogman."

"Ain't right you talk to me like that, Dave. No, suh."

"Maybe not. But why do you want to protect the LeJeune family?"

"I ain't seen what happened after I left the camp. Cain't tell you about what I ain't seen. Don't want to tell you about what I ain't seen, either."

"Somebody saw. Somebody knows."

He breathed hard through his nose, his nostrils flaring in his frustration with me and his own conscience. The wind was cool and wrinkled the bayou's surface, and Hogman's bottle tree rang like spoons clinking on crystal. "There's a man down at Pecan Island stacked time in the same camps as me and Junior. He was a check writer and used to carry the water can when we road-ganged. Him and his gran'daughter sell crabs and vegetables off a truck out on the state road. His name is Woodrow Reed."

"How does he feel about talking to a white man?"

"He don't care what color you are. He climbed up on a power pole to get a cat down and got 'lectrocuted. His eyes cooked in his head. You'll t'ink he's looking at you but don't no light go t'rew his eyes. His eyes scare people. Maybe that's why ain't nobody ever been around axing Woodrow questions about what he seen."

I drove back to New Iberia and on south of Abbeville, where sugar-cane acreage gave way to sawgrass and clumps of gum trees and the miles of wetlands that bled into the Gulf of Mexico, forming the watery, ill-defined coastline of southwest Louisiana. I crossed a bridge onto one of the few remaining barrier islands left in Louisiana, a reef composed of hard-packed shell ground up by the tides, the crest topped with alluvial soil that is among the richest in the western hemisphere. The adjacent islands had been dredged and scooped out of the surf and hauled away on barges decades ago for highway-construction material, but portions of Pecan Island, preserved largely by an oil corporation as a recreational area for its CEOs, contains wooded acreage where the canopy of live oaks rises perhaps two hundred feet into the sky and the sunlight breaking through the moss and branches and air vines is the same color as light filtering through green water in the Florida Keys.

In the midst of duck-hunting camps with wide, screened-in porches and adjacent boathouses was the tiny vegetable farm and blue-point crab business of Woodrow Reed. Stacks upon stacks of collapsible wire crab traps, webbed with dried river trash, stood by the side of his small, paintless house. A middle-aged black woman was chopping up nutria parts on a butcher block a short distance away, the rubber gloves on her hands spotted with brown matter.

Woodrow Reed's eyes were large, round and flat, unblinking, like painted facsimiles that had been cut out of paper and pasted on the face of a mannikin. They stared at me intently, the pupils dilated and black, although it was obvious Woodrow Reed was sightless.

"I'm Dave Robicheaux, with the Iberia Parish Sheriff's Department," I said. I opened my badge holder and held it aloft so the middle-aged woman in the side yard could see it.

"I knowed you was coming," he said, rising from where he sat on the front steps.

"Hogman called you?" I said.

"Yeah, but he didn't have to. I knowed somebody was coming one day. Want to come in, suh?" He opened the rusted screen door to his front porch and waited for me to enter.

He could not have been over five feet. His skin was the color of a razor strop that has yellowed with wear, his body compressed and hard looking, his cheeks and chin scrolled with gray whiskers. But I could not get over his eyes. I had seen eyes like his only once before, in the body of a man who had been exhumed from a grave in northern Montana where he had lain for decades under frozen ground.

"How'd you come by your farm, Mr. Reed?" I asked.

"You already know the answer to that."

"Can you tell me how Junior Crudup died?" I asked.

Woodrow Reed was sitting on what looked like a motion-picture theater seat mounted on a wood block, his palms propped on his thighs. His denim pants were neatly pressed, the cuffs and pockets buttoned on his long-sleeve work shirt.

"The doctor give me another year. I already put my farm in my daughter's name. Ain't a whole lot can touch me no more. I got cancer, just like Jackson Posey, although I never smoked like he did or had no problems with my skin," he said.

"Tell me about Junior, sir."

"Junior was gonna be Junior. He didn't wear no other man's hat. That was Junior," he said. For the first time he smiled.

In the waning days of summer, when the amber light at evening turned the countryside into a yellowing antique photograph, Junior

Crudup took his twelve-string Stella guitar out on the steps of the cabin in the work camp and began composing a song whose lyrics he penciled on a paper bag flattened down on the board plank beside him.

"What you calling your song?" Woodrow asked, sitting down next to him in the dusk.

"'The Angel of Work Camp Number Nine,'" Junior replied.

Woodrow rubbed the whiskers that grew like black wire on his chin. "T'ink that's a good idea, Junior?" he asked.

"Gonna record it up in Memphis one day. You gonna see," Junior replied.

"I seen her car out here last night. Parked right there on the road. She was smoking a cigarette behind the wheel and playing the radio in the dark."

"You better not be fooling with me, Woodrow."

"It was her. Cap'n Posey walked up to her window and axed if anyt'ing was wrong. She said she was just taking a drive. Then she drove on down the road toward the li'l sto' by the bridge. A li'l while later I seen her drive on back to the big house. She was drinking a bottle of beer, tilting her chin up each time she took a sip."

"Why didn't you come get me?"

"You spent too much time up Nort', Junior. You're having t'oughts ain't no nigger in Lou'sana ought to be having."

"Maybe it was that way at first. But not now. You know what she got that make her special?"

"Her tits ain't bad."

"Don't be talking that way, Woodrow. She's special 'cause she got respect for other people."

Junior adjusted the belly of his guitar on his thigh and slipped his three steel finger picks on his right hand, then corded the neck of the guitar and began singing:

> *At Camp Number Nine it's "Roll, nigger, roll,*
> *No heaven for you, boy, the state own your soul."*
> *They took my home and family,*

Give me chains, fatside, and beans,
Bossman making me a Christian,
God Almighty, hear that Betty scream.

"You risking your ass for somebody don't know you alive," Woodrow said.

"Rich ladies like that got all kinds of things they got to do, places they got to travel to, Woodrow. She cain't be coming down here all the time."

"Don't let Boss Posey hear that song."

"When she invites me back up to the house?" Junior said.

"Yeah?"

"That's the first song I'm gonna play."

There was drought in the fall and the fields hardened and cracked under a merciless sun and an empty sky that by noon was like white glass. The leaves of the cane baked in the wind and frayed into thread on the ends and rattled dryly on the stalks, and by evening the sky was cinnamon colored with dust and the convicts filling mule-drawn water tanks with buckets they flung into the bayou on ropes had to tie wet handkerchiefs across their nostrils and mouths. To conserve water the convicts bathed in the bayou, then sat listlessly on the porches of their cabins until lock-up. Every third or fourth evening, while the cicadas sang in a grove of cedar trees near the camp, Junior worked on the song he was composing in tribute to Andrea LeJeune, waiting for the invitation to play on her lawn again, telling himself she was contacting the governor and that any day a parole order for his release would be delivered at the camp's front gate.

At bell count on a September morning Jackson Posey saw the folded brown paper sack covered with penciled lyrics sticking from Junior's back pocket.

"What you got there, Junior?" he asked.

The early sun was already a dull red inside the dust blowing out of the fields. At the bottom of the slope that led down to the bayou, the water was low and swarming with gnats, algae-webbed snags protruding from the surface, all of it smelling of dead fish that lay bloated and fly-specked on the banks.

"Just li'l notes I keep for myself, boss," Junior replied.

"Let's see it," Jackson Posey said, fitting a pair of glasses on his nose. He took the bag from Junior's fingers and studied the words on it, his lips moving slightly as he read. The sores on his arms seemed deeper, more black than purple now. His eyes fixed on Junior's. "You got Camp Number Nine in here?" he said.

"Yes, suh."

"Camp Number Nine is us."

"It is and it ain't, boss."

The guard read both sides of the paper bag, then shook a Camel loose from his cigarette pack and slipped it into his mouth. He laughed to himself and handed the song lyrics back to Junior. "I ain't a big judge of poetry, but I'd say keep this one."

"Thank you, suh."

"To wipe yourself with. You never cease to entertain me, Junior," Posey added.

At morning bell count two days later Andrea LeJeune got out of her Ford convertible at the camp's front gate, wearing a polka-dot sun dress and dark glasses and a blue bandanna tied tightly on her head, the wind whipping her dress around her legs.

"We're taking Junior to a recording studio in Crowley, Mr. Posey. Make sure he brings his guitar and his harmonica and a sack lunch. Y'all will follow me in your truck," she said.

Jackson Posey involuntarily looked toward the big house. "Mr. LeJeune at home, ma'am?" he asked.

"No, he's not, and I resent your asking," she replied.

Junior wrapped his Stella in a blanket, tied string around the belly and the neck, and slipped his E-major Marine Band harmonica in his shirt pocket. Before they left the camp, Posey put chains on Junior's ankles and handcuffs on his wrists, and set the guitar in the bed of the truck. As they drove away Junior looked out the back window at his friend Woodrow flinging a bucket into the bayou on a rope under the gaze of a mounted gunbull.

Then Junior and Jackson Posey were on the highway, driving

through a long tunnel of oak trees behind Andrea LeJeune's purple convertible, the broken sunlight flicking by overhead, the wind cool in their faces.

"You gonna make the big time, huh?" Posey said.

"Don't know about that, suh."

"Think it's coincidence she's taking you to Crowley?"

"I ain't following you, boss."

"That's where she meets a man I wouldn't take time to spit on. Castille LeJeune should have invested some of his money in a chastity belt. Know the difference between rich people and us?" Posey said.

"No, suh," Junior answered.

"They don't get caught."

When they pulled into the Crowley town square Andrea LeJeune parked her car next to one of the old elevated sidewalks and went inside the dime store, one with a popcorn machine in front, to use the pay telephone. Then they drove out into the countryside again, through rice fields that were separated by hedgerows, to a white-painted, flat-top building constructed entirely of cinder blocks that was located inside a grove of cedar and pine trees like a machine-gun bunker.

This was the same primitive studio where a few years later Warren Storm and Lazy Lester would record and Phil Phillips would cut the master for "Sea of Love," which would sell over one million copies. The equipment was prewar junk, the resonator for Junior's acoustic Stella a chunk of storm sewer pipe with a microphone on the other end. But each person working in the studio knew who Junior Crudup was, and his identity as both a black man and a convict seemed to melt away as the session progressed.

He recorded eight pieces, the last of which was "The Angel of Work Camp Number Nine." As he sang the lyrics he looked through a greasy side window and saw her by the front fender of her convertible, talking to a tall white man who had just gotten out of an Oldsmobile with grillwork that resembled chromium teeth. The white man was thin, dark haired, his crisp shirt tucked tightly inside his seersucker slacks. He rested one foot on the bumper of his car and removed a blade of grass from the tip of his two-tone shoe, then took his car keys from his pocket and inserted his finger through the ring and spun them in the air.

He drove away toward town in his Oldsmobile and Andrea Le-Jeune followed him. Junior's voice broke in the middle of his song and he had to start again.

Later, Junior and Jackson Posey rode back through the town square of Crowley, past the colonnaded storefronts and tree-shaded elevated sidewalks inset with iron tethering rings, past the dime store with a popcorn machine in front from which Andrea had made a phone call.

Junior was hunched forward on the seat, his wrists cuffed, the chain between his ankles vibrating with the motion of the truck, his expression concealed from Jackson Posey.

"I'll show you something," Posey said, and cut down a side street and out onto a state road, past a shady motor court that featured a swimming pool in back and a supper club in front. Posey slowed the truck so he and Junior could have a clear view of the stucco cottages inside the trellised entrance.

"Don't need to be seeing none of this, boss," Junior said.

"There's his Oldsmobile. There's her little Ford. What do you reckon he's doing to her right now?"

Junior stared at the tops of his cuffed hands and did not speak again until they were back at the camp.

But his day was not over. Just after supper Jackson Posey came for him again. "She wants to see you," he said.

"Wore out, boss."

He was alone, sitting on an upended Coca-Cola box in the corner of the dirt yard, next to the fence topped by five strands of barbed wire tilted back at an inward angle, his guitar still wrapped with a blanket and tied with string on top of his bunk inside. The sun was only a smudge on the western horizon and the lilac-colored sky throbbed with the droning of cicadas.

"Get your skinny ass up before I kick it up between your shoulder blades," Posey said. "One other thing?"

"What's that, boss?"

"You tell her I drove you past that motor court today, I'm gonna take you out to a stump, nail your balls to it, and leave you there with a knife. Ain't storying to you, Junior. I seen my daddy do it when I was a boy," Posey said.

But Junior did not get up from the Coca-Cola box. "I ain't playing no more today," he said.

Posey raised his fist and knocked him to the ground.

"Whup me or put me on the bucket. I ain't going to play no more," Junior said.

"I don't have to whup you. I'm gonna do it to Woodrow Reed instead," Posey said.

On the way to the house of Castille and Andrea LeJeune, Junior wondered what he had done in this world to earn the grief that seemed to be his daily lot.

He waited on the patio with his guitar and harmonica for Andrea LeJeune to come downstairs and through the French doors. When she emerged she was still wearing the polka-dot dress she had worn earlier. Her face looked haggard, somehow thinner in the evening light.

"I wanted you to know the producer at the studio called to say how thrilled he was. I'm just sorry I didn't get to hear you perform," she said.

"I understand, ma'am," he replied.

"I have to go away, Junior. But I'm going to do everything I can to see you released from prison. What happened to your head?"

"Fell down the steps," he replied, his face empty.

She gave a long, hard look at Jackson Posey standing by the pickup truck in the driveway. "Come in the house," she said.

"That ain't a good idea, Miss Andrea," Junior said.

She walked to the edge of the drive. "Mr. Posey, Junior is coming into the living room for a few minutes. We're not to be disturbed," she said.

"I cain't allow that, ma'am."

"You can't what?" she said.

She stared him down, then turned on her heel and marched inside her house, curling one finger for Junior to follow her.

"Sit down," she said.

"Miss Andrea, Boss Posey ain't an ordinary man," Junior said.

"I'm going to call every week and have someone check on you. You have nothing to be afraid of."

"It don't work like that."

She sat down in an antique chair with an egg-shaped crimson pad inset in the back and folded her hands in her lap. "The producer said you wrote a song called 'The Angel of Camp Number Nine.' Is that about me?"

He hesitated, then said, "Yes, ma'am, I reckon it is."

"That's one of the most touching compliments I've ever received. I'd appreciate it very much if you'd play it."

He slipped the guitar over his neck and began to sing:

> *White coke and a red moon sent me down,*
> *Judge say ninety-nine years, son, you Angola bound,*
> *It's the Red Hat Gang from cain't-see to cain't-see,*
> *The gunbulls say there the graveyard, boy,*
> *If you wants to be free.*
>
> *Lady with roses in her hair come to Camp Number Nine,*
> *Say you ain't got to stack no mo' Lou'sana time,*
> *Gonna carry you up to Memphis in a rubber-tired hack,*
> *Buy you whiskey, cigars, and an oxblood Stetson hat.*
>
> *Miss Andrea is an angel drive a li'l purple car,*
> *Live on cigarettes, radio, and a blues man's guitar—*

Even before he looked through the front window and saw the automobile of Castille LeJeune approaching the house, he knew there was something terribly wrong. Andrea LeJeune's face seemed repelled, as though someone had touched it with a soiled hand.

"You don't need to sing anymore," she said.

"Ma'am?"

"What you've done is very nice, but I don't think this song needs to be recorded."

"I don't rightly understand," he said.

"This particular composition would probably be better deleted from your recording session. I think that's clear enough, isn't it?"

He felt his mouth pucker as though a nerve ending had been cut in his face. From outside he heard a car door slam, then footsteps on the gallery. He lowered his eyes. "Why ain't it supposed to be recorded?" he asked.

"I don't think I should have to explain that to you," she replied.

His throat felt as though he had swallowed a handful of needles. "I'm ready for Boss Posey to take me back now," he said. He pulled the Marine Band harmonica from his shirt pocket and set it on a flower-patterned couch by the French doors.

"I'm not in the habit of having people return gifts to me," she said.

"I'd really appreciate it, ma'am, I mean appreciate more than anything else in the world, if you could just yell at Boss Posey for me, tell him *I'se* on my way," Junior said.

Just then Castille LeJeune opened the front door and walked into the living room, a Panama hat hanging from his fingertips, his mouth twisted in an incredulous smile.

"Please explain it to me, or I'll have to conclude I've either lost my mind or walked into the wrong house," he said.

I heard the cell phone ring on the front seat of my truck. I went outside and picked it up.

"Where are you?" Helen Soileau's voice said.

"Pecan Island."

"What are you doing at Pecan Island?"

"Interviewing a man who did time with Junior Crudup."

She exhaled her breath into the phone. "We've got a submerged car in West Cote Blanche Bay. The driver's still in there. A witness says he heard firecrackers going off before the car went into the water. Then the car drove off a pier."

"How about sending someone else?"

"Dave, your separate itinerary ends right now. Get your butt over there."

"Soon as I can," I said.

"Not good enough."

I turned off the ringer on the cell and went back inside to finish my interview with Woodrow Reed.

Chapter 17

Mr. LeJeune and Miss Andrea had a big fight that night," Woodrow said.

"How do you know?"

"My cousin was the maid. She tole me later, that was after I was out of the joints, she tole me Mr. LeJeune went crazy that night. He picked up Miss Andrea's clothes off the flo' and smelled them."

"He did *what*?"

"He smelled her clothes and knowed she was messing around on him. He was yelling all over the house, saying his wife went to bed wit' a nigger. My cousin was so scared she run out the do' and hid in the trees down by the bayou. She said Mr. Castille come crashing out of the house and drove his car down to the work camp."

"Looking for Junior?"

"No, suh. He was after Boss Posey. A man like Castille LeJeune don't go after a nigger convict. It was Boss Posey he took it out on."

"I don't understand. Jackson Posey knew Junior was innocent, that Andrea LeJeune was having an affair with a man in Crowley."

"What was Boss Posey gonna say? 'Your wife been sleeping wit' another white man and I knowed about it and I ain't said nothing'? Boss Posey was caught, just like Junior. Boss Posey was gonna save his job and his ass only way he knew how."

Woodrow Reed stopped his account, his hands fixed rigidly on his thighs, staring at me with his flat, sightless eyes. The pupils were overly large, like black dimes, as though they contained thoughts and remembered images that were bursting inside his head.

"Save his ass how, Woodrow?" I said.

"I got great shame about this, Mr. Robicheaux. The story of Judas ain't only in the Bible. Thirty pieces of silver can come to you in lots of ways."

He looked at me a long time while fireflies sparked in the darkness outside and moths thudded softly against the screens, then he told me the rest of it.

Two weeks passed at the camp, and still there was no rain, only heat and dust blowing from the fields and dry lightning at night and the rumble of distant thunder over the Gulf. Cigarettes thrown from automobiles and pickup trucks started roadside grassfires that spread into the cane, and after sunset Woodrow and Junior sat on the front steps of their cabin and watched the dull red glow inside the clouds of brown smoke on the horizon.

Junior no longer played his guitar or sat in on bouree games or sassed the guards. Until lock-up he loitered in the corners of the yard, or sat on his up-ended Coca-Cola box, which everyone now called "Junior's box," or sat on the steps with Woodrow, staring at the empty dirt road that led down to a small general store by the drawbridge.

"You tearing yourself up over somet'ing that was never real," Woodrow said. "Miss Andrea is a nice white woman. But that's all she is. She ain't sent down by God to take care of Junior Crudup."

"Shut up, Woodrow," Junior replied.

"Sure, I can do that. Then you can talk to yourself 'cause everybody else around here t'inks you done lost your mind."

Woodrow took a worn pack of playing cards out of his shirt pocket, shuffled them, then cupped and squared them in his palm. "Here, I'm gonna give you one of my readings. Won't cost you a cent," he said.

"Don't be giving me none of your truck," Junior said.

But Woodrow went ahead and turned the cards over one at a time, placing them in a circle in the space between him and Junior. "See, there's you, the one-eyed Jack. Slick, wit' a li'l thin mustache, got the mojo going on the rest of the world. Up top there is the queen of hearts. Guess who that is. Over here is the king of diamonds. Guess who that is. Notice the king and the queen ain't interested in whether the one-eyed Jack is playing pocket pool wit' himself or not. What that mean, Junior, is that rich white people don't care about what goes on down here in this camp."

"Ain't got time for this, Woodrow."

Woodrow peeled three more cards off the deck and snapped them down in a vertical line traversing the circle. "See, there's the joker, right over the head of the one-eyed Jack. That means our man, the one-eyed Jack, is a full-time fool. Sure you don't want to rename your song 'The Dumbest Nigger in Camp Number Nine'?"

But Junior only stared at the fires and brown clouds of smoke on the horizon and the buzzards that were slowly descending in a vortex toward a woods on the far side of the bayou.

Woodrow put three cards down on the step in a horizontal line, completing a cross inside the circle. Junior expected another ridiculing remark but instead there was only silence. He glanced sideways at Woodrow. "Why you got that look on your face?" he said.

Woodrow started to scoop the cards up. But Junior held his wrist. "Answer me, Woodrow," he said.

"It's just a card trick. Been playing it on people for years. Don't none of it mean anyt'ing," he replied.

Junior peeled loose a card that was cupped inside Woodrow's palm. "How come you trying to hide the Jack of spades?" he asked.

Woodrow rubbed one eye with the heel of his hand and stared sadly at the bayou. "It's Boss Posey, Woodrow. Lawd Gawd, it's Boss Posey. Why you gone and done this to yourself?" he said.

Then he rushed away to be by himself, leaving his deck of cards scattered on the steps.

The next day Junior received a contract in the mail from the recording studio. He sat on the edge of his bunk and read the letter that accompanied it, then walked to the fireplace and held a match to the letter, the contract, and the envelope they came in and watched the pages blacken and curl into ash on the hearth. The next morning at bell count Junior stood unshaved and dirty in the front row of men who were about to go into the fields to trench firelines around unburned cane and shovel dirt over stubble that was still smoldering. Jackson Posey looked at the puffiness around his eyes and sniffed at his breath. "Where'd you get the julep?" he said.

"Don't remember, boss," he replied.

"Woodrow, run back to the shed and bring me a case of them empty pop bottles," Posey said.

Woodrow started toward the rear of the camp.

"I said run, boy."

"Yow, boss," Woodrow said.

He ran to the shed and lifted a wood case of Royal Crown Cola bottles by the handles and closed the door behind him with his foot, the bottles clinking between his hands. Then, as though a choice lay before him that would forever define who he was and the place he would inhabit in the world, he hesitated. On the perimeters of his vision he could see the LeJeune home high up on the slope, built to resemble a steamboat, surrounded by live oaks and palm trees; he could see a bulldozer and scooped out hole between the camp and the house where a damaged gas storage tank had just been removed; he could see the soot and brown smoke blowing out of the fields, the buzzards circling in the sky, the barbed wire that surrounded the camp, the tin roofs of the cabins already expanding against the joists with the heat of the day, the hard-packed clay smoothness of the yard, the gunbulls and trusty guards already mounted on their horses, most of them armed with double-barrel, cut-down shotguns whose steel was the color of a worn five-cent piece, and in the midst of it all, Woodrow's best friend, Junior Crudup, drunk on julep made from yeast, raisins, and cracked corn boiled in a syrup can, about to be destroyed by his own pride.

Drop the bottle case on the ground, he told himself. Let them ship you back to 'Gola. Do cain't-see to cain't-see on the Red Hat Gang, take the sweatbox treatment on Camp A, but don't hep them to hurt Junior. Please, Lawd, make me be strong when I am weak, he prayed.

"Goddamn it, boy, move your ass!" Jackson Posey shouted.

"I'm coming, boss!" Woodrow said, running, the empty pop bottles rattling inside their wooden slots.

Junior sat down on the ground, pulled off his shoes and socks, and mounted the pop bottles, extending his arms out sideways for balance. The other men marched out the front gate, their eyes straight ahead, and began climbing into the trucks that waited for them. When the trucks drove away in the dust, Woodrow looked through the slats in the tailgate and saw his friend quivering like Jell-O atop the rows of R.C. Cola bottles, his pain sealed inside his closed eyelids.

Junior was still there when the trucks returned in the evening. Except he didn't look like Junior anymore. There were skinned places on his face and knots on his head; one eye was swollen shut and his denims were dark with his own urine.

At sunset Junior was allowed to come off the box and sit in one corner of the yard. As the other men passed on their way to the mess shack, they saw the bottoms of Junior's feet and had to look away. But Junior's trial by ordeal was not over. Jackson Posey stood over him, thinking private thoughts, touching at the corner of his mouth with one finger. Posey looked up the slope toward the gouged hole in the landscape where a gas storage tank had been pried out of the ground.

"Get your shoes on, Junior. Woodrow, bring a spade from the shed and get my lunch bucket and a chair from my office," Posey said.

The three of them walked together up the slope in the twilight, Junior limping like he had glass in his shoes, while purple martins darted through the haze of smoke in the air. A fat, thumb-buster .45 revolver creaked in a holster on Boss Posey's hip. Woodrow set down the chair for Boss Posey to sit in and speared the spade into a huge mound of wet clay by the hole, then set down Posey's lunch bucket on the ground by the chair. For just a moment he thought he smelled rain inside the wind.

"You don't need me no more, huh, boss?" he said.

"Hunker down on the dirt pile and keep me company," Posey replied, opening his lunch bucket and removing a pint of whiskey.

He wants you to attack him, Junior. Then he's gonna kill you. He brung me to be a witness and cover his ass, Woodrow said to himself. Look at me, Junior. Can you hear the words I'm t'inking?

"Dozer man run out of gas today, Junior. So you got to fill up that hole for me. Better get on it," Posey said.

"Stood all day on the bottles, boss. Ain't got nothing left," Junior said.

"You done this to yourself, boy." Posey unscrewed the cap on his whiskey bottle and took a sip, rolling it in the corners of his mouth before he swallowed. Then he seemed to think a long time before he spoke again. "You believe you're better than me, don't you?"

"No, suh," Junior replied.

"Smarter, been more places, slept with better-looking white women than I have. Been wrote up in northern magazines. A man like me don't get his name in the paper lessen it's in the obituary."

Junior pulled the spade out of the clay mound and began shoveling into the hole, keeping his bruised feet stationary, swiveling his back to throw each spadeful. Boss Posey drank from the bottle again, then removed a piece of waxpaper-wrapped chocolate cake and a slapjack from his lunch bucket. The slapjack was perhaps eight inches long, thin, mounted on a spring, lead-weighted and swollen at the tip, like the head on a snake. He rested it on his thigh and ate part of the cake, then put both the slapjack and the remnant of the cake back in the lunch bucket.

The sun dipped over the rim of the earth and the fields went dark and nightbirds began calling to one another in the woods across the bayou. At first Woodrow tried to close his eyes and sleep on his feet. Then, without asking permission, he sat down on the back side of the pile Junior was spading into the hole. But Boss Posey didn't seem to mind. He was drinking steadily from the bottle now, bent slightly forward in the chair, the cancer on his arms like small poisoned roses buried in his skin.

Off in the distance Woodrow heard the dry rumble of thunder and saw a tree of lightning splinter across the sky. Junior's movements with the shovel became slower and slower, then it slipped out of his hands and clattered down into the darkness.

"I had it, boss. You gonna shoot me, go 'head on and do it," he said. He stood erect, his face slick with sweat, his body glowing with stink, one eye swollen into a knot with a slit in it.

"I'm about to lose my job 'cause of you. My pension goes out the window with it. That's what you done, you black sonofabitch. Now, you fill that goddamn hole."

"Know what the problem is, boss?" Junior asked. "It ain't Miss Andrea. It ain't Mr. LeJeune, either. It's 'cause you ain't no different from us. You eat the same food, stack the same time, kiss the same pink ass the niggers do. Maybe it's time you wise up."

The first blow with the slapjack caught Junior across the temple, splitting the skin to the bone. Then Jackson Posey whipped him to the ground, just as though he were chopping on a piece of wood.

But Woodrow believed it was the first blow that killed Junior and that the others were visited upon the body of a dead man, because Junior made no sound as the slapjack whistled down on his head and neck and back, thudding to the ground on his knees, his eyes already rolled upward in his head.

And while his friend died Woodrow stood by impotently, his fists balled in front of him, a cry coming from his throat that sounded like a child's and not his own.

Jackson Posey's chest was heaving when he looked down at his work. He flung the slapjack aside. "Damn!" he said. He paced up and down, staring back at the camp, then at the lights burning in the LeJeune house. Woodrow was so frightened his teeth knocked together in the back of his mouth.

Posey steadied his foot against Junior's shoulder and tried to shove his body over the edge of the hole. But Junior's body fell sideways and Boss Posey couldn't move it with his foot. In fact, Woodrow could not believe how weak Posey was.

"Get a holt of his feet," Posey said.

"Suh?"

"Pick up his feet or join him. Which way you want it?"

Woodrow gathered up Junior's ankles while Boss Posey lifted his arms, and the two of them flung Woodrow's friend over the rim of the hole. The *thump* it made when it hit the bottom was a sound Woodrow would hear in his sleep the rest of his life.

"Go over there and set on the ground," Posey said.

Posey mounted the bulldozer and started the engine. With the lights off he lowered the blade and pushed the huge pile of clay into the hole, backing off it, packing it down, scraping it flat, until the hole was only a dimple in the landscape. When he cut the engine Woodrow could hear the first drops of rain pinging on the steel roof over the driver's seat.

"Junior transferred out of here tonight. Ain't none of this happened. That's right, ain't it, Woodrow?"

"If you say so, boss."

"There's a half inch of whiskey left in that bottle. You want it?"

"No, suh."

"Have a Camel," Posey said, and shook two loose from his pack. "Go ahead and take it. It's a new day tomorrow. Don't never forget that. Sun gonna be breakin' and a new day shakin'. That's what my daddy always used to say."

How'd you come by this little farm here?" I asked Woodrow.

"Mr. LeJeune sold it to me. Give me a good price wit'out no interest," he replied.

"To shut you up?"

"He sent a black man to me wit' the offer. Never saw Mr. LeJeune." Woodrow stared at me with his flat, sightless eyes that could have been large painted buttons sewn on his face. Lightning jumped in the clouds over the Gulf.

I slipped my business card between his fingers. "Let me know if I can do anything for you," I said.

His hand folded around the card. "Whatever happened to Mr. LeJeune's li'l girl, the one named T'eo?" he asked.

"Theodosha? She's around."

"My cousin, the maid for Mr. and Miz LeJeune? She always worried about that li'l girl. She said t'ings wasn't right in that house."

I asked him what he meant but he refused to explain.
"How long were you inside?" I said as I was leaving.
"Five years."
"What'd you go down for?"
"Fifty-t'ree-dol'ar bad check," he replied.

Chapter 18

As I drove back toward New Iberia a thunderstorm blew in from the Gulf and marched across the southern tip of Vermilion Parish, thrashing the sugarcane in the fields, the rain twisting in my headlights. I could not shake the tale told me by Woodrow Reed, nor the sense of needless death and cruelty and loss that it instilled in the listener. I turned on my radio and tried to find a station that was playing music, but my radio went dead, although it had been working fine earlier.

I tried to get Helen again on my cell phone, but I couldn't raise the wireless service and gave it up and tossed the cell phone on the seat. I passed flooded rice fields wrinkled with wind and lighted farmhouses that looked like snug islands inside the storm. Then I passed a billboard on a curve and my lights flashed across a woman standing by the side of the road.

She wore blue jeans and an unbuttoned tan raincoat that whipped back in the wind. Her hair was honey colored, tapered on her neck, her skin almost luminous in the glare of headlights. *Hey, G.I., give a girl a ride?* I thought I heard a voice say.

I braked the truck to the side of the road, my heart beating, and looked through the back window. The woman stood on the shoulder of the road, silhouetted against a light that shone on the face of the billboard. Don't buy into this, I told myself. It's not her. Your wife is dead and all the delusions and misery you inject into your life will not change that inalterable fact.

Then I put the truck in reverse and began backing toward the figure on the side of the road.

She glanced back over her shoulder once and began running. I accelerated faster, swerving on and off the pavement, until I was abreast of her. Through the rain-streaked glass her face stared at me, beaded with water, eyeshadow running down her cheeks, her mouth glossy with lipstick. I closed and opened my eyes, like a man coming out of darkness into light, her face forming and reforming in the rain.

I shoved open the passenger door and held up my badge holder. "Get in," I said.

She hesitated a moment, then sat down in the passenger seat and slammed the door behind her. She gave me a hard look in the glow of the dash panel. Her cheeks were pitted and heavily made up, her clothes reeking of cigarette smoke and booze. "Thanks for the ride. My old man threw me out," she said.

"Where do you want to go?" I asked.

"First bar we pass," she said. "For a minute you scared me. I had trouble with a couple of black guys last night. You stopped just 'cause you saw me in the rain?"

"I thought you were somebody else," I said.

She gave me a look. "There's a bar past the curve. Right by the motel," she said.

I put on my turn indicator and began to slow the truck. I knew the bar. It was a ramshackle, sullen place owned by a man who ran dog fights.

"I left my purse at the house. The sonofabitch I live with has probably drunk it up by now," she said.

I stopped in the parking lot and waited. She took a cigarette from her shirt pocket and lit it with a plastic butane lighter. She continued rubbing the striker wheel under her thumb. "Look, I can't drink in there for free. You want some action or not?" she said.

"Get out," I said.

"I can really pick them," she said. She stepped out into the storm and slammed the truck door as hard as she could.

Lesson? Chasing a nighttime mirage on a rain-swept highway has no happy ending for either the quick or the dead.

. . .

The one-car fatality at West Cote Blanche Bay seemed to lack any plausible explanation. The witness, an elderly Cajun hired to pick litter out of the ditches along the roadside, had seen an expensive, large car parked next to a compact in a grove of pine trees. Children had been lighting fireworks all evening, shooting Roman candles and rockets over the bay. Then he had heard firecrackers in the trees, just before the compact had driven away. When he looked again at the grove of pines, the large car started up and drove out onto a pier, snapping the supports on the guardrail into sticks, finally plunging off the end of the pier into the water.

Helen Soileau had arrived at the bay only a few minutes before me. She walked with me up a shell ramp and introduced me to the witness. As with most elderly Cajun men, his handshake was as light as air. "How many firecrackers did you hear?" I asked him.

"Two, maybe t'ree," he replied.

He was a tiny man, dressed in neat khakis, with cataracts and a supple face that resembled brown tallow. He seemed nervous and kept glancing over his shoulder at the bay and at the splintered guardrail on the pier and at the wrecker that so far had not been able to pull the sunken car off a submerged pipeline, all of it lit in the glare of searchlights mounted on a firetruck.

"Is anything wrong?" I asked.

"I seen a big man behind the wheel. Seen him go crashing right off the end of the pier there. I cain't swim, me. I keep t'inking maybe there was air inside the car. Maybe if I'd brung hep sooner—"

"You have no reason to feel bad about anything, sir. Who was in the compact?"

"Just somebody driving a li'l car. It was an old one. I ain't sure what kind."

"Was a man or woman driving?"

His shook his head, his face blank.

"What color was the car?" I asked.

"I just ain't paid it much mind, no."

"You see a license tag?" I asked.

"No, suh."

"The firecrackers you heard, those were in the pine trees? You're sure about that?" I said.

"No, suh, I ain't sure about none of it no more."

I patted him on the shoulder and walked down to the water's edge. The bay was black, dimpled with rain rings, and the tide was pushing small waves that glistened with gasoline up on the sand. Two scuba divers, both of them sheriff's deputies, had already been down on the wrecked car. They were sitting on the running board of the firetruck in their wetsuits, sharing a thermos of coffee.

"What's it look like down there?" I asked.

"The vehicle landed on its side. Driver's face is down in the silt. The ignition is on and the gearshift in 'Drive,'" one of them said. His name was Darbonne. He was unshaved and had curly black hair, his throat prickled with cold.

"Any chance air was trapped in there?" I asked.

"The front windows were down. The driver's arm is tangled up in the seat belt, like he couldn't find the release button. All that water probably hit him like a hammer," Darbonne said.

"The witness blames himself for not getting back with help sooner. Tell him about the air situation, will you?" I said.

Darbonne nodded and yawned. "When they drive off bridges or piers, they're drunks, nutcases, or suicides," he said. "If a guy in a Caddy ices himself, he should have the courtesy to do it without inconveniencing people who make twenty-five grand a year."

"Say again?"

"The whale who just offed himself. I wish he'd gone to a heated, indoor pool to do it," the driver said, then looked at my expression. "*What*, I just spit on the floor in church?"

A few minutes later the divers went down again to reset the hook on the Cadillac's frame so the car could be flipped over on its top and slid off the pipeline it partially rested on. Helen and I stood by the water's edge and watched. The moon had broken through a slit in the clouds, and far out on the horizon there were whitecaps that looked like tiny bird's wings.

"Castille LeJeune's lawyer called again. He's talking about a harassment suit against the department," she said.

"He'd like my job?"

"What did you find out down at Pecan Island?" she said, ignoring my question.

"Castille LeJeune had Junior Crudup killed. He was beaten to death by a prison guard, a guy named Jackson Posey," I replied.

She looked at the black surface of the bay and at the slickness of the wrecker cable as it extracted the submerged car from the water. Her face did not change expression. She wiped away a raindrop that had caught in her eyelash. "Where's Crudup's body?" she asked.

"Probably still buried on the LeJeune's property," I said.

"Get a search warrant," she said.

The wrecker man winched the Cadillac upside-down out of the shallows and slid it up on the bank, the front windows gushing with water and oil-blackened silt. The body of a huge man hung against the safety strap, his shoulders and neck pressed against the roof, his face twisted toward the open window so he appeared to be staring at a bizarre event taking place outside his automobile.

I squatted down to eye-level with him and shone a flashlight on his face and inside the rest of the car. There was a small entry hole in his neck, his cheek, and the side of his head. The wounds had bled out and had washed clean in the water and had started to pucker around the edges.

"Ever think anybody could sucker-drop Fat Sammy Figorelli?" Helen said behind me.

"No," I said. I reached inside the car and closed Sammy's eyes. The inverted weight of his massive buttocks and thighs had curved his spine so that his back and neck were compressed like a gargoyle's.

"Don't waste your sympathies, Streak. He was a pimp and a pusher and the world's a better place every time one of these shitbags gets stuffed into a hole," Helen said.

"I guess you're right," I said. But I could not help remembering the stories of a French Quarter fat kid who had spent years being the butt of people's jokes.

Helen stood up from the spot where she had crouched behind me. "Wrap it up here. At oh-eight-hundred tomorrow go to work on the warrant. It's time Castille LeJeune learned this is the United States," she said.

"You got it, Top," I said, referring to her old rank in the U.S. Army.

"Call me that again and I'll tear off your head and spit in it," she replied.

I think even Fat Sammy would have enjoyed that one.

We had the warrant by late Tuesday afternoon. Without announcement and with a balmy breeze at our backs and a sky the color of a ripe peach, two cruisers from the Iberia Sheriff's Department, three from St. Mary Parish, a front-end loader, and a bulldozer chain-boomed on a flatbed tractor-trailer rig all came down Castille Le Jeune's front drive, raking through the lone tunnel of oaks, right into the middle of an outdoor dinner party LeJeune was holding on his terrace.

Helen and I and a plainclothes from the St. Mary sheriff's office served the warrant on him in front of his guests, who included, among at least a dozen others, Theo and Merchie Flannigan. Le-Jeune tried to feign an amused dismay and the good cheer of the professional bon vivant, but Theo imposed no such restraints on herself.

She wore a low-cut white evening dress and a necklace of red stones around her throat. Her skin was flushed with either the challenge of the moment or the glass of bourbon and crushed ice with a sprig of mint she had been drinking. She placed her small fists on her hips, as a drill instructor might, and turned her face up into mine. "You're an idiot," she said.

"Excuse me, madam, but you need to sit down and stay out of this," Helen said.

"And you need to work on your sexual-identity problems before you lecture other people in their homes," Theo said.

Helen gazed through the trees at the bayou and the deserted shacks that had once housed prison inmates, her breasts hard-looking as softballs against her shirt. She reread the warrant to herself, seemingly indifferent to Theo's insult. Then she lifted her eyes into Theo's. "Repeat what you just said."

"You have no business here," Theo said.

"Where do you think the burial site is?" Helen said to me, ignoring Theo.

"On a line between here and what would have been the front gate of the prison camp. I'd put it pretty close to that pond inside the fenced area," I said.

LeJeune raised his hands. "Listen to me," he said. "I don't know anything about this man Junior Crudup or whatever his name is. My wife befriended the convicts who worked out their sentences on our farm. She was a kind, gentle, decent person. How in God's name can you accuse us of hiding the remains of a murdered man on our property?"

Helen walked out into the yard. "Take out that fence and start in a circle. Drain the pond if you have to," she said to the two heavy-equipment operators.

Helen went back to her cruiser and I began walking down the slope toward the old work camp. Inside the evening shade of the trees I could hear the conversation and tinkle of glasses resume among LeJeune's guests on the patio.

"Dave, stop," Theo said, catching my arm.

She'd just had her hair cut and it was thick and even and shiny on the whiteness of her shoulders. The bourbon and smell of ice and mint on her breath touched my face like the tracings of a kiss.

"Your father commissioned a murder," I said.

"You have it all backwards," she said.

"Then why are you afraid to go down to the pond?"

"For reasons you don't understand."

"You can tell the jury that at your father's trial."

"Why do you hate him so much?"

"Because he's a sonofabitch."

"I'll remember you said that to the day I die."

"Go back home, Theo. Your guests are waiting."

"I can't believe I slept with you. I want to peel my skin off."

Perhaps her response was justified, but at that moment I didn't care one way or another. Down below, the bulldozer and front-end loader were tearing apart a white-rail fence and a sloping green pasture, looking for the bones of a man who had been beaten to death so a cancer-ridden prison guard could keep his pension and a cuckolded husband his pride.

The heavy-equipment operators worked by gasoline-powered light until midnight, blading away the grass and topsoil, pushing it into water-beaded, black-green mounds. They came back at sunrise and started in again, scooping huge amounts of wet clay and feeder roots from the oak trees onto LeJeune's lawn, trenching a drainage into his fish pond, smashing his dock into kindling. By noon the entire landscape between the trees in his backyard and the cluster of cabins by the bayou was an ecological disaster, water oozing from the substrata, perch and catfish fighting for survival in small pools, a cow's ribs arching out of the clay like a woman's comb.

A half dozen uniformed deputies in rubber boots raked and probed for hours but found no sign of a human burial. By Wednesday afternoon the excavation area had become a giant, water-filled pit. Since the previous day I had slept three hours. My eyes stung, my jaws were like sandpaper, and a stale, clammy odor rose from my clothes. The heavy-equipment operators shut down their machines and waited. Helen shook her head and the operators climbed down and began packing up.

"We're in the Dumpster, bwana," Helen said.

"That body was here. He moved it," I said.

"Ride back with me. You look like a car wreck," she said.

"He's not going to get away with it. I'm going to fry that bastard."

"You probably will. Even if you have to take everybody down with you. You might give that some thought," she said.

I opened and closed my mouth and felt my ears popping, the horizon tilting slightly, a buzzing sound inside my head, as though my old companion the malarial mosquito was having its way with me again.

Helen cupped her hand around my upper arm and kneaded the muscles in it. "Come on, Loot, give a girl a lift," she said.

"What? What did you say?" I said.

She looked at me strangely, her eyes filled with a mixture of pity and sadness.

Not far away, just outside the little town of Jeanerette, Clete Purcel drove down a back road past three antebellum homes that were so stunning in appearance, the tree-shaded lots they sat on so perfect in arboreal and floral arrangement, they looked like Hollywood movie fabrications rather than homes that people of enormous wealth actually lived in. He turned at the green, embanked property corner of the last house in the row, crossed a steel bridge over the Teche, and passed, within fifty yards of the last antebellum home, a rural slum composed of rusted trailers, desiccated sheds, and junker cars that could have been replicated from a photograph taken in Bangladesh.

He removed a pair of binoculars from his glovebox and went inside a cafe from which his line of sight allowed him to see the trailer slum that spilled haphazardly to the edge of the bayou. It had not been a good day for Clete. Early that morning he had picked up a bail skip for Wee Willie Bimstine in Opelousas and was about to transport him back to New Orleans, when the skip began jerking against the D-ring anchored on the floor of the Caddy, his face twisted with visceral pain, threatening to soil himself and the convertible if he wasn't allowed to use the bathroom. Clete cuffed him to a pipe next to the toilet in a filling station and waited outside. In less than two minutes the skip managed to put seventy-five cents in a sexual-enhancement dispenser, smear his wrist with a desensitizing lubricant, slip the cuff, and escape out a window.

Score one for the meltdowns, Clete thought.

A half hour later a woman did a hit-and-run on his convertible in a church parking lot; the investigating traffic officer gave him a citation for an expired inspection sticker; and while Clete argued the situation a flock of robins lit in a tree above his car, the top of which was down, and defecated all over the seats and upholstery.

He drank coffee and focused his binoculars on a trailer that was broken in the center and had vinyl garbage bags taped across the windows. It was the home of the skip's one-time fall partner, an Angola parolee who had been down twice for sexual battery against children. There was no movement inside the trailer, but next door a woman in faded jeans, tennis shoes without socks, and peroxided hair that was waved on only one side walked down to the school-bus stop and waited for her child. Then she escorted the child, a boy of about eight, back home and closed the door behind her.

A moment later she reemerged with a tall, equestrian-looking man who had a hard, flat stomach and a purple birthmark that seeped from his hairline to the corner of his eye. They kissed on the mouth and the man put on a yellow hard hat and got into a waiting car driven by another man wearing an identical hard hat. The two men parked in front of the cafe and came in and sat down in the booth next to Clete's.

"Kid come home a little soon?" the driver of the car, a truncated, moon-faced man, said.

The man with the birthmark didn't reply but instead snapped his fingers repeatedly for the waitress's attention. After she took the order and went away, he said, "This guy Robicheaux is a walking hemorrhoid. You should see the old man's property. It looks like a bombing zone."

"Tell me about it," the other man replied. His blond hair was combed straight back from a receding hairline, and he kept leaning forward, reverentially, each time the other man spoke. But the man with the birthmark was silent now, not interested in whatever the blond man had intended to say. The blond man, who wore a pair of electrician's wire snips in a leather case on his belt, tried again. "His house was so dried out a popcorn fart could have set it on fire but he blames me for it. He tried to screw me with the Better Business Bureau and get my license pulled."

But the man with the birthmark, whom Clete had now connected with the name Will Guillot, only sipped his coffee and looked out the window at the bayou and the antebellum home on the far side of the steel bridge.

"You think he sent that doctor to your house?" the moon-faced man said.

"Probably."

"You're a mean machine, Will."

"Nope."

"The guy came at you with a sawed-off shotgun?"

"He thought he could go into a man's house and kick ass. He lost. End of story," Will Guillot said.

"*Pow!*" his friend said.

Both men became silent, eating slices of apple pie, drinking their coffee, picking their teeth. Clete went to the rest room, then waited for his check. The men in the other booth were talking about football now. Go home, he thought. You don't need any more bad luck today.

He looked out the window and saw the child of Will Guillot's girl-friend playing on a swing set, a cheap one that was probably bought at Wal-Mart. The skip's fall partner, the sex predator, pulled up next door, talked to the boy briefly, tousling his hair, then went inside his trailer.

Clete paid his check and started toward the door. He paused, thinking to himself, then reset his porkpie hat and walked back to Will Guillot's table. He grinned without speaking, his Hawaiian shirt partially unbuttoned on his chest, his eyes flicking sideways as though he did not know how to introduce himself.

"Help you?" Guillot said.

"You guys were in the Crotch?" Clete said.

"The *what*?" the blond man said.

"I heard you say something about a 'mean machine,' so I thought you were talking about Mother Green's Mean Machine. See, jarheads call—"

"Yeah, I know all about that. What can I do for you?" Guillot said.

Clete cleaned an ear with one finger, looking sideways again as he did it, his face filling with thought. "I think I know who you are," he said.

"You do?" Guillot said.

"You popped a doctor from Loreauville in your driveway. Guy was some kind of weirded-out Vietnam vet, right? That's some kind of irony, huh? Guy probably had a thousand AK rounds shot at him, then loses his Kool-Aid and gets smoked in the suburbs."

Guillot looked across the table at his friend and tapped his finger-nail on the cover of his wristwatch. The two men started to get up.

"Whoa," Clete said.

"Whoa, *what*?" Guillot said.

"The lady up there in the trailer, the one you're banging? She's got a little boy. The guy next door happens to be a sex predator. So while you're getting your twanger taken care of, the freak who was just pat-ting her kid on the head is figuring out ways to sodomize him. My suggestion is you take your mind off your dick long enough to move the lady and her son out of that shithole before the kid's life is ruined. Can you relate to that?"

"You've got some fucking nerve," Guillot said.

The owner of the cafe had come from behind the counter and was standing behind Clete now, resolute, his feet planted, his thumb raised in the air.

"Out," he said.

"No problem," Clete said. He pulled two one-dollar bills from a brass money clip and dropped them on his table.

But outside Clete could not give it up, standing by his car door, flipping his keys back and forth, his face growing darker. He watched Will Guillot and the electrical subcontractor with him get in their car. "Hold on a minute," he said.

"Get a life, queer bait," Will Guillot said from the passenger win-dow as his car rolled past Clete.

Clete watched the two men cross the steel bridge over the Teche and turn down the tree-shaded back road that led past the row of an-tebellum homes. In his mind's eye he saw himself running them off the road, strolling back to their car, his blackjack in his side pocket, moving the situation on up to the full-tilt boogie. Why not? he thought. The day couldn't get any worse than it was already.

He got into his Caddy, slammed the door, and turned the ignition. He heard a dry, clicking sound, then nothing. The battery was as dead as a butcher block.

It took an hour for a filling station a half block away to send a truck that gave him a quick-start. He sat behind the wheel, revving the en-gine to charge the battery, oil smoke pouring from under the frame, bird-shit smears on his clothes, all immediate hope of squaring the beef with Will Guillot gone.

He looked through the windshield at the trailer slum by the bayou and the parolee who was now drinking a can of beer on his steps and talking to the little boy from next door.

Clete retrieved a pair of leather work gloves from under the seat and put them in his pocket, then dropped the Caddy into low gear and rolled into the trailer slum, gravel and oyster shells ticking softly under his tires.

"You Bobby Joe Fontenot?" he said.

The man on the steps was relaxed, smoking a cigarette with his beer, barefoot in the sunshine, his arms flecked with blue tattoos done by an needle improvised from the guts of a ballpoint pen. He wore imitation black leather pants and a tie-dyed strap undershirt, his black hair scalped on the sides and braided into a matador's pigtail in back.

"I'm gonna take a guess. Casting director from, what's that TV show called, *Survivor*?" he said, squinting against the sunlight.

Clete grinned and got out of the Caddy, opening his badge holder briefly. "Looking for your friend who jumped his bond with Wee Willie Bimstine and Nig Rosewater," he said. "Slipped his cuffs this morning and left me with shit on my nose."

"Haven't seen him."

"Mind if I look inside?"

"Get yourself a beer. It's in the icebox."

"Thanks," Clete said, and gave him the thumbs-up sign.

Clete stepped inside. The garbage can in the small kitchen was overflowing, the counters covered with pizza and fried-chicken cartons. A television set was playing without sound, the VCR under it lighted, a cassette pushed halfway into the loading slot. Clete shoved the cassette all the way into the unit with his thumb and waited for the video image to transfer to the screen. Then he clicked off the set and the figures on the screen shrank to a small dot. He slipped on his work gloves and called through the screen door: "Did you know you have a gas leak in your stove?"

Bobby Joe stepped inside the trailer, sniffing at the air. Clete drove his fist into Fontenot's stomach, burying it to the wrist, so deep he actually felt bone. Then he kicked the wood door shut, flung him headlong into a wall, and pulled a shelf filled with carnival midway ceramics down on top of him. He ripped the cassette from the VCR and bounced it off Bobby Joe's face, then rooted in the refrigerator's freezer compartment and pulled out a box of Popsicles and threw them in Bobby Joe's face, too.

"You get the kids in here with cartoons and ice cream?" he said.

Bobby Joe tried to raise himself up against the wall, spittle running from the corner of his mouth. "I'm in treatment. Ask my P.O.," he said hoarsely.

Clete opened and closed his huge hands, breathing hard, his cheeks pooled with color. He lifted Bobby Joe by his shirt and belt and threw him into the narrow bathroom at the back of the trailer. Bobby Joe grabbed the side of the lavatory and tried to raise himself up again, his face bewildered.

"What did your P.O. tell you about putting your hands on little kids, asshole?" Clete said.

"I ain't put—"

Clete locked one hand on the back of Bobby Joe's neck and drove his head down on the toilet bowl, smashing his mouth against the rim, plunging his head into the water, scouring the bottom of the bowl with his face. It should have been enough but he was beyond controlling it now or even trying. He slammed the toilet seat down on Bobby Joe's neck and head, then grabbed the top of the shower stall and mounted the toilet, crushing the seat down on Bobby Joe's head, tap dancing on it like an elephant on hallucinogens while Bobby Joe's legs thrashed on the linoleum.

Outside he heard children playing and through the top of the window he saw a little girl chasing after a Frisbee that sailed above her head, and like a man descending from an electrical storm high up on a mountain he stepped back down on the floor and pulled Bobby Joe from the toilet bowl, dripping with water and blood.

He tossed a towel in Bobby Joe's face and leaned back against the wall, out of breath, his fists still knotting. "I'm going to make regular checks on the kid next door," he said. "If I find out you've been near him, you'll wish you were a bar of soap back in 'Gola. The same goes if you dime me. Maybe you think you got a bad deal here today, but pervs don't get slack. You hearing me on this?"

"You fat fuck," Bobby Joe said, pressing the towel to the blood that ran off his chin, looking at it in disbelief, his words muffled, his mouth still trembling. "You like family values? That kid's mother used to be an army whore over by Folk Polk. I'm gonna find out your name. If I ever offend with a kid again, I'm gonna say it each time I poke him. How's that, *asshole*?"

When Clete got back to the motor court, he stayed under the shower until the hot water tank went empty, burned his clothes in a barbecue pit, drank a quart of whiskey-laced eggnog, and still could not feel clean.

Chapter 19

Father Jimmie Dolan had done six months federal time for demonstrating at the School of the Americas and probably considered himself jailwise. But in reality, like all people who are intrinsically decent, he was incapable of the cynicism that passes for prison-acquired wisdom.

On Thursday morning he was in Franklin, in black suit and Roman collar, collecting signatures on his petition to ban the sale of mixed drinks from drive-by windows. During three hours of approaching people in front of strip malls and grocery stores, he had amassed a total of six signatures, one from a retarded man, and two from people who signed their names with an *X*.

He bought a take-out lunch from a McDonald's and ate it in his car under the trees in a small park, then fell asleep. The day was unseasonably warm, the live oaks flickering with wind, but he dreamed of snowmelt in the Cumberland Mountains, the bright air of early spring, tea-colored streams that leached out of limestone cliffs, dogwood blooming purple and white on a hillside. When he awoke, children were running by the front of his car, kicking a soccer ball in the leaves, the spangled sunlight racing across their bodies, but somehow there was a continuity between the beauty of the Appalachian spring in Jimmie's dream and the joy of the children at play.

He got out of his car and began walking toward the public rest room. He had no reason to pay attention to a nervous, agitated plainclothes detective by the name of Dale Louviere, who was parked in a Ford by the swing sets, the same detective who had investigated the killing of Dr. Parks by Will Guillot and called it an open-and-shut case of self-defense.

Nor did Father Jimmie pay attention to a man known as Cash Money Mouton standing by the lavatory inside the rest room.

Cash Money's last name was French but he was actually a peckerwood product of north Louisiana. He used to sell fire and accident and term life insurance from door to door in black and poor-white neighborhoods, and was infamous for both his sweaty enthusiasm and his carnival sales rhetoric. He would pull clutches of papers and brochures from a vinyl briefcase, his face bursting with sincerity, tapping his seated listener, usually the man of the house, on the kneecap, saying, "You run your lawnmower over your foot and chop your toes off, I'll give you twelve-hunnerd dollars, cash money, boy. You stick your hand in your skill saw, I'll pay you five-hunnerd dollars, that's cash money, for every finger you cut off. Splash muriatic acid in your eyes and go blind, I'm talking five-thousand bananas, cash money, boy."

Then Cash Money Mouton's uncle became police chief and Cash Money began a new career.

Father Jimmie stood at the urinal and relieved himself. He could feel the man at the lavatory staring at the side of his face. He started to look at him, then thought better of it and kept his eyes straight ahead. But when he tried to get to the lavatory the man known as Cash Money stood in his way.

"Excuse me," Father Jimmie said.

But Cash Money did not move. He wore sideburns, a Tabasco tie, an American flag in his coat lapel. He smelled of deodorant, hair tonic, and fear. There was almost an iridescent shine on his skin.

"Is there some difficulty here that I don't quite grasp?" Father Jimmie asked.

"Repeat that?" Cash Money said.

"Could I be of some assistance to you?"

"That's it," Cash Money said.

He stepped into the rest room doorway and waved at the man in the Ford automobile. Father Jimmie rinsed his hands, shook them off, and tried to walk around him.

"You're not going anywhere, buddy boy," Cash Money said.

"Push me again and we're both going to regret the next couple of minutes," Father Jimmie said.

But Cash Money was looking over his shoulder now and not at Father Jimmie. "He just threatened me," he said to the man approaching the rest room.

"What else did he do?" the plainclothes detective named Dale Louviere said. Even in the open air a gray fog of nicotine and ash seemed to enclose his body. Clusters of veins, like tiny pieces of green string, pulsed in his temples.

"He said he wanted to help me. He was fooling with his fly when he said it," Cash Money said.

"You're a liar," Father Jimmie said.

"We saw you watching those kids, Father," Louviere said.

"How would you like to have your teeth knocked down your throat?" Father Jimmie said.

"Hook him up," Louviere said.

"I ain't putting my hands on him," Cash Money said. His eyes jumped sideways when Father Jimmie looked him directly in the face.

At the police station Father Jimmie was charged with sexual solicitation and threatening a police officer and locked in an empty holding cell that was in full view of anyone, male or female, in the booking area. He made a pillow out of his coat, pulled off his collar, and lay down on a wood bench. He stared up at the graffiti and scratched drawings of genitalia that covered almost all the painted surfaces in the cell, and remembered the admonition of the blues singer Lazy Lester: "Don't ever write yo' name on the jailhouse wall."

He could see Louviere punching in numbers on a phone, calling up first the local newspaper, then a television station in Lafayette and one in Baton Rouge, the Associated Press in New Orleans, and finally the diocese.

Louviere walked to the cell door. "Want your phone call now?" he asked.

"I'd like to ask you a question first," Father Jimmie replied.

Louviere unlocked the door and pulled it open. "If you're wondering whether I'm a Catholic, yeah, I am. And it's perverts like you who give the church a bad name," he said.

"Call yourself whatever you wish, but you're not a Catholic. The real issue is whose pad are you on. Who's paying you to do this to other people, sir? What price have you gotten for your soul?" Father Jimmie said.

I was at the office when Father Jimmie called.

"How much is your bond?" I said.

"I haven't been arraigned yet," he replied.

"Why'd you have to take your petition into St. Mary Parish?"

"What's wrong with St. Mary Parish?"

"It's a fiefdom. They think it's the year 1300 down there."

I heard him laugh. "A fiefdom? With serfs in iron collars and that sort of thing? That's an interesting observation. I see," he said.

No, you don't, Jimmie, I thought. But martyrs and saints fly low with the angels, colliding with telephone poles and the sides of buildings, and consider harm's way their natural environment. Who was I to contend with them?

Max Coll didn't like gambling; he loved it and all the adrenaline rush and glittering ambiance that went with it, as passionately as a man could love a woman or a religion. All men had a vice, his father used to say. It was recognition of our moral frailty that allowed us to retain our humanity, he said. The man who wasn't tempted by drink or women or betting the ponies could easily set himself on a level above Christ, and hence become guilty of the most pernicious of the seven deadly sins, namely arrogance and pride.

Max had always remembered his father's words. Drink robbed a man of his intelligence and his organs; women gave a man satiation for only a little while, and memory of it immediately rekindled lust for and dependence on more of the same.

But gambling gave a man control, allowed him to choose his battleground and make use of his knowledge about both people and mathematics. The losses were only monetary ones, and since gambling was never about money, what difference did the loss make, particularly for a single fellow whose occupation was a bloody affair that should allow for a sybaritic excursion once in a while?

He was discriminating in the games he played. The slots, video poker, and electronic keno were created for natural-born losers. Jai alai was fun and fast, but what reasonable person would bet on players who all came from the same part of Spain and were related to one another? With the ponies you could dope out the morning line, study the track conditions and the animals in the paddock, and have a fair chance at the windows. Craps was for showboats, roulette for Côte d'Azur faggots, and dog tracks everywhere strictly for the dogs.

Not to say he didn't bet ball games, boxing matches, and national elections. In fact, Max once bet a window washer on the thirty-first floor of a Chicago hotel that he could climb out on the sill and clean the window faster than the professional washer. He not only won the wager, he enjoyed the experience so much he washed four more windows out of goodwill.

But the game that got Max in trouble was blackjack, the one game that gave the casino player a running chance at beating the house. Max's memory bank was almost like a computer's, and even when going up against a houseman dealing out of a five-deck shoe, Max's ability to count cards and to successfully stay put or risk another hit was uncanny.

Max's weakness at the blackjack table was his inability to put principles ahead of personalities. He didn't resent losing to a machine or to corrupt jai alai players wanting to keep their family members out of the tomato patch. Max did not like to lose to individuals, particularly stolid and dispassionate people who were paid by the hour and could not wait to get off work. To count cards until his brain was bleeding, then have a joyless clod turn up a blackjack on him out of sheer luck made the scalp recede on his skull.

He would retaliate by playing multiple hands, progressively increasing his bets, doubling up on splits, until he was broke, exhausted, and depressed, staring out the window at the ragged edges of dawn in

Vegas or Reno or Atlantic City, wondering if he could get the casino manager to open a credit line for him.

Max depressed was Max out of control. He would telephone sports books all over the country and lay down fifty thousand dollars in bets without blinking an eye. Then he would dress in a pair of pressed pink pajamas and lie spread-eagled on his back in the center of his hotel bed, the world spinning around him, his heartbeat decreasing, a strange serenity washing through him, as though he had descended to the bottom of a vortex and was no longer at its mercy or required to control it.

Usually his sports-book binges were harmless and his wins canceled out his losses. But contrary to all his wisdom he went in heavy on an insider tip at the jai alai fronton in Dania and took a bath for a hundred large he couldn't pay. Not only was the sports book in Miami unsympathetic with Max's financial situation, they sold his debt to shylocks who informed him the vig was four thousand a week, none of which applied to the principle.

Or he could take out a Catholic priest.

So he had come to Louisiana on a gray, rain-swept, cold day, trudging through flooded streets floating with garbage, himself no different in aspect than a poor sod on his way to work in the peat bogs. But there had been an upside to it all. He'd found out he didn't have it in him to shoot a priest, which meant perhaps part of his soul was still intact. Secondly, he had discovered a new identity and gambling ambiance.

Wearing Father Dolan's black suit and rabat and collar, he had entered a bingo parlor on an Indian reservation in south-central Louisiana and had suddenly found himself a celebrity. People smiled at him, shook his hand, offered him their chairs at the tables, patted him affectionately, brought him beer and sandwiches from the cafe. He began to feel like a mascot being trundled from hand to hand by five hundred people. In fact, he was pinched and pulled and squeezed so many times and places he couldn't concentrate on his bingo board and finally gave it up.

Then he was asked to stand on the stage and call out the bingo numbers. Why not? he thought. It was a grand evening. The weather had turned balmy again; palm trees strung with colored lights were rustling in the breeze outside the windows; the faces of the people around him were warm and filled with goodwill. Maybe his clerical role was a bit cosmetic, but it was still a fine way to be.

Then at 10:00 P.M. he went into the bar and ordered a cup of coffee and sat down to watch the nightly news.

The lead story was the arrest of one Father James Dolan, charged with sexual solicitation in a public rest room that was located close by a children's playground.

The arresting officer, Dale Louviere, was interviewed on camera. "We had this area under surveillance because of previous complaints," he said.

"Regarding the children?" the reporter asked.

"Yes, that's exactly correct," Louviere replied.

"Regarding this particular suspect?" the reporter asked.

"I'm not at liberty to say that. We're currently involved in a deep background investigation," Louviere replied.

If I ever saw a bull carrying around its own china shop, Max thought. Oh well, it was the good father's cross to bear, not Max's. Maybe Father Dolan would have a little more empathy for professional criminals now that he'd gotten himself jammed up by coppers on a pad, Max told himself.

He finished his coffee and went back to the bingo game. But the fun was gone and the clothes on his body suddenly felt foreign on his skin, superheated, sticky, smelling of the priest.

He found himself biting his knuckle, oblivious to the stares around him. What was it that bothered him? The priest was a hardhead, determined to see himself buggered with a posthole digger. Max had nothing to do with it, no obligations to him.

Wrong, he thought, lowering his eyes, staring into his lap.

He had set out to murder an innocent, decent man, something he had prided himself on never having done. In addition, the priest had bested him at every turn; that thought didn't go down well, either. In fact, all of Max's thoughts were like thongs on a flagrum whipping down on his head.

It was depressing.

He walked outside into the wind and the sweep of stars overhead and the glow of Christmas lights strung around palm trees and started up his rental Honda. He removed a .45 automatic wrapped in an oily cloth from under the seat and set it beside him. As he drove down the two-lane road toward the interstate, he rested his right hand on the .45 and felt his heart rate decrease and his breath grow quiet in his chest.

Then he looked up through the windshield at the stars and for the first time in years found himself addressing an ancient deity with whom he had once had a relationship.

Sir, if you're going to drop problems of conscience on a man like me at this time in his career, he prayed, *would you mind doing so in a gentler manner so I don't have to feel I'm being crunched inside the iron maiden? I would very much appreciate it. Thank you. Amen.*

It rained the next morning and Jimmie Dolan was still in jail, waiting to be arraigned at 11:00 A.M. I had just sat down at my desk when I saw an unmarked vehicle of the kind used by N.O.P.D. pull to the curb and Clotile Arceneaux, wearing Levis, a knit sweater, and blue-jean jacket, get out and run through the rain to the courthouse entrance, her hand raised in front of her brow.

She came into my office, out of breath, her denim jacket streaked with rainwater. She sat down without being invited and said, "Wow! You're a hard man to catch!"

"I don't follow you," I said.

"I left three messages yesterday afternoon," she said.

"I was in Franklin. Father Dolan is in jail," I replied.

"Yeah, I know all about it. Guy really walks into wrecking balls, doesn't he? Look, what have you got on the death of Sammy Figorelli?"

"Nothing."

"Nothing?"

"He was killed with a .22. He probably knew the shooter. That's about it," I said.

I could see her anger at losing months of work rekindling itself in her face. She bit a thumbnail and looked at the rain hitting on the window, then looked back at me. "I came here for another reason as well. In fact, I'm off work today," she said.

"What is it?"

"You already have breakfast?" she said.

"No," I lied.

"It's on me," she said.

"Your accent seems to come and go."

"See, I knew you were a smart man." She smiled, her mouth pressed into a small flower.

We got a take-out order at Victor's Cafeteria on Main and drove across the bayou to a giant crab-boil pavilion next to an exhibition hall where, believe it or not, Harry James, Buddy Rich, Willie Smith, and Duke Ellington's arranger, Juan Tizol, performed during the 1950s. The camellias along the bayou were in bloom and looked like red paper flowers inside the grayness of the day, and a tug was moving a huge iron barge loaded with dredged mud through the drawbridge up by Burke Street.

"So what's the haps?" I said.

"I came down on you pretty hard when you and Purcel scared Fat Sammy out of town," she replied.

"Your feelings were understandable."

There was a fried-egg-and-ham sandwich on French bread in her Styrofoam container but she hadn't touched it. "I talked to Purcel. He told me about your wife's death," she said.

I raised my chin to straighten my collar and looked at the tug moving the barge down the bayou.

"So what I'm saying is—"

"Got it. You don't need to explain."

"How about shutting up a minute? My husband was killed in Iraq in '91. He was in a tank. The army said he died instantly but I don't believe them," she said.

"I'm sorry."

"For a long time I thought I saw him at a football game or in a bar or in a crowd at a department store. That ever happen to you?"

"No."

"You're lucky. What I'm saying, Robicheaux, is I think you're a good cop and you don't need another cop yelling at you." She picked up her sandwich and took a bite out of it. I heard the tug blowing its whistle at the next drawbridge.

"It's Friday. You want to hang around town, maybe catch dinner and go to a movie?" I said.

"What's playing?" she asked.

"Really hadn't checked it out."

"Father Dolan's being arraigned at eleven," she said.

"I thought you'd cut loose of Father Jimmie's problems."

"A girl's got to do something for kicks," she said, and watched me over the top of her cup while she drank her coffee.

Dale Louviere liked being a city police officer, especially since he had been promoted to plainclothes and given his own office, a travel account, and membership in two civic clubs. The pay was nothing to brag about, but good things happened if a man did his job and accorded people respect and made sure he was available to serve in whatever capacity he was needed.

Anything wrong with that? he asked himself.

He lived a bachelor's life in a freshly painted bungalow out in the country, enclosed by sugarcane fields, cedar trees, flower beds and vegetable gardens tended by a trusty from the parish stockade. The radical priest's accusation that he was on a pad still rankled him. Dale Louviere never accepted a bribe from anyone; he didn't have to. He took care of his own side of the street and the other things took care of themselves. A mortgage or car loan was approved upon application; his drinks were put on a tab at local bars but he was not expected to ever pay the tab; a land developer gave him forty-yard-line tickets to LSU's home games whenever he wanted them; and at Christmastime cellophane-wrapped baskets of candy, fruit, and wine were delivered to his door.

The people who owned the sugar mills, drilled the oil wells, and governed the parish's affairs paid most of the taxes, didn't they? They gave other people jobs. The parish would be a giant rural slum without them. So a civil servant had to pay attention to the needs of rich people who could locate elsewhere anytime they chose.

Anything wrong with that?

Early the same morning Father Jimmie Dolan was to be arraigned, Dale Louviere rose at first light, put on his warm-up suit, and drank coffee and smoked a cigarette at the kitchen table, waiting for the chill to go out of the room. Through the front window he saw a Honda pass on the state road, then return, going in the opposite direction.

He washed his cup and saucer in the sink, put his spare set of house and car keys around his neck on a braided lanyard, and began his early-morning aerobic walk down the state road. Two hundred yards from his bungalow he crossed a wood bridge over a coulee and entered a long, cleared slash between two unharvested cane fields. The rain had quit temporarily, but fog hung like smoke in the cane and the thatch under his feet was sodden and mud coated, squishing each time he took a step, soaking the bottoms of his sweat pants.

One of his shoes went down ankle-deep in water. Bad day for aerobics, he thought.

He heard a car stop on the road. When he looked behind him he saw the Honda again, and a priest with a map spread across his steering wheel, rolling down his window now, his face expressing his obvious need for directions. But secretly Dale Louviere neither liked nor trusted the clergy, and off the clock he gave them no time. He pretended to tie his shoe until he heard the sound of the Honda's engine thinning in the distance.

It started to sprinkle again and Dale Louviere headed home, walking fast along the edge of the road, through ground fog that welled out of the ditches, his arms pumping the way he had learned in an aerobics class. He wondered if he would ever successfully quit smoking. He had tried many times, but within three days he would be so irritable and agitated his colleagues would toss cigarettes on his desk blotter by way of suggestion. Now the best he could do was pump the smoke out of his lungs and the nicotine out of his blood with a hard, early-morning walk that left his head spinning and his nervous system screaming for another cigarette.

Fortunately he had stuffed a pack in his jacket pocket. Just as he fished one out he saw the Honda coming in his direction again. The driver pulled alongside Dale Louviere and rolled down the window with the electric motor. He wore a golfer's cap pulled down on one eye, and had a tight face and small ears, like a fighter who had spent too many years in the ring. A road map was crumpled on the dashboard. His black suit and rabat were dry, his shoulders narrow, his hands round and pink on the steering wheel.

"Could you be directing me back to Highway 90, sir?" the priest said.

"Go to the four corners and turn left," Louviere said.

The priest screwed his head about, his eyebrows raised into half-moons. "That simple? I must have made a complete circle. I think the bishop served too much of the grog last night."

But instead of driving away he started fiddling with his map, running his finger along a line that marked Highway 90, peering down the road, then through the back window again. Dale Louviere thought he heard a knocking sound in the trunk.

"What's that?" he asked.

The priest clucked his tongue. "I'm afraid I ran over a dog. I'm taking him to a veterinary if I can find one," he said. "Turn at the crossroads, you say?"

"Correct. You can't get lost. Got it now?" Louviere said impatiently. He lit a cigarette and drew the smoke lovingly into his lungs.

"I don't see that on this map," the priest said.

"Look, it's not that hard. You see the state road here—" He held his cigarette to one side and leaned in the window.

That was as far as he got. The priest grabbed the lanyard around Louviere's neck and rolled up the window on his throat, trapping his head at the top of the glass like a man caught in an inverted guillotine.

He pressed down on the accelerator and drove his car down the road and into Louviere's driveway, while Louviere held onto the door handle and tried to extend his body like a crane's to keep from being decapitated.

"Be a good fellow and toggle along as best you can. We'll have you safe and snug in your digs before you know it," the priest said. "Oops, a little bump there. Hang on."

Dale Louviere felt his head being torn loose from his torso as he tripped over his feet, fighting to find purchase. The Honda moved past the side of his house, his gardens and flower beds and across the thin, wintergreen stretch of grass that comprised his backyard, into a paintless cypress barn left over from an earlier time.

The priest lowered the window glass and Dale Louviere fell backward into a smell of rotted straw, hard-packed, damp earth, and horse manure that powdered into dust. The priest cut the engine on the car and got out, a .45 automatic hanging from his right hand. "I have nothing against coppers. Except those who are no better than me and pretend otherwise. On which side of the line would a fellow like you fall, sir?" he said.

Again Dale Louviere heard a kicking sound in the Honda's trunk but could not think of anything except the violent pounding in his own chest.

At 10:55 A.M., while Father Jimmie Dolan sat in a St. Mary Parish courtroom, cuffed to a wrist chain with a collection of drunks, pipeheads, prostitutes, and wife batterers, the prosecutor's office received a call from Dale Louviere. He indicated he was resigning his job and, for personal reasons, moving to an undisclosed city out of state. He also said there was no substance to the charges against Father James Dolan and that his colleague, Cash Money Mouton, who had made the arrest in the public rest room, would confirm the same, provided he could be found.

Clotile Arceneaux, Father Jimmie, and I walked out the front door of the courthouse together. The rain had stopped and the town looked washed and clean, the trees green against the grayness of the day, the ebb and flow of the traffic on a wet street somehow an indicator of the world's normalcy.

"What happened in there?" Father Jimmie said.

"I wouldn't worry about it," I said.

"Max Coll is behind this, isn't he?" he said.

"Who cares? Those guys deserve anything that happens to them," I said.

"I thought New Orleans was tough. Y'all have death squads over here?" Clotile said.

I started to make a flippant reply, but saw the troubled expression on Father Jimmie's face. "I have to get my car from the pound," he said.

"We'll see you at the house. Let it slide, Jimmie," I said.

"One of those men may be dead," he replied.

He walked down the street, his black suit rumpled and stained from sleeping overnight on a cement jailhouse floor.

"Your friend isn't easily consoled, is he?" Clotile said.

"Ever hear about the Jewish legend of the thirteen just men who suffer for the rest of us?"

"No. What's the point?"

"Some people have to do life in the Garden of Gethsemane," I said.

She picked up my left hand and looked at it, her fingers cool on my skin. "This is where those greaseballs put the pliers to you?" she said.

"Yes."

She patted the top of my hand and released it. "Take care of your own ass for a change," she said.

Chapter 20

Father Jimmie had not been back at my house ten minutes when the phone rang in the kitchen. He picked it up but did not speak, his breath audible in the silence.

"Ah, you're a clairvoyant as well as a spiritual man," the voice on the other end said.

"Leave me alone. Please," Father Jimmie said.

"I got you, didn't I?"

"What do you mean?"

"Oh, you *know* what I mean, sir. It took a bastard like me with blood on his hands to get you out of the slams. Now it's you who owe me."

"What did you do with those men?"

"They're both alive and probably enjoying a cool drink in a warm climate by now. I think one of them mentioned Ecuador. Have to say, though, I was tempted to release them from their earthly bonds."

Father Jimmie sat down in a chair and tried to think. "Perhaps you mean well, but you cannot use violence to solve either your problems or mine," he said.

"What do you know of violence, sir? What do you fucking know of it?"

"You're full of hatred, Max. Get it out of your life. You injure yourself with it more than others."

"If I came into your confessional, would you give me absolution?"

"Yes."

"There are a couple more house calls I'd like to make."

"You don't negotiate the terms of forgiveness. . . . Max? Did you hear me?"

But Max Coll had hung up. Father Jimmie leaned his head down on his hand, the stink of the jail still on his clothes, Snuggs the cat pacing back and forth on the table, his tail dragging across Father Jimmie's face. He felt more tired than he had ever been in his life, vain and used up, now sullied by the accusation of molester, even though it was a lie.

He knew the rumor would always follow him, regardless of where he went or what he did. A wave of revulsion and anger washed through him and made him clench his fists. Is this what all the years in the seminary, the struggles with celibacy and bigots and dictatorial and obtuse superiors had been about? To end up with his name and life's work soiled by an accusation that made his skin crawl?

Why didn't he quit running a game on himself? He posed as the altruist, but other people constantly had to get him out of trouble. If he had wanted to be a true missionary and take real risks, why hadn't he joined the Maryknolls? He disdained the role of the traditional priest, but in his self-imposed piety he had become little more than a noisy gadfly dedicated to causes Carrie Nation might have supported.

He had just lectured a tormented man on his violence, although he, Jimmie Dolan, had just profited from it, and if truth be known he was glad he was on the street and perhaps secretly glad his false accusers had gotten their just deserts.

Better to marry than to burn, St. Paul had said. Better to be a bourbon priest or a diocesan sycophant than a self-canonized fool, Father Jimmie thought.

"What do you think, Snuggs?" he said.

Snuggs answered by nudging his head into Father Jimmie's chin.

Father Jimmie went into the bedroom, flung his clothes in the corner, and got under the shower. The water coughed in the pipes, then seemed to whisper the word *hypocrite* in his ear.

The South has changed dramatically since the civil rights legislation of the 1960s. Anyone who says otherwise has either not been there or wishes to keep old wounds green and tender as part of a personal agenda. And nowhere has the change been more visible than in the once recalcitrant states of the Deep South.

But that evening, when I took Clotile Arceneaux to supper on East Main, I tried to convince myself otherwise. I told myself the furtive glances at our table, the awkwardness of friends who felt they should stop by and say hello, were expressions of narrowness and latent racism to be expected in our culture.

The truth was no one took exception to Clotile's race. But they did take exception to my being out with another woman in less than a year of Bootsie's death.

It had turned cold again when we left the restaurant. Stars were spread across the sky, the horizon flaring with stubble fires, smoke boiling out of the electric lights at the sugar mills.

"You a little uncomfortable in there about something?" Clotile asked.

"Not me," I replied.

She opened the door to my pickup by herself and got in and closed it behind her, although I had tried to help her in. "You're really out of the past, aren't you?" she said.

"Probably," I said.

She smiled and didn't say anything. We drove toward the draw-bridge and the theater complex on the other side of Bayou Teche. She had checked in to a motel out by the four-lane that afternoon.

We crossed the bayou and turned in to the theater parking lot. It was filled with teenagers, long lines of them extending out from the ticket windows.

"Friday night is a bad night for the movies here," I said.

"We don't need to go," she said, looking straight ahead.

I turned around in the parking lot, recrossed the bayou, and drove up East Main, without destination. The street seemed strangely empty, the stars shut out by the canopy of oaks overhead, my rented shotgun house dark and blown with unraked leaves. I hesitated, then pulled into my driveway and cut the engine. The ground fog in the trees and bamboo glistened in the lights from City Park across the bayou.

"Where's Father Dolan?" she asked.

"Staying with friends in Lafayette."

"You have a lot of regrets in your life, Robicheaux?" she said.

"All drunks do," I replied.

"How do you deal with them?"

"I don't labor over them anymore."

She still looked straight ahead. "I don't want to be a regret in somebody's life," she said.

"Want to meet my cat?" I said.

And that's what we did. I introduced her to Snuggs; then we ate ice cream in the kitchen and I drove her to her motel.

Afterward I went to the cemetery in St. Martinville and sat on the steel bench by Bootsie's tomb and watched the moon rise over the old French church on the bayou.

That night I dreamed I was in New Orleans in an earlier era, riding on a streetcar out to Elysian Fields. The streets were dark, the palm fronds on the neutral ground yellow with blight. No one else was on the car except the motorman. When he turned and looked back at me his eyes were empty sockets, the skin on his face dried and shrunken into little more than gauze on his skull.

Oftentimes police cases are not solved. They simply unravel, by chance and accident. With good luck there will even be an appreciable degree of justice involved, although it often originates from an expected source.

Early the next morning, Saturday, my lawn was white with frost and the bamboo on the side of the house was stiff and hard and rattled like broomsticks in the wind. I put on my sweat suit, ran three miles through City Park, then showered and drove down to Clete's cottage in the motor court.

He sat on the side of his bed in the coldness of the room, sleepy, shivering slightly, wearing only a strap undershirt and pajama bottoms. The wastebasket in his kitchen was stuffed with fast-food containers and beer cans.

"You want to do what?" he said.

"Eat breakfast at McDonald's, then maybe knock down some ducks at Pecan Island," I said.

"I'm busy today," he replied.

"I see."

It was quiet in the room. His eyes lingered on mine. "What's bothering you, big mon?" he said.

I told him about the dream, the motorman with the skeletal face, the darkness outside the streetcar, the yellowed palm fronds that clattered like bone. "You ever have a dream like that?" I said.

"I used to dream I was on a Jolly Green that was going down. But that was in the hospital in Saigon. It doesn't mean anything. It's just a dream."

"I can't shake it," I said.

He got up from the bed and began dressing. "Turn on the heat, will you? It feels like it's thirty below in here," he said.

We ate at the McDonald's on East Main. Outside, the sky was blue, the leaves of the live oak in the adjacent lot flickering in the sunlight. "Can't tempt you into a duck-hunting trip?" I said.

He wiped his mouth with a crumpled napkin and dropped it onto his plate. "That perv I told you about, Bobby Joe Fontenot, the one in the trailer court? I couldn't stop thinking about what he said to me."

"Said what?"

"That if he reoffended, he was going to use my name every time he stuck it to a little kid. So I called the perv's P.O. Guess what? The P.O. is on vacation. So I told the guy handling his case file about the little boy in the trailer next door. He did everything except yawn in my ear."

"Call Social Services," I said.

"I already did. I think that kid is shark meat."

He gathered up the trash from both our meals and stuffed them angrily into a bin.

"Take it easy, Cletus," I said.

"Screw the ducks. Time to spit in the punch bowl," he said.

· · ·

The mother of the little boy in the trailer court was named Katie Goltz. She sat with us in her tiny living room, still not connecting the reasons we were there, even though Clete mentioned he had been chasing down a bail skip who was the fall partner of Bobby Joe Fontenot, a convicted sex predator living next door.

She wore no lipstick, old jeans, Indian moccasins, and a colorless pullover. Her hair was cut short, and had probably been brown before it was peroxided and waved on one side to resemble a 1940s leading lady's.

"Where's your son?" Clete said.

"At the strip mall," she replied.

Clete nodded. "He went with some friends?" he asked.

"Bobby Joe took him. To buy him a comic book for helping clean his trailer," she said.

Clete leaned forward in his chair. "Ma'am, we have a Meagan's Law in Louisiana. You must have been notified about Bobby Joe Fontenot's record," he said.

"People change," she said.

"You listen to me. That guy is a degenerate. You keep your son away from him," Clete said.

She focused her eyes on a neutral space, her hands folded in her lap. Her arms were muscular, as though she had grown up doing physical work, her complexion clear. Behind her, framed on the wall, was a black-and-white photograph of her and a man who looked like a power lifter. His hair was shaved on the sides, curly in back, his face impish, like a cartoon drawing of a monkey's.

I stood up and looked closer at the picture. It was inscribed "To Katie Gee, the girl who made my own screen role a real pleasure, Your pal, Phil."

"That's Gunner Ardoin," I said.

"'Gunner' is his nickname. Phil is his real name. You know him?" she said.

"He was involved with the beating of a priest in New Orleans. You made a film with him?" I said.

She frowned, unable to process all that she just heard. "I made just one film. My screen name is Katie Gee. The producer said 'Gee' looks better than 'Goltz' on the credits. Phil was my costar. What was that about a priest?" she said.

"You were in one of Fat Sammy Figorelli's porn films?" Clete said.

"They're art films. They're shown in art theaters. Listen, nobody has hurt my little boy. I wouldn't let that happen. I have to go to the washateria now," she said.

There seemed nothing left to say. Her mindset, formed out of either desperation, ignorance, or just plain stupidity and selfishness, was armor-plated, and in all probability no amount of attrition in her life or her son's would ever change it.

Bobby Joe Fontenot pulled up outside, wearing a foam-rubber collar, his face marbled with bruises. When the little boy got out of his car, Bobby Joe cocked his index finger at him, as though he were pointing a gun, and said, "Come over and watch some TV tonight. I got some Popsicles."

Clete and I got up to go, our mission by and large a failure. Her son rushed past us into his bedroom, a new comic book rolled tightly in his hand. Clete twisted the handle on the front door, then stopped and turned around. "It's not coincidence you let that geek be alone with your kid. There's a financial motive here, isn't there?" he said.

"Coincidence?" she said.

"You've got more than a neighborly relationship with that asshole next door. He knows you were working the trade around Folk Polk," Clete said, tapping the air with one finger. "Fontenot's in porn films, too, isn't he?"

"I'm not saying any more. I have to go to the washateria and fix lunch and do all kinds of things I don't get no help with. Why don't y'all just leave now? I didn't do anything to cause this, and you can't say I did," she said.

She stared at us indignantly, her arms folded across her breasts, as though the irrefutability of her logic should have been obvious to anyone.

Clete and I crossed the Teche on the drawbridge behind the trailer court and headed toward New Iberia on the back road, past the row of oak-shaded antebellum homes that belonged on a movie set. Then he mashed on the gas, one hand on top of the steering wheel, the sugarcane fields racing past us, a crazy light in his eyes.

"What are you thinking about, Clete?"

"Nothing. I'll drop you off," he said.

"Clete?"

"Everything is copacetic. Just hang loose. I'll check in with you later," he said. He whistled an aimless tune under his breath.

Chapter 21

At 10:15 Monday morning I received a call from Clotile Arceneaux. "Did you hear from the FBI yet?" she asked.

"No," I said.

"You will. They just left here. They want to put a net over Max Coll real bad," she said.

"A guy crossing state lines to commit a homicide? I guess they would."

"No, you've got it wrong. It's face-saving time. Because he's IRA, he's on a terrorist watch list. In fact, he's been on one for three years. Except he's been going back and forth across the Canadian border like a yo-yo, making a lot of people look like shit."

"That's their problem," I said.

"You're not hearing me. The Feds believe Coll is . . ." She paused and I heard her shuffling papers around. "They say he's a nonpathological compulsive-obsessive with paranoid and antisocial tendencies."

"Antisocial tendencies? This is the kind of crap that comes out of Quantico. Don't buy into it."

"Will you shut up? They're saying Coll kills people because he feels he has a right to. He's not a psychopath or a schizophrenic or anything like that. He's just a very angry man. Have I got your attention?"

"Yes," I said.

"He had a wife and son in Belfast nobody in law enforcement knew about. They used a different name so Coll's enemies wouldn't find them. But about five years ago a Protestant death squad of some kind put a bomb under their car and killed both of them. They were on their way to Mass."

The subject wasn't funny anymore.

"Is there a tap on my home phone?" I asked.

"We're in the George W. Bush era. I'd keep that in mind," she said.

Fifteen minutes later Helen came into my office, a clutch of fax sheets in her hand. "Did you hear anything about an explosion on the drawbridge in Jeanerette?" she asked.

"No," I said.

She sat on the corner of my desk and studied the fax sheets in her hand. "This is from the St. Mary's sheriff's office. See what you think," she said. Her jawbone flexed against her cheek.

I took the sheets from her hand and read them, trying not to show any expression. The details of the investigator's report were incredible. In the early A.M. someone had evidently slim-jimmed a wrecker that was parked in a filling station located a half block from the trailer court by the Jeanerette drawbridge. After hot-wiring the ignition, the perpetrator drove the wrecker down to the trailer court, hooked up the winch to a trailer owned by one Bobby Joe Fontenot, and ripped it off its cinder blocks, tearing loose all the plumbing, electrical, phone and cable connections.

According to witnesses, the owner tried to exit the trailer but discovered the door had been sealed shut with a bonding adhesive used to repair the bodies of wrecked automobiles. The perpetrator skidded the trailer out of the court onto the surfaced road, bouncing it across a drainage ditch, smashing mailboxes and parked cars. When the trailer toppled on its side, witnesses thought they saw the owner trying to climb out of an exposed window. But the driver of the wrecker accelerated, knocking Fontenot, the owner, back inside. The driver then dragged the trailer across the steel grid of the drawbridge, geysering rooster-tails of sparks in the darkness.

A liquid blue flame enveloped one of the butane tanks on the rear of the trailer. The explosion that ensued blew burning paper, fabric, and particleboard all over the bayou. The owner, who by this time had broken out a window and cleaned the glass from the frame with a hammer, barely escaped with his life.

The perpetrator abandoned the wrecker and burning trailer, which was tightly wedged between the steel side beams on the bridge, and disappeared into the darkness on the far side of the bayou. A moment later an ancient Cadillac convertible was seen speeding down the road toward New Iberia, the engine misfiring, leaking oil smoke, the driver wearing a small, short-brim hat perched on the front of his head.

"Wow, that's something, isn't it?" I said, handing the fax sheets back to Helen.

"Any idea who could pull a stunt like that?" she said.

"There're a lot of old gas guzzlers like that around," I replied, my eyes drifting around the room.

"Right," she said.

"No mention of the Cadillac's color?"

"Nope," she said.

"It's not in our jurisdiction, anyway. Let St. Mary Parish do some work for a change."

"You get Clete Purcel in here right now," she said.

But Clete did not answer his phone, and when I drove by the motor court, the manager told me he had not seen Clete's car in the last day or two. I called Clete's office in New Orleans. The temporary secretary he sometimes used was an ex-nun by the name of Alice Werenhaus who put the fear of God in some of Clete's clients.

"You *are* Mr. Robicheaux?" she said.

"I was when I got up this morning," I replied, then quickly regretted my mistake in attempting humor with Alice Werenhaus.

"Oh, it is you, isn't it? I should have immediately recognized the quick wit at work in your rhetoric," she said. "Mr. Purcel left a message for you. Would you like me to read it to you?"

"Yes, that would be very nice, Ms. Werenhaus," I replied.

"It says, 'Give Alice a pay phone number and a time. Fart, Barf, and Itch probably have you tapped.'"

"What's going on?" I said.

"I suspect that's why he'd like to talk with you, Mr. Robicheaux. To explain everything to you. I'm sure by this time you're rather used to that," she said.

I walked downtown and got the number off a public telephone and called it back to Alice Werenhaus. "I'll be at this number at one P.M.," I said.

I expected another rejoinder at my expense. But she surprised me. "Mr. Robicheaux, be careful. Watch after Mr. Purcel, too. Under all his bluster he's a vulnerable man," she said.

At 1:04 P.M. the payphone across from Victor's Cafeteria on Main Street rang. I picked it up and didn't wait for Clete to speak. "Have you lost your mind?" I said.

"About what?" he said.

"You stole a tow truck out of a filling station. You almost burned Bobby Joe Fontenot to death in his trailer. The drawbridge in Jeanerette is still closed with the melted wreckage you left on top of it. Boat traffic is backed up ten miles."

"Oh, yeah, *that*," he replied. "Things got a little out of hand. Look, big mon—"

"No, you look, Clete. Helen wants to feed you into an airplane propeller."

"She's emotional sometimes. I talked with Clotile Arceneaux. She says your phone is tapped."

"I already got that. Listen to me—"

"You think the Feds are tapping a cop's phone because they're worried about an Irish button man whacking out a couple of greaseballs? These guys still haven't found Jimmy Hoffa. It's Merchie Flannigan and his wife they're worried about."

"You're making no sense."

"That broad's been giving you a hand job. I did some checking on Merchie's company. He's in line for some big drilling contracts in Iraq after Shrub turns it into an American colony. That means his father-in-law, what's-his-face, Castille LeJeune, is probably mixed up in it, too. The Feds are after Coll because he's about to pop somebody with a lot of juice, not because they're worried about Coll trying to kill a Catholic priest or smoking the Dellacroce brothers."

It was pointless to argue with Clete. He was the best investigative cop I ever knew, his blue-collar instincts for deception and hypocrisy and flimflam always on target. But his antipathy toward Federal law enforcement agencies, particularly the FBI, was unrelenting, and at best he considered them bumbling and inept and at worst lazy and arrogant.

"Why'd you say Theodosha Flannigan was giving me a hand job?" I asked.

"She and her husband are business partners. She set you up to either get drunk or clipped, she didn't care which. Rich broads look after their money first and think about the size of your Johnson second. You think she's going to let a guy like you screw up her family's finances?"

"You really know how to say it, Cletus."

"You want to be a dildo for this broad, that's your choice. She's dirty, Streak, just like her husband and her old man."

"What are you up to?"

"I told you before, I'm going to make cripples out of the shitheads who hurt you. Get this. I saw a guy in Franklin who looks just like your description of Max Coll."

"Stay away from him, Clete."

"Lose a resource like that? By the way, what's the name of that electrician who burned down your house?"

I started to give him the name, then refused.

"That's all right. I already had a talk with him. He might be contacting your department, but don't believe anything he says."

Later, I went into Helen's office. She was on the phone, nodding, while someone on the other end talked, her eyes on mine. "All right, we'll take care of it. . . . I agree with you. Absolutely. . . . This isn't the Wild West. You got it," she said, and hung up.

Her face looked scorched.

"Who was that?" I asked.

"The Lafayette sheriff. An electrical contractor by the name of Herbert Vidrine was pulled out of his house at around six-thirty this morning and worked over in his backyard," she said.

She looked down at the yellow legal pad on her desk, widening her eyes, as though she could not quite assimilate what she had just heard and written down. "By 'pulled out,' I mean just that. His attacker was wearing work gloves of some kind and grabbed Vidrine by the mouth like he was picking up a bowling ball," she said. "He swung him around in a circle and threw him into the side of a garbage truck. Vidrine is in Our Lady of Lourdes now. A neighbor got the tag number of the attacker's car. A lavender Cadillac convertible. Guess who it belongs to?"

"I just talked to Clete on the phone. He's not coming in," I said.

"The electrical contractor is too scared to file charges. But Clete's not going to use Iberia Parish as his safe house while he goes around kicking people's asses."

I nodded.

The heat went out of her face. "What's the score on this electrical contractor?" she said.

"He's the guy who installed bad wiring in my house. He works for Will Guillot."

"I'm fed up with the stuff, Dave. Clean it up or you and Clete can start making your own plans," she said.

I took the old highway through Broussard into Lafayette and hit a rainstorm just outside of town. By the time I got to Our Lady of Lourdes Hospital the streets were flooding. I ran past a row of blooming camellia bushes into the side entrance of the hospital and asked at the nurse's station on the second floor for directions to Herbert Vidrine's room.

"Three rooms past the elevator, on your left," the nurse said.

I thanked her and started down the hall. Then I stopped and went back to the station. I opened my badge holder. "How's Mr. Vidrine doing?" I asked.

"A concussion and a broken arm. But he's doing all right," the nurse replied. She was young and had clean features and brown hair that was clipped on her neck.

"Has anyone else been in to see him?"

"Not since I've been here. I came on at eight A.M.," she said.

"Could I use your typewriter?" I said.

I had taken a fiction-writing course when I was an English education major at Southwestern Louisiana Institute. I hoped my old prof, Lyle Williams, would be proud of the letter I was now composing. I typed rather than signed a name at the bottom, folded and put the letter in an envelope the nurse gave me, then printed Herbert Vidrine's name on the outside.

"Would you wait ten minutes, then deliver this to Mr. Vidrine's room?" I said.

"I don't know if I should get involved in this," she replied.

I placed the envelope on her desk. "You'd be helping out the good guys," I said.

Vidrine was sitting up in bed when I entered his room, one arm in a cast, easing a teaspoon of Jell-O past a severely swollen bottom lip.

"How are you, Herbert?" I said.

He put his spoon back in a bowl that rested on his bed tray. "You're Iberia Parish. What are you doing here?" he said.

"We're looking for the guy who hurt you but on different charges," I said, laying my raincoat and hat on a chair.

"Maybe you're here to rub salt in a wound, too," he said.

"You burned my house down, partner. But I'm like you, I'm a drunk. I can't carry resentments. Did you ever go back to meetings?"

His eyes left mine. Even though he was a hard-bodied man, he looked small in the bed, his spoon clutched in a childlike fashion. "I never had that big a drinking problem. It was just when I was married," he said.

"The man who attacked you didn't have the right to do what he did," I said.

He frowned and ran his tongue over the swelling in his bottom lip. "Just leave me alone," he said.

"One day you're going to have to do a Fifth Step on the injury you caused me and my family. My father built that house in the Depression with his own hands. My second wife was murdered in it. Her blood was in the wood," I said.

"I'm sorry," he said.

"Maybe you are," I said. I put my business card on his nightstand. "I think you have a lot of information about the dealings of some bad people, Herbert. Why take their bounce?"

"I haven't done anything wrong," he replied.

I drummed my fingers on top of the chair where my raincoat rested and looked out the window at an oak tree whipping in the wind, its leaves shredding high in the air. Then I picked up my raincoat and left, just as the nurse entered with the letter I had typed at the nurse's station.

"This was left for you, Mr. Vidrine," I heard her say behind me.

I waited five minutes, then reentered Vidrine's room. "I forgot my hat," I said, picking it up from the chair.

The letter I had written lay unfolded on top of his bed tray. He was staring into space, his expression disjointed, like a man at a bus stop who has watched the bus's doors close in his face and the bus drive away without him.

The letter I had typed at the nurse's station read as follows:

Herbert,

Sorry you got your ass stomped by that queer bait we had trouble with at the cafe in Jeanerette. But if you can't deal with a fat shit like that, I don't need you on the job. Take this as your official notice of termination. Also be advised you are forfeiting all fees due on uncompleted work.

Will Guillot

"Something wrong?" I asked.

"Yeah, there is. You want to know about Sunbelt Construction?"

"Yeah, what's up with these guys?"

"They got connections with gangsters in New Orleans."

"That's not real specific."

"Maybe they're selling dope. I'm not sure. But Will Guillot is going to take over the company. He's got something on the old man."

"Castille LeJeune?"

"Yeah, him. The war hero."

"What does Guillot have on him?"

"I don't know. I asked him once and all he said was, 'I finally got the goods on both him and that cunt.' I asked him which cunt he meant. He told me it wasn't my business."

"Ever hear the name of Junior Crudup?"

"No," he said.

It had stopped raining outside. The sky was gray, the sun buried in a cloud like a wet flame, the hospital lawn blown with camellia petals. "That's all you got for me, Herbert? It's not too much," I said.

"I'm an electrician. People don't confess their sins to me."

"See you around," I said.

"One time I told Will Fox Run was a beautiful place. He said, 'Don't let it fool you. All these places got a nigger in the woodpile.' I wasn't sure what he meant, though." He tilted his head inquisitively, waiting for me to speak, as if somehow we were old friends.

So Vidrine repeated a racist remark that confirms what you already knew," Helen said in her office an hour later. "Maybe a convict was killed on the LeJeune plantation fifty years ago. Or maybe not. We didn't find a body, bwana."

"That's the point," I said. "How could Will Guillot be blackmailing Castille LeJeune about the death of Junior Crudup? Guillot has something else on him."

"I'm glad we cleared that up. Now get out of here," she replied.

I couldn't blame Helen for her feelings. The real issues were the murders of the daiquiri-store operator and Fat Sammy Figorelli, and in both instances we had no viable suspects. In the meantime I had gotten myself abducted, gotten deeply involved in a murder case from a half century ago, and had helped bring Max Coll to our community.

As a member of Alcoholics Anonymous, the axiom "keep it simple" was supposed to guide my daily life.

What a joke.

But Helen herself had said the real problem lay in the fact we were dealing with Dagwood and Blondie. Amateurs hide in plain sight. They also do not feel guilty about the misdeeds they commit. They attend church, Kiwanis meetings, belong to the Better Business Bureau, support every self-righteous moral cause imaginable, and float like helium balloons right over whole armies of cops looking for miscreants in off-track betting parlors, triple-X motels, and crack houses.

The word *criminal* is more an emotional than legal term. Go to any U.S. post office and view the faces on the wanted posters. Like Dick Tracy caricatures, they stare out of the black-and-white photographs often taken in late-night booking rooms—unshaved, pig snouted, rodent eyed, hare lipped, reassuring us that human evil is always recognizable and that consequently we will never be its victim.

But every longtime cop will tell you that the criminals who scared him most were the ones who looked and talked like the rest of us and committed deeds that no one, absolutely no one, ever wants to have knowledge of.

Five or six years ago Helen and I had to fly to Deer Lodge, Montana, and question a kid whose execution was scheduled in three days. We were not prepared for what we saw when he was brought into the interview room in a short-sleeve, orange jumpsuit and leg and waist chains. His first name was Kerry, and the softness in his name was like both his features and his North Carolinian accent. He had no cigarette odor, no tattoos, no needle tracks. His auburn hair was shampooed, clipped on the ends, and kept falling across his glasses, so that he constantly twitched his head to shake a loose strand out of his vision.

While we questioned him about a murder in Iberia Parish, his large glasses wobbled with reflected light and a strange, almost self-effacing smile never left his mouth. If he bore anger or resentment toward anyone, I could not detect it.

He had been sentenced to death for tying a rancher and his wife to chairs in their kitchen and butchering them alive. While on Death Row he helped organize a riot that resulted in the convict takeover of the entire maximum-security area. Kerry also was a chief participant in the fate of five snitches who were pulled out of protection cells, tortured, and lynched with wire loops from the second tier of a lock-down section.

He said he knew nothing of the homicide in Iberia Parish.

"Your fingerprints at the murder scene indicate otherwise. Maybe the victim had it coming. Why not get your interpretation of events on the books?" I said.

He flipped his head to clear a strand of hair from his glasses and smiled at a joke that only he seemed to understand.

We gave it up. But before we left the interview room I had to ask him another question. "What do you think lies on the other side, Kerry?" I said.

He had a slight cold and couldn't wipe his nose because his hands were manacled at the waist, so he huffed air out of his nostrils before he answered. "You just move on to another plane of existence," he said.

The afternoon of his injection he had to be awakened from a sound sleep. Minutes later the death warrant was read and he was videotaped by a member of the medical examiner's office on the way to the execution chamber. He grinned at the camera and said, "Hi, Mom," and jiggled all over with laughter.

Chapter 22

I went to bed early that night and listened to the rain hitting the tin roof of my rented house. The fog was white in the trees, a lighted tugboat out on the Teche, its gunnels hung with rubber tires, glistening inside the rain. I slept the sleep of the dead.

The time on my alarm clock was 4:16 A.M. when I heard the unmistakable sound of Clete's automobile engine dying in my driveway. A moment later he tapped softly on the front door. He was wearing gloves and a beat-up leather bomber jacket. The jacket was unzipped, and I could see his nylon shoulder holster and his blue-black, pearl-handled .38 revolver inside it.

"Where have you been?" I said.

"At a fish camp on Lake Fausse Pointe. Get dressed. I know where Max Coll is," he said.

"No more cowboy stuff, Clete."

"Me?" he said.

"Where is he?" I said.

Clete stepped inside the living room and started to explain, looking back over his shoulder at the street, then got vexed at being conciliatory. "You want in on this or not?" he said.

I left a note on the kitchen counter for Father Jimmie, then Clete and I headed out in the predawn wetness for New Orleans, a thermos of coffee and a box of beignets on the seat between us. The old homes along East Main were still dark, the live oaks dripping on the sidewalks. I was still not quite awake.

"Run it by me again," I said.

"Janet Gish is trying to get off the nose candy without a program, so she spends most of the night at Harrah's. She says a guy with a Mick accent was in the casino until early Saturday morning, then he left just before seven. He came back at eight-thirty, ate a plate of steak and eggs, played some more blackjack, and drove off in a Honda."

"Why was she paying so much attention to a guy with an accent?" I asked.

"One, I'd already described Coll to her, and, two, she still hooks a little on the side and thought he'd be an easy trick. Here's the rest of it. He had on black dress pants, like a priest might wear."

It was raining and still dark when we crossed the high bridge over the Atchafalaya at Morgan City. Down below I could see shrimp boats in their berths, the red-tiled roofs of the town, and the great, cypress-dotted expanse of the wetlands in the south, all of which were being eaten away by saltwater intrusion at a rate of hundreds of square miles a year.

"Doesn't your heater work?" I said.

"It's full blast, mon."

Clete's cell phone rang. He answered it, listened, then said thanks to someone and clicked it shut again. "That's Janet. The guy who looks like Coll is still there. By the way, she's got a porn lead for us, too," he said.

We crossed the wide sweep of the Mississippi just as the first cold band of light, like the blunt edge of a sword, appeared on the eastern horizon. Then we were rolling down I-10 past the northern shore of Lake Pontchartrain, into the heart of the city, the welfare projects, the cemeteries where the dead were entombed in white brick, the homeless and the hopelessly addicted gathered around fires next to the cement pillars that supported the elevated highway.

At the head of Canal Street stood the casino, the royal palms at the entrance beaded with rainwater in the graying of the dawn. The gamblers inside were not a group that took note of changes in either weather or clocks. The rain might beat against the windows and lightning flicker on the streets outside, but the blacks and Hispanics and blue-collar whites who crowded the tables or fed the endless banks of slot machines were committed to their own form of solipsism, one in which the amounts that were lost or gained were far less important than the gamblers' desire to stay in the game, to be a part of the action, at the table or in front of the machine, until they were physically and emotionally sated in a way no sexual or narcotic experience can equal.

Janet Gish was at the bar, a scotch and milk in front of her. Her hair was currently orange, stiff with spray, the tops of both breasts tattooed with a blood red star, her skin rough grained, freckled, layered with makeup. But in spite of all the cosmetics and chemicals she used on herself, she had one natural gift that was unimpaired by the life she lived. Her eyes were like a doll's, with weighted lids that clicked open suddenly, so that she always seemed surprised, somehow still vulnerable.

She turned on the stool, drew in on her cigarette, and looked at us without expression. "Lend me twenty bucks, Streak?" she said.

I took out my wallet and found fifteen. She took it and slipped it under her glass. "I got to get out of this shit. I just dropped three hundred in a half hour. How about lunch at Galatoire's? God, I hate this place," she said, although I had no idea which place she meant.

"On the clock today. You know how it is," I said.

She was obviously stoned or drunk or both, staying off coke with booze and baccarat, paying the rent with fifty-dollar tricks, starting her daily routine at 4 P.M. with eyewash, thirty-minute hot showers, and white speed on the half shell. Anyone who thinks prostitution is a victimless crime needs his head drilled with a brace and bit.

"Where's our Irish friend?" I asked.

"Just went out the door. Like *voom*," she replied.

Clete's face reddened with exasperation. "Why didn't you call?" he said.

"It's been a long night. I don't need criticism right now. I just don't need that kind of unjustified negativity in my morning," she said, a thin wire quivering in her throat.

"Right," he said, glancing up and down the bar.

"Because if that's why you two are here, I'll just go back to the tables," she said. She gestured at the bartender. "This milk is curdled. Give me a tequila sunrise."

"We appreciate everything you've done for us, Janet. How long has our man been gone?" I said.

"Ten minutes," she said.

"You saw him drive away?" I asked.

"No, he was walking. Right up Canal. Like he was in a hurry," she said.

"When he left Saturday morning for an hour or so, did he walk or drive?" I asked.

She thought about it. "He walked down Canal. Just like this morning," she replied.

"Stay here, Cletus," I said.

"Oh, I got it. I just drive people around, then turn into an ashtray. I'm glad I'm your friend, Dave, because otherwise I don't think you'd have any," he said, screwing an unlit Lucky into his mouth.

I didn't try to explain. I hurried down Canal, past smoking sewer grates and gutters dark with rainwater, to the side street that led into the dilapidated downtown area where Father Jimmie Dolan's church was located, like a fifteenth-century fortress inside which its inhabitants refused to accept a tidal wave of ecclesiastical change.

The early-morning Latin Mass had already begun when I entered the vestibule and dipped my hand in the holy water fount. In a back pew, hard by a marble pillar, I saw the diminutive form of Max Coll, next to a group of elderly, head-covered women, all of whom had rosary beads threaded through their fingers. He wore black trousers and a puffy, tan down jacket that was zipped halfway up his chest.

My cell phone was in my pocket, my .45 automatic in a clip-on holster attached to my belt. I started to punch in a 911 call on the phone, then thought better of it and instead genuflected at the end of the pew and knelt down next to Max Coll.

"Walk out of here with me," I whispered.

He glanced at me and showed no sign of either recognition or alarm. "Bugger off," he said.

"No one needs to get hurt here," I said.

He ignored me and concentrated on the missal in his hands.

"I know some evil men killed not only your natal family but your wife and son as well," I said. "Both my mother and my second wife died at the hands of murderers. I can understand the feelings you've had to deal with over the years. I think many of the people you killed were bastards and deserved what they got. But it's time to give it up. Take a walk with me, Max. You know it's the right thing to do."

Other people were beginning to look at us. "You're disturbing the Mass, Mr. Robicheaux. Now show some respect and shut your 'ole," he replied.

Parishioners who had come in late, one of them weighing at least three hundred pounds, began bottling up the open end of the pew. I was trapped with Max Coll. I thought I might have a chance at him during communion, but as soon as the communicants began filing toward the front of the church, Max helped an elderly woman into a wheelchair and pushed her to the altar.

I stayed right behind them, received the Host myself, which he did not, and followed them back into the pew. Through the concluding prayers he kept his eyes straight ahead, one thumb hooked inside his half-zipped jacket. Just as the priest gave the final blessing to the congregation, Max turned to me and calmly whispered, "Got a Beretta nine-millimeter, fourteen rounds in the mag, all tucked nicely under my armpit. Try to take me and, House of the Lord or not, I'll leave hair on the walls."

With that, he wheeled the elderly woman down the center of the aisle and through a crowd in the vestibule, like a mummy wrapped in black cloth being trundled along a cobbled street. He and two other men lifted her down the steps and fitted her chair into a waiting van, then suddenly Max Coll leaped into the traffic.

I went after him, my shield held up above my head, a wall of water from a passing truck striking me full in the face, horns blowing, a taxi missing me by inches. Somewhere on the edge of my vision two vehicles crashed into each other. Max was now somewhere on the opposite side of the traffic, hidden behind a city bus or a Mayflower van or a refrigerator truck, all of which were moving through the intersection.

I reached the opposite sidewalk and looked in both directions.

No Max Coll.

I saw the bus stop briefly on the next block, then it turned a corner and headed in the direction of Lee Circle. I started running, threading my way through pedestrians, truck drivers off-loading food for restaurants, winos sitting in doorways with their legs outstretched on the sidewalk. I turned the corner and saw the bus at the curb in the middle of the block, the door opened to allow a passenger to exit.

I ran toward it, breathless, waving my arms at the driver. As the bus pulled away from the curb I struck the side with my fists. Behind the elongated glass windows in the back door I saw Max Coll standing in the aisle, holding a support strap with one hand. He grinned, unzipped his jacket, and pulled out the sides to show me he had no weapon on his person.

The bus sped through the next intersection and disappeared down the street. I reached for my cell phone to punch in a 911 call, then remembered hearing it clatter across the sidewalk two blocks behind me.

I stopped in the men's room at the casino and tried to dry off with paper towels before I went in search of Janet Gish and Clete Purcel. A few minutes later, my clothes glued to my skin, I found the two of them eating breakfast in the restaurant, Janet looking half revived by food and coffee. Clete chewed his food thoughtfully, his eyes traveling up and down my person. "I'm not even going to ask," he said.

"He was at Mass. He got away," I said.

"At Mass? A stone killer?"

"I just told you."

"So instead of calling the locals, you decided to talk him in?" he said.

"Something like that," I replied.

"Couldn't have used any backup from me, of course?"

"Lay off it, Clete," I said.

He took a coffee cup and saucer that was set up on an empty table, poured the cup full, and pushed it toward me. "Sit down, big mon, and let Janet tell you how Fat Sammy was shipping porn out and crystal in," he said.

"It all had to do with those Mideastern degenerates," she said.

"Those what?" I said.

"Those Muslim lamebrains or whatever who crashed the planes into the towers. Sammy Fig said he was going to round them up for the FBI," Janet said.

I gave Clete a look.

"You're going to love this, Streak. Sammy straightening out Fart, Barf, and Itch," he said.

It seemed a grandiose and bizarre tale, but in truth no more peculiar than many in New Orleans' long history of political intrigue, from William Walker's military adventurism into Nicaragua during the 1850s to Lee Harvey Oswald's involvement in the city with the Fair Play for Cuba Committee.

According to Janet Gish, Fat Sammy felt tainted by a past association with a mobster who had been an enforcer in Brooklyn and later one of the Watergate Plumbers. The mobster was part of a blackmail sting involving Cuban prostitutes in Miami, and just before Kennedy's visit to Dallas on November 22, 1963, the mobster showed up in New Orleans with a hooker and stayed at a motel owned by Sammy's uncle. As soon as Sammy heard John Kennedy had been shot, he was convinced New Orleans had been the staging area for the assassination.

From that time on, Fat Sammy did everything in his power to demonstrate his patriotism and disassociate himself from the people who he believed had murdered the president.

"The night before the planes crashed into the towers, these Mideastern guys were in Sammy's club by the airport. They told one of the girls they were pilots," Janet said.

"Maybe they were," I said.

"Except they were sweating so bad the janitor had to scrape the

B.O. off the furniture. They had another problem, too. Like keeping napkins over their boners."

"Sorry, I'm just not following all this," I said.

"Sammy calls the FBI. They send some guys out and Sammy looks at all these photos and says that's not the guys who were in the club. One of the FBI guys says, 'Well, these are the hijackers who died in the planes.'

"Sammy says, 'Yeah, but there must have been other hijackers whose planes got grounded. The guys in my club are the ones who probably never got off the tarmac.' Even while he's talking you can already hear the toilet flushing.

"Two weeks go by and Sammy calls the FBI in Washington. He tells some agent there they're looking in the wrong place for terrorists. He says these guys are not Muslim revolutionaries, they're degenerates and losers, just like the other jack-offs who come into the club. Sammy says to the FBI agent, 'Use your fucking head. These guys weren't hanging in mosques or living in Nebraska. They were holed-up in Miami and Vegas and hanging in dumps like mine 'cause they want to get laid. You want to nail 'em, float some cooze out on the breeze and see what happens.'"

People at other tables were turning to stare.

"Maybe we should move to a quieter spot," I said.

"Well, *excuse* me. Here's the briefer version so I don't offend anybody," she said, her eyelids fluttering. "The FBI agent blew Sammy off, so he set up an Internet site out in Arizona to sell his movies. He was using a P.I. to run the credit card numbers of anybody with a Mideastern name who bought from the site."

"Who were his partners?" I said.

"You met a couple of them," she replied.

"The Dellacroces?" I said.

She raised her eyebrows innocuously.

"Tell him the rest of it, Janet," Clete said.

"Sammy got paid in crystal. It's cooked across the border and comes through Tucson," she said. Then she looked at nothing, the whites of her eyes veined, her facial skin like flesh-colored clay that had been molded on bone. "Sammy wasn't a bad guy. He took us all to Disney World once. He wore a Mouseketeer hat on the plane all the way back home."

"Who popped him, Janet?" I said.

"I don't know. Sammy always said it was the normals you got to watch out for, 'cause they never learn who they really are."

She stared through the front windows at the palm trees beating in the wind and the rain slashing on the glass.

Chapter 23

It was afternoon when Clete dropped me off at the house. The sky was a cold blue, dense and flawless in texture and color, the lawns along the street ridged with serpentine lines of leaves where the rainwater had receded into the streets. I shaved, showered, changed clothes, and went to the office.

Helen listened quietly while I told her of what had happened in New Orleans, her gaze fixed out the window on the crypts in the old cemetery.

"You called N.O.P.D. about Coll?"

"Yes."

"When?" she said.

"When we left town."

"I don't think you wanted to arrest him."

"Then why would I have chased him across town?"

"You should have called N.O.P.D. as soon as you saw him inside the church."

"Picture this scene, Helen. A couple of hot dogs coming through the vestibule with M-16s and 12-gauge pumps and Max Coll with a nine-millimeter," I said.

"Coll saved your life. You think you owe him."

I started to speak but she raised her hand for me to be quiet. "The state attorney's office put us on notice this morning. We're going to be investigated for harassment of Castille LeJeune, destruction of his property, and for deliberately damaging his reputation. What do you think of that?" she said.

"You warned me," I replied.

"You never understand what I'm saying, Dave. You were right about the murder of Junior Crudup. LeJeune was behind it. He thinks we've got information that in reality we don't. Find out what it is. You're a handful, bwana."

She folded her arms on her chest, shaking her head, a smile tugging at the corner of her mouth.

At quitting time I drove to the home of Merchie and Theodosha Flannigan. It was almost the winter solstice now, and the sepia-tinted light in the trees and on the bayou seemed to emanate from the earth rather than the sky. Merchie greeted me at the door, wearing glasses, a book in his hand, his long hair like white gold against the soft glow of a living room floor lamp. "She's not here," he said.

"It's you I want to talk to," I replied.

"Why is it you keep finding reasons to put yourself in my wife's path? Just doing your job?"

"You're out of line, Merchie."

"Could be. Could also be you'd like to get into Theo's pants. If that's the case, good luck, because she's out drunk somewhere."

I cleared my throat and shifted my eyes off his face. His thoroughbreds were nickering inside a pecan orchard beyond a white fence, their bodies barely distinguishable in the shadows. "The murder of Junior Crudup isn't going away. His remains were moved, but eventually we'll find out what happened to them. If I have anything to do with it, your father-in-law is going to have an opportunity for on-the-job training in soybean farming," I said.

"So why tell me about it?"

"Because I think you wouldn't mind seeing that happen."

"You want to dip your wick, go do it. But leave us out of your personal problems."

"I think Theodosha knows what happened to Junior Crudup's body."

"My wife is a sick person. That's why she's spent a hundred thousand dollars on psychiatrists and clinics. But I think you like stirring her up. I think you like feeding on our troubles."

He started to close the door but I held it open with one hand. "Your wife's frigid, isn't she?" I said.

He released the tension on the door, slipped off his glasses, and dropped them in his shirt pocket. "If you weren't already an object of pity and public ridicule, I'd splatter your nose all over your face. Now go home," he said.

The door clicked shut. I stared at it stupidly, my ears ringing in the silence.

Early the next morning Clete picked me up for breakfast, cheerful, wearing his utility cap low on his brow, a Hawaiian shirt under his bomber jacket, driving with one hand down East Main toward Victor's Cafeteria.

"You moved back into the motor court?" I said.

"Yeah, why not?"

"You burned a guy's trailer. You assaulted a man in Lafayette."

"They're not filing charges. Not if they want to stay on the planet. So I don't see the big deal. Things get out of control sometimes. I'm cool with it," he said, fiddling with the radio.

Clete was Clete, a human moving violation, out of sync with both lawful and criminal society, no more capable of changing his course than a steel wrecking ball can alter its direction after it's been set in motion. Why did I constantly contend with him? I asked myself.

But I knew the answer and it wasn't a comforting one: We were opposite sides of the same coin.

I told him about my visit to Merchie Flannigan's house.

"That punk said that to you?" he asked.

"I got a little personal about his wife," I replied.

"That's another question I have. You actually asked him if his wife wouldn't come across?"

"I guess that sums it up."

"I can see that might piss him off. Particularly when he knows you bopped her."

"Can't you show some subtlety, just a little, once in a while?"

"You bump uglies with a guy's wife, then tell him she's an ice cube, but it's *me* who's got a problem with language?"

"She was drunk. We both were. Stop harping on it."

He looked at me, then turned into the parking lot across from Victor's. The old convent across the bayou was still in shadow, the live oaks speckled with frost. "Why get into Flannigan's face about his wife's sex life?" he said.

"A psychiatrist would probably say she has trouble with intimacy. So she gets it on when she's drunk, usually with strangers or people she doesn't care about. It's characteristic of women who were molested as children," I replied.

"You're really going to hang LeJeune's cojones over a fire, aren't you?"

"You better believe it," I said.

Later I signed out a cruiser and drove to the Lafayette Police Department to see my old friend Joe Dupree, the homicide cop and airborne veteran who had investigated the gunshot death of Theo Flannigan's psychiatrist. While I talked he sat behind his desk, picking one aspirin, then another, then a third out of a tin container, swallowing them with water he drank from a cone-shaped paper cup. His tie was configured to the shape of his pot stomach, his hair combed like strands of wire across the bald spot on top of his head.

"So you think this guy Will Guillot is blackmailing Castille LeJeune and it has something to do with LeJeune's daughter?" he said.

"Right."

"About what?"

"Molestation."

Joe leaned back in his chair and rubbed his mouth. Through the window I could see a chained-up line of black men in orange jumpsuits being placed in a jail van. "Well, Ms. Flannigan's file was missing from Dr. Bernstine's office. But I found out several other files were missing, too. Maybe Bernstine took them home and they got lost somehow. Or somebody could have stolen several files to throw off the investigation. Anyway, it's been a dead-end case," he said.

"You checked out the secretaries, any reports of forced entry?" I said.

"If Bernstine was burglarized, he didn't report it. The alarm company never had to do a 911, either. The secretary is a church-going, family woman, with no reason to steal files from her employer."

"How long was she there?"

He looked down at the torn notebook pages that were clipped inside a case folder. "Seven months," he said.

"Who was the secretary before this one?" I asked.

He looked again at his notes. "A woman named Gretchen Peltier. But she quit before Ms. Flannigan starting seeing Bernstine."

"What was that name again?"

I drove to the alarm company that had serviced Dr. Bernstine's office. Like most alarm companies, it was an electronic shell that didn't provide security but instead relayed distress signals to the fire department or a law enforcement agency. In other words, the chief expense of home security was passed on to the taxpayers and the alarm company was able to maintain its entire system, which monitored several parishes, with no more than a half dozen technicians and sales and clerical employees.

But the assistant director of the company, a black woman named Dauterive who had been an elementary school teacher, did her best to help me. A computer record of all electronic warning signals originating during the last year at Dr. Bernstine's office was laid out on the desk. "See, there were a number of power failures. Those were either during an electrical storm or when a power line was knocked down. These other dates are the times the customer didn't disarm the system fast enough. The dispatcher had to call and get the password."

She was heavyset and wore glasses and a pink suit with a small corsage on the lapel. She glanced at her watch.

"Am I taking up too much time?" I asked.

"Oh, no. It's my anniversary. My husband's meeting me for lunch," she replied.

"Who's the dispatcher?"

"We use the Acadiana Ambulance Service. When they receive an emergency signal, they call the residence or the business and clear it up, or they notify the appropriate response service," she replied.

"When was the last time you received an alarm that could have indicated an unauthorized entry?" I asked.

"Here," she said, and tapped her finger on the computer printout. The date was one day after the gunshot death of the psychiatrist, Dr. Bernstine. "But the dispatcher called and got the password."

I ran my finger up the column on the printout to a billing notation for July and a description of services that amounted to two thousand dollars. "What's this?" I asked.

"It looks like the customer changed out the system. If I remember correctly, a power surge fried the main panel and the customer decided to use the opportunity to upgrade," she replied.

I was getting nowhere. "Let me think about this stuff and come back," I said.

"I don't know if this is of any help to you, but the customer changed his keypad code when he got his new system. See?" she said, and tapped the notation again.

"Yes?"

"He didn't change his password. Sometimes people don't like to change the password, particularly if it's a pet name or part of a private joke in the family," she said.

She looked me flatly in the face.

"That's a hole in the dike, isn't it?" I said.

"You might say that," she replied.

"Did you say today was your anniversary?" I asked.

"That's correct. Our twenty-seventh."

"Have a great anniversary, Ms. Dauterive."

I headed straight for Abbeville, twenty miles south on the Vermilion River, and the insurance company that employed Gretchen Peltier, the woman who had given Will Guillot his alibi for the night the drive-by daiquiri shop operator was murdered and who had also turned out to be a former employee of the slain psychiatrist.

She was terrified. Like most people who lead ordinary lives and stray across a line, usually in concert with someone far more devious than themselves, she could neither defend herself nor lie convincingly. Instead, she began to perspire and swallow like someone in an elevator hearing steel cables snap a strand at a time.

"I don't think you're a bad person, Ms. Peltier. But you're taking the weight for a bad guy," I said.

"Taking the weight?" she said, more confused and frightened than ever now, her eyes flicking to the open door of her employer's office.

"You're about to take Will Guillot's fall. That means you'll go to prison. You'll live behind razor wire and cell with murderers and sexual deviates of every stripe. Snitch one of them off and you get glass put in your food. That's where Will Guillot has taken you."

My rhetoric was cruel. She was a sad woman, her eyes etched with mascara, her clothes obviously bought at a discount store. I could only guess at the means of seduction Will Guillot had used to entice her into cooperating with the systematic destruction of her own life.

"I knew the code numbers to the alarm system in Dr. Bernstine's office," she said. "Dr. Bernstine had shot himself in the park. I gave the numbers to Will because he said his wife, the one he's divorcing, told Dr. Bernstine a lot of lies that were going to be used in court against him. I gave him the password, too."

"How did he get into the building?" I said.

"A man who works for him, an electrician, opened the door. But the numbers on the keypad had been changed. The alarm went off. If Will hadn't had the password, the cops would have come out."

Her eyes were wet. She rested her forehead on the heel of her hand.

"You told me Guillot was with you the night the daiquiri store operator was killed. Was that a lie?"

"No."

"You sure?" I said, looking down into her face.

"I thought I was helping Will. Why have you done this to me?" she replied. She found a handkerchief in her purse and pressed it against her eyes.

"What's going on out here?" her employer said, standing in the doorway of his office, his tie printed with hundreds of tiny blue stars against a red background, a small American flag pinned on the lapel of his suit.

I walked to my cruiser, which was parked on Abbeville's town square. The sun was already deep in the west, the light thin and brittle on the old brick cathedral in the square and the cemetery behind it, where the bodies of Confederate dead from Shiloh and Port Hudson lay in crypts stained with lichen and split with fissures, as though the earth were determined to absorb them and their contents back into itself. I could hear traffic crossing the steel bridge over the Vermilion River and smell the odors of diesel oil and water and shrimp husks piled behind a restaurant, and as I looked at the bare limbs of the willows along the river I was suddenly filled with the sense the sun was not simply completing part of its cycle across the sky, it was about to descend over the rim of the earth for the last time.

In psychoanalysis it's called a world destruction fantasy.

Were my irrational feelings connected to the fact I had just helped dismantle a woman's life? Or were the rats' nests of rags and bones in those crypts reminders that Shiloh was not a grand moment in history, but a three-day meat-cutter that soaked the hills with the blood of farmboys, most of whom never owned a slave or knew anything about the economics of northern textile mills? Or was the sum total of my own life finally being made apparent to me?

The streets were almost empty, swirling with dust and pieces of newspaper, the water oaks bare of leaves, many of the old stores permanently closed. The world in which I had grown up was gone. I wanted to pretend otherwise, to find excuses for the decay, the strip malls, the trash strewn along the roadways, the century-old live oaks that developers lopped into stumps with almost patriotic pride. In my vanity I wanted to believe that I and others could turn it around. But it was not going to happen, not in my lifetime nor in my child's.

It was 4:45 when I got back to the department and rain had begun falling in big fat drops on the sidewalk that led into the courthouse. I pulled my mail out of my pigeon hole and went into my office. A few minutes later Helen came in.

"So what happened today?" she asked.

I told her.

"Will Guillot creeped the psychiatrist's office and stole Theo Flannigan's file so he could blackmail Castille LeJeune?" she said.

"It's more serious than that. I think he murdered the psychiatrist on orders from Castille LeJeune. He was probably supposed to deliver the file back to LeJeune, but he either didn't do that or he xeroxed it and is using it to take over the old man's business."

Through the window I saw a hearse pass on its way to the funeral home on St. Peter Street. I got up from my desk and let down the venetian blinds. My office suddenly seemed hermetically sealed, artificially lit, shut off from the rest of the world.

"You unhappy about something?" Helen said.

"No. Everything is fine."

She looked somberly at my face. "Have dinner with me, Pops," she said.

"Why not?" I said.

Chapter 24

That evening I walked into the kitchen while Father Jimmie was on the phone. Unconsciously he turned his back to me, rounding his shoulders, as though somehow creating a shell around his conversation.

"I believe you, but we'll do this on my terms. No, you have my word. I'll be there. Now, good-bye," he said. After he hung up he turned around and grinned sheepishly. "I get calls from a neurotic parishioner once in a while," he said.

"Was that one of them?" I asked.

"Let's don't clutter up the evening, Dave."

"You're meeting Max Coll?"

"He's ready to change his way. I can't deny him reconciliation or communion."

"Coll is planning to kill somebody. But you're supposed to repair his soul so he can sneak into heaven through a side window?"

"That last sentence describes two thirds of my constituency," he said.

He picked up Snuggs and a box of cat food and went out on the back steps to feed him.

"I already fed him," I said.

"He's a warrior. He needs extra rations," Father Jimmie replied.

There was no moon that night. Screech owls were screaming in the trees and the humidity was so thick I could hear moisture ticking in the leaves on the ground. Father Jimmie had gone out, although I had no idea where. I went into the small office I had created in my rented house and sat at the desk and began writing a letter to Alafair.

Dear Alf,

We're going to have a swell time at Christmas. Clete's in town and is anxious to see you, as of course am I. How is your novel going? I bet it's going to be a fine one. Hope you're through exams by now. Don't be too worried about grades. You always did well in school and college is not going to be any different. Would you like to take a ride out on the salt if the weather permits? Batist says he's found a new spot for redfish by Southwest Pass.

The images out of the past, created by my own words, made my eyes film. I saw Bootsie, Alafair, and me in the stern of our boat, with Batist at the wheel, the throttle full out, slapping across West Cote Blanche Bay at sunrise, the salt spray like a wet kiss on a spring morning.

I put aside the letter and stared at the guns mounted on the gunrack I had screwed into the wall: an AR-15, a sporterized '03 Springfield, and my old Remington twelve-gauge, the barrel sawed off even with the pump, the sportsman's plug long ago removed from the magazine.

I knew what had been on my mind all afternoon and evening. Since I had interviewed Gretchen Peltier at the insurance office in Abbeville I'd had little doubt about Will Guillot's involvement in the burglary of Dr. Bernstine's office and Bernstine's death by gunshot in Lafayette's Girard Park. I also had no doubt he was mixed up in pornography and narcotics and the blackmail of Castille LeJeune. The problem was his crimes had all been committed in other parishes, and there was no way to hang the killing of either Sammy Figorelli or the drive-by daiquiri store operator in New Iberia on him.

In order to get at him and subsequently Castille LeJeune, I would have to work with at least three other law-enforcement agencies. Then the legal processes of indictment and prosecution would be turned entirely over to others, perhaps in a parish Castille LeJeune controlled.

I turned off the light and sat in the darkness with the twelve-gauge across my lap. The steel and the wood of the stock felt cool against my palms. I opened the breech and smelled the odor of the machine oil I had used to clean the chamber and the magazine, then set the stock butt-down between my legs, moving my thumb along the edges of the barrel where I had sawed it off and sanded it smooth with emery paper. I thought about my dead wife Bootsie and the systemic corruption of the place I loved and the inhumanity and cruelty that had been visited upon a great blues artist like Junior Crudup.

I removed a box of double-ought buckshot from my closet shelf and began pressing a handful of shells one at a time into the magazine of my Remington. I sat in the darkness a long time, the gun resting on my knees, my mind free of all thought, a strange numbness in my body. Then I ejected the shells and replaced them one by one in their box, set the shotgun back in the rack, and took a walk down by the drawbridge. A lighted tug was waiting for the bridge tender to raise the bridge. I waved at him in the pilot house and he waved back at me, then I walked back home and went to bed, with Snuggs sleeping at the foot.

The next day, Friday, I contacted Joe Dupree in Lafayette, and we went to work on getting a search warrant on Will Guillot's home and place of business. But it was going to be a long haul. The warrant request was based on statements made by Gretchen Peltier, the psychiatrist's former secretary, about a break-in committed in Lafayette by a man who lived in Franklin. Also, Will Guillot was probably many things, but stupid wasn't one of them. It was highly unlikely he would keep the stolen case file, which he was using to blackmail Castille LeJeune, in either his home or office.

There are days in law enforcement, just like those at the craps table, when you think the dice have no combinations on them except treys and boxcars. Then suddenly they magically bounce off the backboard, all elevens and sevens.

Just before quitting time Helen opened my door and leaned inside. "The sheriff in St. Mary just called. Will Guillot made a prowler report last night. The city cops who responded told him there'd been a peeping Tom in the neighborhood, but Guillot seemed to think it was someone else."

"Who?"

"He was walking around in the yard with a gun and not saying."

"Thanks for passing it on," I said.

I continued with the paperwork I was doing, my expression flat. I thought she was about to close the door and go back to her office but instead she approached my desk, her eyes on mine.

"My words don't have much influence on you. But be careful, Dave. Don't give power to a guy like Castille LeJeune," she said.

"I hear you," I said.

"Yeah," she said.

At 5 P.M. I went home, reloaded my cut-down twelve-gauge, locked it in the steel box that was welded to the bed of my pickup truck, and drove to Clete's cottage at the motor court.

He was outside, grilling a chicken, drinking from a quart bottle of beer, his eyes watering in the smoke, the collar of his jacket pulled up around his neck, his utility cap cocked sideways.

"What's shakin', big mon?" he said.

"Think the Bobbsey Twins from Homicide should make a house call down in Franklin?" I said.

"Oh my, yes indeedy," he replied, as though the statement were one word.

The shrubs and gazebo and wide gallery of Will Guillot's house were threaded with Christmas lights, and sequined cutouts of reindeer, with tinted floodlamps aimed at them, were spiked into the lawn. We pulled into the driveway and parked just inches from where Dr. Parks had bled to death on the cement. I unlocked the steel box in the truck bed, removed my cut-down twelve-gauge, and tossed it to Clete. He went into the shrubbery with it, deliberately silhouetting against the Christmas lights and tinted floodlamps, the barrel held at an upward angle. As I walked up on the gallery I saw Will Guillot pull aside a curtain on a tall window and look outside. I hung my badge holder on the breast pocket of my sports coat and banged hard on the door with the flat of my fist.

Everything I did in the next few minutes would be based on my belief that Gretchen Peltier had truly been sickened by her experience with Will Guillot and had not gone back to him or confessed she had given him up.

He jerked open the door and stared into my face. He wore a burgundy corduroy shirt and gray slacks and loafers, and in the dim light the birthmark on his face looked like a scar from a hot iron. Behind him I saw a woman get up from the couch and go into the back of the house. "Do I need to call the cops?" he said.

"I'm the least of your troubles, Mr. Guillot. I think your electrician wants to park one in your brainpan," I said.

"*What?*" he said, his eyes shifting from me to Clete, who had just walked out of the yard, stepping up on the gallery with the twelve-gauge resting in the crook of his arm.

"It's clear," Clete said to me.

"What's clear? Why are you walking around in my yard with that shotgun?" Guillot said.

"Your electrician, Herbert Vidrine, gave you up. But I guess that wasn't enough for him. Evidently he hates your guts. What'd you do to the poor guy?" I said.

"I already found out about that letter you or somebody else sent him with my name on it. It didn't work," Guillot said, his eyes flicking from me to Clete and the shotgun again.

"Try this. You got Herbert Vidrine to help you break into Dr. Samuel Bernstine's office the same weekend Bernstine took two .25

caliber rounds in the head. You set off the alarm, then found out you had the wrong code numbers for the keypad. But fortunately for you somebody had given you the password and you were able to give it to the alarm service when they called."

Guillot tried to let my words slide off his face, biting down with his back molars so his jaw didn't sag. "Then arrest me so I can sue you into the next dimension," he said.

"You think this is about some pissant B&E?" Clete said.

"Who is this guy?" Guillot said to me.

"There's my buzzer," Clete said, opening his P.I. badge, then flipping it closed again before Guillot could look at it carefully. "The G doesn't spend its time on nickel-and-dime farts who make dirty movies. But unlucky for you, a guy we do care about, a psychopath named Max Coll, is in the neighborhood, and it's got something to do with you and the cocksucker you work for."

Guillot looked behind him, as though he did not want our words heard by the woman who had gone into the back of the house. If he had closed the door in our faces and called his attorney, it would have been over. But Clete had set the hook and Guillot couldn't pull it out. He stepped out on the porch with us and pulled the door shut behind him, shivering slightly in the cold.

"What's the deal on this guy you mentioned, what's his name, this guy Coll?" he said.

"He blows heads for the IRA or the Mob or just because he can't get it up in the morning," Clete said.

"He's here, in Franklin?" Guillot said to Clete.

"You tell us," Clete said.

Guillot looked out into the darkness, as though trying to see beyond the Christmas lights that partly illuminated his yard. "None of this has anything to do with me," he said.

"Let me ask you this question: When the warrants are cut, or if Max Coll is in town, looking for the people who put the whack on him, whose grits are going into the fire, yours or Castille LeJeune's?" I said.

Clete pumped a shell out of the shotgun's chamber and dropped it into Guillot's shirt pocket. "Twelve-gauge double-ought bucks. Load up your bird buster and stick it under your bed. Better than a warm glass of milk. You'll sleep like a baby. I guarantee it," he said, and gave Guillot the thumbs-up sign.

Ten minutes later we turned into Fox Run and drove down the long, oak-lined driveway to Castille LeJeune's front entrance. Almost the entire house was scrolled with white Christmas lights, so that the house glowed like a nineteenth-century paddle-wheeler inside a fog bank on the Mississippi. My guess was that Will Guillot had called LeJeune as soon as we had left his house, and I hoped, in an undeniably mean-spirited fashion, that for the first time in his life Castille LeJeune was genuinely afraid.

I parked at the end of the drive and cut the headlights on my truck. A solitary shadow moved across the windows in the living room. I started to get out, but Clete hadn't moved, the shotgun propped at an angle between his legs, the chamber open.

"Dave, Guillot's a sex freak and a lowlife and dirty up to his elbows. I'm not so sure about the guy in that house," he said.

I looked at him.

"All this crap isn't adding up for me," he said. "The war hero didn't pop the drive-by daiquiri guy and neither did Guillot, not if you buy his alibi. But for one reason or another we keep looking at the war hero. No matter what happens, it's always the war hero. Meanwhile Merchie Flannigan's old lady gets a free pass, the same broad who got you kidnapped."

"Theodosha is south Louisiana's answer to Bonnie Parker?" I said.

"Be a wise-ass if you want. You hate the guy in that house and the class of people he comes from."

"*I* do? You've been at war with these people all your life."

He took off his utility cap, looked at it as though he had never seen it before, then refitted it on his head. "He really bagged Bed Check Charley?" he asked.

"That's the story."

"I'd like to get his autograph. Hey, I'm serious," he said.

He got out of the truck, trying to suppress his grin, and followed me onto the porch. A white-jacketed black houseman answered door, a broom and dustpan in his hands.

"Is Mr. LeJeune home?" I said.

"Took his guests to the country club a half hour ago. I'm still cleaning up," the houseman said.

I opened my badge. "Did you receive a phone call in the last ten minutes?" I said.

"Yes, suh, I sure did," he answered.

"From whom?"

"My wife. She tole me to bring home a loaf of bread."

On the way to the country club Clete was still grinning.

"Why is all this funny?" I said.

"I miss the Mob. Shaking up a bunch of Kiwanians just doesn't cut it."

"You're too much, Cletus."

In that mood we pulled into the tree-bowered entrance of a small tennis and golf club outside the city limits. It wasn't hard to find Castille LeJeune. He and his friends were having drinks under a pavilion and driving golf balls on a lighted practice range dotted in the distance with moss-hung live oaks that smoked in the mist. The range looked hand clipped, immaculate, with neither a leaf nor wind-blown scrap of paper on it.

The pavilion seemed as isolated and disconnected from the outside world as the golf range was from the trash-strewn roads beyond the hedges that bordered the club. Deferential black waiters brought LeJeune and his friends their buttered rum drinks on silver trays; a Wurlitzer jukebox next to the bar played Glen Miller and Tommy Dorsey recordings; a rotund, cherry-cheeked man was speaking affectionately about "an old nigger" who had worked for his family, as though the waiters would take no offense at his language.

We locked the truck, with the twelve-gauge inside, and walked past the clay tennis courts, all of them deserted, the wind screens rattling in the breeze, just as Castille LeJeune whacked a ball off a tee and sent it downrange in a high, beautiful arc. The people at the tables or teeing up from wire buckets filled with golf balls showed no recognition of our presence. LeJeune positioned himself, swung his driver back, and once again lifted the ball surgically off the tee, high into the darkness, a testimony to his health, the power in his wrists and shoulders, and the maturity and skill he brought to his game.

Clete used a toothpick to spear a peeled shrimp from a large bowl of crushed ice on the bar, dipping it in hot sauce, inserting it in his mouth. His badge holder was stuck in his belt, mine in the breast pocket of my sports coat. But still no one looked at us.

"Give me a Jack straight up with a beer back," he said to the bartender.

"Right away, suh," the bartender replied.

"That's a joke," Clete said.

LeJeune's friends were not people who had to contend with the world. They may not have owned it, nor would they take any part of it through the grave, but while they were alive they could lay rental claims on a very large portion of it.

"Mr. LeJeune, we'd like for you to come with us to the Iberia Parish Sheriff's Department," I said.

"Why should I do that, Mr. Robicheaux?" he replied, addressing the ball on his tee, his feet spread, his thighs flexed tightly.

"We need you to answer some questions about the murder of Dr. Samuel Bernstine and the fact Will Guillot has been blackmailing you about your molestation of your daughter when she was a child," I said.

In the silence I could hear leaves scraping across the surface of the tennis court. LeJeune seemed to gaze at an isolated thought in the center of his mind, then he sighted downrange and smacked the ball in a straight line, like a rifle shot, so that it did not strike earth again until it was almost to the oak trees smoking in the electric lights.

"You need to talk to my attorney, Mr. Robicheaux, not to me," he said.

"Did you hear what I said? We're investigating a homicide, the second one that happens to be connected with your name. We don't call attorneys to make appointments," I said.

He turned and dropped his driver in an upended leather golf bag.

He wore a silk scarf around his neck, as an aviator might, the ends tucked inside a sweater with small brown buttons on it. In the corner of my eye I saw two security guards walking from the club's main building and a man at the bar punching in numbers on a cell phone.

LeJeune began chatting with a woman seated at a table as though I were not there. Then I started to lose it.

"You had Junior Crudup beaten to death," I said. "You turned your daughter's childhood into a sexual nightmare. You sell liquor to drunk drivers and probably dope and porn in New Orleans. You think you're going to walk away from all this?"

"Mr. Robicheaux, I don't know if you're a vindictive man, or simply well-meaning and incompetent. The truth is probably somewhere in between. But you need to leave, sir, to let this thing go and give yourself some peace," he replied.

His detachment and his pose as a chivalric and charitable patriarch were magnificent. As Clete had always said, some people have no handles on them. Castille LeJeune was obviously one of them, and I felt like a fool.

Then Clete, who all night had been the advocate of reason and restraint, stepped forward, his thick arm and shoulder knocking against mine. "You were a fighter pilot in the Crotch?" he said.

"In the *what*?" LeJeune said.

"I was in the Corps, too. Sunny 'Nam, class of '69, smokin' grass and stompin' ass with Mother Green's Mean Machine. See?" He removed his utility cap and pointed to the globe and anchor emblem inked on the cloth. "We used to have a Bed Check Charley, but he was a guy who'd start lobbing blooker rounds in on us at about oh-two-hundred so nobody could get any sleep. Do you have any autographed photos? No shit, it'd mean a lot."

"Sir, I don't ask this for myself, but there're ladies present. Let's don't have this kind of scene here," LeJeune said.

"I can dig it," Clete said, putting his cap back on, his eyes cocked up in his head as though he were meditating upon a metaphysical consideration. "The problem is some greaseballs kidnapped and tortured a police officer and pissed all over his face while he was blindfolded. So how about taking the corn bread out of your mouth? It's getting to be a real drag."

"I apologize for any offense I may have given you," LeJeune said. "Tell me something, that badge you have hanging from your belt? I have the feeling you're not a police officer."

I could see the heat climbing into Clete's face. "Dave, hook up this prick. Work out the legal stuff later," he said.

The situation was deteriorating rapidly now. Two security guards had just walked into the pavilion and were standing behind us, awkward, unsure what they should do next. I turned so they could see my badge. "It's all right. Iberia Parish Sheriff's Department," I said.

They tried to be polite, their eyes avoiding mine. I felt sorry for them. They made little more than minimum wage, paid for their own uniforms, and possessed no legal powers. They waited for Castille LeJeune to tell them what to do.

But I raised my finger before he could speak. "We're leaving," I said.

"Screw that," Clete said.

Two cruisers from the St. Mary Parish Sheriff's office had pulled into the parking lot and three uniformed deputies, one black, two white, were walking toward us, their faces filled with purpose. I slipped my hand around the thickness of Clete's arm and tightened my grip. "We're done here," I said.

But it was too late. The three deputies went straight for Clete, with the collective instinct of pack hounds who had just gotten a sniff of a feral hog. At first he didn't resist. When they walked him toward a cruiser, he was seemingly in control of himself again, grinning, full of fun, back in his familiar role of irreverent trickster, ready to let it all play out.

Maybe I should have stayed out of it. But I didn't.

"Let's slow it down a little bit," I said to the black deputy, a towering man with lieutenant's bars on his collar.

"Best let us do our job, Robicheaux," he replied.

"What's the beef?" I said.

"Impersonating a police officer," he replied.

"That's bogus. He never claimed to be a police officer."

"Work it out at the jail. We just deliver the freight," he said.

It should have all ended there, a routine roust to appease a rich man, a discussion down at the sheriff's department, maybe a few hours in a holding cell, at worst an appearance in morning court where the charge would be kicked.

But one of the white deputies, an angry man with corded veins in his neck who had been fired in another parish for abusing a prisoner, had pushed Clete into a search position against the hood of the cruiser and was running his hands down Clete's left leg.

"Ease up, my man," Clete said.

"Close your mouth," the deputy said.

"That's a slapjack in my right hand pocket. I'm not carrying," Clete said, twisting around.

"I told you to shut up," the deputy said, and slapped Clete's utility cap off his head.

Clete ripped his elbow into the deputy's face, breaking his nose, then caught him in the jaw with a right hook that lifted him off the ground and knocked him the full length of the cruiser.

"Ouch," he said, trying to shake the pain out of his hand, trying to step back from his own misdeed.

Then they were on him.

Chapter 25

It rained at sunrise and kept raining through the morning. Clete was in jail and Father Jimmie had not returned to the house. Because it was Saturday Helen was at home. I called her and told her how it had gone south at Castille LeJeune's golf and tennis club.

"What did you plan to accomplish over there?" she said.

"Not sure."

"I am. You wanted to provoke a confrontation and blow pieces of Castille LeJeune all over the golf tee."

"That's a little strong."

I thought she was going to give it to me but she didn't. "As far as you know, Guillot didn't try to call LeJeune after you went to Guillot's house?" she said.

"When we went to LeJeune's house, the man cleaning up said nobody had called except his wife. She wanted him to pick up a loaf of bread."

"Maybe LeJeune is not the guy we should be after."

"He's the guy."

"I think I'm going to do something more rewarding today, like have a conversation with a pile of bricks," she said.

"Did you just hear something on the line?"

"Hear what?"

"A friend in New Orleans said I probably have a federal tap on my phone."

"Have a nice weekend, Dave."

Clete was in serious trouble and would not be able to bond out of jail until he was arraigned Monday morning. The impersonation beef was a gray area. A person does not have to specifically claim to be a police officer in order to be guilty of impersonating one. He simply has to give the impression of being one. But Clete had licensed P.I. status and ironically, as an employee of a bail bond service, possessed legal powers that no law officer did, namely, he could cross state lines and even break into residences without a warrant to arrest a bail skip who was a fugitive from a court proceeding.

The assault-and-battery beef was another matter. With luck and some finesse, an expensive, politically connected lawyer could probably get the charge kicked down to resisting. But it wasn't going to be easy. Clete's reputation for violence, destruction of property, and general anarchy was scorched into the landscape all the way across southern Louisiana. His enemies had longed for the day he would load the gun for them. Now I had helped him do it.

I went to Baron's Health Club, worked out with free weights, then sat for a half hour in the steam room. When I came back outside it was still raining, harder than before, litter floating in the ditches that bordered the streets. I went to an afternoon A.A. meeting above the Methodist church by the railroad tracks and listened to a man talk about nightmares he still had from the Vietnam War. His face was seamed, unshaved, his body flaccid, his clothes mismatched. He had been eighty-sixed out of every bar in the parish and he had been put out of two V.A. alcoholic treatment programs. He began to talk about a massacre of innocent persons inside a free-fire zone.

I couldn't listen to it. I left the meeting and drove home. When I pulled into the driveway my yard was flooded halfway to the gallery and Theodosha Flannigan was waiting for me by the door, a rain-spotted scarf tied on her head, her face filled with consternation. Snuggs was turning in circles around her ankles.

"I know all about last night," she said.

"Not a good day for it, Theo," I said, unlocking the door.

I went in the house without inviting her inside, but she followed me anyway, Snuggs racing past us toward the food bowl in the kitchen.

"My father didn't molest me. It was a black man. That's why I was seeing Dr. Bernstine," she said.

"Don't do this, Theo."

"When I was a little girl a black convict got in our house and hurt me. He was killed running down toward the bayou."

"Killed by whom?"

"A prison guard. He worked at the labor camp. He and the other guards buried him in back. I saw the bones when the fish pond was dug. They were sticking out of the dirt in a front-end loader."

"You've been fed a lie."

"It's the truth. I went over every detail of it with my father."

"Bernstine told you your father raped or molested you, didn't he?"

"It doesn't matter. I know what happened."

"When you first told me about Bernstine's death, you said you thought you had something to do with it."

"I was confused. I know the truth now."

I gave up. Through the kitchen window I could see steam rising off the bayou in the rain. Theodosha picked up Snuggs, set him on the counter, and rubbed her hand down his back. "Merchie is leaving me," she said.

"That's too bad."

"We're not good for each other. We never were. I'm too messed up and he's too ambitious."

"I have some things to do today, Theo."

I could hear an oak branch slapping against the side of the house, water rushing out of a gutter into the drive.

"We had fun together, didn't we?" she said.

"Yeah, sure," I replied.

"Know why we're alike?"

"No."

"We both live in the cities of the dead. We don't belong with other people."

"That's not true. Why did you use that term?" I said, my heart quickening.

But she didn't answer. She lifted up Snuggs and set him back down on the floor, then touched me on both cheeks and kissed me on the mouth. "So long, baby. I never told you this, but you're the only man I ever slept with and dreamed about later," she said.

She went out the front door, letting the screen slam behind her, then ran for her car. I had to force myself not to go after her.

I lay down on my bedspread, with my arm across my eyes, and listened to the rain on the roof. I drifted off to sleep and suddenly saw an image out of my past, one that had no catalyst other than perhaps the story told by the war veteran at the noon A.A. meeting. I saw the members of my platoon marching at night through a rain forest that had been denuded by napalm. Their faces and uniforms and steel pots, even the green sweat towels draped over their heads like monk's cowls, were gray with ash. They cast no shadows and made no sound as they marched and their eyes were all possessed by the strange non-human look that soldiers call the thousand-yard stare.

I sat straight up in my bed, my throat choking.

The phone was ringing in the kitchen. I went to the counter and picked it up, the dream still more real than the world around me. "Hello?" I said.

"Is Father Dolan there?"

"Coll?"

"Sorry to be a nuisance, Mr. Robicheaux. I just wanted to pass on something to Father Dolan."

My mind began to race. Castille LeJeune had remained untouchable and was about to skate. Will Guillot could probably not be charged with any crime more serious than breaking and entering, and the evidence against him was problematic and subject to easy dissection by a defense attorney.

"I owe you one, Max. That means I don't want to see you taken off the board by a couple of local scum wads," I said.

"Could you be speaking a little more plainly, sir?" he replied.

My pulse was beating in my wrists, the veins dilating in my scalp. "I think the clip on you came down from a couple of homegrown characters in the porn and meth trade. Maybe you should stay out of Franklin, Louisiana, and spend more time at Biscayne Dog Track," I said.

"A couple of local fellows, you say? Now, that's interesting, be-

cause I'd come to a very different conclusion. I thought the porn connection was the woman, the screenwriter, Ms. Flannigan. She's the
brains in the family, not her father. The colored people hereabouts
say he may have had his way with her when she was a child. This fellow Guillot is trying to take over the business, so Ms. Flannigan does
the daiquiri fellow, draws a lot of attention to her father's selling grog
to teenagers and drunk drivers, and uses Guillot's gun to do it. Perfect way to screw both her daddy and her business rival."

"Why would Theo Flannigan be the porn connection?"

"I'm ashamed to say I'm well acquainted with a number of low-
lifes in the underworld who say Sammy Figorelli's films were successful because they were written by a famous woman author. It's
not a big reach to figure out who that might be. . . . Hello? Are you
there?"

"Yes," I said weakly.

"I've never harmed a woman, sir, so I let the matter go. But I'll be
reamed up the bung hole with a spiked telephone pole if you haven't
made me reconsider the LeJeune and Guillot fellows."

"Hold on, Coll."

"No, you've done me a favor. I've got to cancel my flight reserva-
tions and give it all a good think. Tell Father Dolan thanks for his
help. A tip of the hat to yourself as well."

The line went dead. I replaced the receiver and wiped my face with
a dish towel. I tried to sort through the conversation I had just had
with Max Coll. My head was a basket of snakes, my mouth dry, my
thoughts suddenly centered on a jigger of Beam poured into an iced
mug of draft beer inside a Saturday-afternoon bar that was only two
blocks up the street.

Father Jimmie Dolan's car pulled into the driveway, pushing a
wave of water under the house. When he entered the front door he
was smiling, his tan, wide-brim hat dripping. "Any calls for me?" he
asked.

I drove downtown to the restaurant that used to be Provost's Pool
Room. It was warm and cheerful and crowded inside, and I sat at the

hand-carved mahogany bar and looked out the window at the wetness of the day and the traffic passing in the street. As a boy I used to
come to the pool room on Saturday afternoons with my father, Big
Aldous, in a era when the plank floors were strewn with football betting cards and green sawdust and the owner served free robin gumbo
out of big pots that he set on an oilcloth-covered pool table. The
stamped tin ceilings and mahogany bar and old brick walls still remained, but the building was an upscale restaurant now that catered
to tourists who came to see a world that no longer existed.

The bartender wore his hair slicked back and black pants and a
white jacket and black tie. "You just gonna have coffee, sir?" he asked.

"How about I buy you a drink?" I said.

"Sir?"

"It's not a complicated question." It sounded bad but I grinned
when I said it.

He shrugged. "I get off in a hour," he said.

I put several one-dollar bills on the bar. "Make sure it's Beam or
Jack," I said.

"You got it," he said, scooping up the bills.

Then I drove back home and went into the kitchen, where Father
Jimmie was reading the newspaper. He lowered the paper, then
looked curiously at my face. "It can't be that bad, can it?" he said.

So I told him how bad it was, or at least how bad I thought it was;
but I was to learn my education about my own obtrusiveness was on-
going. After I finished he sat for a long time without speaking, his
gaze turned inward, unable to conceal his disappointment at either
me or his own missionary failure, or the world as it really is. I suspect
I wanted absolution, like a child going to confession on a Saturday afternoon, leaving behind his imaginary sins, bounding down the
street as though a stricken world has just been made whole again. But
that wasn't to be.

Father Jimmie had a look of sadness in his eyes that I cannot ade-
quately describe. "You don't know what you've done," he said.

"Maybe I have at least a fair idea," I replied.

"Max met with me outside Franklin. He expressed what I think

was genuine remorse for the evil he's done in his life. I gave him absolution. But you hung the bait in his face and energized him. My God,
man, we're talking about his soul."

I felt light-headed, as though I were coming down with the flu.
When I tried to speak I couldn't clear the obstruction in my throat.
Father Jimmie filled a glass with water but did not hand it to me.

"Listen, Coll changed his direction because he didn't want to kill a
woman," I said.

"It makes no difference."

"It does. I never thought about Theo being involved. Even though
Clete kept warning me, I never thought about Theo."

Father Jimmie realized I had already moved on from my own irre-
sponsibility and was now concentrating on another matter, one that
showed a degree of obsession beyond his grasp. He set down the glass
and turned on me. I saw his right hand close. His next words were
spoken through his teeth: "Don't deceive yourself. You're a violent
and driven man, Dave, just like Max Coll."

His eyelids were stitched to his brows, his throat bladed with anger
and rebuke.

That evening the sky was as dark as I had ever seen it. Lightning rip-
pled like quicksilver across the thunderheads in the south, and the
sugarcane in the fields along the road to St. Martinville thrashed and
flickered in the wind and rain, the oak canopy blowing leaves that
stuck like leeches on my windshield. I went to Mass in the old French
church on the square in St. Martinville, then when the church was
empty put five dollars in the poor box and removed an unlit votive
candle in a red glass receptacle and took it with me down to the
cemetery on the bayou.

It was a foolish thing to do, I suspect, but I had long ago come to
view the world as an unreasonable place, not to be contended with,
better left to pragmatists and the mercantile who view the imagination and the unseen as their enemy. I parked under the streetlight,
opened an umbrella, and walked between the crypts toward Bootsie's

tomb. A generic compact car passed behind me, turned at the corner, and disappeared down a side street.

The bayou was high, dented with rain rings, yellow in the lights from the drawbridge. I placed the votive candle next to the marble tablet on Bootsie's tomb, wedged the umbrella so that it sheltered the candle from the rain and wind, then lit the wick.

The same compact car came out of the square and crossed the drawbridge, but I paid little attention to it. An event I had never seen in my life was taking place in front of me. Two huge brown pelicans drifted out from under the bridge, floating south on the tidal current, their wings folded tightly against the wind, their long yellow bills tucked down on their chests. I had never seen pelicans this far inland and had no explanation for their presence. Then I did something that made me wonder about my level of sanity.

I rose from the steel bench I was sitting on, pointing at the two birds, and said, "Take a look, Boots. These guys were almost extinct a few years ago. They're beautiful."

Then I sat down and folded my arms on my chest, the rain clicking on my coat.

That's when I saw the compact in plain relief against the streetlight at the corner. It was pulled into a careless position at the curb, steam rising from the hood, the driver moving around in silhouette, as though he were having trouble with his safety belt.

Dave! a voice said, as audibly as a voice speaking to you on the edge of sleep, as defined as a stick snapping inside the eardrum.

I rose from the bench just as the streetlight glinted on the lens of a telescopic sight and the muzzle flash of a rifle splintered from the passenger window of the compact car. The bullet whanged off the steel bench and blew pieces off a statue of Jesus's mother.

I ducked down between the crypts and pulled my .45 from my belt holster and sighted with two hands on the compact. But there were houses on the far side of the street and I couldn't fire. I started running toward the compact, the .45 held at an upward angle, zigzagging between the crypts, my eyes locked on the driver, who was fighting to straighten the car's wheels so he would not hit the curb.

He pulled around a parked pickup truck and floored the compact down the street. In seconds he would be beyond any safe angle of fire that I would have. I left the sidewalk and ran toward the corner of the cemetery, jumped on top of a crypt, and went over the chainlink fence into the street. The compact was twenty-five to thirty yards away, headed down the bayou in the direction of the church, the license plated patinaed with mud. I stood in the center of the street, both arms extended, and aimed low on the trunk.

I squeezed off three rounds, the recoil knocking my forearms upward, the muzzle throwing sparks into the darkness, the spent shells tinkling on the pavement. I don't know what I hit inside the compact, but I heard the hard slap of all three hollow-point rounds bite into metal.

The compact swerved around a corner and disappeared down a tree-lined side street that looked like an illustration clipped from a 1940 issue of *The Saturday Evening Post*.

I went back to my truck and used my cell phone to punch in a 911 on the compact, then walked to Bootsie's tomb, my ears still ringing from the explosions of the .45. The umbrella had not been disturbed by the wind and the candle was burning brightly inside its red receptacle, but the pelicans had flown or drifted southward on the current.

I heard your voice, I said.

But there was no reply.

I don't care who else knows it, either. That was your voice, Boots, I said.

Then I said a prayer for her and one for me and headed back for the truck, wishing the pelicans had not gone.

Don't worry, they'll be back. One of these days when you least expect it, you'll see them on Bayou Teche, she said.

I turned around, my jaw hanging, the clouds blooming with electricity that made no sound.

Chapter 26

I rose before dawn Sunday morning and ate a breakfast of Grape-Nuts and coffee and hot milk in the kitchen. When I opened the front door to leave I saw an envelope on the porch with a footprint stenciled across it and realized it must have fallen out of the door-jamb the previous night and been stepped on by either me or Father Jimmie.

The letter inside was handwritten and read:

> Dear Mr. Robicheaux,
>   I must talk to you. I don't know why all this is happening. We moved here to live in a decent environment and look what everyone has done to us. I also do not understand this new development. Nobody will answer my questions. I think all of you people suck. Call me at home. Do it right now.
>
> Sincerely,
Donna Parks

In my memory I saw a stump of a woman, with dyed red hair and perfume that was like a chemical assault on the senses, a ring of fat under her chin. She was the mother of Lori Parks, the teenage girl who had died with two others inside their burning automobile on Loreauville Road. I did not look forward to seeing Mrs. Parks again.

I put away her note and drove to Franklin. The parking compound for Sunbelt Construction was located behind a house trailer that served as a company office. In the lot were trucks of every kind, front-end loaders, bulldozers, and grading machines but no compact car that resembled the shooter's.

I drove back to New Iberia and parked in Merchie and Theodosha Flannigan's driveway. Their faux medieval home was shrouded in fog puffing off the bayou, their horses nickering and blowing inside the pecan orchard. The morning newspaper was still inside the metal cylinder at the foot of the drive, but woodsmoke was rising from a living room fireplace. There was no compact car anywhere in sight, but I did not expect to see one. In fact, I did not know why I had come to the Flannigans' home. Perhaps it was to prove somehow that Theo was not involved with a criminal enterprise, that she was a victim herself and not capable of setting me up to be kidnapped and tortured by the Dellacroce brothers. Maybe I just wanted to believe the world was a more innocent place than it is.

I got out of the truck and rested my hands on the top rail of the white fence that bordered the pecan orchard and watched the Flannigans' thoroughbreds moving about in the fog. I could hear their hooves thudding on the soft earth, smell the fecund odor of the bayou, like the smell of humus and fish roe, and the pecan husks and blackened leaves that had been trodden into pulp in the trees, and I wondered how it was that a place this beautiful would not be enough for anyone, why each morning would not come to the owner like a blessing extended by a divine hand.

Theodosha opened the front door and walked down the drive in her bathrobe and slippers, her hair black and shiny in the grayness of the morning. "What are you doing out here?" she asked.

"How bad would you be willing to screw an old friend?" I said.

"It's pretty early in the morning for your craziness, Dave."

"Your novels were nominated twice for Edgars but they didn't win. If your script-writing career was on track, I think you'd be out in the Hollywood Hills, not on the bayou. Maybe Fat Sammy Figorelli's skin films were a shortcut to being back on the big screen."

"You're sickening," she said.

"Somebody shot at me last night."

"I can't imagine why."

"Did you set me up with the Dellacroces?"

She walked past me and pulled the morning paper from the metal delivery receptacle, then started back up the drive toward her house. "Too bad it's Sunday," she said.

"Why's that?"

"The state mental hygiene unit in Lafayette is closed. But if I were you, I'd jump right on it first thing in the morning," she said, opening the paper, not bothering to even glance at me as she spoke.

When I got back home, Father Jimmie was gone, his closet empty. He had left a recording for me on my message machine, its brevity like a shard of glass: "So long, Dave. Thanks for your hospitality. I hope everything works out for you."

There was also a voice message from Donna Parks: "Why don't you answer my goddamn letter, you callous fuck?"

It was going to be a long day.

I tried to eat lunch but had no appetite. As I washed my dishes and put away my uneaten food, I looked through a window and saw Helen Soileau pull into the driveway. She got out of the cruiser and walked to the gallery, wearing faded jeans, boots, and a mackinaw, her jaw set. I opened the door before she could knock.

"I was out of town, so I just got the report on the car sniper," she said, walking past me into the warmth of the living room. "Go over it for me."

I went over each detail with her and also told her I had been to Franklin that morning to look for the compact car I had put three rounds in.

"Anybody from St. Mary Parish contact you?" she asked.

"No," I said.

"Yesterday somebody got past the alarm system at both Castille LeJeune's and Will Guillot's house. In the middle of the afternoon. A real pro. Know who it might be?"

"Max Coll," I said.

"What was he looking for?"

"Evidence they put a hit on him."

"I hate to even ask this question. How would you know this?"

"He called here yesterday. I more or less told him there were two local guys behind the contract on him and they lived in Franklin."

She stood at the ceiling-high living room window and stared out at the street and at the rain dripping through the canopy of live oaks that arched over it, her fists propped on her hips. "Want to tell me your motivation for doing that?" she said.

"I owed him one."

"We don't owe criminals. We break their wheels and put them out of business. We don't make individual judgments on the people we need to arrest."

"I don't see it that way."

"There are a lot of things you don't see," she replied, turning to look directly at me. "I'm pulling your shield, bwana."

I nodded, my expression flat. "It's been that kind of day," I said. I slipped my badge holder out of my pocket and handed it to her. "Coll thinks Theo Flannigan may have been the porn connection to Sammy Figorelli. Maybe she was the shooter in the daiquiri drive-by. In case you want to follow that up."

Helen flipped my badge holder back and forth in her hand while she listened, then she tucked it into her pocket. "Sometimes you break my heart," she said.

I had been suspended before, put on a desk, investigated by Internal Affairs, locked up on at least three occasions, and years ago fired by N.O.P.D. But this time was different. The suspension came not from a career administrator but from my old partner, a woman who had been excoriated as a lesbian and who had never allowed the taunts and odium heaped upon her to diminish either her integrity or the dignity and courage that obviously governed her life.

The fact that it was she who had pulled my plug made me wonder if indeed I hadn't gone way beyond the envelope and become one of those jaundiced and embittered law officers whose careers do not end but flame out in a curlicue of dirty smoke that forever obscures the clarity of their moral vision.

But that kind of thinking is what we call in A.A. the paralysis of analysis. In terms of worth it shares commonalities with masturbation, asking a rage-a-holic for advice on spiritual serenity, or listening to your own thoughts while trapped by yourself between floors in a stalled elevator.

I went into the kitchen and called Donna Parks at her home. There was no answer. I left a message on her machine and drove to Franklin to visit Clete Purcel in jail.

A turnkey walked me down a corridor to an isolation cell, one with horizonal bars, flat cross-plates, and an iron food slit in the door, but with nothing inside except a stainless steel toilet and a metal bench bolted to the floor. Clete was sitting on the bench, still in his street clothes, his wrists locked to his hips with a waist chain, another chain locked between his ankles. His right eye was swollen into a puffed knot, his forehead and chin scraped raw. The cement floor outside the cell door was splattered with red beans, rice, two pieces of white bread, and coffee from a broken Styrofoam cup.

"Who did that to his face?" I said.

"He come in like that," the turnkey said.

"That's a lie," I said.

"He wouldn't put on his jumpsuit. He threw his tray at a deputy. You got issues with it, talk to the boss. I just clean up the mess," the turnkey said, and walked away.

I hung my hands through the bars. "How you doin', Cletus?" I said.

He stood up from the bench and shuffled toward me, his chains clinking on the cement. "I'm going to look up a couple of these guys when I get out of here," he said.

"Why do you have to provoke them?"

"It's fun."

"I'm suspended. I don't have any clout to help you."

"What'd you do?"

"Fired up Max Coll and pointed him at LeJeune and Guillot. I figured my line was tapped and I might get the Feds in here."

"I keep telling you, it's the broad."

"Maybe it is."

Then his eyes went away from mine and looked into space. "Nig and Wee Willie won't go bail," he said.

"Why not?"

"They're pissed because of that dinner I charged on their card at Galatoire's. Plus two of the girls skipped their court appearances and Nig's putting it on me."

"What kind of bail are we talking about?" I asked.

"A screw tried to do an anal search on me. He's going to need some dental work. So I've got two separate A&B's on a law officer."

I touched my forehead against the bars and closed my eyes. Clete kicked the door with the point of his shoe, rattling it in the jamb. "Listen up, Dave. We're the good guys. The problem is nobody else knows it. But that's their problem, not ours," he said.

I left the jail and parked my truck on an oyster-shell road down by Bayou Teche, just outside the Franklin city limits. Rain was falling on the trees around my truck, and across the bayou were a cow pasture, a collapsed red barn, and a solitary black man in a straw hat, sitting on an inverted bucket, cane-pole fishing under a live oak. I got out of the truck, tossed a pine cone into the current, and watched it float southward toward the Gulf.

Clete had made a point, one which I don't think was either vituperative or vain. Legal definitions had little to do with morality. It was legal to systemically poison the earth and sell arms to Third World lunatics. Politicians who themselves had avoided active service and never had listened to the sounds a flame thrower extracted from its victims, or zipped up body bags on the faces of their best friends, clamored for war and stood proudly in front of the flag while they sent others off to fight it.

The polluters and the war advocates are always legal men, as the Prince of Darkness is always a gentleman.

The John Gottis of the world make good entertainment. The polluters and the war advocates can be seen at prayer, on camera, in the National Cathedral. Unlike John Gotti, they're not very interesting, but they cause infinitely more damage.

The chances were I would never take down Castille LeJeune for the murder of Junior Crudup. Nor did it look like I would solve the shooting of the drive-by daiquiri store operator or Fat Sammy Figorelli. The people who had committed these crimes did not have patterns and to one degree or another operated with public sanction. They might go down for an ancillary offense, but at worst they would do minimum time, if not get probation.

But regardless of what occurred in the lives of others, I was going to clear my conscience of a problem I had created because of my desire to control a situation in which I had failed.

I drove through the wet streets of Franklin, out to Fox Run, and lifted the false knocker on the front door that activated the chimes deep inside the house. A moment later Castille LeJeune answered the door, dressed in sweat clothes, a towel twisted around his throat, surprisingly pleasant, his face ruddy from riding an exercise bike by the sun room that gave onto the back patio, the same patio where Junior Crudup had entertained him and his wife fifty years ago.

"Come in, sir," he said, opening the door wider.

"I don't know if you'll want me in your house after you hear what I have to say," I said.

He laughed and closed the door behind me. "Go ahead. I know a determined man when I see one. But excuse me just a minute. I have to use the bathroom," he said.

He went into a hallway and closed a door behind him, then I heard him urinating into a toilet bowl. Through the French doors I could see the long slope of his backyard tapering down to the bayou, a yellow bulldozer parked by the area we had excavated during our search for Junior Crudup's remains. Much of the dirt had been filled in, smoothed and tamped down, so that the lawn was now a mottled brown and green, in patterns like camouflage.

I heard LeJeune washing his hands, then he came back into the living room.

"I couldn't stick you with Junior Crudup's death, so I tried to sic a psychological nightmare by the name of Max Coll on you," I said.

"Ah, a mea culpa because you've put me at risk. Let me clarify something for you—"

"If I can finish, please. Using Coll was a gutless act on my part. If I had wanted you smoked, I should have done it myself instead of exploiting a headcase."

"I admire your candor, Mr. Robicheaux. But I'm not bothered by Coll's presence in the community. I walked in on him and he fled. If this fellow is indeed a soldier for the IRA, which is what I've been told, then I understand why the British are still in control of northern Ireland."

"Wait a minute. You saw Coll?"

"I just told you that." He stared at me, his eyes probing mine.

"Was he armed?"

"He might have been. It's hard to say. I didn't bother to ask."

"Where did he go?"

"Out the back door. I've reported all this."

"You might drop by the church today and light a candle, maybe offer a prayer of thanks that a guy like Father Jimmie Dolan is a minister in the Catholic Church," I said.

"As always with you, Mr. Robicheaux, I have no idea what you're talking about. But if this man Coll comes back around, he'll rue the day he left his little shanty back in the peat bogs or wherever he comes from. . . . Am I losing your attention?"

"Hubris has always been my undoing, Mr. LeJeune. Maybe it will be different with you. Anyway, my badge has been pulled and I'm done. Run your happy warrior act on somebody else," I said.

When I got back home I put on sweat pants and a hooded jersey, tied on my running shoes, and jogged down East Main, past the Shadows and the plantation caretaker's house across the street, which now served as a bed-and-breakfast, and crossed the drawbridge into City

Park. I ran along the winding paved road through the live oak trees, my clothes soggy with mist, then cut across the closely clipped grass and ran along the edge of the bayou. In our area the sugar mills are fired up twenty-four hours a day during the cane-grinding season, and in the distance I could see a huge red glow on the horizon, like fire trapped inside a thunderhead, and I could hear the heavy thumping sound of the machines, like the reverberation of giant feet stamping upon the earth. There was not another soul inside the park, and for just a moment my heart quickened and I felt more alone than I had ever felt in my life.

I sat down on a bench, my palms propped on my thighs, my breath coming hard in my throat. What was it Theodosha had said? We were alike because we both lived in the cities of the dead? I wiped the sweat off my face with my jersey and fought to get my breath back, widening my eyes, concentrating on the details around me, as though my ability to remain among the quick depended on my perception of them.

Is this the way it comes? I thought—not with a clicking sound and a brilliant flash of light on a night trail in Vietnam, or with a high-powered round fired by a sniper in a compact automobile, but instead with a racing of the heart and a shortening of the breath in a black-green deserted park smudged by mist and threaded by a tidal stream.

My head hammered with sound that was like helicopter blades thropping overhead, and for just a moment I was back on a slick piled with wounded and dying grunts, AK-47 rounds vectoring out of the jungle canopy down below, the inside of the airframe crawling with smoke.

I put my head down between my knees, my hands on the pavement, the world spinning around me.

I looked up and saw from out of the mist a pink Cadillac convertible headed toward me, one with wire wheels, tail fins, Frenched headlights, and grillwork that was like a chromium smile, the radio blaring with 1950s Jerry Lee Lewis rock 'n' roll.

The Cadillac passed me and behind the wheel I saw a man with an impish face, the features cartoonlike, as though they had been sketched with a charcoal pencil, the hair shaved on the sides and left long and curly on the neck.

"Gunner?" I said out loud.

But the driver did not hear me, and the Cadillac wound its way out of the park, the only piece of bright color inside the failing light.

Gunner Ardoin in New Iberia? I asked myself. No, I had let my imagination run away with itself. The year was 2002, not 1957, and the rock 'n' roll days of pink Cadillacs, drive-in movies, Jerry Lee Lewis, and American innocence were over.

At 10:00 P.M. I turned on the local news. The lead story involved a homicide inside a Franklin residence. The television camera panned on a tree-lined street and a Victorian home where paramedics were exiting a side door with a gurney on which a figure inside a body bag was strapped down. The reporter at the scene said the victim had been shot once in the temple and once in the mouth and, according to the coroner, had been dead approximately twelve hours. The victim's name was William Raymond Guillot.

Chapter 27

It was still raining Monday morning, the air cold, the fog heavy among the crypts in St. Peter's Cemetery as I pulled into the parking lot at the courthouse.

Wally, our leviathan dispatcher, made a face when he saw me come through the front door. "Dave, you ain't suppose to be here," he said.

"Pretend I'm not," I said.

"Don't jam me up here. I'm your friend, remember?"

"Is anybody working the Guillot homicide?" I said.

"I didn't even hear you say that. I'm deaf and dumb here. Go home," he replied.

Helen's door was ajar. I went inside without knocking. "What's happening in Franklin with the Guillot shooting?" I said.

"None of your business," she said.

"They made Max Coll for the hit?"

"One in the temple, one down the throat. The signature of a pro," she said.

"I don't buy it."

"What you need to buy is a hearing aid. You were suspended as of yesterday. Now haul your ass out of here."

"I talked with Castille LeJeune late yesterday afternoon. He says he walked in on Coll while Coll was creeping his house. If Coll was going to pop anybody, he would have done it then."

"You went out to LeJeune's, after I pulled your badge?"

"I told him I was suspended. It was a personal visit."

She shook her head, nonplussed. "We have an attorney in lawyer jail right now. I'm about to put you in there with him," she said.

"Coll isn't the shooter."

"Don't be on the premises when I get back." She walked down the hall and into the women's restroom, glancing back at me just before she pushed open the door, as though my argument for Coll's innocence had just sunk a hook on the edge of her mouth.

Louisiana is a small state, with a comparatively small population. In the year 2002 over 950 people were killed and 55,000 injured on our state highways. Booze was a major factor in most of the fatalities. Hence, the presence of a drunk person behind the wheel of an automobile in Louisiana is hardly an anomaly. So I had no reason to be surprised when I picked up the phone in my kitchen and heard a woman's voice say, "Why don't you do something about this goddamn traffic light out here on the four-lane?"

"Who is this?" I asked.

"Donna Parks, who does it sound like? The man in front of me is driving a shit box that's smoking up the whole town. He won't turn left because there's no arrow on the traffic light and I have to breathe his goddamn exhaust fumes."

For just a moment I had the uncharitable thought that her husband, Dr. Parks, was better off dead.

"What could I do for you, Ms. Parks?"

"I want to file rape charges."

"You've been sexually assaulted?"

"Like my deceased husband said, you people are really dumb. I'll come over there and explain it to you. Where are you?"

"Since you dialed me at my home number, I think we should both conclude I'm at home."

She belched softly, then I heard what was probably her car horn blowing just before the line went dead.

With luck she would have an accident before she got to my house, I thought.

I looked at my watch. Clete's arraignment was at 11:00 A.M. I wrote a note for Donna Parks, included my cell phone number on it, and stuck the note inside the grill on the front screen. Eventually I would have to deal with her, but it would be easier to do by phone than in person. I put Snuggs on the back porch, slipped my checkbook in my pocket, and started out the door, just as Merchie Flannigan pulled into the driveway, blocking my truck. He worked his way around the puddles in the yard and stepped up on the gallery, raking back his long, white-gold hair with his fingers.

"Hang on, old buddy. Need to clear up my remarks to you when you came by the house," he said.

"I'm in a hurry, Merchie," I said.

"Let's face it. I was jealous. Theo and I haven't had the best marriage. You said I was out of line. You were right." He extended his hand, his jaw square, like an imitation of an athletic, educated, country club millionaire, one he had probably seen on a movie screen as a child and had spent a lifetime trying to become.

I didn't take his hand. "I think you're here covering your wife's ass. Will Guillot got popped and the cops are going to be taking a hard look at his enterprises. I believe Theo is part of a porn operation in New Orleans," I said.

The smile died on his face. "You're actually serious? You believe Theo is involved with pornography?" he said.

"The word is she wrote scripts for Fat Sammy Figorelli. Where was she the night the daiquiri store operator got shot?"

He slipped his hands into his pockets and looked at the rain falling through the live oaks onto the street, as though any conversation with me was useless and the problem was mine, not his. "Theo and I are taking a cruise to the Islands. I came by here to do the right thing. But I can see it was a mistake."

"Where'd it go wrong for you, partner?"

"Wrong about what?" he said.

"You were Jumpin' Merchie Flannigan, a stand-up kid from the Iberville who did the crime and stacked the time. Why'd you become a hump for a bum like Castille LeJeune?"

The skin of his face seemed to crinkle, like a sheet of yellow paper held against a hot light bulb. He raked his hair back over his head again and started to speak, his eyes tangled with thoughts I could

only guess at, then stepped off the gallery and walked through a water puddle to his Mercedes.

I headed down the four-lane toward Franklin and five miles outside
New Iberia felt a front tire on my pickup go soft and begin to wobble.
I pulled to the shoulder and changed the tire in the rain. It was almost 11:30 when I got to the St. Mary Parish Courthouse. Across the
street I saw the restored pink Cadillac I had seen in City Park the
previous night. A curious black man holding an umbrella was bent
down by the driver's window, admiring the interior.

"Do you know who owns this?" I asked.

"A man who got a lot of money," he replied.

I went inside the courthouse and peeled off my raincoat in front of
a coffee stand run by a blind man. I had no way of knowing the
amount of Clete's bail, but obviously it would be high, and the 10
percent bondsman's fee would probably clean out my checking account and part of my savings. Of course, my paying a bondsman's fee
was predicated on the assumption a local bondsman would be willing
to write a bond on Clete, whose past record included fleeing the
United States on a murder warrant.

"You want a cup of coffee, Dave?" the blind man behind the
counter said.

"Yeah, sure, Walter," I said, distracted by a brown-haired little girl,
no older than six or seven, sitting on a bench by the courtroom entrance. A small teddy bear, a red ribbon with a silver bell on it tied
around the neck, was perched on her lap. Where had I seen her before? Then I remembered, with a rush of shame. It had been at Gunner Ardoin's house, on the morning I had rousted him last fall,
chambering a round in the .45, sticking it in his face, causing him to
soil himself while his little girl watched.

I walked up to her, my raincoat slung over my arm. "Is your daddy
here?" I asked.

"He's inside the big room," she replied.

"What's he doin' there?"

"Helping Clete."

"You remember me?" I asked.

"You're the man who pointed a gun at my daddy."

I went inside the courtroom just as the morning's proceedings were breaking up. Clete was talking to a local attorney while a deputy put cuffs on him for his trip back to jail. The judge left the room for his chambers, and among the people filing out in the corridor I saw Gunner Ardoin.

"Clete's going back to lock-up?" I said.

"Just till he bonds out," Gunner said.

"How much is his bond?"

"Fifty grand," he said.

"How'd he put it up?"

"He didn't. I did."

"You went a fifty-thou bond?"

"You don't watch the news? I hit the Powerball last week. Three million bucks. I bought him that pink Caddy out front, too."

I looked at him, stupefied. He walked past me and took his little girl by the hand. "Want something to eat? Clete's going to meet us outside in a few minutes," he said.

"Why not?" I replied.

A half hour later the four of us were eating gumbo at a checker-cloth-covered table inside a cafe one block from the courthouse. The pink Cadillac convertible was parked outside, rainwater standing up in beads as big as marbles on the waxed surface.

"I appreciate it, Gunner, but I can't accept it," Clete said.

"The title's already in your name, man," Gunner said.

"We'll have to change that," Clete said.

Gunner looked at a spot on the far wall of the cafe. "There's something I didn't mention. A couple of guys I was inside with needed a place to crash. Remember Flip Raguzi, used to run a chop shop for the Giacanos over in Algiers? He started a grease fire on the stove. It sort of changed the way your kitchen and the ceiling look."

"You let Flip Raguzi stay in my place? This guy has diseases scientists haven't found names for," Clete said.

"What's he talking about, Daddy?" the little girl asked.

Clete shut his eyes, then opened them. "Give me the keys," he said.

One of my favorite lines of all time, one excerpted from a 1940s song understood readily by all those who experienced the human and economic realities of the Depression and war years, goes as follows: "You don't get no bread with one meatball."

"What's funny?" Gunner said.

"Nothing," I said. "Take a walk with me, will you?"

We went outside and stood under a canvas awning, the mist blowing in our faces.

"That's a decent thing you did for Clete, Gunner," I said.

"I don't use that name anymore," he said.

"How about Father Jimmie? You do the right thing by him, too?" I said.

"Matter of fact, I did. But that's my business."

"I respect that, Phil. But I need your help, too. Know a woman named Theo Flannigan?"

"Jumpin' Merchie's old lady? I know who she is, but I don't know her personally."

"Was she writing scripts for Fat Sammy Figorelli?"

He shook his head. "No, but she might as well have. Her books were lying around the set. The director would lift the dialog from the love scenes in her books. So a bunch of degenerates, that includes me, were doing sixty-nines on each other and talking like Shakespeare."

"Why would the director pick her work to steal from?" I asked.

"A guy named Ray was involved. His girlfriend was my costar. I never saw him, but I think he was the same guy who'd call me and tell me where to pick up my meth delivery to the projects."

Ray?

Why hadn't I seen it? William Ray Guillot, lately of Franklin, Louisiana, now having his blood drained and replaced with formaldehyde.

"You're sure Theo wasn't part of Fat Sammy's action?" I said.

"Ever see one of Fat Sammy's films?"

"No."

"You don't want to," he said. "Let's go inside. Clete needs to drive me and my daughter to the airport in Lafayette. I'm buying a Mexican restaurant in San Antonio. You get to town, have a free dinner on me."

"You're a stand-up guy, Phil."

"I'm out of the life. I'm a millionaire. What's a few bucks to show some gratitude?"

I started to say something else, but he cut me off.

"I got your drift. Give it a rest," he said.

I drove back to my house on East Main and tried to put the LeJeune family and Junior Crudup out of my mind, but I couldn't rest. I did not believe Max Coll killed Will Guillot, and I couldn't shake the feeling that Castille LeJeune had been unduly happy when I went to his home, as though with a broad sweep of a broom he had gotten rid of a large problem in his life. In fact, I believed Castille LeJeune was about to get away with at least one if not two additional homicides.

And I also felt I had a problem of conscience about Theo Flannigan. I had falsely accused her of involvement in the shooting of the daiquiri-store operator and the production of pornographic films.

In fact, I rued the day I had ever heard of the LeJeunes or Junior Crudup.

On top of my more elevated level of problems, Batist stopped by the house with another one, namely Tripod, Alafair's three-legged raccoon, whom Batist carried up on the gallery inside Tripod's wood-frame hutch.

"Cain't keep him at my house no mo'," he said.

"Why can't you?" I asked, looking down at Tripod, who was standing up in the hutch, his claws hooked on the wire screen, his whiskered snout pointed at me.

"He's old, like me. He went to the bat'room on the kitchen flo'," Batist said.

"Thanks, Batist."

"You welcome," he replied, and drove off.

I opened the wire door on Tripod's hutch and he stepped out on the floor and looked up at me. "How's it hangin, 'Pod?" I said.

He responded by running into the kitchen and eating Snuggs's food out of the pet bowl.

But I could not distract myself from my problems with the world of play and innocence represented by animals. I wanted to believe I'd been dealt a bad hand. There was even some truth in my self-serving conclusion. But unfortunately I had dealt the hand to myself, beginning with the day I stepped into the unsolved disappearance of Junior Crudup, a man who had probably sought self-immolation all his life.

I called Theo at her house and apologized for my accusation.

"Drunks are always sorry. But they do it over and over again," she said.

"Could you define 'it,' please?"

"Acting like an asshole."

"I see."

"Have you apologized to my father?" she asked.

"Are you serious?" I said.

She hung up.

I called Helen Soileau at the department and told her I'd been wrong about Theo.

"How'd you clear her?" she asked.

"A porn actor told me a guy named Ray, as in William Raymond Guillot, was responsible for lifting material from Theo's books for Sammy Figorelli's movies. Theo had nothing to do with it."

"Thanks for telling me."

"Can you get another warrant to search Castille LeJeune's property?"

"No."

"I want to resign from the department, Helen. I'll have a formal letter on your desk by tomorrow."

"That's the way you want it?"

"Absolutely."

"I love you, bwana, but I don't trust you. And I . . ."

"What?"

"Want to kill you sometimes."

I got in my truck and backed into East Main. The bamboo and gardens in front of the Shadows breathed with mist that blew into the street, and as I looked at the old, massive brick post office on the corner, where a Creole man sold sno'balls and chunks of sugarcane off a canopy-shaded wagon when I was a kid, and as I watched the traffic turn at the next light onto the drawbridge, just past the Evangeline Theater where my father, mother, and I went to see cowboy movies in the 1940s, I had the feeling, not imagined, not emotional in nature, that I would never see any of these places or things again.

Chapter 28

As I approached Fox Run I could see sleet marching across the barren cane fields on the far side of the Teche, the same fields where Junior and Woodrow Reed labored a half century ago under the watchful eyes of Boss Posey and the other mounted gunbulls, all of them, one way or another, controlled by the man who lived across the bayou in the great white house that resembled a Mississippi paddle-wheeler.

I parked by the carriage house. The automobiles were gone and even though the sky was dark, no lights burned inside the main house. I dropped my cell phone in the pocket of my raincoat and walked down the slope toward the bayou, where the yellow bulldozer sat, huge, mud smeared, and clicking with soft white hail.

Helen had said we were looking for Dagwood and Blondie, whose advantage was they did not feel guilty and hence hid in plain sight. But amateur criminals have another kind of problem, one that professionals do not. They're arrogant and they presume. They're psychologically incapable of believing the system was not constructed to benefit them, and consequently they cannot imagine themselves standing in front of a law-and-order judge who can send them away for decades.

The bulldozer blade was partially raised, the tractor-treads pressed deeply into the earth, fanning back off the rear of the dozer in patterns like horse tails, as though the operator had been involved intensely with one particular area of repair rather than the entire environment.

The keys were hanging from the ignition. I turned over the engine, revved the gas once, and clanked the transmission into reverse. As I backed up the dozer, a different kind of topography began to emerge from under the suspended blade—an unevenly filled depression, one that had not been graded and tamped down, so that the surface was spiked with severed tree roots and ground-up divots of grass.

I dropped the blade, shifted into forward gear, and raked off the top layer of the depression, then backed up again so I could see where the blade had cut. The dirt was loose, sinking where there were air pockets, water oozing from the subsoil that had been compressed by the weight of the tractor-treads. I dropped the blade lower, this time cutting much deeper into the hole, trundling up a huge, curled pile of mud, blue clay, and feeder roots that looked like torn cobweb. But this time, when I backed off the hole, I saw something I hoped I would not find.

I cut the engine, pulled loose a shovel that was behind the seat, and walked around the front of the blade to a spot where a human arm, shoulder, and the curved back of a hand protruded from the soil, the hail rolling down the sides of the depression, pooling around them.

I pushed the shovel under the back of the person and wedged the torso and the face free from the soil. The skin had turned a bluish gray, either in the water or because of the clay in the alluvial fan of the bayou, but his eyes were open and still emerald green, his small ears tight against the scalp, his shoulders somehow far too narrow for the violent and dangerous man he had once been.

There were entrance wounds in his face, under one arm, and in his left temple.

I speared the shovel blade into the clay and reached for the cell phone in my raincoat pocket, just as the cell phone began ringing. I flipped it open and placed it against my ear. "Dave Robicheaux," I said.

"Are you trying to avoid me?" a woman's voice said.

The hail was hitting hard on my hat and the steel frame of the bulldozer and I could hardly hear her. "Ms. Parks, I'm no longer with the sheriff's department. You need to call—"

"I found a diary under Lori's mattress. There were hearts all over the last page and drawings of a man's face. It wasn't some kid's face, either. There was a phone number, too." Her voice was starting to crack. "You know who that number belongs to?"

"No, I don't."

"A pipeline company in Lafayette. It's owned by that man who lives in that phony piece of medieval shit across from the junk yard."

"Say his name, Ms. Parks."

"Flannigan. Merchie Flannigan. I'm filing charges for statutory rape."

"Ms. Parks, Lori might have known someone who simply worked at the pipeline company."

"This number goes into Flannigan's office. It's his extension. Why are you covering up for him? I hate you people," she said.

She was obviously still drunk, but I couldn't fault her for her rage. Her daughter had burned to death in an automobile after being sold liquor illegally, and her husband, who had survived a tour as a combat medic, had been killed with impunity by Will Guillot, the investigation written off by a cop on a pad. But family survivors of homicide victims are seldom mentioned in follow-up news stories, even though the grief they carry is like the daily theft of sunlight from their lives.

The window on my cell phone cleared. Donna Parks was off the line now, but either because of the weather or my location I was losing service as I tried to punch in a 911 call. I heard someone's feet crunch on the hailstones behind me.

"You must have been a Marine, Mr. Robicheaux. I think you're the most determined man I've ever met."

I turned and looked into the face of Castille LeJeune. He wore a silver shooting jacket, one with ammunition loops sewn on the sleeves, a flat-brimmed, pearl-gray Stetson hat, and khaki trousers tucked inside fur-lined, half-topped boots. In his right hand he held a blue-black revolver with walnut grips. But he did not point it at me. Up on the slope, by the carriage house, I could see Merchie Flannigan's Mercedes.

"You got the jump on me, Mr. LeJeune. You and your son-in-law just pull in?" I said.

"The question is what do I do with you, Mr. Robicheaux."

"You didn't just pop ole Max, did you? You executed him."

"Could I see your search warrant?"

"Don't happen to have it with me."

"Ah."

"Merchie has been screwing both you and your daughter, Mr. LeJeune. He stole a single-action Army colt from Will Guillot and used it to kill the daiquiri store operator. Then he threw the gun down so we'd put it on Guillot and by extension on you and your enterprises."

"Why would he kill a liquor salesman?"

"Merchie was banging a seventeen-year-old girl by the name of Lori Parks. She died in a car wreck after she bought booze from a drive-by store you own."

I could see the connections coming together in LeJeune's eyes. Behind him Merchie Flannigan was walking down the slope, his hands in the pockets of his jacket, his shoulders hunched under an Australian flop hat.

LeJeune glanced over his shoulder, then focused on my face again. "You uncovered evidence in a homicide without a warrant, which destroys the probative value of the discovery," he said. "But you're not a stupid man. Something else is going on here. You quit the sheriff's department, didn't you?"

I shrugged my shoulders. "We've got your ass in the bear trap, Mr. LeJeune. How's it feel?" I said, and actually laughed.

Up on the slope I saw Theodosha Flannigan park her Lexus and walk into the front of the house, carrying a guitar case.

"Open your coat," LeJeune said, raising his pistol toward my chest. "Use your left hand, unsnap the strap on your sidearm, and drop it on the ground."

"Nope," I said.

"Say again?"

"A police officer never surrenders his weapon."

"You're not a police officer anymore."

"Old habits die hard."

I'd like to say my behavior was brave, my principles inviolate, but in reality I didn't feel personally threatened by Castille LeJeune. He didn't care enough about me or the social class I represented to hate or fear me, and in all probability he still retained some of the fatalistic views that had allowed him to survive the Korean War as a decorated combat pilot. The system had served him for a lifetime—why should it fail him now?

But on another level I misjudged him. He could abide a professional enemy such as myself, but treachery inside the castle walls was another matter. He pulled back my coat, removed my .45 from the clip-on holster I wore, and tossed it in the mud.

Merchie Flannigan was standing now on the rim of the depression, his face disjointed as he stared down at the half-exhumed body of Max Coll. "Who's this dead guy? What's happening here?" he said.

"You were having an affair with a seventeen-year-old girl?" LeJeune said.

"Hold on, there, Castille," Merchie said.

"I always told Theo you were trash, with your blow-dried hair and Thesaurus vocabulary. You shot my sales person at the drive-by window?"

"I think I'm going to boogie and let you and Dave work it out. Maybe y'all can tell each other war stories. But I'd say from the looks of things here, you're genuinely fucked, Castille," he said, and began walking back up the slope.

The temperature had dropped, and the air was bitter, like the taste of copper coins, the tin roofs of the old convict cabins speckled with frost. I could see a lump of cartilage working in LeJeune's jaw. Merchie was halfway up the slope when LeJeune raised the revolver and fired three times, *pop, pop, pop.*

Either his hand shook from cold or anger or he was simply not a good shot, because he missed with all three rounds, and I heard the bullets break glass in the French doors that gave onto his patio.

Merchie ran past the carriage house and down the drive, hunkered low, the brim of his Australian flop hat angled down over his neck. I walked up behind LeJeune, slipping my hand down his forearm, removing the revolver from his grasp.

"You killed Will Guillot and were going to put it on Max Coll?" I said.

"I have nothing more to say," he replied.

"Guillot killed both Bernstine and Sammy Figorelli and took a shot at me, didn't he?"

"Can't help you, sir," he replied.

Up at the house there was no sound or any movement behind a window or the French doors. I snicked open the cylinder on Le-Jeune's revolver, ejected all the shells into my palm, then retrieved my .45 from the mud.

"My vision isn't very good anymore. You know I tied Ted Williams' gunnery record? Highest ever set by a Marine or Navy aviator. That's God's honest truth," he said.

"I believe you. Better take a walk with me," I said, punching in 911 on my cell with my thumb.

"Of course. We're going up to my house. I'll fix coffee for us. I have no personal feelings about this," he said.

He walked up the slope beside me, his chin lifted, his hands stuck in the pockets of his silver shooting jacket, his nostrils flaring as he breathed in the fresh coldness of the afternoon. I studied the back of the house, but still there was no movement inside. I felt LeJeune's attention suddenly refocus itself on the side of my face.

"Why are you so somber, Mr. Robicheaux? It should be a red-letter day for you," he said.

"My father taught me to hunt, Mr. LeJeune. He used to say, 'Don't be shooting at nothin' you cain't see on the other side of, no.' He was a simple man, but I always admired his humanity and remembered his words."

"As always, your second meaning eludes me."

"Is that Theo's car in the driveway?"

He stared at the rear end of the Lexus that protruded just past the edge of the carriage house. His eyes began to water and he rushed across the patio through a cluster of winter-killed potted plants and tore open the French doors.

Theodosha Flannigan sat in an antique chair, with a crimson pad inset in the back, her guitar perched on her lap, her trimmed finger-nails like shavings from seashell, her knees close together, at a slight ladylike angle, her mouth parted in mild surprise, a hole with a tiny trickle running from it in the center of her forehead.

Through the front window I saw a half dozen emergency vehicles turn off the state road and come roaring up the drive through the long tunnel of live oaks, their flashers beating with light and color, their sirens muted, as though the drivers were afraid they might wake the dead.

EPILOGUE

My daughter Alafair and I flew to Key West for Christmas and hired a charter boat I could scarcely afford and scuba-dived Seven Mile Reef. The water was green, like lime Jell-O, with patches of hot blue floating in it, the reef swarming with baitfish and the barracuda that fed off them. At sundown we set the outriggers and trolled for a stray marlin or wahoo as we headed back into port, the gulls wheeling and squeaking over our wake, the sun bloodred as it descended into the Gulf.

Alafair looked beautiful in her wetsuit, her body as sleek and hard and tapered as a seal's, her Indian-black hair flecked with seaweed. As she stood in the stern, watching our baited hooks skip over our wake, she reminded me of Theo Flannigan and all the innocent victims of violence everywhere, here, in this country, where friends clasped hands and leaped from flaming windows into the bottomless canyons of New York City, or in the Mideast, where a storm of ballistic missiles and guided bombs would rain down upon people little different from you and me.

But it was the season of Christ's birthday and I did not want to dwell upon all the corporate greed and theological fanaticism that had rooted itself in the modern world. We attended Mass in a church James Audubon had sat in, strolled Duval Street among revelers with New York accents, ate dinner at a Cuban cafe by the water under a ficus tree threaded with Christmas lights, and visited the home of Ernest Hemingway down on Whitehead Street. The sun was gone, the sky full of light, the incoming tide wine dark against the horizon, and bottle rockets fired from Mallory Square were popping in pink fountains high above the waves. How had Hemingway put it? The world was a fine place, and well worth the fighting for.

As Alafair and I walked back toward the happy throng on Duval Street, the yards around us blooming with flowers, the air touched with salt and the smell of firecrackers, I thought perhaps the world was more than just a fine place, that perhaps it was a domed cathedral and we only had to recognize and accept that simple fact to enjoy all the gifts of both heaven and earth.

Castille LeJeune was sentenced to Angola Prison for manslaughter in the shooting of Max Coll and for first-degree homicide in the death of Will Guillot. Because of his age, he was transferred to an honor farm, where he did clerical work in an office. The correctional officers at the farm admired him for his genteel manners and military bearing and his fastidiousness about his dress. In fact, they came to call him "Mr. LeJeune" and often sought his advice about financial matters. But a visiting prison psychologist put an evaluation in his jacket that indicated LeJeune was not only experiencing depression and self-loathing over the death of his daughter but perhaps intense levels of guilt characteristic of a father who has sexually molested his daughter.

An inmate's jacket is confidential only until the first trusty clerk reads it.

Castille LeJeune became what is known as a short-eyes in the prison population. Other inmates shunned him; the correctional officers became distant and formal in their dealings with him. He was transferred back to Angola after he bit into pieces of broken glass that had been mixed into his food.

Ironically, he was placed in a segregated unit within viewing distance of the levee built by the Red Hat Gang on which Junior Crudup had pulled what Leadbelly called his great, long time.

We couldn't make our homicide case against Merchie Flannigan and he got away with the murder of the daiquiri-store operator. At least legally he did. But Castille LeJeune nailed him from jail by having his lawyers file a wrongful death suit against him, freezing his personal and corporate accounts, then using Donna Parks to bring statutory rape charges against him. Merchie's reputation was ruined and his pipeline business went bust. For a while he ran a welding service, then began hanging out at a bar frequented by Teamsters in Baton Rouge. I ran into him one day by the capitol building, where Huey Long was shot down in 1935.

"Hey, Dave, no hard feelings, huh?" he said.

"Not on my part," I replied.

He smelled of cigarettes and was fat and puffy, sporting a mustache and goatee, driving a junker car that was parked at the curb, a young girl in the passenger seat.

"That's my niece," he said.

"Right," I said.

"Putting together a drilling deal in Iran, can you believe it?"

"That's great, Merch."

"Good seeing you, Dave. I mean that," he said, taking my hand, trying as hard as he could to hold my eyes without averting his. The girl tossed a beer can out of the window as they drove away.

Father Jimmie and I and two employees of a funeral home made up the entire retinue at the graveside ritual for Max Coll in a Catholic cemetery outside Franklin. I felt partly responsible for his death, but had he not died, Castille LeJeune would not have gone down, nor would Castille LeJeune have utilized an opportunity to take Will Guillot off the board. Ultimately I came to think of Max Coll in another fashion. In his way he was a brave man who made his own choices, and it was an arrogance on my part and a disservice to him for me to pretend that somehow I was the designer of his fate.

Father Jimmie went back to his conservative parish in New Orleans and worked as a chaplin at Central Lock-Up. After Alafair returned to college in Portland, I invited both him and Clotile Arceneaux to dinner at a Mexican restaurant off the upper end of St. Charles.

"Pretty slick how you took down LeJeune, searching his property without a warrant," she said.

"It was dumb," I said.

"You never flinched, even though LeJeune had a pistol on you and you thought you didn't have backup," she said.

"Say that again."

"I watched you through a pair of field glasses. An FBI sharpshooter watched LeJeune through a scope on a rifle." She put a forkful of food in her mouth and raised her eyebrows at me.

"Y'all were using me as bait?"

"Got a job for you with the state if you want to start putting away bad guys again."

"I'm out."

She placed her foot on mine under the table and squeezed. "Come see me sometime and we'll talk about it," she said.

"Am I missing something here?" Father Jimmie said.

"Dave likes to pretend he can stop being a police officer. Make him go to confession, Father," she replied.

Clete Purcel spent three months in the St. Mary Parish Prison, paid twenty-thousand dollars in damages to the sheriff's deputies he had busted up with his fists, and upon his discharge moved in with me, saying he was going to start up another P.I. office in New Iberia. We fished for sac-a-lait and bass at Henderson Swamp and Bayou Benoit, and Clete tried to appear light-hearted and unaffected by his time in jail. But I knew better. Clete was a natural-born cop and despised the new breed of criminals and literally washed himself in the shower with peroxide when he got out of the bag.

But out on Bayou Benoit, with the spring breezes up and the bream spawning back in the bays, the levee sprinkled with buttercups, we didn't talk about the bad times of the past or the present. I had never looked to the skies for great miracles, and, as St. Augustine once indicated, to watch a vineyard soak up the water in a plowed row and produce a grape that could be translated into wine was all the proof we needed of higher realities. But when Clete and I were deep in the swamp, the lacy green branches of the cypress trees shifting back and forth across the sun, I fell prey to a new temptation as well as hope.

I waited to see a pair of pelicans drift down off the windstream, their wings extended and pouched beaks bulging, their improbable presence a harbinger of better times. I waited for them daily and sometimes in the flapping of wings overhead I thought I heard Bootsie's voice, reminding me of her promise about the pelicans, only to discover that a white crane or blue heron had been frightened by our outboard and had flown through the cypress trees back onto open water.

But I'm sure one fine day, when I least expect it, the pelicans will return to Bayou Teche, and in the meantime I share my thoughts about them with no one, except perhaps Snuggs and Tripod, who, like me, sleep little and wake before first light.